Praise for Jessica

"This captivating tale from Kate explores a woman's pain and hardship as she questions her faith . . . With believably flawed characters, this affecting tale of deceit and redemption, which questions what it means to forgive, will elicit strong reactions from Christian inspirational readers interested in stories with strong moral themes."

—*Publishers Weekly* on *Love and Other Mistakes*

"A stunning debut. Clever and well written. I love how Jessica Kate breathes new life into romance. This tale of love and redemption will stay with you long after you've closed the book. A must-read."

—Rachel Hauck, *New York Times* bestselling author of *The Wedding Dress*, on *Love and Other Mistakes*

"Witty. Charming. Heartfelt. I could go on and on about Jessica Kate's debut novel. From its highly relatable characters to its pitch-perfect dialogue, *Love and Other Mistakes* is a delightful, romantic read filled with just the right amount of sass. I lost count of the number of times I laughed out loud as I watched Natalie and Jem navigate their relationships, careers, and faith. Definitely one of the most enjoyable books I've read lately, and I can't wait to see what's next from Jessica Kate!"

—Melissa Tagg, Carol Award–winning author of *Now and Then and Always* and the Walker Family series

"*Love and Other Mistakes* wraps a poignant and warm look at relationships within a smart, sly, and knowing comedic voice. Readers of Sally Thorne and Bethany Turner will be immediately at home with Natalie: an all-too-real heroine who balances whip-smart agency with an endearing vulnerability and whose intersection with long-lost Jeremy helps her forge a path to confidence and discover the woman she was always meant to be. Kate's unputdownable debut recognizes that all human relationships—familial, friendship, romantic—are worth the keen eye and clever insight of her talented pen."

—RACHEL MCMILLAN, AUTHOR OF
THE VAN BUREN AND DELUCA MYSTERIES

"If you're looking for a story with sass on top of style, or a fresh voice pumped full of fun, you need to read *Love and Other Mistakes*. Then after you've enjoyed this—and I'm confident you will—make a date with whatever this exciting new author writes next!"

—DAVID RAWLINGS, AUTHOR OF *THE BAGGAGE HANDLER*

Love
and
Other
Mistakes

A Novel

JESSICA KATE

THOMAS NELSON
Since 1798

Love and Other Mistakes

Published in Nashville, Tennessee, by Thomas Nelson. Thomas Nelson is a registered trademark of HarperCollins Christian Publishing, Inc.

Thomas Nelson titles may be purchased in bulk for educational, business, fund-raising, or sales promotional use. For information, please email SpecialMarkets@ThomasNelson.com.

Scriptures taken from the Holy Bible, New International Version®, NIV®. Copyright © 1973, 1978, 1984, 2011 by Biblica, Inc.™ Used by permission of Zondervan. All rights reserved worldwide. www.zondervan.com. The "NIV" and "New International Version" are trademarks registered in the United States Patent and Trademark Office by Biblica, Inc.™

ISBN 978-0-7852-2959-9 (e-book)

Library of Congress Cataloging-in-Publication Data

Names: Kate, Jessica, author.
Title: Love and other mistakes / Jessica Kate.
Description: Nashville, Tennessee : Thomas Nelson, 2019.
Identifiers: LCCN 2019000983 | ISBN 9780785229582 (paperback)
Subjects: | GSAFD: Love stories. | Christian fiction.
Classification: LCC PR9619.4.K366 L68 2019 | DDC 823/.92--dc23 LC record available at https://lccn.loc.gov/2019000983

Printed in the United States of America

19 20 21 22 23 LSC 5 4 3 2 1

Mum and Dad
Words can never express the impact you've had on my life,
so I won't even try—except to say thank you, and I love you.

God
You made me, saved me, and love me.
You're everything.

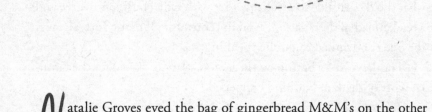

Natalie Groves eyed the bag of gingerbread M&M's on the other side of the office meeting room and prayed for a divine intervention of Red Sea proportions.

In forty-five minutes, two goons from the head office of Potted Plants 4 Hire would walk through the door and give her fifteen minutes to convince them not to close the Charlottesville branch—the last in this half of Virginia. In forty-five seconds, she might topple out of her office chair, curl up in a ball under this wobbly table, and hide.

"Natalie." Frank, one of the salesmen, plugged Natalie's five-year-old laptop into the projector. A muscle jerked in his sandpapery cheek. Was that meant to be a smile? Hard to tell. "Those corporate idiots won't know what hit them."

Natalie manufactured a smile in return. "Thanks, Frank."

He opened the laptop lid. "You look like you're about to throw up. Just get it over and done with before the presentation."

She took a deep breath and ignored the Mexican jumping beans in her stomach. Nothing mattered now except her presentation notes.

Suck it up, buttercup. This isn't about you.

No, it was about eight coworkers' jobs and her ability to pay Dad's medical expenses. The bills kept coming, and between her parents'

1

increasing copay and dwindling savings, money was beyond tight. The past seven years had been a never-ending Monday morning.

Ever since Dad's doctor said, "It's cancer."

By rights, their boss, Maria, should have been giving this presentation—not the girl who answered phones. But Maria had an epic case of food poisoning, and Natalie was the one who'd written a business plan to save their office-plant hire service. It was amazing what she'd been able to piece together with half a business degree and a bucketload of desperation. And in return for all that effort, she was the one condemned to public speaking.

Frank pressed a button on the laptop. Natalie waited for the familiar whir of the fan. Nothing happened.

Uh-oh.

She peered over at him. "Did you press the right button?"

He picked up the computer and shook it. "Three times. Why do you have such an old laptop?"

Because this week's budget was down to whatever coins she could scrounge from the back of the sofa. But he didn't need to know that.

She dropped the notes on the table and walked toward him, smoothing her borrowed business jacket as she went. She'd hoped a power suit would boost her confidence. She'd even donned black pumps and straightened her rebellious hair. Though it'd started to frizz again when she spent her first hour of the morning scrubbing graffiti off their business sign. Kids always found it hilarious to black out the "ted" in their name and draw illustrations of just what kind of plants they'd prefer to hire.

But who needed perfectly straight hair when you had bulldog determination?

Her cell rang, vibrating against the chipped wood veneer of the table. Probably Mom. She paused, tempted to ignore it. Mom knew how important this morning was—someone had better be dying.

Her mind's eye flashed to her father's once strong hand trembling as he'd waved goodbye to her from his patchwork-covered bed yesterday morning. He was technically in remission, but even the Three Blind Mice could see the way he'd deteriorated this year.

Had that been their last farewell?

Fear punched her in the chest as she lunged for the phone, swiped a finger across the cracked screen, and hit the voice-message icon. Unfamiliar number, but that did nothing to soothe the throat-closing sensation that enveloped her. She set the phone to speaker. Her normal speakers had decided to take a vacation this week, but her speakerphone remained loyal.

An unfamiliar male voice glitched in and out, poor reception chopping the message. "Gregory . . . looking for Natalie Groves . . . here, called . . . ambulance . . . corner of Harding and Davis Streets." *Beep.*

She froze. It had to be about Dad. No one would call her about anybody else. But why had a stranger called? Where was Mom? Had something happened to her as well?

"Natalie." Frank's deep voice rumbled across the room. "You should go." His tone carried a heaviness that told her he, too, assumed it was her father.

Most folks in this town had heard of her evangelist father. Everyone also knew that each unexpected phone call could be announcing very bad news.

Or just another false alarm. And those head-office guys would be here in forty-one minutes . . .

Frank placed a hand on her back and pushed her to the door. "We'll be fine. It might be nothing, and you'll be back in time. If not . . ." He paused, having maneuvered her to the threshold, and met her eye. "There's more important things than this store. Go."

She reached into her pocket for her keys. If she missed saying goodbye to Dad, she'd never forgive herself.

"Thanks, Frank." She sprinted from the room.

"And don't take that hunk of junk you call a car," he shouted after her as she reached the end of the corridor.

She paused, and he tossed her his keys.

"Good luck, Nattie."

She nodded and darted out into the parking lot. The muggy late-summer air triggered an instant sweat, and the morning sun made her squint. She hit the beeper and ran past her rusted VW Bug toward flashing headlights. Thank heaven for Frank. He knew her car was as likely to break down as not.

Natalie jumped into the driver's seat of Frank's SUV and pulled a fast-food bag off the dash before she threw the vehicle into reverse. The scent of stale fries lingered in the air. She twisted in the seat to look out the back window, and a flash of color caught her eye. Discarded Happy Meal toys lay in a child's car seat, strapped in next to a baby seat. Frank must've had his grandkids for the weekend again.

She rocketed backward, then out of the parking lot and onto the road. She'd go to the address the mystery man mentioned first—it was just around the corner. She might even beat the ambulance.

If there was nothing there, she'd head to Martha Jefferson Hospital.

A man lay splayed out on the footpath ahead. More than six feet of pale skin and freckles. Unmoving.

The sharp twist in Natalie's gut eased as she slowed the SUV and flashed her turn signal. That man definitely wasn't her seventy-one-year-old father.

Thank you, God.

She swiped a stray tear that had gathered in the corner of her eye, then squinted at the figure on the ground. It sure looked like . . .

Movement caught her eye. An older man, standing behind the

guy on the footpath, holding a baby with one arm as the other flagged her down.

She whipped the car into a parking space fifteen yards from the man prone on the ground. She couldn't see his face from this angle. But recognition tickled the edge of her mind. Mouth dry and stomach on spin cycle, she jumped out.

The older man rushed toward her, Colonel Sanders without the smile. She tried not to stare.

"Natalie?"

She gestured to the man on the ground behind the colonel. "What happ—"

He dumped the baby into her arms. It squirmed and squealed, and she recoiled half a step as the child wobbled in her tenuous grasp. She clutched a handful of blue jumpsuit while the baby arched his back against her, kicked his chubby legs, and reached toward the man on the ground. "What is going on?"

"You know this guy, right?"

The Colonel Sanders look-alike blocked her view, so she couldn't confirm or deny.

"He was jogging from that building there, back to his car with his kid." He pointed to the wriggling child in her arms. "And whacked his head against that." His finger indicated a tree branch that stretched six feet above the sidewalk. "I stopped to check he was okay, but the cut on his forehead bled and he got dizzy and passed out. Guess he hates blood. I called an ambulance, but there's a crash on the other side of town, and they've been held up. So I grabbed the emergency contact card in his wallet."

He paused for breath as he held up the card. It was misshapen and discolored with age, like he'd pried it from the depths of a wallet that should've been retired last decade.

Colonel Sanders finally stepped aside so she could see who lay on the sidewalk. The man on the ground shifted, groaned.

Natalie's brain begged her eyes to admit they were lying. She scanned the man from head to toe. Brown hair with red highlights that caught the sunshine. Boyish freckles. Broad shoulders.

Jeremy Walters, her ex-fiancé.

I'm outta here.

Fumbling with her keys, she turned to the colonel to return the baby. Instead she encountered his retreating back. "Wait! You can't leave me."

The man spun to face her but kept walking backward toward a truck parked by the roadside. "You have no idea how late I am. He's only been out for a minute or two. Take him to the emergency room if you're worried." With those words, he hauled himself into his vehicle.

"You can't go." Desperation edged her voice as Natalie stepped toward him, trying to hold out a crying handful of baby.

His revving engine drowned her plea. A puff of exhaust fumes tickled her nose as he pulled out, and she sneezed. The truck drove away as she watched.

Turn back, turn back, turn back . . .

It rounded a corner and disappeared.

Unbelievable. Natalie huffed a breath and swiveled with the enthusiasm of a vegetarian at Outback Steakhouse.

Jem hadn't crumpled to the ground. He lay flat on his back, long limbs stretched in every direction. One hand lifted to rest on his bleeding forehead, and his eyelids twitched but remained closed.

No one would call him a bodybuilder, but neither did he have that gangly look anymore. He'd grown his hair longer than the military-style cut his dad used to do at home every month, and his face sported more freckles.

But it was him.

She ground her teeth against the warm rush of memories that

poured into her mind. Sure, she hated his guts, but he wasn't just the guy who'd broken her heart seven years ago. He was the tang of lemonade after they raced their bikes down the street. He was the crinkle of comic-book pages as they hid from his dad under the back porch. He was the smell of lavender in Mr. Holbert's jewelry shop, where her nineteen-year-old self had pointed to a diamond and said, "That one." He was every good memory before life got complicated.

So much had changed—though not all. Blue ink still smudged his palm. Jem without a pen was like a Saturday night without chocolate. Had he fulfilled his journalistic dreams?

She scrubbed a sleeve across her face. Time to focus. The man burned faster than forgotten eggs on a stove, so she should get him out of the sun.

Or better yet, leave him there.

God, what did I do to deserve this?

Running into the guy who'd dumped you ten weeks before your wedding was always bad, but especially like this. She was broke. Single. Going nowhere.

He'd take one look at her and thank his younger self for leaving.

She shifted on her feet. She'd give up anything, even pumpkin-spice M&M's, to jump in the car and meet the head-office representatives. She had a store to save.

But there was a baby in her arms, and she couldn't plop him on the ground and leave.

Jem lurched to a sitting position. "Oliver!"

Natalie jolted.

The motion seemed to catch the corner of Jem's eye. He swung his head toward her and squinted into the sun. When he jumped to his feet, he swayed.

"Whoa." Stepping forward, she grabbed his arm with her free hand, then dropped it.

Jem leaned back against the tree trunk—the one supporting the branch that had put that red gash on his forehead. After a few seconds, he raised his gaze and did a double take.

"Natalie?"

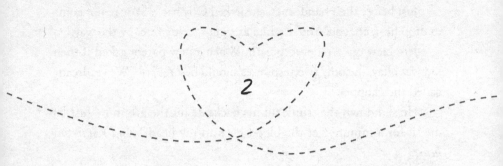

2

J em blinked against the waves of dizziness as he stood and tried to
focus on the five feet six inches of woman radiating resentment
toward him. Gorgeous as ever.

Even if her brunette hair was frizzing and his nine-month-old
son's flailing hand was smearing her pink lipstick.

He steadied himself against the tree behind him, pressed his hand
into the scratchy bark to check he was really awake. Natalie was standing
in front of him. For the first time in seven years. And she'd found him
passed out and drooling on the sidewalk.

Terrific. Just the look he'd been going for.

He fought for focus as his vision narrowed. "Olly. Is he okay?" A
bubble of panic popped inside him. He'd been holding Olly when
he whacked his head, saw the blood, and the dizziness swallowed his
consciousness. Had he hurt his son?

Natalie looked at Olly, fussing in her arms. She held him out.
"Here."

That wasn't a "Yes, he's fine." Nausea flooded Jem for a second
time. He tried to blink away the fuzzy static on the edges of his vision
as he reached for his son.

Just before their hands met, she jerked Olly back. "You're not going to drop him, are you? You're white as a ghost. He's fine, by the way."

Jem blew out a relieved breath. When a new parent asked if their kid was okay, the only two responses should be "Yes" or "We've already called the chopper."

He slid down the trunk till his backside hit the ground. "Just let me sit for a minute, get the blood back to my head." *And restart my heart.*

He rested his throbbing forehead on his knees and willed the rushing in his head to go away. Olly was okay, so now he needed to deal with problem number two: salvaging his first conversation with Natalie in seven years, two months, and—if memory served correctly—about three weeks.

In the thousands of times he'd pictured this moment, he'd envisioned the full spectrum of scenarios, from the sting of her slap to the sweet taste of her kiss. But not one of those scenarios had included a tree branch and a throbbing skull, nor the distinct possibility of throwing up at her feet.

If he could stay conscious for five seconds, he could figure out why she was here and how he could stop her from punching him in the teeth. From the sparks shooting from her green eyes, he was in imminent danger.

Maybe he should let her hold Olly till he got his reflexes back.

After a minute, his tunnel vision cleared and equilibrium returned. He sent up an emergency prayer for help, faced Natalie, and offered a small smile. "Let's start over. Hi."

She plopped Olly onto his lap. "Let's not. Goodbye." She spun toward an SUV parked by the sidewalk.

A jolt of loss shot through him. He'd missed this woman for years and today had woken up on a warm concrete footpath to find her holding his son. She couldn't vanish now.

He scrambled to his feet, off balance with Olly in one arm and residual dizziness swirling in his brain. "Hey, wait! Where are you going?" He managed to get to her car without falling over.

"Not that it's any of your business, but I'm late for an important presentation."

He leaned against the side of the car and studied her face. She'd matured from his bright-eyed college-student fiancée into a professional twenty-six-year-old woman. Freckles faded. Eyelashes as dark as ever.

And he didn't buy her excuse for a second. The Natalie he'd known would swear off sugar before she'd speak in public.

Not that he could blame her for avoiding him. He'd be mad at him too.

She opened her door, and he placed a gentle palm on it. "Hold on. Just let me give you a heads-up. I'm moving back to town. Moved, actually. Yesterday. The boxes are at Mike and Steph's."

Reconnecting with his brother, Mike, and niece, Lili, had been the best part of yesterday. His sister-in-law, Steph—not so much.

Natalie paused. Her brow furrowed, her lips pursed, then the flash of emotion disappeared. "Whatever." She jumped up into the SUV and started it without closing the door, then looked over her left shoulder, away from him, like she was checking for cars. Her hand reached toward the door handle that his body blocked.

Not so fast. He owed her a proper apology, and he couldn't exactly yell it at her fleeing car.

He edged closer to her, almost leaning into the vehicle. "You're just going to leave me here with a concussion and a baby?"

She whipped her head around so quickly her long ponytail slapped him across the eye socket. "You're really going to say that to me?"

Ouch. Not that he didn't deserve it.

She pushed him back from the door and slammed it shut, but the window was down. He poked his face through it. Her perfume filled his senses—that and the salty scent of what looked like old

McDonald's on the passenger seat. "Which road is the hospital on again?" he asked in his most innocent voice. "I'll take myself there, but I can't remember." He gave his forehead a dramatic rub. "Must be the knock to the head."

She glared. "Liar. And it's called Google Maps."

He held eye contact, and after a moment she looked away. Sighed. "You shouldn't drive anyway."

Bingo. Chink in the armor.

"It's okay. I'm fine." He fished his keys from his back pocket with one hand, Olly now content in his other arm. "I'll figure it out. See you later."

He walked toward his Camry. *Three, two, one* . . .

"You should call your dad," she yelled after him.

He stopped. "Doesn't know I'm here yet." And he'd put that unpleasant moment off for as long as possible.

"Mike, then. That's what big brothers are for."

He waved off her concern. "He's busy. Minister stuff."

"An ambulance."

"They have actual emergencies to go to. I'll cancel the one that was called." Somewhere in his semiconscious haze, someone had mentioned that an ambulance had been contacted.

He turned back to his car. Not that he had any intention of driving. But she didn't know that—

Behind him, the car clunked into gear. Maybe he was wrong. He sighed. He could sit here awhile, make sure he really was okay, before he drove anywhere.

Though that wouldn't help him say what he had to say to Natalie.

Gravel crunched beside him. He glanced up. Natalie's SUV slowed to a stop.

He couldn't stop his smile. She might be mad at him, but ol' Nat's dependability never changed.

"Get in the car." She didn't even look at him, but he'd take what he could get.

"I'll grab Olly's car seat."

"Already got one."

He froze. "You've got kids?" No way. He would've heard if she'd married. Surely.

"Borrowed car."

Relief flooded him—a ridiculous reaction as, kids or no kids, he had as much chance with her as Adam Sandler did of winning World's Sexiest Man. But still.

"Seriously, hurry up. I told you I've got somewhere to be."

Oops. Maybe she hadn't lied. But too late now. He buckled Olly in and jumped into the passenger seat. At least the hospital wasn't far.

She pulled out from the curb at an alarming speed while he gripped the door handle and prayed his son wasn't about to be orphaned at nine months old. When the tires stopped screeching, the silence rubbed his nerves like a cheese grater.

Well, it was now or never.

He took a deep breath and faced her profile. "Nat, I owe you an apo—"

"Why are you back, anyway?" Her eyes stayed on the road, expression tense.

He settled back in his seat, gaze bouncing off his blood-stained hand. In the back seat, Oliver grizzled. "Work transfer."

"That doesn't make sense. Weren't you in Chicago?" Her cheeks flushed a little after her words.

Interesting. He grinned.

"I wasn't keeping tabs on you."

He grinned wider. She now had a serious case of tomato face. "I know."

She shifted her hands on the steering wheel, still looking flustered. "Then what's with the move?"

He cleared his throat. "I was about to get fired, so I found another job. Here."

She slid a glance toward him like she was waiting for more.

He shrugged. No point being anything but honest. They'd always told each other the truth. "When your ex-girlfriend tells you she's pregnant and then you become a single dad, work . . . suffers." Ending the pregnancy had run counter to both Chloe and Jem's beliefs, but neither had his ex been ready to face motherhood. It'd been just him and Olly from day one.

A beat of silence. "That's, uh, unfortunate." Her understatement carried a note of sympathy.

"It's okay. Olly and I are the dynamic duo. The first few months were a bit rough, but the old lady next door was a lifesaver. We made it."

He risked another glance at Natalie. "So, how are you?"

She took the corner five miles an hour faster than she should have. "I'm fine."

He swept his gaze from her face to her feet and back again. Worry lines had carved their way across her forehead. "Really? Because you look awful."

Her jaw tightened. "That better be the concussion talking."

He rolled his eyes. "I didn't mean it like that. I mean you're stressed. I can tell." He'd dated her for four years—it wasn't like he'd forgotten how to read her expressions.

No matter how long it'd been.

She jerked the car right and jammed on the brakes. His seat belt snapped tight. He threw one hand against the dash and looked for whatever she'd braked to avoid. It took a moment to realize they were in front of the hospital.

Natalie yanked the parking brake up and turned to face him. If looks could kill, he would've just been incinerated. "Why don't *you* try getting a mystery phone call about someone being taken to the hospital? No wonder I'm stressed. I thought it was Dad!"

Jem's insides flipped at the mention of her father. A man he'd been far closer to than his own father. "Phil? What's wrong with him?"

"It's a little too late to pretend you care."

Her phone rang. She snatched it from her pocket and hit the answer button without checking the screen. "Hello?" She angled her body away.

"Natalie?" A man's voice blared through the speakerphone.

"Hold on, Frank. I've got to—"

"Nat, the head-office rep just left. They came early. We're all out of a job."

A pit of dread opened in Jem's chest. Had that been the important presentation she'd mentioned? Had he cost Natalie her job?

Natalie stared at her phone, blinking rapidly. "I've got to go."

"Nat, wait."

"Get out of the car, Jem." The words didn't sound angry, just sad. And that ripped him far more than her fury ever would.

He did as she asked, pulled Olly from his car seat, and stood back on the sidewalk. She drove away without a backward glance.

Just like he had seven years ago.

♡

A police car whizzed by, and Jem ducked into the doorway of Charlottesville Christian Church's old hall, hiding his face from the street. He couldn't risk his dad, a captain in the Charlottesville Police Department, seeing him.

Especially as he broke into his brother's church.

One hundred Irish dancers pounded on his brain as he worked a credit card into the aged lock. Since the hospital had released him twenty minutes ago, his body screamed for home and a nap. A long list of jobs—shifting boxes and childcare hunting at the top—waited for his attention. Oliver would wake up hungry soon. And he'd promised his niece, Lili, that he'd study up on math today and help her with homework tonight.

But after the taxi dropped them at his abandoned car, Jem had driven straight here. He couldn't be back in town for more than a day without visiting Mom.

The lock clicked, and he eased the squeaky door open. No sign of anyone. Just him and his private sanctuary.

Jem picked up Olly's carrier, closed the door behind him, and walked down a long corridor to the third storeroom on the left. The 1950s structure had become a storage facility when the church built its bigger building in the early 2000s. Most people visited a grave site to "talk" with long-gone family members. Jem came here.

"Hi, Mom." Jem paused before a plaque and photograph beside the storeroom door.

IN LOVING MEMORY OF BARBARA WALTERS, AND
IN RECOGNITION OF BARBARA'S SERVICE TO THIS
CHURCH AS A SUNDAY SCHOOL TEACHER.
THE LORD GIVETH, AND THE LORD TAKETH AWAY.

The photo wasn't the formal wedding shot Dad had embedded in her headstone, but rather a candid snap of Mom kneeling beside first-grader Jem, smiling at a painting he'd drawn. Her red hair was twisted into an old-fashioned bun—her attempt at an Anne of Green Gables look. She'd apparently been obsessed with the character, even nicknaming Jem after the fictional woman's oldest son.

Or so he'd been told.

He ran a finger along the photo's warped wooden frame. He had no memory of Mom teaching Sunday school or reading novels. Few memories of her at all. He'd been five when a drunk driver killed her, and it wasn't like Dad had been big on sharing memories.

Jem plucked the photo from its nail on the wall, grabbed Olly's carrier, and ducked into the storeroom. Spare chairs filled most of the space, but he squeezed into the corner by the door.

Resting Oliver beside him, he used the edge of his gray Chicago Bulls T-shirt to wipe dust from the frame. Particles tickled his nose. He sniffed and studied the image. "Well, Mom, I'm back."

He cast his gaze around the room. When he left Charlottesville, he'd never thought he'd see the inside of a church building again. After five years and a lot of mistakes, he'd returned to the fold—but he'd still never expected to be back inside this particular church.

His brain turned to static. He needed this chat, needed her support for the weeks that lay ahead—even if he was only talking to a photo. "I, uh, I broke into the church. Sorry about that. I didn't really want to explain to Mike why I needed a key."

He had to see a photo of his mother. His father had put them all away the day after the funeral. Only this faded image and the one at the cemetery remained.

And cemeteries were spooky. But he didn't plan to tell his older brother that.

"I ran into Natalie today. She's still gorgeous, if you're wondering." He grinned at the memory of her rumpled state. "She's still mad at m—"

The storeroom door flew open. He jolted and almost dropped the photo onto Oliver.

A dark-haired man loomed in the doorway. "I thought I might find you here."

Jem huffed out a relieved breath. "Mike. How'd you know?"

Jem's senior-pastor brother, twelve years older and twenty times more sensible, folded his arms. "You tripped the silent alarm. I knew you'd break in sometime this week."

"I always suspected you could read my mind."

"You think I never saw you do it when you were a kid?" Mike grinned. "You're not as sneaky as you think. Now you've got about five seconds to scram if you don't want Dad to catch you here."

"He's here?" Jem scrambled to his feet, scooped up Oliver's carrier, and hung Mom's photo back on the wall.

"He was pulling up as I walked out of the church, and he's probably followed me. Go out the other door."

Jem scooted out of sight as Dad's deep voice echoed down the hall. "Mike? You here?"

Jem made it outside, then leaned against the outer door's weathered wood. It had been seven years since he'd left, three since they'd spoken. He'd gone through college. Started a career. Become a father.

When he'd realized the only decent job he could find at short notice was in his hometown, he'd tried to look at the positives. Set goals. Like finding a way to talk to Dad again. But at the sound of that voice he was ten years old again, locked in his room writing lines of Bible verses, wondering if his dad had it out for the whole world . . . or just him.

Jem reached into his pocket. Poking past a pacifier, three sticks of gum, and his favorite pen, he dug out his keys and headed for the car.

At the end of their last conversation, Dad had said not to call again. So he wouldn't.

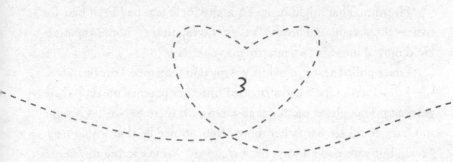

3

Sixteen-year-old Lilianna Walters dropped a math textbook into her backpack and jerked the zipper closed. "My whole relationship with Dad could be riding on this mocha-and-raspberry gelato."

The only good thing about having math last period on a Friday was that it made her that much more ecstatic when the bell rang and the weekend started. But on this Friday, she couldn't shake the anxious energy that kept her toes tapping as she tried to solve quadratic equations.

Her best friend, Grace, shrugged from her perch on a school desk, coloring her latest tattoo design in blue pen on her forearm. Around them, other tenth graders stuffed laptops and notebooks into bags and chattered about their weekend plans.

Grace blew on the ink. "I still don't get the problem in the first place, Lil."

Lili jammed her phone into her orange denim skirt pocket and searched for room in her tie-dyed backpack for a calculator. "He's been super distant lately. Ice cream Friday has been a tradition since forever. But this is the first time this month he's remembered."

"Maybe he's distracted because your Uncle Jem just got back in town."

Hmmm. That might be it. Though Uncle Jem had been here for two weeks already, and he wasn't even staying in their house anymore. He'd moved into his own apartment yesterday.

Grace pulled a face. "I'm lucky if my dad remembers my birthday."

Lili winced. Grace had struggled since her parents' breakup three years ago. Though her mom was about to shift them to North Carolina so Grace could see her father more often, so maybe that would help. "Yeah, but your dad's always been that way. Mine's acting different." Lili hefted the backpack. The textbook weighed a ton. As if it wasn't bad enough math was determined to destroy her brain, now it would destroy her back.

Grace slid off the desk and exited the classroom with her. "Why don't you take your art project to show him? He always loves your art."

"Good idea. I'll ask Miss Kent—*Ooof.*" Something small, blonde, and familiar plowed into Lili's gut. "Riley? What are you doing here?"

The ten-year-old girl from Lili's Sunday school class removed her face from Lili's diaphragm. "I was sick, so Nick came to pick me up early. But he forgot some stuff and came back to get it."

Lili glanced around the hallway. So Nick Kent *was* an official student here now. He used to go to Charlottesville High, but it couldn't have been easy after the business with his brother. She'd seen him around the school lately. But he could have been visiting his aunt, Lili's favorite art teacher.

Lili smoothed down Riley's mussed braid and hunkered to her level. "You don't look too sick to me."

"I'm sick of my teacher." Riley's eyes filled. "She yelled at me for falling asleep again today."

Lili's insides tightened. Riley couldn't sleep because her parents spent their nights screaming at one another. Lili opened her arms, and Riley buried herself in them. "I'm sorry, kiddo."

Grace gave a goodbye wave over Riley's head, and Lili wiggled her fingers in response.

"Riley?"

A pair of sneakers shuffled into view, gaping holes showing where the soles came away from the fake leather. Lili moved her gaze upward, past stained jeans cuffs to a torn flannel shirt, until a face with hazel eyes and messy brown hair replaced the scruffy clothes.

Nick knelt next to her in the emptying corridor and studied what little he could see of Riley's face. "Is she all right?"

"Um, yeah. Just upset about—"

He nodded before she had to say it, then rubbed Riley's back. If anyone understood Riley's home situation, it was Nick. Riley never stopped talking about him. According to her gushing stories, he was her next-door neighbor, official chauffeur, and unofficial guardian angel.

According to town gossip, he was the son of an alcoholic and brother of a drug dealer.

"Do you come to school here now?"

"Yeah."

Lili could fill in the blanks. Miss Kent had come to Dad last year after Charlottesville High expelled Stephen Kent. Dad pulled strings to get Stephen into rehab. They probably figured out a way to get Nick into a different school as well.

Riley relaxed her hold on Lili but kept her face hidden. Lili fished a tissue from her pocket.

Nick tweaked the end of one of Riley's braids. "Do you want a piggyback ride to the car?"

When she hiccupped and nodded, he stood and offered his back. Lili lifted the child up until she latched her legs around Nick's waist and wrapped a stranglehold on his throat.

"Whoa. Easy on the windpipe."

Riley readjusted, and Nick sucked in a breath. Lili passed him his bag.

"You're her Sunday school teacher, right? I've seen you around church." Nick asked the question as Riley bounced and ordered him to march. He marched, and Lili followed.

"I just help Mrs. Dunkitt teach the class, but yeah, that's me."

"Riley talks about you a lot."

The tension in Lili's muscles lessened. She rolled her neck till it popped. "She talks about you too. She's kind of obsessed."

The little girl poked her tongue out at Lili, who poked hers right back.

"I am pretty awesome." Nick puffed out his chest, then burst out laughing. "Nah, I just bribe her with raspberry lollipops." He pulled one from his pocket, and Riley snatched it up. Lili laughed, then the sound faded into an awkward silence.

"So, uh, how do you like the new school?" She glanced at their surroundings. Her college preparatory school for gifted students would be an adjustment for anybody.

"It's different." He shifted his grip on Riley, bouncing her as he did so, and she squealed. "But different is fine. It'll help me get into business school."

Lili tilted her head, her gaze trailing over the length of him.

The ripped flannel and flappy sneakers didn't exactly scream "future businessman," and neither did his family's reputation. But the obstacles just made his ambition way more impressive . . . and kinda hot.

He held Riley up with one hand and used the other to open a door for Lili.

Ambitious and sweet. Grace was going to hear about this tonight.

Nick followed her through the door. "I've got some catching up to do, but actually, art's the only thing really killing me. And Aunt Trish is no help. Apparently if she teaches my class, she can't do my homework for me." He rolled his eyes, but a smile tugged at his lips.

"How is art your problem when our math teacher is an evil alien in disguise?" She rolled her eyes so hard she almost saw her brain.

"Crunching numbers is no problem. But stick figures are my only artistic strength."

Lili grinned. "Art is my jam. We might have to do a tutoring swap sometime."

"Seriously? That'd be awesome."

Lili paused at the turnoff to the art classroom. "Well, um, I guess I'll see you around?"

"Yeah." He nodded. "See ya later." He sounded like he planned to.

Riley waved, and the two headed on their way.

Lili shook her head as she double-timed it to the classroom door. A businessman math genius? Nick Kent was a surprising guy, and that tutoring would sure come in handy. The way things were going, she wasn't going to pass without a magic concentration secret.

A flicker of movement caught Lili's eye as she passed the internal art-classroom window. Was Miss Kent talking to someone?

Lili backtracked a step to peek through the open window.

Dad!

The room was too dark to make out his features, but she could recognize him from his frame alone. He must've come to talk to Miss Kent about Nick. Hopefully Miss Kent had talked up her art project.

Lili shuffled closer to see Dad's face. Her project—what did he really think? She peered through and squinted, trying to make sense of the forms in the darkened room. Vision sharpening, the images cleared. Her project rested on the desk, right in front of Dad—but he wasn't looking at it.

Her breathing labored as she stared at her dad, his face mushed up against Miss Kent's, fingers intertwined in her hair.

"Dad?" The word slipped from her mouth and echoed through the empty corridor and—whoops—the open window. She tensed.

But he didn't respond. He just attacked Miss Kent's mouth again and pushed her up against her desk.

The sucking noise made Lili gag. She dropped her bag on the ground with a thud.

"Dad!"

He ripped from Miss Kent and spun around. When his gaze locked on Lili, he froze. Behind him, Miss Kent wiped a hand across her face, eyes wide like she was horrified at what she'd done—or just at being caught?

Dad jolted out of his zombie state and surged in Lili's direction, his hand hitting a switch and flooding the room with light. "Lili! I— Um, we . . . we have to go."

Red stained the teacher's cheeks as she smoothed her blonde hair. Her black claw clip dangled from the frizzy strands. It looked like one of Mom's—

Mom.

Dad moved toward the closed door between them. Some invisible force field pressed against Lili's throat, and her breath came in short gasps. Inching back, she shook her head while shock waves rolled through her chest, swelling through her body to her fingers and toes. A ground-shifting sensation, like the California earthquake she'd once cowered through.

The art room door opened, and Dad took a step toward her, expression pleading, but tripped over her deserted backpack. He almost fell but managed to keep his feet beneath him.

"Get away from me." Her voice wobbled as she took a big step back.

Dad straightened and held out a hand. "Lili, it's not—"

"Get away from me!" The scream erupted from deep in her throat.

Miss Kent jolted and bumped the desk. Lili's project—a painted plaster cast—crashed onto the floor, shattered.

Dad's outstretched hand lowered a little.

Tears fogged Lili's vision. Striding past Dad, she slapped his hand aside and sprinted for the double door at the end of the hallway, her mind too full of lights and sirens to form a coherent thought.

She sidestepped a slow-moving body and burst through the door into the outside world.

"Lili!" A male voice came from behind.

High-octane fuel replaced Lili's blood. A burst of speed had her halfway down the block before Nick's face appeared in her mind's eye. It was his voice she'd heard, not Dad's.

At the corner, Lili glanced behind her. All clear. She dove left and powered down the sidewalk.

After the initial my-chest-is-a-pincushion pain of her sprint, she settled into a rhythm. Her lungs prioritized air over tears, so she stifled the sobs as she dodged pedestrians. Sweat drenched her black button-up shirt. Doc Martens made terrible running shoes.

After several minutes, she reached the town's outdoor mall. Chairs resting in front of the children's museum called to her suddenly heavy limbs, and she flopped into one.

She wasn't far from the school, but she'd zigzagged in case Dad tried to follow her. She gulped in a few big breaths to satisfy her muscles' demands for oxygen and bit her lip to stop the oncoming sobs. Leaning over, she rested her elbows on her knees and covered her face with her hands. Maybe people would think she looked more like a winded jogger than a world-falling-apart teenager.

Though not many joggers wore purple-patterned stockings with orange skirts.

Children's laughter floated toward her from the museum. She wiped her eyes as kids dashed into the building. This had been her favorite place on earth as a child. On the last Friday of every month, she'd visit with Grace and Grace's mom while her own parents enjoyed an afternoon date.

Her nose tickled with remembered chalk dust. She'd spent as much time scribbling on the freedom of speech wall—a seven-foot-high chalkboard in the mall—as she had in the museum. One of the museum workers had been the first person to comment on her artistic talent.

She rubbed her nose, and the tickle stopped. The visits had ended with the completion of elementary school. Come to think of it, so had the dates.

Her phone buzzed. Dad's face flashed on the screen, the silly selfie he'd taken while dressed in a sumo-wrestling fat suit at youth group last year.

Lili's thumb swiped and rejected the call. The fifth time the phone rang, she caved. "What?"

"It's not what you think." Dad's breathless voice bounced at regular intervals, like he was jogging.

"What do you think I think? I just saw you jamming your tongue into—" She couldn't finish the sentence.

"It's not—it wasn't—it was the first time. I'm not cheating. I swear."

"What, so just 'cos you haven't slept with her yet it's all okay?" Lili's voice verged on ultrasonic, and a few parents in front of the children's museum glanced at her. She wilted in her seat and lowered her voice. "Anyway, I don't believe you."

"Lili, I'm sorry. It wasn't meant to happen. I went there to talk. I don't know what happened. I never kissed her before."

"What about Mom?"

A pause. "You know your mom and I have been having some . . . problems." He sighed. "I'm just stressed. We'll work this out."

"Does she know?"

"There's nothing to know. What you saw was the extent of it. We—we just need some time to work our stuff out."

"I have to tell her."

"It'd be better coming from me. I know it's hard to understand, but these things are difficult. Your mother is— It's tricky."

She rubbed her eyes. How could she not tell Mom?

"Lili?"

The voice didn't come through the phone. She swiveled her head. Dad stood behind her, collar loose and sweat dampening his blue business shirt. Her bag dangled from his hand.

"How did you—"

He held up his cell. "Find My Phone service."

She stared at him, and the moment stretched. Thoughts stampeding through her mind quieted to one thing: for the past sixteen years, he had been her hero, her knight in shining armor. Now she couldn't pull her gaze from the lipstick smudging his face.

"You're the last person I thought would do this," she whispered.

He rubbed a hand through his hair. "I know. Same here."

She rose and followed him, and they drove toward the house in silence. She'd rather go to math class than home, but what choice did she have? At least Mom would be out at basketball all afternoon.

As streetlights flicked by, the storm grew in Lili's mind. Did she even know her father? For the love of chocolate gelato, he was *Pastor* Mike Walters! Didn't he care about God? Or had their whole lives been a lie?

She glanced at him, his hand on the wheel of their BMW, the other massaging his temple. She bit her lip. Would he leave?

Lili pressed back in her seat and held her eyelids down. She couldn't cry. She'd only make things worse.

Ten minutes passed before she could open them again. He didn't seem to notice, just fixed his eyes on the road and occasionally scrubbed his sleeve over his lips.

She shook her head and turned to the window.

Dad, do you even care what this is doing to me?

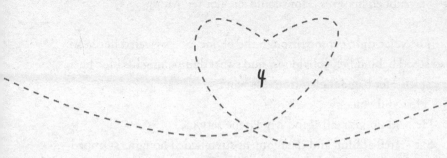

4

I'm going to kill my mother.

The squeak of rubber soles on the court echoed around Natalie as she froze in the doorway of the recreational center's basketball court, two weeks after leaving Jem on the hospital sidewalk.

Three guys raced toward the far end of the court, chasing their opponent, whose long legs propelled him down the court at a lightning pace.

Jem.

After another depressing day of job hunting, the last thing she'd wanted to do on her Friday afternoon was play in the weekly social basketball league. But Mom had convinced her to get off the computer—she'd been researching weird M&M flavors to buy—and instead run off the stress, all with a twinkle in her eye Natalie hadn't quite deciphered.

Now she recognized it—the cunning of a woman determined to get grandchildren. Mom had been single minded toward that endeavor ever since Natalie made the mistake of telling her why she missed the head-office rep meeting.

But if the dream involved Jem, it had to die.

Cheers swelled from the handful of bystanders as Jem leapt through the air and dunked the ball. Even the opposing team members clapped.

"Way to go, Jem!"

The corners of her mouth lifted. She'd practiced with him for countless afternoons till he mastered that move. From that day on, every time he nailed a dunk his eyes would search her out, whether she was beside him on the court or cheering in the stands. His lips would pull into a grin that seemed to combine *Did you see that?* with *Couldn't have done it without you, babe.*

Her mind landed back in the present at the same moment Jem's gaze locked with hers.

She froze.

He grinned. *Did you see that?*

The corner of her mouth twitched upward.

Another thought slammed into her mind. *He has a baby with someone else.*

She whirled and headed out the door. How could he grin at her as if the last seven years hadn't happened?

Her ire built with each step, threatening to spill over into frustrated tears. He had a baby. She'd felt sick each morning when she woke and remembered that the man she'd thought would raise her children now had one with someone else. And the fact it bit so deep dragged her self-esteem down another three notches. He'd obviously not missed her at all, and here she was still affected by him. After seven years.

Pathetic.

Natalie rounded a corner and pulled her keys from her pocket. She needed time with Jeremy Walters about as much as she needed a cockroach under her pillow.

"Nat! Wait up!" Jem's voice echoed down the hall.

The open door to the sports equipment storage room presented the perfect hiding place. She flew in and dove behind a pile of dusty gym mats.

"Natalie?"

She fought a sneeze as his footsteps approached, then paused.

"Your foot is sticking out." Laughter rumbled in his voice.

She wriggled her way upright, brushing a monstrous dust bunny from her blue-and-gold uniform.

"I was just, uh, looking for something." *Like peace and quiet.*

He nodded. "There's a dead moth in your hair."

"Blagh-eek!"

"Just kidding." He smirked.

Trying to claw back some dignity, she crossed her arms and surveyed him. How was it fair that, even after so long, those mischievous blue eyes hadn't lost one ounce of their charm? Time to go on the offensive. "What are you doing on my team? Don't you have an article to write or a baby to take care of?"

"Didn't realize you owned the team. Or still played." He quirked an eyebrow. "Is it a problem?"

Rats. No good way out of that one. "Of course not. You'd better be able to pull your weight, is all. You've got a bit of a dad bod going on." An utter lie. Curse his physique.

He slapped a hand on his stomach. "Didn't know you'd been checking my bod out." The words were laced with laughter, but Natalie just stared. Not going there.

The mirth drained from Jem's expression under the weight of the silence. "Okay, I can't do fake nicety-nice with you." He ran a hand down his face, pulling his cheeks. "I talked to your mom."

The air left her lungs.

"She told me about your dad. I'm sorry. I knew he was sick, but I didn't know how bad."

She flinched at the mention of Dad. *He's in remission.* She fought the urge to shout the words. Yes, technically he was in remission. But the writing was on the wall, and barring a miracle, they all knew what the future held. The question was when.

"And she said you can't find a job and will have to move back in with them."

Natalie sucked in a deep breath, pressure building in her brain. "Why would—"

"I need someone to take care of Olly."

She gaped at him. "Have you lost your mind?" The man had told her he loved her. Asked her to marry him. Dumped her and disappeared for seven years.

And now he wanted to be her boss?

"I would never ask if we weren't both desperate. But I start my new job on Monday, and so far my best childcare option is the place on James Street. The woman smelled of cigarettes and had gross fingernails." He pretended to gag.

"Do you know how weird this is?" Her voice jumped about a hundred octaves.

He searched her face. "Just think about it, okay? It's only school hours. I can't afford to pay you full-time. Lili's gonna have him from three thirty till I get home. At least until I can figure something out."

Natalie's brain spun. How could he even pay for this? His brother had to be helping him. And was he serious about . . . "Lili?"

"She's sixteen. We babysat at her age."

"Yeah, and look how that went."

"Come on. The kid's eyebrows grew back. No biggie."

"Where is Olly, anyway?"

"There's a childcare service for parents during the game. Unfortunately, they're not available from eight till six every day."

Footsteps sounded in the hall outside.

"Jem? Nat? We're starting in five."

"Coming." Natalie snatched a basketball off the shelf and scrambled past Jem. He followed her, and the fabric of her shirt shifted as he plucked something off it.

"What was that?"

"You don't want to know."

A shudder rippled through her. For the first time in seven years, she was thankful for something Jem had done.

Would working for him really be so bad?

Whoa. Alarm bells blared in her mind. No. Never again.

A step from the gym door, still out of sight from their teammates, she spun and sank a finger into Jem's chest. "The answer's no. And don't ask again."

Before he could react, she stalked onto the court.

The opposing team had already taken up their positions, ready for the jump ball. Three of Natalie's teammates waited at half court, each sporting their blue-and-gold team colors. Steph, Natalie's old mentor from when she was a teen—and Jem's sister-in-law—was closest, hair in a perky ponytail and Nikes gleaming white. She bounced on her toes, warming up, then spotted Natalie and Jem and did a double take. "Are you okay?"

Natalie barely caught the murmured words as she took up her position. Jem headed to the ref, ready for the jump ball.

"Talk to you at halftime," she muttered.

The referee held out the ball and gave his usual spiel about playing fair. Natalie shut out all other thoughts and focused on the ball.

The whistle blew.

The basketball flew into the air. Jem slapped it, and she snatched it and fired it back to him in a move they'd perfected years ago. They were halfway down the court before the other team could blink, and a minute later he scored. Some guy Natalie didn't know, but who apparently played for their team, smacked him on the back. Jem gave him a thumbs-up and winked at her.

Natalie rolled her eyes and headed for the throw-in.

♡

"Before you say anything about Jem, I have news."

Natalie watched Steph wipe a slight sheen from her forehead as they stood in the bathroom at halftime. Jem's sister-in-law radiated Chanel No. 5 after a brutal half game. Natalie tried not to compare Steph's poised appearance to the dark blotches on her own shirt as she stared at her friend. Stars had been born, twinkled, and died while she waited for the ref's whistle and the chance to vent.

"News bigger than Jem moving back and asking me to work for him?" Natalie panted, still short on oxygen after her last drive for the basket. Sweat trickled down her calf. "I'll do the fund-raiser again if you want." She'd run the basketball team's annual fund-raiser the past three years and exceeded her record of funds raised each time. She'd tried to beg out of it this year, but Steph had been determined that she was the woman for the job.

"There's no one better at it than you, but that's not what I'm talking about." Steph leaned forward, eyes alight. "Did you see Sam? The new guy?"

"Tall, dark hair—"

"And bulging biceps. He's Samuel Payton. As in—"

"The guy who started Wildfire?" Natalie blinked against the fluorescent glare bouncing from bleached-white tiles. No wonder everyone had flocked to talk to him as soon as the whistle blew. She'd been following the Australian's success with his California-based youth ministry, Wildfire, even before it attracted national attention. Then revival hit the West Coast, and the whole country heard his name when the *Today* show ran the story.

"He's in Charlottesville to run the pilot program for his East Coast campaign. The one on the West Coast last year started a revival in at least a dozen Christian high schools. He's basically the next version of your dad."

Natalie turned to the counter and twisted the faucet, holding back a wince. Her Australia-born father had taken Virginia by storm when he arrived as a young evangelist forty years ago. Up until the last seven years, people predicted *she* would be the next Philip Groves. She and her father shared the same intense work ethic, the same sharp mind. Or so Billy Graham had said when she met him at a youth leaders' conference a dozen years ago.

Ever since she'd had to drop out of ministry, most people in the church didn't even know her name.

And sometimes it felt like God didn't either.

"Dad's been excited about Samuel's work for a while. Especially since he's an Aussie. But how does this compare to my news about Jem?"

"Sam's hired me to help get things going. Administration isn't his strong suit. I'll be part-time for the church and then part-time for Wildfire. But we need more manpower, so we're about to open an internship. It goes for three months, and if Sam likes the intern, he's promising a job at the end of it. They'd even pay for you to finish college. I told him you'd apply."

Natalie's hand slipped as she shut off the water. "Are you serious?" Thoughts exploded like confetti—youth rallies, baptisms, working with Steph, her father's beaming face, social-media buzz, altar calls, discipleship camps, the *Wildfire* logo on her email . . . "It would never work."

A single wrinkle creased Steph's porcelain forehead. "Why?"

"Internships are unpaid. I've got bills." Her mind raced. There had to be a solution. This internship could be her ticket into a career that actually mattered.

"It's minimum wage."

"Still not enough." She calculated the money she'd save by moving into Mom and Dad's spare room. Not much. And her savings were long since tapped out, as she'd secretly paid all the medical bills she could without Mom finding out about it.

Steph puffed up her cheeks. "What if you found a job flexible enough to work around it? It's a lot of nights, weekend work. Our focus at first will be getting Sam in to speak at schools, and we'll brainstorm other strategies from there. It means the hours will be flexible for the time being. I'll email you the official details. Maybe you can look for something that fits with it."

Something twisted Natalie's gut. She picked at a torn fingernail. "Maybe."

"Oh yeah. The Jem thing." Steph wrinkled her pert nose. "He told me he planned to ask you. I told him to stand out of striking range." She squeezed Natalie's forearm. "Believe me, I get it." Something strange entered her tone before she gave her head a little shake. "Brother-in-law or not, in my books he's got a long way to go before he earns a place back in our family. But consider what's at stake. You've always dreamed of carrying on your dad's work, but . . ."

"I knew he wouldn't see it," Natalie finished. Her watch ticked five times before she spoke again. "What if Jem's only offering because of . . . you know, our history?"

"So what? Do the job and take his money. His feelings are his problem." The corner of Steph's mouth twitched in a sympathetic smile. "Just think about it. When will you get another chance like this?" She dropped an eyelid in a wink. "I'm even ninety-five percent sure Sam's single." She patted Natalie's shoulder and left.

Natalie gripped the counter as the marrow drained from her bones. She'd done the same thing in this room before. The Friday that the news broke of her ruined engagement. The Sunday that Dad announced his diagnosis.

She stared at the dark hole in the bottom of the sink, searching for any speck of dirt the cleaners had missed. Her eyes zeroed in on the edge of the metal guard on the plughole, tears clearing as her focus sharpened.

Different day, same grit.

Working for Jem would be like staring at a movie of how her life was supposed to turn out. Longing and revulsion in one twisted pill, like the sweet-and-sour Warheads Dad used to trick her into eating.

There had to be another way to fund her months in the internship. She just couldn't do it with Jem.

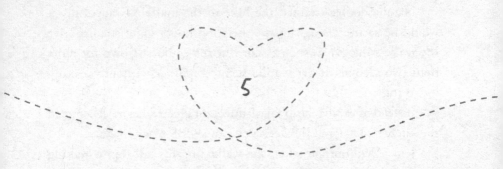

5

*P*ain dug its fingers into Natalie's shoulder as she gave the pedals of Mom's rusting bicycle one final shove and coasted toward her parents' home in the waning evening light. She'd come off second best in a pileup of bodies—including Jem's—when a contest for the basketball went a little too far. Jem had offered her a ride home, but she'd said no before he finished the question.

As she rolled closer, the streetlight illuminated the driveway in front of the 1970s rental her parents now called home. She squinted at the parked vehicle. Not Dad's ancient Volvo.

Dismounting, she walked the bike up the drive and peered into the blue Camry. A baby seat sat buckled in the back.

No, no, no, no—

"Come on in." Mom stood in the open door dressed in a fluorescent-blue sweat suit and too wide smile, her Australian accent a touch thicker than usual. "You're just in time for sweets."

"Mom, what did you do?"

Mom folded her arms. "Natalie Jane, don't you throw a hissy fit. I didn't know you planned to stop by before you went home. Your father asked to see Jem, so here he is." She pointed to the door. "Come inside and help me serve dessert."

Natalie double-chained the bike to the mailbox—hopefully it would be secure enough in this neighborhood—and tried to give Mom the stink eye as she passed. But she couldn't frown for more than two seconds at her vanilla-scented mother without breaking into a smile.

Instead of vanilla, hospital disinfectant greeted her as she entered the kitchen. That and the deep voice of a CBS news anchor.

Jem jerked upright when she walked in, his tall frame making the room seem tiny. Olly fussed in his arms until Jem popped a pacifier into the baby's mouth. "Nat, I didn't realize— I, um . . ."

Natalie eyed him. Where was his previous swagger?

She shuffled farther in, her right hand holding her left shoulder. "Where's Dad?"

"He was just having a little rest before Jem arrived," Mom said. "You serve up and pour the tea, and I'll go get him." She scuttled down the hallway.

Natalie smiled at the ice cream bucket sweating beside an open tin of peaches, her taste buds watering at the Groves household's Thursday night dessert. But she moved to the freezer first and snagged a bag of baby corn. Then she rummaged through the third drawer for Dad's masking tape.

"Sorry again about the shoulder," Jem said from the other side of the counter.

She kept her eyes on her task. "It's fine."

"Need any help?"

"I'm fine."

She balanced the bag on her shoulder, held it down with her ear, and wrapped the tape around and under the armpit, once and then again. She had neither the energy nor the patience to hold the thing on and try to serve dessert at the same time. Tearing the tape with her teeth, she slapped the end down, grabbed a spoon, and slopped peaches into the first bowl.

Jem, still in her peripheral vision, let his gaze wander around the walls crammed with photo frames, knickknacks, and more photos. "It's, uh, different from their old place."

"They had to sell last year."

"Oh."

The news droned on in the background, and Olly rattled Jem's keys, breaking the awkwardness. Tension left her shoulders. She could survive this. Jem just had to keep quiet till she made her escape.

"So how is your dad, uh, doing?"

She usually prided herself on her politeness, but this whole keep-a-distance-from-Jem thing called for an exception.

Make it clear he should stay away. Be tough.

She squared her shoulders. "He's dying. But I thought you knew."

He cleared his throat. "Your mom mentioned it. But I mean how does he feel about—I mean, does he think the same, uh . . ."

Natalie looked up to meet his eyes, but he focused on the photo frame in front of him, the Australia-shaped one that used to contain a photo of Mom, Dad, Natalie, and Jem. She'd swapped it out years ago.

His lost expression matched how she felt.

"Here we come." Mom broke the moment as Dad's wheelchair edged out of the hallway.

Jem tensed. Lines appeared on his forehead, and his skin turned a delicate shade of gray.

Despite her brain's warning signals, Natalie's chest tightened. Jem had been closer to her father than his own family.

Dad's slippered feet peeked around the corner, followed by patchwork-quilt-covered legs with veined hands resting on the knees.

"Jeremy Walters. Get your skinny backside over here. I've got something to say to you." Dad's voice cracked across the room as Mom stopped the wheelchair next to their table.

Jem paled another five shades and stepped closer.

"Sir, I just wanted to say—"

Dad grabbed Jem's free hand before he could finish and squeezed it. "I missed you, boy."

A muscle twitched in Jem's face, and he bent to give Dad an awkward hug.

Natalie's eyes misted.

Jem had adored her father ever since that day in eighth grade when Dad had filled in for Captain Walters at a school Father's Day basketball game. Jem found an excuse to come over all the time after that, and their family had often laughed that they never knew if it was to see Natalie or Dad.

Jem perched on a seat next to Dad and cleared his throat. "I, um, think I should apol—"

"Gimme a look at the strapping young man you've got there. He's a chip off the old block. What a handsome little devil."

Jem surrendered Olly to Dad's outstretched hands.

They chatted about the baby, Jem's new job at the local newspaper, apartment rental prices. The only thing Dad refused to discuss was Jem's apology.

Natalie handed out dessert bowls, shifting a stack of papers so she could place Dad's in front of him as he chatted.

A large red number on the top page of the stack jumped out at her. She did a double take and snatched up the bill, her skin prickling into goose bumps all the way down to her curled toes. She caught Mom's eye and nodded to the far side of the kitchen. Mom moved behind the sink and turned on the water as Natalie joined her.

"What is this?" Natalie held out the page, pointing at the bottom figure. She shot a quick glance at Dad, but the gurgling water seemed to cover their conversation.

She'd managed her parents' finances for the past four years. Mom had a terrible head for numbers and enough stress to deal with already. And Dad . . . Well, they'd all decided it was best if she took care of the paperwork and kept them up to date on the situation.

And so far she'd handled dozens of large bills like this. But not without a job.

Mom grimaced. "It came this morning. We didn't realize this one was coming."

Natalie rested her elbows on the counter and studied the document. Worse than the dollar figure were the words *Due in thirty days.*

"You can't get an extension?"

"Already tried."

Head down, Natalie counted to ten. The beast inside her longed to smash everything in reach. Instead, she reached for the sugar bowl and dumped a teaspoon of granules in Jem's tea. He liked it black, no sugar, and even though this situation wasn't his fault, she felt a smidgen better.

Mom moved closer and lowered her voice. "How much do we have left?"

Natalie shook her head. "Not this much. Not if you want to buy bread and toilet paper in the next month."

Ripples ran through Mom's tea as her hand shook. "Toilet paper's overrated. There's some leafy trees in our backyard." Her upbeat tone couldn't hide the quiver in her voice.

Natalie dumped three more spoonfuls of sugar in Jem's cup. "Not going to cut it."

"And you've had no luck finding a job?"

Oh no. There had to be another way.

She scanned the room, crammed with worn furniture and bric-a-brac valuable only in terms of sentiment. They had nothing left to sell except for Dad's Sean Connery–signed James Bond poster—something he loved only slightly less than her. She'd sell her clothes before she sold that. And her job search had been futile. Savings: gone.

Natalie's eyes slid shut and she massaged her temples. There was no way around it. They needed cash, and they needed it now.

Steel entered her soul. She could do this for Mom and Dad. "Actually, I have a bit of an announcement."

She took a fortifying gulp of tea. It scalded all the way down her throat. Two more spoonfuls went into Jem's cup. She turned to the men and raised her voice. "Tea's ready."

Jem stood and passed Dad's cup to him, then picked up his own.

"Dad, I've got good news." Natalie glanced at Jem as she stepped closer to her favorite man in the world. Dad's weathered face smiled at her.

"Eh, what's that?"

Jem choked on his tea. A small satisfaction in light of the blow about to be delivered to her fragile pride.

"I'm applying for an internship with Samuel Payton's youth ministry, and I'll work as a nanny for Jem at the same time. If I get it, the positions will be flexible enough to work around each other."

"You will? It will?" Jem recovered enough to ask, setting his cup on the table with a grimace.

Natalie braced her hands on her hips. "Take it or leave it."

He beamed at Dad. "Right. I'm your daughter's new boss."

She should have put another six sugars in.

Dad grasped her fingers, and she dragged her death stare from Jem's face. "Nattie, that's terrific. Samuel Payton's a good man."

Her lips tugged into a smile. "Yes, he is. It's an amazing ministry." And she'd dreamed for so long now of taking part in something of such significance.

Putting up with Jem would be worth it. Hopefully. Now she just needed to secure the internship.

Dad's eyes clouded for a moment before he blinked the tears away. "You deserve this chance, more than anybody. After all you've given up."

She clasped his hand with her other one. "I haven't been accepted yet. And I might not get the job at the end of it."

Dad tugged her down to kiss her cheek. "I know you. You'll get it. You always do me proud."

A tiny blossom of hope unfurled in her soul. He was right. She would work harder than any intern ever before. She'd make this ministry thing work. And she'd make Dad proud.

Mom's expression remained the only one uncertain, unlike the grinning Jem and Dad.

Dad turned his attention to Jem. "Thank you, Jem. She couldn't do this without the right kind of job."

Jem shrugged. "I feel bad it's only part-ti—Ow!"

Natalie ground her heel into his toe. No need for Dad to know their financial situation still wasn't ideal.

"What's wrong?" Dad frowned.

"Remember he used to get terrible leg cramps?" She patted Jem on the back as he grasped his foot. "Needs more salt." Technically, it wasn't a lie.

Jem, still bent over and holding his foot, glanced up at her with mutinous blue eyes. She drilled him with a look and prayed he got the message.

He straightened. "Yeah, those cramps. I'll have to eat more bacon."

Natalie licked ice cream from her spoon and smiled at him.

He flexed his sore foot. "Anyway, I should get home and give Olly a bath. I'll see you on Monday, Nat."

"I'll walk you out so you can give me the details."

He collected Olly from Dad, pried his keys from the baby's slobbery hands, and she followed him out the door. As soon as it shut behind them, he spun. "We need a safe word, because I think you just broke my toe."

"Makes up for the shoulder."

"That was an accident."

"So was this."

He shook his head, opened the rear car door, and fastened Olly into his seat. "You don't want your dad to know it's only part-time?"

Natalie shook her head. "He and Mom have enough on their minds. They don't need to think about finances too. But that brings me to my one condition."

"Condition?" He finished clicking Olly into place and faced her.

She put her best negotiating face on and held his gaze. Thank goodness Steph had been able to email her the details straight from her phone after the game. "I'm only interested if I can work it around an internship with Wildfire. Most of it is night and weekend work, but some will be in the daytime. I'll need to bring Olly along with me or do the work from your place while I have him. The hours change, so I'd need to be flexible."

Jem folded his arms and tilted his head, like he was thinking about it. "You'll send me the details when you get them? So I know how many hours we're talking about?"

She brought up the new-contacts screen of her phone and held it out. "I'm guessing you're not still BugsBunny92@hotmail.com?"

His fingers brushed hers as he took the phone from her. "I have a condition of my own." His thumbs flew across the screen, his own phone dinged, and he handed hers back. She checked the screen. He'd entered his contact details under the name *Elmer Fudd* and sent himself a text, presumably to get her number.

She gave a cautious nod. "Shoot."

"You'll consider staying later occasionally, if I need it. You can always say no. Just be open to the possibility. And sometimes, if I need a hand with something, like . . . finding furniture for my apartment, you'd also consider helping out with that. I'd pay you, of course."

His tone remained professional. But it sounded like a plot to entwine her in his life again.

Her hands curled into fists, and she forced them flat. "You can't find your own furniture?"

He reached toward the keys in his pocket. "Take it or leave it."

She gritted her teeth. She'd had nightmares over the years where she met Jem and his new family, or Jem gate-crashed her wedding to a world-famous actor. A girl could dream. But never, ever, in the darkest recesses of her mind, had she imagined agreeing to work for him.

Her eyes shut momentarily. "Fine."

Jem pulled out his phone. "I'll send you the address. Come at seven thirty Monday, and we can work out the finer details then."

She nodded.

He crossed to the driver's side and slid in. She'd turned to go back inside when his window whirred down. "Beetroot," he called.

"What?"

"Our safe word. It's 'beetroot.'"

She pressed her lips together to stop a smile. She was supposed to be mad. "You're sleep deprived. Go home."

He backed out of the driveway, head still poking out the window. "Beetroot! Don't forget!"

"I'll see you Monday."

She made it sound more like a threat than a promise, but his grin looked like it remained as he drove away.

The front door squeaked, and vanilla sweetened the air. "Natalie?" Her mother joined her in the driveway, facing the twinkling lights of Charlottesville and the cool night breeze. "Are you okay?"

The question was quiet, thoughtful.

And difficult to answer.

Natalie injected levity into her tone. "The internship is a great opportunity. One I've been waiting on for a long time."

Mom squeezed her hand. "I know. I just . . . I know how you

throw yourself into whatever you put your mind to. It's going to be a lot of work, especially with Jem—"

"A necessary evil." She hugged her mother. "But nothing I can't handle."

Another lie.

6

"Lili, I ran into Miss Kent the other day."

Lili choked on her grape juice as Mom looked at her across the dinner table, still dressed in her basketball uniform from this afternoon's game.

The evening hadn't been too awful after Lili and Dad arrived home from today's disastrous afternoon at school. Mom had been out at basketball and Dad holed up in his office—probably praying Lili wouldn't say anything to Mom. But now they were all together for a late supper, and the only thing worse than awkward silence was conversation.

Snagging a napkin, Lili blotted the red stains on her plate and tried to sound unconcerned. "Oh?"

"She said she loved your project. Have you received your marks yet?"

Dad kept his eyes on his plate. He hadn't spoken for the entire meal. "Uh . . . no. It, um, it got broken today."

"What? How?"

Dad's eyes flickered up.

She shifted in her seat. "Someone was being stupid and accidentally knocked it off the desk."

"That's ridiculous." Mom's voice jumped an octave. "I hope they were punished. Will it affect your grade?"

Lili glanced at Dad. "It better not."

He cleared his throat and shoved a lettuce leaf into his mouth.

The silence stretched as Mom took a deep drink from her SlimShake, then set it down where her plate should have been. She adjusted her straw. "Today marks two weeks since the Women in Ministry group made our Shake'n'Shimmy pact."

Dad rolled his eyes. "Steph, that diet is a complete fraud."

Mom glared at him. "If you had your way, every pastor's wife would wear potato sacks and no makeup." She twirled an ironed-in curl. Somehow her hairstyles survived even the toughest workout. "Besides, Shauna's doctor told her to lose weight."

Dad shook his head. "It's unhealthy. Those shakes are sawdust and milk, and if Shauna's going to lose sixty pounds, she can't depend on a dance routine for exercise."

"Are you saying you know more than the team of scientists and doctors who endorsed the program?"

Dad acted as if Mom hadn't spoken.

Mom sniffed. "Didn't think so. It wouldn't hurt you to tr—"

"Nick!" Lili jumped in, desperate for a change in topic.

Her parents stared at her.

"I, uh—I made a new friend today. His name's Nick."

Mom tilted her head. "What's his last name? Do we know the family?"

"Kent. Nick Kent." A sinking sensation lodged in her belly. Maybe Mom's healthy-living rant would've been a better topic after all.

"Kent. As in Trish Kent's nephew? Mike, is that the troubled boy you've been helping?" Mom's voice neared levels only audible to dogs.

The words smacked Lili in the face. Of course. It made total sense. Nick and Stephen were the reason Dad and Miss Kent spent so much time together. They were the reason that—

"Don't take that tone, Stephanie. Stephen's the one who was in trouble. We got Nick into that school because he wanted an opportunity. Lili can be friends with him if she wants."

Lili's mouth fell open. Dad never spoke to Mom like that. At least she'd never heard it. But was it in defense of Lili or the Kents?

Mom's lips twisted in that tight smile that fooled most people. Oh boy. She was *really* angry. "Of course she can, Mike. I just want to be certain we're doing what's best for our girl." She nodded toward Lili. "For our family."

The urge to spill the whole story rose up inside Lili. Or was that her dinner threatening a revisit? She threw her napkin on the table. "May I be excused?"

Mom frowned, but Dad spoke first. "Of course."

Lili fled up the stairs, the hounds of truth barking behind her. Grabbing her robe, she dashed into the bathroom, set her phone's music player to Mom's most-hated rapper, and shoved the volume up all the way. Then she turned the shower up as hot as she could stand. Dad hated her using too much hot water.

Hair coiled in a soapy bun on her head, she practiced the dance moves Grace had been teaching her. Without Grace's tutelage she was so awkward on the dance floor. No one would ever think she was attractive, let alone sexy.

She stopped, midshimmy.

Was that how Dad and Miss Kent had started? The woman was also the school's dance teacher. It wouldn't have been hard for her to invite Dad to practice and then seduce—

Ewww. Seduce was such a gross word, especially in reference to parents.

And what if it was the other way around? What if Dad had come on to Miss Kent?

She shoved her head under the spray and washed the soap out. Forget conditioner. She had to know.

She jumped out of the shower and dressed in her pajamas and robe in record time, then stomped in the direction of Dad's office. He stood facing his computer, back to the door, staring at . . . nothing, by the looks of it. She stepped inside and shut the door with a bang.

He jumped. "Lili."

No reprimand for slamming the door. He just sank into his leather chair and sighed. "What do you want to know?"

Lili folded her arms. "Who came on to who?"

"What?"

"Who came on to who? Did she start it? She did, didn't she? That little—"

"No, Lili."

Her arms dropped. *"What?"*

"No one started it. It just . . . One second we were discussing Nick's scholarship, and the next . . ."

"Normal people discuss scholarships from opposite sides of a desk." She shook her head. "I can't do this. It's *killing* me. Dinner was torture."

"Lili, don't. You'll make things worse."

"All you two did was fight, and half of it was fighting over me." Sobs crept into her voice. "Is that what I do? Make it worse?"

"Liliiiiiiii." Dad dragged her name out. "This isn't about you."

That didn't mean she wasn't contributing to the issues. Sobs shook her robe, its tag tickling her neck. "Are you going to move out? Are we going to be like Grace's family?"

"No, honey, I'm not going anywhere." Dad stood and tugged her forearm till she was close enough to hug. "We'll fix this. But I'll be honest, it's going to be a big job."

They stood in silence for a moment, rocking back and forth to an unheard tune.

"What if you went and stayed with your Uncle Jem for a few weeks?" Dad said. "You've already been planning to babysit for him.

We'll tell Mom you thought it would be easier to stay there. It'll be a good chance for the two of you to reconnect."

She shrugged. How could she leave now? She was as shattered as her art project. She'd never needed her parents more.

"I've been trying to get Mom into couple's therapy for a long time, but she won't go. I think she's embarrassed to admit to anyone we have problems, even to you. It'll drag up things we've been hiding, and well . . . Our arguments may be a little louder than the usual whispers." Dad eased back and placed both hands on her shoulders. "Just stay with Jem for a little while. Give us a chance to get started on the right track again. If we work on this, instead of ignoring it, it's going to be painful at first. Things will get worse before they get better. I don't want you to see that."

Her lip trembled. She couldn't stop it. She placed both hands over her mouth as two more tears squeezed out of her eyes.

"I'm sorry, Lili. I never wanted this to happen." Dad's voice was low. "But now that it has, I'm just trying to think about what's best for you. For all of us."

And that was for her to leave.

She scrubbed her hands over her face. "You won't leave me there?"

"Of course not."

"It's just for a little while?"

"I couldn't bear it any longer than that."

She scrunched up her eyes and gave a single nod.

I can do this. I have to do this.

Otherwise, it sounded like her family would never make it through.

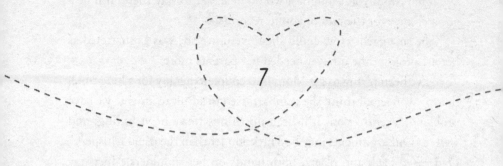

7

Natalie was walking into a trap.

Pacing in the corridor outside Jem's apartment at 7:29 a.m. Monday, she rubbed her hands together. Her spark of hope from Friday had dissolved into a sense of impending doom.

Deep breaths, Nat. Just take some deep breaths.

Jem had hurt her too much last time. She'd spent the first six weeks stunned, believing he'd come back, and the next six weeks in bed.

She could never give him that kind of power again.

She shook off the thought, straightened her no-nonsense gray T-shirt for the bazillionth time, then rapped on the door. And waited.

It flew open as her hand drew back for another knock. Eyes barely open, Jem stood before her with his shirt untucked and just two buttons in their holes. A fully awake Olly clapped his hands and squealed.

Natalie smiled, then caught herself. "He woke you up early?"

"Yup."

"I see you're still a morning person."

"Yup."

Jem passed her the baby and walked into the apartment's small dining area, fingers trailing the bordering kitchen's brown Formica countertop straight from 1974. Eyes totally shut.

She looked around for Lili. Jem had texted her yesterday to say his niece would be staying for a couple of weeks so she could help babysit Olly and reconnect with Jem—her only uncle. Now it was nearly time for school. Natalie ran her eyes over the kitchen on her right and the dining/living area in front of her. No teenager. "Where's Lili?"

Whatever Jem mumbled escaped her as he disappeared into a doorway off the living room.

Natalie focused her attention on the baby. With blond hair sticking out at crazy angles, he had dribbles of milk and drool running down his chin. He bounced in her arms, threw his weight forward, and face planted into her shoulder. A milky-wet patch remained when he pulled away.

A half-empty baby bowl rested on the counter, so she pulled up a wooden stool and scooped a tiny spoonful of mushy cereal.

This wasn't so bad. Yet.

Lili appeared from a doorway off the kitchen, wearing an oversized *Bazinga!* T-shirt. "What's all the noise?" She yawned halfway through the question.

The microwave clock flashed above Lili's head. "Why are you sleeping? Shouldn't you get ready for school?"

"In-service day." Lili disappeared back into the room she'd come from, colorful artwork already plastered all over the door. Natalie smirked at the Dumbo-eared caricature of Jem.

Jem popped his head out from what must have been the bathroom, because a toothbrush poked out of his mouth. "I didn't realize she had the day off till after I messaged you last night, but it's good you're here. Her having Olly after school is okay, but all day is too much."

She glanced at the door Lili had closed behind her. She still wasn't sure about leaving the baby with Lili at all. And what would happen when the teenager went back home? She couldn't be staying more than a week or two.

Olly grabbed the cereal bowl. Natalie dropped the spoon and snatched it away. He smeared her cheek with a glob of cereal.

Jem strolled over, black business shirt in place and tie shoved into his pocket. The scent of his deodorant wafted over, a mixture of cedar and cinnamon. Her mouth watered like he was a six-foot-two pecan pie M&M.

"You've got a little somethin'." He pointed to his own cheek, then plucked Olly from her lap.

She swiped the mush away as her cheeks heated.

Jem hoisted Oliver up to eye level and spoke into his chubby face. "You be nice to Natalie, okay? Stay out of the liquor cabinet and no wild parties."

She rolled her eyes.

He gave the baby a loud kiss, then set him on the ground and offered him a plush Oscar the Grouch before he straightened. "I know I said we'd discuss the details of this arrangement today, but I've gotta go. If you've got time, I can do it tonight."

Olly dropped Oscar on the floor and crawled over to a pile of toys. Natalie kept one eye on him and shrugged in Jem's direction. "Sure."

"And can you do me a favor?"

A favor . . . That was running into personal territory. Natalie pursed her lips. Today was strictly business. "Will it be legal?" Flashbacks of their childhood escapades ran through her mind.

The corner of Jem's mouth pulled up. "This time, yes. I'm cashing in on my one condition. Can you take my credit card and buy us a couch? And a little dining table? We only moved in on the weekend, and I haven't had time."

She peeked past him to take a second look at the living room. Nothing but ugly gray walls, toys on the floor, and one photo of Olly hanging lopsided. One smallish TV sat on the mustard-colored carpet.

"Okay." Not in her plan for today, but this was the deal they'd struck last night. Still, that didn't mean she had to be enthusiastic about it. "Any particular style? Budget?"

"Classic, comfortable, and cheap. I'm not fussy. It can be second-hand. Just be your usual stingy self." Jem dropped his card on the counter. "And . . . is it okay if you stay till five thirty today instead of three thirty?" He moved closer and lowered his voice. "Lili hasn't spent a whole lot of time with Olly yet, and I'm nervous about leaving her alone with him without backup. Can you just see how she does with him? Tell me if there's any truly heinous red flags?"

His eyes were wide, genuine, pleading. A nervous dad.

A piece of her softened.

"Five thirty, but not a minute later." She tapped a finger on the counter to make her point. "Part of the Wildfire application process is co-leading a youth Bible study with Sam tonight. He wants to see the applicants' skills before he decides anything." After submitting her application on Saturday morning, she'd been ecstatic to receive a call from Steph by lunch saying that Sam wanted to see her in action. Apparently Steph had talked her up, and Sam had loved the fact that Natalie had been working with her evangelist father since she was a teen.

"Not a problem. Thanks." Jem snagged an apple as he moved toward the door.

She picked up the card and called out to him as he exited. "And I'll take that stingy comment as a compliment."

"As it was intended!" His chuckles drifted through the closed door.

She frowned at the place he had been. She hadn't meant to banter with him. Laughter meant friendship, and that had died years ago.

She turned her attention to the baby who wasn't hers playing on the floor. Now his blond hair had clumps of cereal in it.

His mother must be blonde.

♡

A superstitious man might hesitate to declare his first day at work a success with two minutes left on the clock. But as Jem's fingers on the keyboard raced the minute hand to five o'clock, he couldn't quell a sense of optimism at having not just one but three articles filed on day one.

In the open-plan office around him, advertising reps discussed budgets, two sports reporters debated the upcoming Nationals vs. Mets game, and the police scanner crackled in the background. Jem inhaled a lungful of musty air—the result of filling an old building with hundreds of copies of newspapers—and smiled. It was good to be back in the bullpen. It'd been a lean month transitioning between his Chicago job and this one, and for some heart-stopping moments at 3:00 a.m. he'd questioned whether he'd ever work again in the shrinking industry that he loved.

But he was here. And he'd give up his signed Justin Timberlake CDs before he'd turn his back on this chance to make something of himself.

Four fifty-nine p.m. Article finished with a minute to spare. He clicked over to an online copy of last week's op-ed. He needed to be more familiar with the local conversation if he was going to succeed here, but his mind kept drifting back to the checklist in his head.

A checklist titled *Stuff to Sort Out Before I Contact Dad.*

With Natalie's assistance, his apartment was transitioning from his current "broke college student" decor to "an actual adult lives here." Olly's childcare situation was under control, at least temporarily and with some financial assistance from big brother Mike. Another reason to excel at this job: he needed to find a permanent solution for Olly's care and pay Mike back ASAP.

He scrolled down the page. Whoops. His eyes might've glanced over the last three paragraphs, but he hadn't read them. He scrolled up again.

If he could just keep his life drama free for a bit, he could get himself sorted and somewhere in the vicinity of Dad's exacting standards before he attempted to rebuild that relationship. Were he on his own, he wouldn't try. But with no mother in the picture, the number of people in Olly's family was few. A kid should have family. A grandfather.

Jem would do his best to accomplish that.

The police scanner crackled to life. Hit-and-run, Oakview Street.

In Jem's peripheral vision, his editor, Samson, lifted his head and scanned the reporters' desks. Several journalists avoided eye contact.

Jem grabbed his messenger bag and stood. "I can go on my way home, boss."

Samson nodded and waved him out the door. Jem hustled to his car. Calculating for traffic, he had a ten-minute buffer between now and when he needed to be home to relieve Natalie.

He zipped across town and slowed as he entered the cul-de-sac named on the police scanner. The street was easy to find—it was a main road, and he'd had a high school friend who lived here back in the day. A variety of emergency vehicle lights flashed up ahead, clustered around the driveway at house number—he checked the surrounding homes—nine.

Unease built as Jem scanned the home. Yep, that'd been Jason Whittaker's place. What had happened? Did Jason's family still live here?

He left his notebook in the car and stepped onto the footpath, noting skid marks on the road. His vantage point gave him an unobstructed view of the paramedics working over a small body on the ground.

Oh no.

A pacing man caught his eye. Jason. He had one hand fisted in his hair, the other covering his mouth as the paramedics worked on what appeared to be a child. Jem hit the beeper to lock his car and walked toward his friend.

8

Jem tried to find the energy to run up the stairs to his apartment. He was one hour and six minutes late. Natalie would be livid. But the fastest he could manage was a trudge.

He jiggled his key into the finicky lock and tried to think of the fastest way he could explain his tardiness before Natalie committed some act of assault. One day without drama and a chance to get his life in order. That's all his goal had been this morning. One day.

He jiggled the lock again.

The door was yanked open. He flinched.

Natalie. Nostrils flared, glare fierce enough to melt a glacier.

Oh boy.

"Natalie, I—"

She jerked a finger to her lips. "Shush!"

"I'm sorry but—"

"Your devil baby is finally asleep." She hissed the words. Her mussed hair, yoga pants, and a T-shirt that appeared to be wearing some of Olly's lunch did nothing to detract from her crazy-lady vibe.

He edged past her into the apartment, ears pricked for any sounds

from Olly. "Asleep? What do you mean asleep? It's almost seven."
Oliver had two naps every day like clockwork, and a bedtime of nine
o'clock. "Didn't Lili tell you his routine?" He'd given her a rundown
last night with instructions to pass the message onto Natalie.

"Steph picked her up this morning. I've barely seen her all day.
She should be back soon."

That was the last time he entrusted any communication to a teenager. He moved to his bedroom door, eased it open. Olly, in his crib
next to Jem's bed, sound asleep. Totally out of routine.

There went his sleep for the next week.

He moved forward to wake Olly up. He'd be going to bed after
midnight at this rate.

Natalie grabbed his hand. "What are you doing? He just spent
ninety minutes screaming himself to sleep. Which you'd know if you'd
been here."

Jem looked back at her. "Ninety minutes? So you decided to put
him down for a nap after five o'clock?" He'd assumed she'd know
better than that. They'd babysat as teens.

Deep breaths, Jem.

Natalie's hands went to her hips. "Sorry I'm not a mind reader. I
didn't know he needed a second nap till he was going ballistic."

He moved her back into the living room so their tense whispers
didn't wake Olly. "Why didn't you call me?"

She jabbed a finger in his direction. "I'm not answering another
question until you explain yourself. You're more than an hour late."
She seized her jacket from the back of a chair and stuffed one arm in.
"Do you have any idea what this could cost me?"

"A week's worth of sleep?" It was out before he could stop it.

Jacket on, Natalie stared at him, lips thinning. "That's the last time
I ever do you a favor." She stomped toward the door.

Jem rubbed his forehead. He'd been out of line. "Wait."

She paused, hand outstretched toward the door handle.

"I'm sorry. It's just . . ." He blew out a breath. "It's been a bad day. I apologize for being late, and I'll have better instructions for you tomorrow."

He waited for the open and close of the door. It didn't come. Natalie stood still, indecision written across her face.

Huh. He hadn't expected that.

She rested her bag on a small dining table that she must've bought for him today. "What happened?"

Jem leaned against the counter, the kitchen at his back. "A hit-and-run came over the police scanner."

Halfway through the sentence, Natalie's eyes focused on something behind him.

He paused. "What?"

She pulled her gaze from whatever it was and looked at Jem. "Beetroot."

"What?"

She moved to the kitchen window. He followed her. She leaned closer to the glass pane. "Your dad's here."

"*What*?" Jem jostled her at the window. No. It couldn't be. How did Dad even know where he was?

Below them, a police hat moved from a Charlottesville Police car toward the building's entrance.

Mike must have told him. The traitor.

They jerked back from the window as Captain John Walters tipped his head back and looked up at the building.

A bubble of panic popped inside Jem. Not like this. He wasn't ready. "We have two minutes. Hide the baby stuff."

Natalie gaped. "You haven't told him?"

Jem put steel into his voice. "If you don't help, I'll tell him what really happened to his garden gnome collection."

She lunged for a pile of baby washing and tossed it into the nearest cupboard.

Jem pulled open a kitchen drawer, grasped the drying rack full of Olly's plates and cups, and tipped it upside down.

Natalie had just pulled down Olly's photo as a sharp rap sounded at the front door.

She passed Jem the photo and moved toward the door. "He's going to find out eventually."

Jem opened his door, tossed the photo onto his bed. "You're awfully judge-y for someone with a gnome in their closet."

She narrowed her eyes. "John's never heard the full story of the Great Sewage Incident of 2003."

Yikes. He spun to plead for mercy.

She pulled open the door before he could respond. "John. Hi."

John Walters stood three inches shorter than Jem, thirty pounds heavier, and a hundred times more intimidating. Even Natalie straightened her spine and tucked a wisp of hair behind her ear.

"Natalie." Dad nodded and stepped inside. "Surprised to see you here."

"Uh, yes." She shut the door behind him. "I just came here to . . . yell at Jem."

"It's part of her rage issues," Jem said. "Hi, Dad."

Dad walked into the apartment with measured steps. He swept his gaze up, down, and all around the sparse rooms.

The silence shouted. Jem cringed. Though no baby paraphernalia was in sight, Dad had to know. The man had Spidey senses for such things.

Jem leaned against the wall, crossed one ankle over the other. The tenser he was inside, the more relaxed he tried to appear outside. "How are you?"

The captain folded his arms. Surprising he could, considering the amount of starch he put in his laundry. "You'd know if you called any time in the last few years. I had to find out you were here from Steph."

So this was how it would be. No "Good to see you" or "I've missed you." Straight to the criticism. Jem fought to keep a smart-aleck tone out of his voice. "You said not to call. I figured if you wanted to see me, you'd come."

"I said to call when you'd made some changes in your life."

Ah, yes. A conversation burned into his memory. Jem's muscles bunched at the recollection. "And I said I don't have to explain my choices. You can decide to be in or out."

Dad slashed a hand through the air. "Show some respect. Your mother would—"

Jem rocketed off the wall. He did not get to pull the Mom card. "She would never demand that I lay out my life for her to judge if it's good enough. She would never manipulate—"

"Manipulate? It's called discipline, Jeremy. Something any good parent would do. You can never understand—"

A volcano erupted in Jem's brain. "The door's right there, Dad. If you're so disappointed, just walk out and keep pretending you only have one son left to control."

His father spun toward the door.

Natalie surged between the two men. "Time out."

Jem stared at her, jaw set. She'd refereed them more than once in the past. But now? She had no skin in this game.

Still, she stood between them, hands up. "You two have differences. Those differences have cost you enough years. Just take a breath."

Jem wheeled away and paced a few steps into the living room, then turned back.

Dad stayed stock-still, face granite.

Natalie looked at his father. "John, can I get you a drink?"

"Thank you, no." He never took his glare from Jem.

She folded her arms and mimicked his intense gaze. *"John.* Can. I. Get. You. A. Drink?"

Jem tried not to smirk at the fire in her voice.

Dad twisted to look at her and sighed. "Cold water, please."

She moved over to the kitchen, grabbed a glass, and filled it with tap water. "Here you go."

Jem paced, eyes on Natalie. Gone were the days when they could have a whole conversation about his dad just from facial expressions.

What was she thinking?

♡

What was she thinking? Natalie rubbed her forehead. She was beyond late for the youth Bible study. She should walk out the door right now, leave Jem in the past, and go try to build her own future.

But . . . the glimpse of vulnerability she'd seen on Jem's face when John's harsh words struck him wasn't something she could ignore. There had to be something she could say to help. Quickly.

She rubbed sweaty palms on her yoga pants and went with the easiest question that came to mind. "Let's just catch up on the last few years. Jem, what's new with you?"

Jem crossed his arms, matching his father's posture. "I started as a journalist at the newspaper today."

"And how did your first day go?"

He shifted on his feet. "At five o'clock news came over the scanner of a hit-and-run uptown. My boss sent me, and the address took me to Jason Whittaker's house."

Natalie's breath caught. They'd gone to high school with Jason. Was that what Jem had been saying earlier?

"More specifically, his four-year-old son in the driveway. I left my notebook in the car and spent an hour sitting with him till his wife got there."

Her insides shriveled. Why had she given him a hard time about being late?

John nodded. "I heard about that case at the station. Terrible accident."

Silence stretched for several seconds. Natalie looked between the two of them. "Since we've established that life is short, is there anything you want to say to each other?" She fixed her gaze on the man on her right. "Jem?"

His gaze hovered around a crack in the kitchen plaster rather than his father's eyes. "I missed . . . some aspects . . . of you," he said.

A muscle near John's eye twitched.

Natalie seized the chance. "John, you guys have had your disagreements, but you can't deny your son's a good man."

In her peripheral vision, Jem shot a glance at her.

She kept her eyes on John. "What do you want to say to Jem?"

John fiddled with his cufflinks. "You resent me. I know that. But I did what I thought was best."

A cry sounded from Jem's bedroom.

John jumped like she'd stabbed a cattle prod into his rear. "What was that?"

"I'll get him." Jem slipped away.

John stared at Natalie. Those distinctive blue eyes, shared by his son and grandson, opened wide. Understanding crept in, and they turned to ice.

The crying faded to a whimper as Jem crooned to Olly, muffled through the door.

It'd take him five seconds to return. Five seconds to prevent catastrophe. She grabbed John's arm. "You listen to me." He tensed at her touch. "You react wrong to this, and you'll lose your son forever."

He shook her off with a glare that had reduced criminals to tears.

She lowered her voice as Jem drew closer. "I'm not joking. This is no time for a John Walters judgment special."

Jem appeared, Olly in his arms.

Natalie snapped her mouth shut.

Jem wore the look of a man about to wrestle a crocodile. "Dad, this is Oliver. He's nine months old."

John peered past them, like he expected another person. "And his mother?"

"Not in the picture. Nat's agreed to nanny for me in the short term."

She studied John's face. The muscle next to his eye twitched like crazy.

"Would you like to hold him?" she asked.

Jem narrowed his eyes at her. She shrugged. John didn't move.

"John?"

He held up his hands.

Olly's whimpers stilled as his grandfather held him like an alien specimen. He gave a gummy grin and squealed.

Adorable. With John's wide blue eyes and Jem's dimple, that child was irresistible.

She released a breath. Maybe this relationship wasn't so hopeless after all—

John dumped the child back into Jem's arms. "I'm not going to do this. I need to go." His tone was gruff, face set. He moved toward the door.

Jem stared after him. Natalie winced at the expression on his face. A little boy forgotten at the bus stop.

Jem stepped toward the living room as John reached for the front door. "That's cold, Dad, even for you."

She flinched at his tone, even though the words weren't directed at her.

Jem disappeared into his room.

The captain paused, door handle in his hand. "You think I'm a monster," he said.

Was he speaking to her or Jem? Natalie's feet rooted themselves to the ground.

John opened the door, stepped through the portal, and turned to face her. His eyes were lined with seven years of regret. "But I have my reasons."

He closed the door.

Natalie rested back against the counter. What was she supposed to make of that?

Jem paced back into the room, sans baby, and carrying Olly's Oscar the Grouch. He hurled it at the door. It smashed into the solid wood and fell back against the floor, one button eye hanging loose.

She sighed. "I'm sorry, Jem."

He leaned his hands against the tiny dining table, head hung low. "Olly never did anything to him. But he just—" He shook his head.

Oliver's gurgles carried over from the direction of Jem's room, along with the rattle of Jem's keys.

She watched Jem for a long moment. How many times had she comforted him after a run-in with his father? Too many to count. Her neck prickled at the memory of his face buried against it. She folded her arms.

Jem raised his eyes to hers. She shivered at his expression.

"Thanks for sticking up for me."

Had his voice deepened in the last seven years? Another shiver raced between her shoulder blades. "Don't get used to it." She kept her tone brusque.

Jem came around the table and walked toward her. His gaze never left her face.

Natalie's breathing slowed. Oh man. Sensation rioted through her chest. Was he walking toward her? Yep, he definitely was. She pressed back against the counter.

Three steps away, two steps, one. He leaned in . . . Reached into the bowl behind her and grabbed an apple. Snapped off a bite. "See you tomorrow."

He strolled back toward the living room.

All the energy drained from her limbs. She gathered her belongings and exited.

In the safe territory of the hallway outside the apartment, she leaned against the wall and tapped her head on it. What had just happened? That had to have been one of the weirdest half hours of her life.

Great job keeping a professional distance, Natalie.

If she didn't get this internship, she'd be at the employment office first thing tomorrow. Jem was a quicksand she didn't want to fall into again.

Her phone rang in her pocket. She checked the number. Unknown. "Hello?"

"Hi, Natalie, this is Sam Payton. I'm at the Bible study. Where are you?"

9

Natalie's internship, career, and dreams depended on a story about a sick penguin.

She frowned at her notes for a mother's group devotional talk spread across Jem's kitchen counter on Thursday morning. Sam had been understanding on Monday when she'd told him that she'd been unexpectedly delayed by work. They'd swapped her practice run to today instead. Mommy Time was a church event, not a Wildfire one. But Sam wanted to see her people skills in action this week, and there weren't any more Wildfire events planned till next. Since Steph worked for both organizations, they'd managed to arrange this for her audition.

If her mini sermon at Mommy Time went well today, Steph made it sound like the internship was hers. But if not . . . She pushed the thought from her mind. Three days of preparation, and she'd still been up half the night writing her talk. And it was nowhere near ready.

Now her eyelids weighed fifty pounds, and her concentration went AWOL when the first twinge of cramps shuddered through her abdomen. Was it monthly pain that made her want to vomit or the thought of public speaking?

She needed a distraction. She needed caffeine.

She slid from her stool and walked to the pantry at a pace only grandma sloths achieved. "Jem, where's the coffee?"

Excited baby squeals emerged from his bedroom door. From the thumps and occasional crash in the last fifteen minutes, it sounded like Jem was on the floor again, chasing the baby on all fours. Olly couldn't quite walk yet, but his crawl set land-speed records.

Natalie dug through the pantry, the cupboards, even the fridge—she'd found the saltshaker in there yesterday—but no luck.

She dragged herself over to Jem's door and knocked. "Jem?"

A pause, a *shhh*, a giggle, and the door swung open. "Yes?"

Jem and Olly both wore Daffy Duck underwear on their heads. The room behind them had been hit by a tornado, with clothes and sheets scattered across the floor. Oliver's cheeks flushed pink, and he kicked and squealed in Jem's arms.

"Where do you hide the coffee?" She spoke as if they looked totally normal.

Olly burst into uproarious laughter and clapped his hands. He pulled the undies off Jem's head and tried to eat them.

Jem looked her up and down and smiled. Natalie's insides quivered. The room might have been a wreck, but Jem was not. If anything, his tousled hair and rolled-up shirt cuffs made her mouth go dry.

She needed coffee bad.

"Don't have any, sorry." Jem leaned against the doorpost. "That stuff'll kill you. But I do have OJ."

She dragged herself back to the kitchen. "Are you the only person on earth who hates coffee? I can't believe parenthood hasn't driven you to it."

"I bought juice with pulp," Jem called out.

She swung around, but his bedroom door closed.

Jem had pulp orange juice? His teenage rants about the disgustingness of pulp reverberated in her memory. She quickened her pace and pulled open the fridge.

Two juice bottles rested side by side. Pulp. No pulp.

Jem's door squeaked again, and a moment later he appeared by the fridge. Dropping a final kiss on Olly's cheek, he handed her the baby. "Ready for your talk yet?"

He'd seemed surprised—actually, his jaw hit the ground—on Tuesday when she'd told him her internship involved regular public speaking. Then he'd looked impressed at her determination to trump this irrational fear.

Not that his opinion mattered.

She groaned in response to his question. "Having to talk in front of people is bad enough. But right now, I can't even get this thing written, let alone say it aloud. And if I screw it up, it's all over, red rover." That thought was far more terrifying than her aversion to speaking before a crowd. She had one shot. One.

The corner of Jem's mouth quirked. "'All over, red rover'? One of your dad's Aussie expressions?"

She nodded.

"Why don't you ask him for help? He's the expert."

"My notes are a mess, I only have two hours, and I came on my bike. And he might be asleep." Unless the inspiration fairy paid her a visit, she was in serious trouble.

Maybe it would be better to just end things now rather than make a fool of herself and lose the internship anyway.

Jem fished in his pocket and pulled out his keys. "Take the car and head over there. I'll ride the bus to work. Lili and I have been planning to walk to the bus stop one morning anyway." He set the keys on the countertop, stepped around Natalie, and rapped on his niece's door. "Lili? You ready yet?"

Natalie looked at the keys, then Olly, then the back of Jem's head. "Are you sure? What if you have to go somewhere?"

"I'll take the work car."

Lili's door cracked open and she staggered out, clothed but eyes still shut.

"Come on, sunshine. We're walking today." Jem held the front door open for Lili as she shuffled forward.

Natalie turned back toward the fridge, and the front-door hinge squeaked. Jem's face poked through the doorway.

"Tell your dad I'll pop by tomorrow for a visit. And good luck today. I'll be praying."

He disappeared and the door clicked behind him.

She looked at the baby. "Why does he have to be so sweet? How am I supposed to focus now?"

Olly leaned forward and planted a slobbery kiss on her face.

"That used to be his answer too." She looked at her notes again and sighed. She needed more than two hours to fix this. Had her chance at the internship ended already?

♡

By the time Natalie pulled up at Mom and Dad's house, she had a wedgie, a stain on her shirt, and Edward Scissorhands doing the salsa in her uterus.

Mom's face appeared in the front window as Natalie pulled Olly from his car seat. By the time she got the car locked, Mom was coming down the drive, cheeks glowing—or was it the neon-pink sweat suit reflecting on her face? Nothing could keep Mom from her morning power walk, even if her duties caring for Dad meant it was on her treadmill by the living room window instead of outside.

"I'm glad you're here." She kissed Natalie's cheek and plucked Olly from her arms. "Dad's not having a good day."

The wedgie didn't seem so bad anymore. "Do you want us to go?"

"No, he'd love to see Olly. Just not for too long."

"Okay."

Natalie followed Mom into the house and through the hall. She twisted her notes, dripping with red pen and orange juice, in her hand.

Mom pushed open the bedroom door. Natalie clenched her molars and pushed her lips into a smile.

Dad lay propped on pillows, the bed facing the window so he could see the sun—and the small TV in the corner playing back-to-back James Bond movies. The lines etched into his face were even deeper than usual, and his skin held the yellowish hue of jaundice.

They said he was in remission.

She had her doubts.

He turned his head as they entered, and ten years fell away in his smile. "Nattie! And you've brought the little bloke. Help me up, Karen." He gripped the handle that hung over his bed but only lifted his body an inch before he sagged back against the pillows.

Natalie tugged a chair closer. "Don't worry, Dad, I'm not planning to sit up." She slouched in the seat and propped her feet against the edge of the bed to prove her point.

Mom sat on the other side of the bed, next to Dad, and let him play with the baby. It was a perfect distraction while Natalie swiped a thumb under her eyes.

After several minutes Mom said Oliver was hungry and took him into the kitchen. Dad's eyes followed them out the door, and he sighed. "I wish he could stay longer, Nattie, but I'm all tuckered out."

She slipped her fingers into his hand. "It's okay, Dad, you can rest. I'm staying for a while."

"Good. I . . . wanted . . ." His lids drooped, but he fought the drowsiness. "I wanted to ask if you got the internship."

Natalie nodded, mute, and he closed his eyes. He'd wake before she left for the church, probably, but in this state he wouldn't be able to help her today.

Her internship was doomed. And with it her best chance of carrying on his legacy.

She let her gaze wander the room, desperate for a diversion. Two of Mom's patchwork quilts covered Dad's bony limbs, despite the unusually warm September morning. They were the brightest thing in the dim bedroom, which was barely big enough for a nightstand and the chairs next to the bed. But it wasn't the quilts' bold colors that held her attention. It was the walls.

Photographs hung so thick, it was a wonder the plaster hadn't crumbled beneath the weight. The pictures were ordered by year, the earliest a fifty-four-year-old snapshot of Mom at sweet sixteen, sitting on Dad's lap and laughing. Back then they weren't Mom and Dad, they were Karen and Phil, a dairy farmer's daughter and the son of a minister.

The next photo showed them three years later, Dad in a suit and Mom in her white satin dress, standing out in front of the old Margaret Street church in Toowoomba, Australia.

They'd probably expected the next shot would be of Mom with a big belly, but first there was a brick house with Mom pointing to a *Sold* sign. Then an airplane: their big move to America. Had Dad not had his "come to Jesus" moment at a Billy Graham rally in his early teens, that move would've been to Hollywood for him to pursue his passion for filmmaking. But he'd felt called to preach instead, and the next half a wall boasted shots of him with all different kinds of people—orphan children from his trip to India, a Virginian governor or two, families from the churches they'd started, and dozens of crowd shots from meetings and revivals. Forty years of itinerant ministry and church planting now summed up in fifteen square feet of wall space.

Then, next to the cupboard door, came the big surprise: Natalie. Pregnant for the first time at forty-four, no one was more surprised than Mom when Natalie was born healthy, happy, and pink.

The rest of the room was basically the Shrine of Natalie. Everything from her first loose tooth to her first pimple displayed for all to see. The biggest pictures, with the shiniest frames, were those of her and Dad together at church camps, her running a small youth group Bible study, even delivering her first—and as yet, only—church talk at a youth rally in South Carolina.

That one was her favorite. Dad had traveled to preach so much when she was little, but when he convinced her to give that talk they'd spent so much time together. Drafting her speech. Traveling together to the rally instead of her staying home with Mom. She'd been shaking with fear before she went on the stage, but afterward, when Dad hugged her and told her how proud he was, it'd all been worth it.

That had marked the start of her traveling with Dad on all the trips she could talk her parents into. She avoided public speaking but acted as his gopher and eventually started booking their accommodations and organizing the trips. They were a team.

"I love that wall." Dad's voice spoke beside her.

She jumped, dashed a hand under her eyes. "Even that shot of me swallowing a fly?" She grimaced at the holiday photo of a family trip to her grandparents' farm. Her freckled face had contorted in a disgusted gasp as Mom clicked the shutter. She shuddered. "I don't know how Mom survived growing up on a dairy farm. She's tougher than me."

"You're plenty tough." Dad's voice thickened.

Natalie squeezed his hand and followed his gaze to the corner of the wall—a spot where Dad never let Mom hang a photo. Even in the old house, he'd kept the place reserved. "Leave some room for Natalie. She's not done yet," he'd say. "Who knows what she's going to do next?"

Then the sickness came, the bills, and eventually the monotony.

They stared at the empty space.

"I—I'm so sorry, Nattie." Dad's voice trembled. "I wish I hadn't been a burden. I wish you'd been able to finish college, make some more memories for the wall instead of taking care of this old codger." He lifted a weak hand toward the empty space.

"Shush, Dad. I'm right where I want to be. Next to you."

His grip on her hand tightened, and he cleared his throat. "I'm glad you're getting this chance with Samuel Payton now. It makes me feel better, you know? To be able to go knowing that you've finally got your opportunity. I always knew God meant you for great things. You'll fill the rest of that wall up in no time."

Hope unfurled in her chest, even as her heart shredded. Maybe it wasn't too late to make him proud . . . even if his time was running out.

"You're not going anywhere," she croaked out, even though it wasn't true.

Dad faded in and out for the next half hour. He retold the story of her first day at school, which she didn't think was that memorable—the fire she'd started was quite small—and by nine twenty he'd talked himself to sleep again. Natalie kissed his whiskery cheek and stole out of the room.

She made up her mind. There was only one thing she could do. She'd have to wing it.

Mom sat at the kitchen table when Natalie entered, Olly asleep against her shoulder with a cake crumb on his plump cheek.

"Mom, have you been feeding him junk food again?"

"I seem to remember you grabbing an entire cake and shoving your face in it."

"That was a whole month ago."

Mom grinned, then indicated the baby. "Do you want him back?"

"Let me grab a soda first. I'm in desperate need of caffeine." Natalie's palms sweated at the thought of public speaking in—she checked the clock—fifteen minutes' time. She was probably going to embarrass herself in a major way. But she had to at least try, for Dad.

"I know you have to go, but we need to talk later about Dad's birthday party. I want this one to be special." Mom didn't need to explain why.

Natalie nodded as she grabbed a can of Coke from the fridge. She'd been the party planner of the family since forever. "He'd get a kick out of a Crocodile Dundee theme."

Mom snorted a laugh as Natalie cracked the tab on her Coke. Brown liquid sprayed across the front of her white blouse.

"Mom!"

"Sorry, I just did the groceries, and they shook up on the trip home. Um, let me get you a cloth."

Natalie dumped the can in the sink and pulled her now-ruined shirt away from her skin. "I don't think a cloth is going to cut it. My shirt's totally see-through."

"That's okay, darling, there's not a whole lot there to see."

"That's the pot calling the kettle black, Mrs. A-Cup-Till-Forty." At least Natalie was a B.

"Don't worry. I'm sure I have a shirt that will fit you." Mom scuttled down to her bedroom, Olly still snug against her shoulder, before Natalie could protest.

Fantastic. She was about to do the most important talk of her life dressed like her seventy-year-old mother.

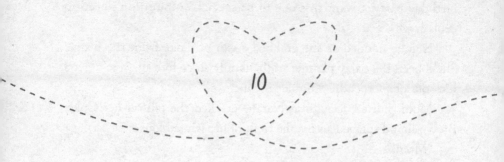

10

Too many cars waited as Natalie screeched into the church parking lot six minutes behind schedule. Why were this many people here?

"Oliver, I think I'm having a panic attack."

Either her bra had shrunk three sizes or unadulterated fear constricted her rib cage. If she screwed this up, it would be straight back to a minimum-wage job and endless hours of wasted life. All Dad's relief at her "one big chance" would be for nothing. And they'd be eating ramen noodles six nights a week just to scrape rent together.

The baby ignored her, asleep and unconcerned with her tight underwear.

Natalie's wooden fingers fumbled with the door handle and opened it. Fresh air revived her, and she managed to get the baby bag and Olly out of the car without hyperventilating.

The church cast its shadow over them as they approached the door. A voice erupted from the doorway, its tone sharing the delicate nuances of air escaping a pinched balloon.

"Natalie! How are you? Pastor Stephanie asked me to keep an eye out for you." Rosemary Dunkitt and her Farrah Fawcett hair smothered Natalie in a too tight hug. Cheap perfume irritated her nostrils as she was dragged inside. "The ladies are nearly ready to start, so I hope you're prepared. We were starting to worry you wouldn't show."

"Yes, we, ah, had a wardrobe malfunction right before I left." Mom's white blouse was two sizes too big and itched against Natalie's skin. But with a belt cinching it around the waist and faux leather jacket over the top, it passed.

"Well, no harm, no foul. Here's Sam. He's been waiting to meet you."

She deposited Natalie next to her potential boss.

"Sam, this is Natalie."

Natalie stood taller. Steph had believed in her enough to recommend her. She could do this.

Sam turned from his conversation with another mother and hit her with a smile that should have belonged to a Hollywood hunk. "Natalie! We officially meet. Well, apart from that basketball game where you showed off your mad skills." He engulfed her in a hug.

Whoa. He must be the touchy-feely type. She mentally shrugged. She could roll with this.

He released her, then offered the same embrace to Mrs. Dunkitt. The older woman stammered another hello and then departed, cheeks rosy.

Sam captured Natalie's hand in a firm but gentle handshake that would've met even Dad's standards. "I can't wait to hear what you've prepared."

His Australian accent held the distinguished rumble of a high-performance car. She sneaked a look at his ring finger. Bare.

Steph materialized on Sam's right and seemed to catch Natalie's quick glance. "Sam, I see you've met one of our church's most eligible bachelorettes." She winked at Natalie.

Natalie swallowed, her face heating.

Sam laughed, a hearty sound that brightened the room. He still clasped her hand in his. The moment stretched.

"Sam, nice to meet you." Jem's voice sounded from behind Natalie's left ear.

She jumped, whipping her hand from Sam's grasp. "Jem! What are you doing here?"

Sam gripped Jem's hand. "Likewise. And you are . . ."

Jem took Olly's weight, and she released him. "The father of this handsome man, and also the journalist you spoke to this morning. Do you have a minute for an interview?"

"Oh, that's right." Sam face-palmed himself. "Do you mind if I join you in five minutes? I just need to chat to Natalie."

"Sure." Jem sauntered off, and Sam turned back to face Natalie.

"You've got a strapping young lad there."

"Oh no, you're not my son—I mean *he*. He's not my son." The horn of an oncoming train filled her mind, and it said one word: *IDIOT!* "He—I—Jem's an old friend, and I nanny his kid." Her tongue fell limp.

"Well, that sounds . . . interesting." Sam indicated the semicircle of women seated to their right. "Are you ready to face the wolves?"

Natalie peeked over at her waiting victims. Several cardigan-clad matrons sipped their tea, seated and waiting. One young mother—whom she suspected wasn't wearing a bra under her hoodie—had fallen asleep in the corner. An older kid, looking bored, bounced a soccer ball off the wall. Cackles of laughter echoed on the far side of the room where a gaggle of women mobbed Jem and Olly.

Natalie straightened her shoulders. "Let's do this."

She should be the president's speech writer.

Natalie barely kept a triumphant grin from her face as she delivered the final lines of her talk, the women staring at her with an intensity usually reserved for chocolate cheesecake. Not even the constant *thump-thump* from Soccer Ball Kid could throw off her rhythm.

Natalie, 1. Irrational fear of public speaking, 0.

"So the next time you feel discouraged as a mother, remember the story of Aunt Esmeralda, the penguin, and the fire extinguisher."

A smattering of applause sounded across the room—a little unenthusiastic, but applause nonetheless. Jem, standing beside a perky blonde woman with a baby girl, let loose a long whistle. The dozing woman in the corner jerked awake and swiped a palm across the drool patch on her neck.

Natalie thanked her audience and stepped away from the podium. She'd done it. And, apart from Jem's whistle, she'd done it with a semblance of dignity.

She floated down the stairs, and Sam approached to take the microphone.

He helped her down the final step, then bounded up the stairs two at a time. "Well, folks, it wasn't quite what we expected, but let's give Natalie one last round of applause."

Wasn't what we expected? Did he mean in a good way? Or—

"Natalie, come over here." Steph took her elbow and pulled her a few steps away from the base of the stage.

"So, what did you think?" Surely she'd done enough to get this internship. Everyone had looked at her with such fascination.

"You had something in your teeth the whole time."

Natalie chuckled, but Steph's mouth stayed flat.

Her chuckle died away. "Seriously?" She swiped a finger across her teeth and dislodged a poppy seed from this morning's breakfast bagel.

"And did you read the attachment on the email I sent you?"

Her soaring spirit—as yet undisturbed by her bloated abdomen and the *incessant* thumping of that soccer ball—smashed into the ground. "What attachment?"

A giggle sounded behind her, and she glanced back. Jem and that trim-yet-curvy mother again. Was she laughing at the poppy seed?

"It explained the theme for today's meeting." Steph drew Natalie's attention back with a hand on her forearm. "Dealing with family illness and loss. You know, because of your dad."

"So that joke about the sick penguin was . . ."

"Wildly inappropriate, yes."

"Oh no." The blood drained from her head. "I need to sit down." She landed on the bottom step of the stage with a thump and rested her forehead on her knees.

Steph lowered herself to sit beside her, no mean feat in a pencil skirt and heels.

"I don't remember an attachment." Natalie scoured her memory and shook her head, forehead brushing her kneecaps. Her temples pounded with the beat of that child's soccer ball. "So they weren't paying attention because my wisdom was inspiring. They were watching a car wreck with morbid curiosity."

Steph shrugged one shoulder.

Ouch. She hadn't even tried to deny it.

As Steph spoke, a young woman approached. She smiled at Natalie.

Natalie looked at Steph.

"Natalie, you should meet Kimberly." Steph beckoned the girl forward.

Kimberly wore peep-toe heels, and the air around her seemed to bounce with energy. Natalie had found her first gray hair that morning and been too tired to contemplate a shoe more complicated than slip-on.

Steph smiled at the two of them. "Kimberly's just signed up as our newest intern."

Natalie blinked. What? They were taking on more than one intern? Or had she lost her spot already?

The woman stepped forward and thrust out a hand. "Great to meet you. We might end up workmates—and competitors." She winked with the last word.

"Nice to meet you." Natalie's words came out with the enthusiasm of a robot.

Kimberly sashayed away, and Natalie whirled to Steph. "What's going on?"

"The board wanted us to take on more than one intern. She applied weeks ago. Your application just got in under the wire."

Natalie swallowed. So even if she got the internship, she'd be competing against someone else for the permanent job.

A young, enthusiastic someone else.

"Great."

Steph stood and tugged her hand. "Come on, let's get the morning tea ready."

Natalie let herself be pulled up and tried to focus on the positive aspect of the morning. "I guess my talk wasn't a total loss. Had it been in the right context, it wouldn't have been so ba—"

Something hard smacked her face. Pain exploded across her right cheekbone and nose. A curse word flew from her lips. Loudly.

A soccer ball bounced away toward the semicircle of fifty women. One hundred eyes lasered in on her as waves of white-hot agony rolled across her skull and she doubled over, face in her hands.

"Nat, come *on*." Steph sounded mortified as she pulled at her elbow.

Natalie eased one hand away from her face. Blood would pour all over Mom's blouse, but that couldn't be helped. She squeezed one eye open, then stared at her hand. No blood?

The pain reduced to a dull pounding. Maybe nothing had been seriously damaged. She stumbled along behind Steph into the kitchen.

Steph hefted open a chest freezer. "Aha." She pulled out a bag of carrots and slapped them against Natalie's cheek.

Natalie jerked away. "Ow!"

"It'll teach you to watch your language," Steph retorted. "Did you see Mrs. Parrish's face? My goodness, Nat. I really don't know about this."

Natalie pulled the carrots from her head, chest tightening, panic rising. "What do you mean, you don't know?" Her throat closed at the look on Steph's face. Pursed lips, two fine lines on her otherwise wrinkle-free forehead. Mad. Definitely mad.

Outside, Sam officially closed the event and the room swelled with chatter.

Steph picked up a tray of cookies and took two steps toward the door. "I have to do some damage control. I'll call you later this week."

"Wait—" Natalie fell silent as Steph strode away. She let her hand with the carrots stay limp by her side. Her face deserved to hurt. She'd just blown her chance.

Seven years ago, her life had derailed in a little town called Missing Out On Everything. The ache now attacking her chest confirmed that no matter how hard she tried, she was never getting out.

Jem strolled over, Olly bouncing against his shoulder. "Hey, there, sailor." His smug smile stung like sandpaper to the eyeball. "I always knew you had a potty mouth."

Her mind filled with the buzz of a million angry bees. Her dream was over. And he thought it was funny.

"Shut up." She shoved the carrots in his chest and stomped away.

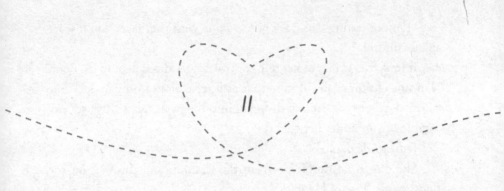

11

Stop being stubborn, Natalie. Just get in the car."

Jem's voice called out to her from behind, but Natalie ignored it. Her stomach had declared mutiny. Her head pounded with every step she took on the footpath outside the church. The fabric of Mom's shirt clung to her still-sticky chest. And her emotions had time-traveled back to nineteen-year-old Natalie, who tried so hard to make something work and was still blindsided when it didn't.

She pretended the old Camry creeping along the road wasn't there.

"*Natalie.*"

"I really need some alone time here, Jem."

Understatement of the century, but she managed to keep her voice calm. Well, relatively.

She threw a cursory glance at Jem's vehicle. "How'd you even get the car? I had the keys. And how did you get here?"

"You left the keys in the church when you stormed out, and I hitched a ride with a workmate and planned to ride home for lunch with you." The Camry kept rolling along beside her, Jem leaning to talk to her out the window. "C'mon, Nat. I'm sorry I laughed at you."

She kept her eyes forward. "It's not about that."

"I'm not letting you walk home alone with that face. You'll scare small children."

It took every fiber of her self-control not to kick a dent in his door. "I'm not bleeding, so I'll take that as a reflection on my looks." She stormed over to the car and dropped into the passenger seat. A squeak sounded from under her backside.

Jem smirked.

She dug a plastic Nemo from the cushion and threw it on the floorboard. "I'm in. Happy?"

"Your eye is purple and green."

"Fabulous."

"I don't know why you're so upset. The soccer ball was bad—I didn't realize how hard it hit you at first—but the rest of the morning wasn't so awful." Jem accelerated into traffic. Yawned. "Even if you don't get this internship, just go try something else."

Steam built up between her ears. "Opportunities like this don't exactly come knocking on my door."

"So go out and make them happen."

Like she hadn't tried. Maybe if he'd stuck around seven years ago, they could've shared the burden of Dad's sickness together, and she wouldn't have had to leave college. She clenched her hands. "I can't."

"Give me one good reason why not."

"Responsibility!" The word spewed forth, seething with seven years of hurt. "I have people depending on me. I can't just run off and do whatever I want."

Oliver jolted at her sudden rise in volume and cried.

Jem's jaw clenched and he slowed the car a little. "Like I did, you mean."

A quiet voice rapped its knuckles on her skull and told her to quit while she could. She told it to shut up. "We don't all have that luxury, Jem."

"Luxury?" Jem jammed on the brakes for a red light, much like she'd done to him a few weeks ago. Natalie's body lurched forward, but the seat belt held tight. Her head banged against the headrest as the car screeched to a halt.

Jem twisted in his seat to face her, his expression thunderous. "You think my leaving was a luxury?"

"What would you call it?"

"I'd call it the worst day in my entire life. And that's including the day my mother died. For Pete's sake, Nat, I—" He bit back what she assumed were some pretty choice words.

Heat swept through her, along with a wave of indignant rage. Her muscles quivered.

The day he'd left hadn't been the worst of *her* life. No, hers was the day Steph sat at Mom and Dad's old dining table, six weeks after Jem left, and told her that Mike had shipped the last box that morning.

He wasn't coming back, and that date marked with love hearts on her calendar wouldn't be her wedding day after all.

Her jaw tightened, and her voice came out as a growl. "Don't you dare play the sympathy card."

He barked a humorless laugh. "Yeah, I left. And that makes me the bad guy."

She gaped. Was he serious? "You bet it does." Did he have any comprehension of what he'd put her through? The crippling insecurity as she grappled with what she'd done to make him leave? The humiliation?

He pulled a hand down his cheeks. "Unbelievable."

Heat rushed into Natalie's face and her voice turned into a screech. "'Unbelievable'? What do you mean, 'unbelievable'? You ran out on me months before our wedding! You—"

A car horn blared. A flash of color caught her eye. "Green light."

"What?"

"Green light!"

He hit the gas and took off.

Shudders rippled through Natalie's body, but she held her breath to prevent a single sob. She pressed her lips together. If she spoke, she'd shout, so she said nothing at all. Olly's screams turned into whimpers, and she twisted in her seat to slip his pacifier into his mouth.

"Don't touch him." Jem's voice cracked.

"What?" Her gaze flew to his face. The granite expression he wore was reminiscent of John.

"If you hate me this much, you don't have to stay. I'll find you another job, and you can go do what you want." He pulled the car into its parking spot at the apartment block and yanked the keys from the ignition.

She fumbled to release her seat belt as he pulled Olly from the car. It gave way and she scrambled out, looked at him over the hood. "Are you firing me?" She'd only worked for him for four days. That had to be some kind of record.

He swung Olly up into his arms and didn't meet her eye. "I'm pretty sure you just quit."

She stomped her foot. "Fine, run away again."

Jem slammed the car door shut and speared her with his gaze. "Let's get one thing straight. You can remember whatever twisted version you want, but I did not run away."

Twisted version? *Twisted* version? She remembered, all right. The strange distance between them for a couple of weeks. Then his incoherent break-up speech on Mom and Dad's porch. Her frantic, unanswered voice messages in the days after. And the unending silence, which made one thing clear: whatever he'd babbled on the porch that night, the simple truth was that he hadn't wanted her anymore.

A passing jogger glanced at them, and Jem turned toward the apartment building. "If you want to yell at me some more, come inside. Unless you want someone to call the police and my dad to join this little party." He walked away.

Nuh-uh. He wasn't walking away from her again. She'd have the last word, and then she'd walk away from *him*.

Jem didn't slow, and the stairs were horrendous to climb in her light-headed state. She caught him as he unlocked the apartment's front door.

"You want a pity party, Jem? Fine, let's go there."

He spread his free arm in a bring-it-on gesture.

She followed him into the living room, riding the momentum of her righteous anger. "Let's bring up the night I had to explain to my mother that she wasn't going to be mother of the bride in ten weeks' time. The day I had to explain to my friends why my fiancé would leave me. How about the day I returned my unworn wedding dress?" She folded her arms. What comeback could he possibly have to that?

Jem plopped a now calm Olly in his playpen and faced her. "I left because that was best for you, for both of us."

She stared. In his warped mind, the months—years—of heartbreak she'd endured were "for her own good"? While he moved on with college, a career, and obviously another woman?

She pointed a finger at him and enunciated each word with precision. "Don't you ever say that to me again." Her voice shook with fury.

While he'd received his education, dream career, and a son, she'd had to drop out of school. Work jobs that turned her brain to oatmeal. Watch Dad shrink into a hundred-and-fifty-pound shell of a human being. And she'd had to do it alone.

To justify his selfish decision with this kind of lie was nothing short of delusion.

Jem closed his mouth, but nothing in his clenched-jaw expression looked like he was backing down.

She lowered her finger and folded her arms tight against her chest. "I'm not only mad that you left. I'm mad that you're the one who did the wrong thing and it was *my* life that derailed."

Jem threw his hands up. "You think I'm not derailed? You think I planned to move back within shouting distance of Dad? To practically get fired? Be a single dad?"

She barked a mirthless *ha*. "You know what people say when they look at you? 'There's Jem. Did you know he was a reporter in Chicago? It's so sweet he came back to his hometown. And he's so good with his little boy.'" She ran a hand through her hair, fingers snagging on each split end. "You know what they say about me? 'Poor Nat. Do you know she was engaged once? And do you know who her father is? Everyone used to think she'd follow in his footsteps. Funny how things turn out.'" She spat the last word out with seven years of bitterness.

The moment stretched, Jem's gaze unreadable.

Natalie swallowed, cheeks burning. What had she done? At least before she could pretend Jem hadn't had the power over her that he did. Now she'd given up the one thing she had left: her dignity.

She pulled her jacket tight around herself and swiveled to leave. It was over. There was nothing left to salvage here.

"I'm sorry."

His quiet words halted her trudge to the door. That was the first sign she'd ever seen that he regretted any part of how things ended between them.

"It's not like I enjoy hating you." Why were these words even coming out of her mouth? But still, she turned to face him, hands jammed into her jacket pockets. "Every day I walk up those stairs and tell myself, 'Unforgiveness only hurts me. God forgave me, so I extend the same to you.'" She shook her head. "And every day it lasts for three seconds before I hate you again."

Jem stared at his toe, expression thoughtful. After a long moment, he met her eyes. "But you try the next day?"

She swallowed. "I do." Not because he deserved it. Not because there could ever be anything between them again.

But because it had been done for her.

Jem shifted on his feet. "Thank you."

Her "You're welcome" stuck in her throat.

"I can't fix the past." Jem pulled his notebook out of his pocket. "But I can help you get this internship."

She sniffed, brain struggling to catch up. "What?"

"What if we make you unfireable?"

"I haven't been hired yet." The words came out scratchy, and she cleared her throat.

"I'm serious." His blue eyes lit with an idea. "Have they given you anything else to help out with? Mentioned anything we could work on to prove how useful you are?"

"Ummm . . ." She tried to focus. "Sam mentioned he wants to plan a new type of event. An outreach that can connect with families as well as teens. But I don't think he's started work on it yet."

"So do it. Work up some ideas, something that convinces him you're too valuable to lose."

"I don't think—"

"I'll help you. Come on, you want this. Let's fight for it."

Her bones felt hollow from lack of energy, her face throbbed, and her brain still screamed for caffeine.

The corner of Jem's mouth pulled up. "I have ten minutes left before I have to head back to work. I'll bet you one diaper change that I think of more ideas than you before then. Then you can go back to hating me."

Competitive Natalie arose from her nap in the corner of her mind and stuffed a sock in Whiny Natalie's mouth. This festival idea could be her chance to get a new photo on Dad's wall, even if the price was working with Jem.

She pulled a pen from the pocket of her jeans, sniffed back the rest of her tears. "Fine. You're on."

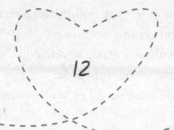

12

W e need to talk."

Natalie's gut somersaulted—not in a good way—at the sound of Sam's voice when she answered her cell. It was 8:00 a.m. on Saturday, and she stood before Jem's front door, finger-combing her windblown hair. "Oh?" Her chance at the internship was down the toilet. She knew it.

"How about we meet at Bodo's for lunch? I want to chat about how Thursday went."

At least she'd get a good bagel out of the meeting that sealed her fate. "Bodo's sounds good. Which one?"

"The one near UVA. I'll meet you there at twelve thirty?"

"It's a date." Her face flushed. Had that sounded flirty? Not that there was anything wrong with flirting . . . was there?

"I'll see you then." The call disconnected, and she stared at the phone for a moment. She and Jem had worked for the past two days on her proposal for Sam's event, but the sick twist of her gut told her it wouldn't be enough.

She shoved her phone into her jeans pocket and rapped on Jem's door.

No answer.

"Jem?"

She knocked once more, then checked her watch. They'd agreed to meet at eight. All their work was on Jem's laptop. And now the countdown had started.

After a moment's hesitation, she pulled out her key and slid it into the lock. She opened the door a crack. "Hello?"

Lili's door remained closed and displayed a crayon reproduction of Van Gogh's *The Starry Night* below a new sketch of Jem and Olly. That girl had more artistic talent in her pinkie toe than Natalie's whole family tree combined.

She tiptoed through the dining nook, a socked foot in view ahead in the living room. Wind howled against the window, covering any noise she made. The sock—covered in pictures of Bugs Bunny—led to the rest of Jem, sprawled across the floor. He lay facedown with his nose buried in the carpet, fingers inches from the laptop sitting before him.

The door to his bedroom stood open. Inside, Olly cooed to himself in his crib.

Her gaze shifted back to Jem, snoring on the floor. No way would she wake him, but maybe if she could just get the laptop . . .

She slipped around him on toes lighter than a ballet dancer. Made it to the laptop. Bent down and closed her fingers around it and—

"Whah?" Jem sucked in a breath and flipped himself over into a half-seated position.

She started and dropped the computer. "Jem." The momentary rush of adrenaline faded, and she scooped up her prize. "Why do you always wake like someone screamed 'fire'?"

His eyes stayed unfocused.

"Jem?"

He jolted, blinked, looked at her. "What time is it?" Without waiting for an answer, he flopped back to the floor and tossed his forearm over his eyes.

Natalie sat down next to him, back against the couch. Her fingers tapped the keys as if she were typing, but she just sat there and looked at him, lying there in his sweat pants and Chicago Bears hoodie. She'd bought him that hoodie for his eighteenth birthday.

They'd reached a cautious holding pattern over the past two days, spending every spare moment on this project. She didn't know if Jem helped her for friendship's sake or because he knew that no internship meant no more nannying or because of . . . something more.

Despite their uneasy truce, questions still swirled like the leaves outside Jem's windows, caught in the forewinds of a coming storm. What did Jem expect from their friendship? Did he feel the stubborn tug of magnetism that she did, despite her logical reasoning against it?

Friday's fight had reinforced one frustrating truth: Jem could still affect her in a big way. And that made this residual attraction all the more infuriating. They had no future. And that was that.

She tapped the mouse pad and logged in with the password Jem had told her yesterday. The screen lit with an employment website. She scrolled down and checked the search terms. *Part-time, flexible hours, no qualifications required.*

She hit the minimize button, but another browser window was open behind it. College scholarships? She minimized again, and a third page popped up: ministry internships.

Jem mumbled something. The words sounded like gibberish, except for the last one—"babe."

She poked her toe into his gut.

"*Ooof.*" He scooted away and cracked an eye open. "What gives?"

"Why don't you tell me, *babe*?"

"I was dreaming about Lola Bunny." He sat up with a groan. Dragged himself to lean against the couch beside her. "Whatcha doin'?" His shoulder pressed against hers as he peeked at the screen. His expression changed. "Oh. You weren't supposed to see that."

"You were looking up opportunities for me?"

He shrugged, eyes guarded. "I wasn't sure if it was something you'd want to look into, but I thought I'd see what's available. You know, if you still wanted to stay working here." A hint of uncertainty entered his voice in the final words.

She paused. Thanking Jem for anything ran against the grain, but this . . . She nudged him. "Thanks." She glanced back at the computer screen. "Even if it looks like there's not much out there."

He flashed her a grin, his face close enough that his breath tickled wisps of hair against her cheek. "I'm a sweet guy." His gaze dropped to her lips.

Natalie's breath caught. Every muscle in her body tensed as old attractions hit her nervous system like a one-ton crate of chocolate strawberries and Barry White records.

Jem moved forward a fraction of an inch.

Oliver cried.

She jerked back from Jem and scrambled to her feet. "I'll get him." She dashed to the crib. What momentary insanity had that been? Two whole days without a fight did not mean she was interested in kissing the man. Whether he fell asleep looking up jobs for her or not.

When she reached the crib, Olly had pulled himself up against the rails. She blinked. "Jem."

"Yeah?"

"Olly's standing."

There was a flurry of movement, a thump, and a bang against the wall. Jem staggered into the room, a hand over his left eye. "I tripped over the computer when I stood up."

A giggle escaped her. Poor Jem, with his sleepy eyes and worn sweat pants. There were moments she wished she could forget the last seven years and pretend they were still overgrown children.

Well, in moments like these, Jem still was.

She picked up the crying baby, and he quieted after a moment. She blew a kiss against his neck. "Who's a clever baby?"

Olly giggled and grabbed her nose. She kissed his palm, and he planted an open-mouthed kiss against her cheek. One hundred percent drool. His little tongue licked her as he pulled away, leaving a wet smear across a quarter of her face.

Jem came up behind her, trapping her between him and the crib. He leaned over her shoulder and brushed a kiss against Olly's blond forehead. "Did you inherit Daddy's kissing skills?"

Her nerves exploded into a full-blown riot.

Jem paused for a moment, and she held still, unable to move and unsure if she wanted to. But he slipped an arm around Olly and took the baby from her. "Come on, little guy, it's time for breakfast. We've got work to do."

♡

Sam was nowhere to be found.

Natalie stretched in her seat to scan the restaurant again. The door opened and she whipped her head around. Three college students stumbled in, looking like they needed a hangover cure more than a bagel.

She checked her watch. Twelve forty. Her stomach rumbled at the smell of bacon and eggs on the table across from hers, but she wouldn't order till Sam arrived. They had agreed on the Bodo's by the university, hadn't they?

The only thing worse than being turned down for her dream internship was being stood up and turned down for her dream internship. She propped her chin on her hand and gazed out the window as storm clouds rolled over the University of Virginia campus. At least it hadn't rained before she arrived. She'd had to slather on the makeup to cover her black eye from that soccer ball. Though now it looked like the effort was in vain.

The doorbell jingled.

"Natalie."

If sound were a chocolate cake, Sam's voice was rich, sweet, and thick with frosting. And it struck a gong of fear in Natalie's heart.

She sat up straight and painted a smile on her face. "Sam. Hi."

He bent down to give her his customary hug, then slid into the seat opposite her, dark hair spiked with water. "Sorry I'm late. I was running a boxing class with some college students and lost track of time."

"Boxing?" That would explain the shower—and the spicy smell of fresh cologne.

"One of our new outreach ideas. Building relationships via sports. Boxing is my specialty, though I'm trying to convince your friend Jem to join me."

She tilted her head. "Jem told you he can box?" As far as she knew, he hadn't touched a pair of gloves since he was seventeen. What else had changed that she didn't know about?

"He mentioned it when he interviewed me for the paper. One of several things we have in common. Including you."

"Me?"

"Well, maybe I'm jumping the gun. You haven't accepted my offer yet."

"Internship offer?" A spark of hope flamed in her chest.

"Yes. Why else do you think I asked you here?"

"I— Well, Steph didn't seem particularly encouraging after Thursday."

He dismissed her concerns with a wave of his hand. "Teething problems. Happens to the best of us. My first sermon, I set the pulpit on fire."

Natalie suppressed a laugh. He sure didn't suffer from false humility.

"I mean literally. A woman put it out by dunking her shawl in the water we had ready for a baptism."

She chuckled, and her rigid posture relaxed. "I thought I'd put together some ideas for that event you mentioned." She slid a manila folder across the table.

Sam picked it up. "Initiative. I like it. But let's get some lunch first. We've got big plans to make."

♡

"And if you're the intern that gets the permanent position in three months' time, Wildfire will pay for you to finish college."

Natalie nodded as Sam pointed to a paragraph on the paperwork in front of her. Times New Roman had never looked so beautiful.

Working for both Jem and Sam would involve many hours, but that concern barely registered. Since she was a teen, she'd worked a succession of mind-numbing, life-wasting jobs. Today she'd start a career and carry on Dad's legacy.

The thought was sweeter than the next bite of her strawberry-cream-cheese bagel.

"So what will the internship—and, if I got it, the eventual job—actually involve?" She leaned forward as she asked.

Sam shrugged. "What will it not involve?" He took a long draw from his second lemonade—the man's sugar addiction seemed to rival hers—and looked to be in thought. "At the moment I spend my time speaking in Christian schools, youth groups, churches—that sort of thing. But I'm open to new ideas. Kimberly, our other intern, suggested a youth drop-in center. The board liked her pitch and agreed to a trial." He held up her folder. "You've got some great ideas here for using a festival as a form of outreach. I say we pitch that to the board as well and try both. They're interested in expanding from just my speaking ministry." He placed the folder back on the table and laced his fingers over his stomach with the smile of a man who'd eaten two bagels. "Apart from that, we're looking for someone to replace Steph. She's made it clear she only wants to help us get off the ground. I need someone to run the administration side of things but also be willing to do some public speaking or lead youth Bible studies."

She finished her bagel and swiped her face for crumbs. It sounded like more public speaking was in her future. Not ideal, but doable. "That sounds good."

He gave a sheepish shrug. "I'm really just making it up as I go along. Wildfire's been a complete whirlwind. Two years ago I was staying with my dad's relatives in LA, working the dinner shift at Sonic and preaching on weekends."

Gorgeous and honest. How was he still single?

She tried to tone her smile down from squealing-excited to enthusiastic-but-professional. "Wow. That's awesome."

A strange expression crossed his face—almost a wince? "There's pros and cons." He shook his head and the expression disappeared.

Natalie made a mental note of it. Looked like there was a story there, but today wasn't the day to push.

"If your boss can spare you for a few hours on Monday, drop by the office and we'll show you around."

She shrugged off his concern about Jem. They'd already agreed that Lili was capable with Olly, so her days now finished at 3:30 p.m. "I'll be there. Jem will be fine with it. He helped me come up with ideas for the festival." He'd even found a group of motocross riders that could headline the event, help draw a young crowd.

Sam folded the papers away. "Sounds like you two have a unique friendship."

He had no idea. "We've got our own way of working together."

"You guys go far back?"

"Since the day he knocked my tooth out in a basketball game. Fifth grade. My first day of school when we moved to Charlottesville." She'd given him a black eye the following week, and their teacher put them on the same team to avoid further injuries.

Sam offered a handshake as they rose from the table. "Hopefully

I can also prove to be an interesting boss-slash-friend." He turned up the wattage in his smile, and a dimple peeked out from one cheek.

Natalie gripped his hand. Solid muscle. He probably had the power to crush her bones, but he held her hand like it was a delicate flower. The twinkle in his eye shone a little brighter than any business deal warranted.

This was going to be an interesting job.

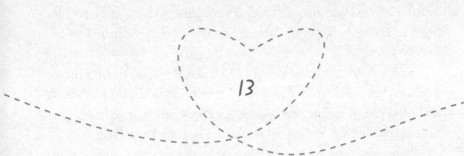

13

"Mom, I'm not pregnant. Or on drugs. Or on a secret spy mission to Mexico."

Lili jabbed her pencil at a math book to punctuate the point. Friday afternoon homework was the pits. Her fingers twitched, dying to throw her cell phone out the window where Mom couldn't nag her.

Instead she leaned back in her desk chair and silently screamed at her bedroom ceiling. Her painting of Emmett Kelly's famous sad clown, *Weary Willie*, stared back at her with sympathy. Two weeks at her uncle's apartment, and she'd already covered the walls of her room with art. When she'd painted Willie last week, she'd had to stick him to the ceiling.

Now his mournful eyes watched her, like he, too, understood the torturous combination that was math homework and uptight mothers.

"Well, what else explains this sudden trouble with school?" Mom's voice faded at the end of the sentence, and an indistinct voice spoke. She was probably at the church, working on yet another project.

"I didn't say I was having trouble at school. I said math is hard and do you know how to do logarithms?"

Any other day she'd have asked Grace, but Grace had moved to

North Carolina yesterday and hadn't yet replied to Lili's message. Not her one about homework, anyway. She'd sent eleven pictures of her new bedroom.

So Mom was the last resort. All Lili had wanted was to ask a simple question, but with Mom it was never that easy. Lili tossed her math book aside and picked up her latest sketch. Her gray pencil skated across the page, darkening the outline of two figures in a shadowy street.

"I ran into your math teacher at church last Sunday." Mom continued as if Lili hadn't spoken. "She said you've been distracted lately."

"Mom, I—"

"I told your father we need to hire a tutor for you. Excelling at art isn't enough to prepare you for a career in this economic climate. I'm putting my foot down. You should come home, and we'll get you some proper help."

Lili dropped her pencil—the sketch wasn't working anyway—and rested her forehead against the windowpane. No afternoon sun to cheer her up. Instead, dull clouds hung around like bored kids, unsure if they wanted to rain or not.

"You don't need to put your foot anywhere, Mom. I'm not failing." Yet.

The important point was she couldn't let Mom run away with the idea of a tutor. Mom and Dad had fought for a week the last time the subject came up. Dad said they couldn't afford it. Mom said he was a cheapskate. Dad said her shoe collection could feed an African village . . . Well, Lili had turned up her stereo at that point.

"Not failing isn't the standard we're aiming for, Lilianna."

She tapped her forehead against the glass.

"It's alright, Mom, you don't have to worry, because . . ." Lili swept her gaze across the room, scanning for inspiration. As she pivoted, her forearm hit a cup on the edge of her desk and knocked it flying. It smashed against the leg of her bed.

"What was that?"

"I just broke a glass. Hold on." She dropped to her hands and knees, scooping up the biggest pieces of the cup. She twisted for a shard that'd landed in the far corner.

Riiiiiiip.

Terrific. Who didn't want a rip in the rear of their favorite jeans? She'd only finished a new screen-print design on them last week.

As she reached the end of her bed, she looked up and encountered a raspberry lollipop poking from her backpack. Nick.

Bingo.

"I, um, was saying you don't have to worry about a tutor, because I'm getting a friend to tutor me. For free. We're doing a swap, art for math."

Well, maybe it wasn't an official arrangement yet, but Nick had mentioned the possibility on the day they met. And they'd hung out over the last two weeks—him, her, and Grace. He should be happy to help.

"Are you sure, Lili? We could get a professional. Don't let your father put you off—"

"Dad's got nothing to do with it."

"I'm just saying, he puts his worries onto you when it's his responsibility—"

"Just drop it—*yeouch!*" A sliver of glass sliced Lili's palm. She jerked to her feet and clenched her teeth as fire radiated from the base of her thumb. Drops of blood, round and red, fell from where she stood over her desk and landed on her sketch. She stared at the red spots on the page, with tiny splashes around them where the droplets splattered. Her stomach rolled.

"Mom, I've got it handled. Don't stress. I've gotta go, okay?" She left her cell on her bed and stomped toward the kitchen, thumb throbbing with every step.

Why did Mom make everything difficult? One simple question about logarithms should not reignite the Great Tutor War. The ground around Mom and Dad was covered in land mines, and she could never tell when she was about to step on one.

The worst part was not being able to tell anybody. Sometimes her brain felt like a pressure cooker.

In the kitchen, Natalie sat at the counter, paperwork scattered before her. She and Uncle Jem had been brainstorming more ideas for her festival ever since he'd gotten home from work. Though Nat wasn't looking at her papers right now. She was rolling her eyes in the direction of the living area.

Uncle Jem's voice bellowed from somewhere in that direction. ". . . move my book?"

"I never touched your book," she hollered back, then shot Lili a wink and pulled a novel from underneath a stack of papers. *Three Bullets and a Broken Heart*. "Did you know he reads sappy love stories?" Natalie whispered. "I read four chapters while Olly was asleep."

Thumb about to fall off or not, Lili cracked half a smile. Though their first week had seemed a bit tense, Nat and Jem had gotten along pretty well this week. Nice to see some playful bickering instead of just . . . bickering.

Lili walked toward the bathroom as Jem padded out into the living room, still dressed in his work clothes. He narrowed his eyes at Nat, who took a sudden interest in her work.

He motioned Lili closer. "Just wait till I find her chocolate stash. It'll be carrots for lunch tomorrow."

Lili pointed to her thumb. "Do you have some tweezers?"

Jem's face paled three shades. "What happened?" He dragged her into the bathroom and sat her on the edge of the tub while he dug through a drawer.

"I knocked a cup off my desk. I think there's a little bit of glass in it."

"Nat! Do we have bandages?"

There was a slight scramble, and Nat poked her head around the doorframe. Her eyebrows scrunched up. "I'll deal with the blood. Just get me something to wrap this up with."

"We've got antiseptic cream and some of those giant Band-Aids." Jem disappeared and returned with the supplies.

Natalie confirmed there was no glass in the cut and unscrewed the jar of germ-slaying goop. The sharp smell pierced Lili's nostrils.

"This is gonna sting."

Jem offered Lili his hand, and Lili gripped it as Natalie slathered the stuff over her thumb.

Two minutes later, her hand was wrapped up and the mess cleared away. Natalie returned to her work as Jem put away the supplies and whistled. "Ouch."

"Yeah," Lili said. Almost as painful as five minutes of conversation with her mother. "While I have your sympathy, can I ask a favor? I want to have a friend over. We're studying together."

"Sure. When?"

"I'll have to call him to find out."

"Him?" Jem dropped to the edge of the bathtub, next to Lili. "What's his name? Social security number? Hottie rating? Do I need my shotgun?"

Her cheeks heated.

"Did someone say hottie rating?" Nat's voice floated from the kitchen.

"Ignore her. Of course you can 'study.'" Jem made quote marks in the air with his fingers and winked. "But it happens at the kitchen table or the living room. No closed doors."

"It's not like that. He's just a friend."

"Sure he is." Jem squeezed her shoulder and stood. "Just let me know when he's coming over."

"Thanks, Uncle Jem." Lili shot from the bathroom.

She had a text message to send.

♡

Lili perched on the edge of her bed and eyed her cell phone.

What if Nick was busy? What if he didn't want to tutor her? What would she tell Mom?

Just get it over and done with.

She typed out the most eloquent message she could think of. *What's up?*

Her phone rang. She grinned. Nick liked to rant about how "kids these days" never spoke on the phone anymore, only texted. Looked like he practiced what he preached. She hit the Answer button. "Hey."

"What's happening?" The background noise on the call sounded like he was in a store.

She flopped back on her mountain of pillows. "I just ripped my favorite jeans."

"An epic day, then."

Her smile grew. "Something like that." She cocked her head. "What's with all the noise? Where are you?"

"Uh . . . I'd rather not say." Laughter hid behind his words.

She propped herself up on one elbow. "Are you in the bathroom?"

"Worse."

"My day has stunk. I think that means you have to tell me."

"Promise not to laugh."

"Yeah, yeah, promise."

"I'm in the ladies' underwear section of Target."

A giggle escaped Lili's lips before she covered with a coughing fit. "Are you perving on the mannequins?"

"I'm, um . . ." His voice dropped in volume. "I'm grabbing stuff for my mom. She's on a bit of a downer and doesn't feel like shopping, but I do the laundry and she— Well, she needs some clothes."

"Oh." Nick had told her about his mother and her struggle with bipolar disorder. "Want some help?"

"You'd be my knight in shining armor."

"I'll be there soon."

Lili disconnected the call, and a second later her phone beeped. A message from Dad. She hadn't seen him in the two weeks since she'd moved to Jem's—her decision, not his.

She tapped her screen and brought up the message. After a long freeze-out, she'd invited him to share a triple-fudge coconut waffle with her tonight. Maybe she could talk to him about how she was feeling, blow off some steam. Apart from Dad, she didn't have many options. Grace would have been the natural choice, even long distance, but she was a blabbermouth who still had a lot of Charlottesville connections. And if this got out, Lili could kiss any chance of a family reunion goodbye.

Dad's sumo suit picture flashed up on the screen, followed by the text.

> Sorry, hon, I'm on my way to meet with Stephen and his caseworker. Rain check?

A fuse lit in the back of her skull. He was still involved with Stephen Kent? Her thumbs flew across the screen.

> Is Miss Kent with you?

No reply.
She jumped from her bed. She had to talk to someone.

Lili picked at her chipped nail polish—a different shade of purple on each finger—as she sat in her uncle's passenger seat on the way to Target. Her phone, plagued with battery problems, burned in her pocket. Just like the secret on the tip of her tongue.

She stole a look at Jem from the corner of her eye. He tapped the steering wheel like a bongo drum, humming along to the tune on the radio. He'd been in the same good mood since Natalie had been coming around.

Lili hadn't been sure of Natalie at first. She had enough adults bossing her around without adding Jem's old girlfriend to the list. But then Natalie offered to teach her to sew, even though Lili knew Nat didn't enjoy the craft. Lili already had an art project planned around a 1940s dress pattern she'd found.

Mom could sew but never found the time to share her skill.

Lili brushed purple flecks from the cute red skirt she'd donned and attacked the next nail.

Natalie was cut from different cloth than most adults. So was Uncle Jem. Could she tell them her family's secret?

"Hey, Jem, can I ask you a question?"

"Sure thing, sweet cheeks."

"If I told you I got a tattoo, what would you say?" Maybe if Jem could be trusted with a little secret like that, he could deal with this too.

He overshot the corner. She grabbed the door and the car's tires squealed as he corrected.

"You mother is going to murder me."

"I didn't say that I actually did it. But what would you do if I had? Would you be cool?"

Jem pulled a hand down his cheeks. "Just tell me it's not of that Bieber guy. I could face your dad as long as it's a tattoo of someone respectable. Like Justin Timberlake."

"NSYNC is over, man. Let it go."

Jem glanced at her. "Seriously, is there something you want to tell me?"

"No tattoos here. I had to watch Grace get her flu shot last month. I woke up on the floor to the sight of the male nurse's man boobs in my face. It was just a random question." Lili forced a light tone to her voice, but her hopes sagged lower than Mr. Munroe's man bosom. If Jem would tell her parents about something like a tattoo, she couldn't trust him with her situation. He'd feel obliged to tell, and Mom would find out about Miss Kent in a bad way. What if this was the thing that totally broke her parents apart?

They rolled into the parking lot, and she checked her phone. Message from Nick.

Mom Shopping List Item #17: personal hygiene products. This. Is. The. End.

She snorted, and texted back. Where are you?

Her phone beeped. Absolute rock bottom.

The car came to a stop and she cracked open her door, thumb still texting a reply.

Jem placed a hand on her forearm. "Two hours, okay? Call me if you want to come back earlier. I'll be here faster than you can say My-Uncle-Is-A-Secret-Ninja-So-Don't-Touch-His-Niece."

"That actually takes a long time to say."

"Not for ninjas."

Lili rolled her eyes and got out of the car. "'Bye, Uncle Jem.'"

"Love you too." He made kissy faces and drove away.

Her throat tightened. Everything in her wanted to chase that car down and blurt the whole story to her uncle. But no. He'd blab. She had to give her parents every chance she could.

A beep sounded from her back pocket, and she checked her messages again.

You'll find me in the tools section. I'm soaking up some manliness.

She smiled. Nick. She'd only known him for two weeks, but he was the only friend she could trust with her burden.

The only drawback: Miss Kent was his aunt.

Lili shoved the thought to the bottom of her pocket, along with her phone. That didn't matter. She had to tell someone, or she would explode.

14

Something didn't look right.

Jem, back from dropping Lili off, closed his apartment door behind him and surveyed his home.

Natalie and her outdated laptop at the counter. That part looked very right, though he didn't fool himself into thinking she was here for his company but rather his free Wi-Fi.

But the rest of the apartment—even with his new couch and dining table—looked too . . . bare? Impersonal?

He couldn't ask his father to dinner here until this got fixed. Dad always said he wasn't responsible enough. This needed to look like the home of a responsible father who was capable of caring for his son.

If only he knew where to start.

"Nat?"

She didn't respond, just stayed hunched over her screen, blue light reflecting off her face.

He flicked the button on the internet modem. After a few seconds her head popped up, reading glasses in place. A new addition since they'd been together. Black frames, very "sexy librarian."

Not that he'd express that thought aloud.

Now they rested over a puckered brow. "What's with the Wi-Fi?"

He lifted the modem and pretended to reset it while actually turning it back on. "That should fix it. While I've got your attention . . ."

Her gaze, already back down at her screen, dragged up with apparent reluctance.

"I need your opinion." Something she usually had no problem giving. Hopefully she'd take the bait.

"On what?"

He smothered a smile. Same old Nat. "I want to try and have Dad over, give him and Oliver a proper introduction. But, well . . ." He indicated the drying rack by the sink, which held two baby bowls and three adult-sized plates. "That's pretty much the extent of my dishes. The whole place needs a spruce-up."

She got a glint in her eye.

"On a budget."

She leaned back on her mismatched stool and twirled a pen between her fingers. "Thrift store. If you buy all their blue-and-white plates, it doesn't matter that they don't match. They look good anyway."

He pulled his notebook from his back pocket and scribbled down the note. "And the rest of the house?"

She surveyed the living area. "It's missing photos."

He palmed his forehead. Of course. "I can do that."

"Get some frames, but do an album too. John's missed the first nine months of Olly's life. Let him catch up."

Jem's pen paused on the notepad. Would Dad *want* to know anything about those first months of parenthood in Chicago? Or would any mention of his life BC—Before Charlottesville—only serve as an unwelcome reminder?

"The first one of Olly smiling on camera." Natalie's soft voice broke through his reverie. "He'll want to see that one." He'd showed it to her the other day.

Jem straightened and stuffed his notebook back in his pocket. "Thanks."

"Maybe cushions and a throw rug wouldn't kill you either."

He rolled his eyes. She loved to decorate almost as much as she loved throwing a good party. He'd seen web pages on her laptop one morning as they worked on her festival proposal. Crocodile Dundee costumes. For her dad's birthday. He sure hoped he was in her good graces by then, because that'd be an event worth seeing.

He checked the time on his phone. Dangerously close to Olly's dinnertime. The predinner hour tended to be Olly's fussiest. Best to save the shopping for tomorrow. But he could sort through the photos now. He pulled up the app on his phone and leaned against the counter as he marked some for printing.

Natalie looked askance at him. "You're doing this for your dad? You really think that'll make the King of Criticism admit you did something right?"

A good point. His thumbs stopped swiping across the screen.

The phone rang in his hand. His editor. What did he want on a Friday evening?

"Samson?"

"Jeremy. Your page-three article that ran today." No smile in his boss's voice.

Jem's hand went to the back of his neck as a chill spread through him. He'd been stoked to see that his report on a major drug arrest made the lead on page three and even had a teaser on the front. But now . . . "Yes?"

"I just had your father on the phone for twenty minutes. He was . . . most displeased. You mixed up the surnames of the accused and the arresting officer."

His nerves stood on end as a flush swept through him. Jem covered his eyes with his hand. *No, no, no, no, no.* How could that have happened? "I am so sorry. I'll come in and load a correction on the website."

"Done already. But not a good start, Walters." *Click.*

Jem lowered the phone.

Natalie, oblivious, closed her laptop with one hand and rummaged around her handbag with the other. "I'll finish prepping this presentation for the board at home, anyway. I have to help my friend Mindy with some bridal shower details." The last part came out as a mumble.

Jem gave a halfhearted wave as she slipped past him to the door, his mind still spinning. How could he have made such a stupid mistake? Dad would never let him forget this.

He slumped down on the stool Natalie had vacated, his photo app still open on his phone. Olly's gummy smile grinned up at him. What was the point of this? He and Dad hadn't seen eye to eye since Mom went into labor with Jem partway through Dad's awards banquet back when he was a sergeant.

A gurgle in the corner caught his attention. Olly, playing with a set of oversized plastic keys.

The baby seemed to notice Jem's gaze on him, because he crawled in Jem's direction. "Da-da-da-da-da-da-da-da."

He'd caught Nat yesterday trying to teach him to say, "Nat-Nat-Nat-Nat." Unsuccessfully.

He reached down and pulled his son up into his arms. "Hey, there, bud." The baby grabbed Jem's nose and squealed. Jem leaned his forehead against Olly's. He couldn't imagine not being a part of Oliver's life when he grew up. And his son deserved to have at least one grandparent. Chloe's absence from their lives meant her parents were out, and Mom was already gone.

Natalie's words about forgiveness last week returned to him.

He'd turned his back on God in far more dramatic fashion than his father had ever done to him. And God had taken him back.

He squared his shoulders.

Every day, try one more time.

He marked another photo to be printed.

♡

"If I flunk art, I'm not going to get a scholarship."

Lili sucked on her blue raspberry Icee as Nick spoke from the other side of their wooden bench out in front of Target, shopping bags stacked around him. He waved his hands as he talked, brown eyes alight. Nick could talk about the growth rate of fungus and he'd look enthusiastic about it.

And since she hadn't yet worked up the courage to tell him about Dad, she let him talk. "That's what you're after? A scholarship?" Another slurp of the Icee.

Nick nodded, lips attached to his own straw. "It's the only way I'll get to a good college anytime soon. Otherwise I'll have to spend a couple years working. Maybe take night classes. This art is killing me."

Lili lowered her Icee. This would be the perfect segue for her tutoring idea. Maybe then she could work up the nerve to tell him about her parents. She leaned forward. "Do you want me to tell you a secret?"

Nick's phone alarm interrupted. He pulled it out and hit a button. "Oh man, I didn't realize what the time was. I've gotta go check my chickens."

Lili choked. "Your what?"

A grin curled his lips. "Wanna see something cute? It's only a couple blocks away."

"Okay." Maybe the interruption was a sign she shouldn't tell. And the boy had chickens. Now was not the time for secrets.

He tossed his empty cup into the trash, grabbed his shopping bags, and led the way. Lili followed him onto the sidewalk, where the cooling air hinted their sweet fall nights were numbered. She buttoned her denim jacket. Nick had no coat, just a flannel shirt over his Nirvana

T-shirt, which peeked out from a tear on his back. She made a mental note of it and quickened her steps to walk alongside him.

"What were you saying about a secret?" Nick asked as she drew level with him.

She scrambled for an answer. "It's . . . it's the secret to art. Art is all about showing someone a story, even if that story is just one thought or emotion."

Phew, that was close.

"What if I don't have many of those?"

Typical boy. "There must be something you want to say with your life. Or something that reflects how you feel."

"You're starting to sound like my counselor."

"You go to a counselor?" Her question came out louder than expected. Oops. He just didn't seem like the counseling type. "Sorry, that was nosy."

Nick shrugged. "No, it's fine. Aunt Trish finally convinced me last year. Unfortunately not before I punched a hole through her wall."

"You punched a hole through her wall?" The pitch of her voice heightened with her surprise.

"It was when my brother's stuff was really bad. I thought he was going to jail."

They reached the front gate of a small house. A rosebush peeked over the fence and white wicker furniture rested on the porch. Nicer than she expected. The scent of freshly mowed grass tickled her allergies.

Nick opened the gate, sat his bags on the concrete path, and reached for an upside-down flowerpot tucked next to the fence. A key rested beneath.

"Aunt Trish always makes sure I can get in. She even leaves a key for her car, just in case."

Lili's legs turned to lead. "This isn't your place?"

"No." Nick laughed the word. "Our place isn't this side of town. And it's not visitor friendly. But most important, it doesn't have these." He nodded toward a box resting by the side door. "Wanna see?"

She moved forward, an eye on the door for any sign of her temptress teacher. "Is Miss Kent here?"

"No, she'll be out for a while." Nick pulled the lid off the box, and a yellow light spilled out from a heat lamp. "Check this out."

She peeked inside. Ten eggs smiled back at her, their faces drawn on with a Sharpie. "These are going to be chickens?"

"Yep. They're for Mom. She's always wanted some."

"Why are they here?"

"I didn't want her to be disappointed if they didn't make it. Aunt Trish is letting me keep them here till they hatch and grow up a little bit, then I'll take them home and surprise her."

"Wow." Words fled Lili's mouth as she stared at the eggs, tucked into a bed of fabric scraps. Warmth caressed her cheeks from the heat lamp attached to the top of the box. The faces even had little eyebrows and ears. "You did her most embarrassing shopping and you're raising her chickens? You're a good son."

"Pretty sure I'm not, but thanks anyway."

"No, I'm serious. I always thought it was weird how . . . normal you are." She knelt by the box, reached in, and stroked the delicate shell of an egg.

"No one's as normal as they look."

He was righter than he knew.

"How do you do it?" Lili's need to know pressed her gut harder than the button of her too tight skirt.

Nick sat on the step and rested an elbow on his knee. "I owe a lot to Aunt Trish. I've lived with her on and off for most of my life, whenever things got bad with Mom. She made sure I got fed, always had enough clothes, had a ride to school. She introduced me to God— not in a 'Jesus loves the lambs' kind of way. Like a 'Next time Mom has a psychotic episode, Jesus will hold your hand' kind of way. And He did."

She pulled her hand away from the egg. God had left her alone. Was something wrong with her? "Anything else?"

"Anything else what?"

"Did anything else help you cope?"

He pointed to the eggs. "I do stuff like this. I'm a fixer. Plus, once I gave up on my weekly staring contests with my counselor, I realized it's way smarter to take action about the junk that happens in your life than to sit there and try to explode the counselor's brain using the dark side of the Force."

Lili bit the inside of her cheek. What action could she take? She was stuck.

Nick pulled a Sharpie from his pocket and reached for an egg. "Want to name one?"

She reached for the Sharpie—and the distraction. "Really?"

"Sure. Anything you want. Actually, you can name five of them. I'll do the others."

She took the Sharpie in one hand and the egg in the other, its warmth seeping through her palm. "What about Leonardo Da Vinci?"

"That old inventor dude?"

"A genius at math *and* art."

Nick grinned. "Perfect."

He found another marker and scribbled names on his eggs while she finished hers. They lined them up in the box for the naming ceremony. Nick's hand brushed Lili's as he straightened an egg.

"Okay, you go first," he said.

She pointed to the first egg. "Leo."

Nick nodded his approval.

"Michelangelo, Donatello, Raphael, and Taylor Swift. All amazing artists."

Nick quirked an eyebrow. "Ninja turtles and T-Swift?"

"Artists. Also ninja turtles."

The smile he gave her sent sparks through her body.

"What about yours?"

"Bruce, Robin, Alfred, Martha, and Thomas."

"A Wayne family reunion?"

"Holy guacamole, Batman, so it is."

She chuckled at his Robin impersonation. The laughter died away, and Nick kept looking at her with that half grin on his face.

She took a breath. It was now or never. "Nick, can I tell you something?"

"Sure."

A Fiat pulled into the driveway. Nick jumped up. "Aunt Trish is back." He jogged to the car.

Lili clambered to her feet, but Miss Kent popped out of the car before she could escape. The teacher swallowed her nephew in a hug, despite being almost a foot shorter and forty pounds lighter than him.

"How's Stephen?" Nick managed to get out around her death grip.

Lili gritted her teeth. Miss Kent *had* seen Stephen . . . with Dad.

No wonder he hadn't replied.

Miss Kent gave a quiet response, and Nick's face wiped of all emotion. He squeezed his aunt, face hidden by her poufy curls. Lili's hands, no longer warmed by the eggs, turned to ice as the wind whipped up. She wrapped her arms around herself.

If Dad had hidden the fact that he'd just spent the afternoon with Miss Kent . . . what else might he be hiding?

The pair broke apart, and Nick bent to retrieve the shopping bags they'd left on the ground. Miss Kent's gaze landed on Lili. Her eyes widened, and she flicked a glance at her nephew.

Lili drilled her with an unblinking stare, then turned to Nick as he straightened with an armful of bags. "I'd better take off, Nick."

"Are you sure? You can come inside till your uncle gets here. And didn't you have a question you were asking me?"

"I, uh, was just going to offer to fix that tear in your shirt. Natalie's teaching me to sew, if you're willing to be my guinea pig."

"That'd be awesome. Last time Aunt Trish tried to sew, she sealed my pockets closed." He grinned at his aunt as he shrugged off his outer shirt and handed it to Lili. She gripped the soft fabric and backed toward the gate.

"My uncle will pick me up from the corner," she lied. "I'll see you at school."

The gate banged behind her as she walked as fast as she dared. She made it around the corner of the block before tears slid down her face and dripped from her chin. But she tried to stay positive.

Maybe Dad hadn't known Miss Kent would be there. Maybe Stephen had occupied all their time.

Or maybe Dad was choosing her over Mom? Over Lili?

Her shoulders shook with sobs as her thoughts swirled up, a waterspout of despair. She'd tried so hard over the past couple of weeks. It hadn't been easy to leave home, but she'd done it because Dad asked her. She'd never demanded her parents spend time with her. She'd worked harder on her studies than ever. She'd helped Jem with Olly and even done a chunk of the housework.

But it wasn't enough.

She pulled out her phone and messaged Granddad. Jem wouldn't be looking for her for a while yet, and Grandad should be knocking off work around now. He liked to take her for rides in the police car. Plus, he was less astute than Jem when it came to tears.

By the time she scrubbed the water off her face and got back to Target, his black-and-white car idled in the parking lot.

"Hi, there, cupcake." Granddad's grizzled face softened when she got in. He held up a small tub and spoon. "Frozen mango treat?"

A tiny piece of Lili's burden lifted. "I love you." She took the gift and poked the spoon in her mouth as she secured her seat belt. Sweetness melted on her tongue.

Granddad put the car into gear and pulled out into traffic. "How are you? Your uncle taking good care of you?"

She swallowed the last of her sobs and adopted a flippant tone. Best to be flippant when the conversation was teetering between Dad cheating and a badly hidden father-son feud. "He told me not to tell you that yesterday we had a Beyoncé karaoke night. He was afraid you'd be jealous."

Granddad grunted.

So much for flippant. "That was a joke. He helped me write a newspaper article for my English assignment." She poked Granddad's knee. "You should come visit us. Jem's not so bad. And Olly's growing fast."

She was the only person Granddad would let nag him about Jem. Up until recently she'd been his only grandchild, and he spoiled her shamelessly.

"I saw the photo you sent me of him walking along the furniture."

She smiled around the spoon between her lips. Cracks were everywhere in this family. Maybe if she could glue together one little piece, it would help the rest.

Granddad glanced at her as they pulled into Jem's parking lot. "You okay? Your eyes look a bit red."

"Allergies." Lili gave her spoon one last lick and unclipped her seat belt. "Will you come upstairs with me? Just to say hello?"

He patted her hand. "Maybe another time."

She stared at him. So polite. So distant. Refusing to make an effort, even for her sake. Was this what the future looked like? Her family in neat little compartments, always tense and never together?

She got out of the car and stood on the sidewalk. "Thanks for the ride."

He gave her a wave and drove off, and Lili watched him go. Uncle Jem had never been enough for her grandfather. What made her think her own family would be any different with her?

Lili dragged herself up the stairs to Jem's apartment and entered with her key. Jem stood in the kitchen as she closed the door, cell phone to his ear.

"I can't hear you, Nat. What did you say . . . ? What kind of emergency?"

15

Natalie stood in her living room, phone to her ear, as she surveyed the carnage around her.

Her little mother-in-law suite, located in the backyard of local proctologist Dr. Dinkle, had been assaulted by a tsunami. The carpet squished beneath her feet, and water continued to pour from a pipe beneath the kitchen sink.

"I said it's a plumbing emergency," she said to Jem on the other end of the phone. "The Dinkles are away, and a plumber will take ages to get here. I just need to know how to shut off the water."

He gave her step-by-step instructions, then finished with, "Lili can watch Olly. You'll need help cleaning up. I'll be there in five minutes."

He hung up before she could respond.

Standing in her doorway, she pulled the phone away and looked at the contact photo he'd installed the one time she'd left her phone unlocked. A close-up of Olly's nostril. Same old Jem.

Doing stupid things to her phone.

Coming to her rescue when she didn't even ask.

Yikes. That was dangerous territory. Back to her flooded apartment.

She wrinkled her nose. She'd left a box of laundry detergent in the bottom of the kitchen cabinet, so the scent of lavender and oriental blossom fought for supremacy with wet-dog smell. Curse that shih tzu of old Mrs. Dinkle.

She lifted her sodden bean bag, which now weighed three times what it should have. A stack of dirty dishes peeked out from beneath the purple polka dot material. Drat. She'd wondered where they went.

A pile of bills on the floor had been saturated, and the legs of her wooden desk were wet. Would they swell? At least the rest of the room was bare, with the exception of one plastic garden chair tucked under her desk. Mindy's bridal shower invitations were safely on top of her desk. Her friend, overwhelmed by organizing a wedding in just three months, had talked Natalie into helping out. Thankfully the invitations were safe, and she owned little else that could get ruined.

Her plans for the night were another matter. She'd intended to get home, eat a piece of toast, and spend the evening finding a potential venue and attractions for the festival she'd pitched to Sam.

She scratched her scalp, and frizzy hair strands tickled her palm. Sweat dampened her blue T-shirt from her bike ride home, and water soaked through her tennis shoes. She was going to look fabulous when Jem arrived, and the place was a mess even without the water.

Not that it mattered what Jem thought.

But first things first. Shut off the water.

She followed Jem's instructions to find and shut off the valve under the sink. Within a few minutes Jem stood in her doorway, toolbox in hand. He wore a gray top and orange board shorts. And he'd never looked more wonderful.

A sympathetic smile tugged his lips as she let him in. "I've heard of a coastal theme for interior design, but this is taking it a bit far."

"Speaking of coastal, you look dressed for the beach."

"I figured there was a good chance I'd be getting wet. Damp denim is no fun."

She leaned against her dining table and resisted an old memory of their spontaneous beach trip. Unprepared, she'd swum in some gym gear she had in the car, while Jem went in nothing but his jeans. He'd laughed about the chafing all the way home. That'd been a week after they got engaged.

She folded her arms. They'd struck a truce in the past few weeks, nothing more. Any melting would be confined to the chocolate bar stashed in her pocket. "Thanks for coming."

He winked. "It's worth my time to get a peek into your apartment." He made a show of scanning the room.

She winced. She was proud of the wall full of quotes from inspirational women. Less so of the dead potted plant, five dirty cups on her desk, and the drying rack of unmentionable laundry. She grabbed the rack and opened her bedroom door to throw it inside.

"Oh no." The water had seeped under the door and saturated the carpet in there too. Plus the pile of clothes on the floor beside her bed.

Jem peeked over her shoulder. "Is that *The Cowboy and the Princess*?" He nodded toward the book on her bedside table.

She tried to cover a smile. "Um, no?"

"I've been looking for that all week."

Natalie gave him a cheesy grin, charm her only defense.

He rolled his eyes and walked into the kitchen.

She turned back to her bedroom. Besides the clothes, nothing looked too—

Jem gave a short laugh, and she turned. Oh no. He was reading the sticky notes on her fridge.

"Call Sam about venue. Feed Dr. Dinkle's goldfish when he's on the cruise. Return Jem's book." Jem slid her a look. "Bring sewing machine to Jem's for Lili. FEED GOLDFISH. Find new hiding place for M&M's at Jem's. Buy new goldfish." He tugged the last note from the fridge and held it up. "Should I be leaving my son with you?"

"Lili told me about the cockroach incident last week. He's better with me than you."

"Come on, I got to him quick. He only ate one leg."

She shuddered and pulled open the kitchen cupboard to expose the offending pipe.

"Research art?" Jem held up another sticky note.

She knelt before the cupboard and pulled Jem's flashlight out of the toolbox. Water soaked the knees of her jeans. "Lili loves it so much, I wanted to learn something so I could talk about it with her." She resigned herself to a wet backside, sat on the floor, and poked her head into the cupboard.

Jem's bare feet splashed across the tiles. He lowered himself beside her, stretching his body across the cold floor. She gripped the flashlight and tried not to think about the fact he was eight inches away.

Jem's face appeared on the other side of the S-bend. His hand closed over hers on the flashlight. "*That* is why I leave my son with you." His gaze never leaving hers, he repositioned her hand to shine the light in the right spot.

Her palms, already slick with soapy water, added sweat to the mix.

Jem turned his attention to the pipe between them and grabbed a tool from his box while Natalie scoured her mind for a normal thing to say. "How are we going to dry the carpets?"

"We'll have to rent some industrial fans or a shop vac tomorrow. In the meantime, I hope you have a lot of towels."

"Not really."

"I brought extras."

She leaned against the cupboard wall and propped her flashlight arm up with her spare hand. "How can I ever thank you?" The words came out with some difficulty. Did she appreciate the fact she wouldn't have to go begging to Mom or Mrs. Dinkle for towels? Yes. Did she enjoy owing Jem? Not at all.

Metal clinked on metal as Jem rummaged around for another tool. The pipe was almost done. "You can feed me dinner. I hadn't eaten yet when you called."

She grimaced. "Ummm . . ."

"I'm not fussy. Whatever you've got in the cupboard." He ran his hand over the pipe. "That should do it. Turn the tap on to test." He turned the valve back on.

Natalie backed out of the cupboard and flicked the tap on and off.

"Success! Now, dinner." Jem righted himself with a satisfied smile and opened her panty. His smile faded. He stepped back so she could see the shelves, bare except for a jar of coffee, a bag of sugar, peanut butter, and half a loaf of bread. "Babe."

She bristled. "It's not as bad as it looks. I eat a lot at your house. And why do you keep calling me 'babe'?" He'd done it on Saturday too—though she still wasn't sure if he'd been talking to her or Lola Bunny.

"Old habits die hard. I've been saying it in my head." He closed the pantry door. "And you might eat at my house a bit, but you never have dinner there."

"By the time I get home I just heat up noodles and work on Wildfire stuff or Mom and Dad's bills."

"That's not healthy. No wonder I've been showing you up on the basketball court."

She punched his arm.

"That would have hurt if you ate greens once in a while." He picked up his toolbox. "We'll clean this up, take you home, and get you some decent food. In the morning we can get the fans and go grocery shopping."

"No."

"Okay, then, join us for dinner every night. That would save you time shopping and cooking. We can take turns for who cooks."

"No, I mean the tonight thing. I have to get this presentation to Steph and Sam." Kimberly had been killing it lately. The woman's proposed youth drop-in center was gaining community support, and her organizational skills had whipped the next six months of Sam's speaking schedule into shape. Natalie needed an edge, and this presentation to the board to gain support for her festival outreach was her chance.

Jem looked around the house. "I don't think that's gonna happen, babe."

She sighed. "I can work late."

"No point. Once you're tired, you become inefficient. Might as well take a night off with your favorite boss and start again tomorrow."

"Who says Sam isn't my favorite boss?"

"Is he the one here saving the day?"

"Touché." But she didn't move toward the door.

He kept looking at her.

She huffed. She shouldn't take a night off. But she *was* starving. Sick of peanut butter toast. And . . . maybe his company wouldn't hurt. "Fine, I'll come to your place for dinner."

Jem headed for the car. "I'll get the towels. Let's get this place fixed up."

The corners of Natalie's mouth tipped up as he walked away. Maybe some downtime wasn't such a bad idea.

She walked across the tiles to her linen cupboard. Her left foot slid out from under her and she nearly toppled as Jem entered the room again.

"Careful." He dropped the towels and grabbed her arm.

Natalie latched onto his shirt with one hand as her right foot also lost traction, her other arm sweeping over the kitchen counter and knocking her lifeless miniature rose into the air. "*Blaaar-eep!*" She clutched Jem's arm and pulled her feet back under her. He grasped her upper arms until she found grip.

"Are you okay?"

She tested her balance and, once convinced she was secure, reached for her plant.

"That's got a bud on it," Jem said as she placed it on the bench.

"What?" She inspected the rose. Sure enough, a tiny green bud sprouted from the end of the brown stick that had once been a plant.

"Huh. I'd given up on this one. I gave it one more chance and watered it last week, but I didn't think it would make any difference."

Jem smiled at her. "Surprises happen."

Warmth spread through her core. She tucked a curling piece of hair behind her ear. "Yes, they do."

♡

Three missed calls flashed on Natalie's phone.

She frowned at the screen, still half asleep as she watched cartoons on Jem's couch. What did Steph need so badly at 9:15 a.m. Saturday?

She'd bunked on the floor of Lili's room last night, as Mom and Dad would've already been in bed and she had no desire to sleep in her wet-dog-scented apartment.

Jem's fingers closed around hers on the phone and tugged it from her grasp. "No phones during Looney Tunes." He set the phone on the coffee table beside him and turned the volume up a little.

She eyed him. He was rumpled and delicious, with his eyes half open and boyish delight on his face. Oliver, sitting in his lap and dressed in a *Despicable Me* minion onesie, only increased Jem's appeal.

Olly wriggled in Jem's lap.

He put him down on the floor, and the baby crawled straight to Natalie's feet and whined.

"What?" Jem looked from his son to her.

She scooped him up with a triumphant smile. "Hey, little man. Did you want to upgrade?"

"Traitor." Jem flopped back against the couch.

"I'm surprised you two don't have matching minion onesies."

"Mine's in the wash."

Lili tugged her blanket closer. "He's not joking."

The cartoon ended after ten minutes, and Jem peeled himself off the couch to go start the pancakes. Lili had gone to shower, so Natalie muted the TV and dialed Steph's number. The scent of cooking pancakes teased her senses.

"Hey, Steph, what's up?"

"Where are you? Are you up? Can you be here in five minutes?" Her words shot from the speaker, rapid-fire.

Natalie jumped up from the couch. "Why? What's wrong?"

"Sam got overexcited at the board meeting and pitched your festival idea early. We've only really got half a pitch here. I'm assuming you've got more details with you, but . . . Anyway, it's done now. The board members are having a quick break, but we need to get the second half of this pitch, and fast."

She face-palmed herself. She'd not finished her presentation last night. "I'm not . . . Um, I didn't realize . . . My house flooded." She took a breath. Whole sentences would be helpful. "I'm not at home at the moment. How soon do you need me?"

"You're already out at nine thirty on a Saturday?" Steph's tone changed from business Steph to friend Steph—a tone she heard less and less these days.

Natalie held her breath.

Lord, I will never roll my eyes at my mother again if you stop her from asking what I'm doing right now.

"What are you doing?"

Natalie placed Olly in his playpen and walked toward the shelf Jem had labeled "Natalie's junk" on a piece of masking tape. "I'm heading to grab my laptop right now," she said to Steph. Still the truth—part of it.

But the shelf just held her grocery sack, toothbrush, about fifty sticky notes, and eleven green M&M's. Second face-palm moment. "It's at home. I'll go there now."

"Natalie?" Jem's voice called out from the kitchen. "Do you want choc-chip pancakes or plain?"

She cringed and braced.

"You're at *Jem's*? What's going on?"

"Nothing. My apartment flooded and he helped."

"Uh-huh, sure." Steph's tone was loaded with suggestion. "Look, Nat, you've got a chance here to really impress the board. So if my brother-in-law values his life, he'll deliver you to our front door in ten minutes. Fifteen tops."

Uh-oh. She dragged a hand down her face. Yesterday's jeans were dry—well, dry-ish—but her shirt had picked up a mud stain somewhere along the way. The Wildfire office was close, but to go home first . . . "I'll be there. Just let me figure something out." Her pulse quickened. A chance to impress the board—this opportunity was too good to miss. She'd make it work.

"See you soon." Steph ended the call, and Natalie pressed the phone to her forehead. She could come up with ideas on the fly. But she had to get there first.

"Jem?"

He turned at the mention of his name, spatula in hand and clad in Lili's red-checked apron.

"Can you take me home?"

"Pancakes are in the pan and Lili's in the shower." Jem frowned. "What happened?"

"I just got a chance to impress the board. They love the festival idea. But they need me there to pitch it in ten minutes."

His face lit up—until his gaze flew to the clock. "Is Steph crazy? It's nine thirty on Saturday morning."

"The board is all volunteers. They meet when they can." She ran last night through her memory. "We didn't bring my bike, did we?" Even without the bike, she could splurge on an Uber.

"No. And don't even think about it, Nat. Your jeans are still damp, and you're wearing One Direction pajamas. Give me twenty minutes, and I'll take you home."

She zipped into Lili's room as he spoke and yanked on her jeans, then pulled last night's hoodie over Harry, Liam, Louis, Zayn, and Niall and popped back out into the kitchen. "It's early on a Saturday. They'll forgive the hoodie."

She ran out the door.

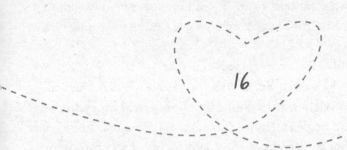

16

Natalie twisted her fingers together as Steph gave her a rundown on what Sam had pitched to the board so far, the two of them huddled in the corridor outside the Wildfire conference room. It was hard to hear anything past the voice in her head reminding her that in her haste she'd forgotten to put a bra on under that hoodie and PJ top.

"Nat." Steph snapped her fingers. "You listening?"

She started. "Sorry. Just—nervous." At least half the people would be on the conference room's big-screen TV, teleconferencing in from various locations across the country. It'd be difficult for them to assess her attire from the screen. Still . . . "Are you sure the hoodie's alright?"

Steph shrugged. "Sam told them he was calling you in unexpectedly to talk about it."

Nevertheless, it was difficult not to compare her wardrobe to Steph's sleek black pants, heels, and silk top.

Steph nudged her arm. "He likes you, you know."

Natalie blinked. "Who?"

"Sam. I told him to ask you out." A smug smile accompanied the words.

A door closed nearby. Natalie lowered her voice, brain scrambling. "I—he—um, but he's my boss."

Steph waved the concern away. "I told him you were fine with it. You can thank me later. You don't want people getting the wrong idea about you and Jem."

"Me and Jem?" Her voice jumped an octave.

"Exactly. It's ludicrous. But there's your history, you're there all the time . . . Sam might get the wrong idea." She raised her eyebrows at Natalie. "You're single and quite the catch. You need to act like it."

Act like it? She'd be lucky if she could tie her shoes in front of Sam now. And in five minutes she had to walk in there and give this presentation.

She pretended to flick through the notes in her hand while turning the thought over in her head. Could Sam really be interested in her? A thrill tickled her nerves at the thought. No man had spared more than a passing glance at her since Jem, despite what the movies said about being single and in your twenties. And Sam was . . . well, Sam. Australian. Genuine. Warm. Talented. Australian. Passionate about the very field she wanted to work in.

And Australian.

Okay. She could do this. She straightened her shoulders and entered the board room. Most board members were still out on a short break, but a woman in smart skinny jeans and a form-fitting gray blouse occupied a chair on the edge of the room.

Kimberly.

Natalie's stride faltered.

Kimberly shot her a smile. "Hey."

Natalie pasted her smile back on. "Hi. I didn't know you were coming."

Kimberly shrugged. "I wanted to hear about your idea. Sam's been really enthusiastic about it. And I like to see how other people pitch. It's not my strongest suit."

Steph joined them. "Kimberly's being modest. She pitched business ideas back in LA all the time, and her pitch to this board was terrific." To Natalie: "Did you know she worked with start-ups in Silicon Valley?"

No, she did not. And wasn't that just a great confidence boost? She gave a feeble, "That's awesome."

Kimberly shrugged it off. "It was Mom's company. But this is what I want to do." Certainty filled her voice.

Like the job was already hers.

Board members filed back in. Kimberly nodded to the front of the room. "Break a leg."

Natalie walked to the front of the room on wooden limbs.

Sam strode through the door, all broad shoulders and flannel. The man's vibe could be summed up as "preaching lumberjack." He sent her a thumbs-up and took his seat.

Natalie gripped her notes.

God, please help me.

She took a deep breath. Okay. Professional mode. She clicked to her first slide, and her brain slipped into its groove.

Ten heart-pounding minutes later and she was done. She exited the room, head high, legs wobbly. Leaned against the wall. She'd done it. The rest was out of her hands.

A door quietly opened and closed. Sam joined her in the corridor, a smile stretching from ear to ear. "That was fantastic!" He offered his hand in a high five.

She slapped it with a relieved laugh.

He gestured to the room. "I'll be tied up here for another hour or two, but are you hanging around? Celebratory lunch?"

Natalie hesitated. Was this a date? Did she want it to be? What exactly had Steph told him?

Snap out of it, Natalie. It's just lunch.

And lunch with an attractive single man never hurt.

She smiled. "Sounds great."

17

Something was wrong with Lili.

Jem sat at his dining table, fingers suffering the death of a thousand paper cuts, and watched his niece staple schedules and pass them to Natalie on the girls' side of the table. Stacks of fliers, balloons, and lollipops for the Wildfire festival promotional bags covered the room in preparation for the announcement of the event at church on Sunday—just one week after Natalie's festival pitch got the green light from Wildfire's board.

Packing goodie bags wasn't his favorite Friday night activity, but this was the first time they'd drawn Lili from her room in the last week.

Besides, in the days since Natalie's apartment flooded—which had dried out with minimal damage to the carpet-over-concrete floor—the only way he could get Natalie's attention was by working with her. She'd been busy since the board endorsed her pitch last Saturday, planning budgets with Steph, organizing volunteers, and having coffee with some of the town's biggest church leaders. She seemed so excited about this opportunity the festival was giving her, she'd worked 24/7 to make sure everything was perfect.

Even now, after folding sixty million festival fliers for the woman, he was losing to his niece and a dead painter.

"So why did Picasso start painting everything blue?" Natalie asked Lili as she stuffed another bag full and dropped it on the growing pile.

"He had this friend called Casagemas who committed suicide over a girl who didn't love him."

Lili went on to explain a love triangle that made a soap opera seem tame, but Jem's brain got stuck on Natalie's question . . . and the dried paint on Lili's forearms. Flecks speckled her skin, as usual, but her normal riot of colors had disappeared. A streak of gray blue ran up the inside of her forearm, left over from her latest artwork. She'd painted that freaky sad clown about six times in the last week. All blues and grays, no bright color.

He picked up another blasted flier, slapped the edges down to form rough thirds, and ran his mind through recent days. Lili hadn't been the same since he'd taken her to Target to meet Nick. Was it boy trouble?

If it was, she hadn't told Nat. He'd managed to distract her from work for twenty minutes yesterday to strategize about Lili. Natalie offered to talk to her, but Jem had learned one thing from growing up with teenage Natalie: when bringing up a touchy topic with a girl, do your homework first. You never knew when you were going to hit a trip wire. He'd left a message with Mike yesterday but still hadn't heard back.

He reached for another flier and cursed himself for suggesting these bags in the first place.

"So when did his Rose period begin—"

"My left butt cheek lost feeling ten minutes ago, if anyone's interested," Jem said.

"You're such a crybaby." Natalie formed her lips into a mock pout.

His eyes focused on those lips, as pink as those roses she'd just mentioned and softer still.

It took a moment to realize Natalie was snapping her fingers.

"Earth to Jem."

"What?"

"Your phone's ringing."

The girls smirked to each other as he grabbed for his phone. His brother's name flashed up on the screen.

"Mike?"

"Hey, sorry, I left my phone at Dad's and just got your message from earlier," his brother said. "I've got time to chat now, if you want. Come on over."

"Sounds great."

He grabbed a notepad, scribbled *Can you watch the kids? 1 hr* and held it up in front of Natalie.

She gave him a thumbs-up, and he resisted the urge to fist pump. His big brother had just saved his numb rear. "Where do you want to meet?" Jem shifted the phone closer to catch the background noise coming through the speaker. Rhythmic, dull thuds that almost sounded like—

"I'm at Dad's. We're doing a few rounds in the ring. Join us?"

The words froze in Jem's throat. Besides some awkward politeness at church each week, he hadn't spoken to his father since Natalie's first day on the job. He'd purchased and hung photo frames. Created an album. Even bought three cushions and a throw rug.

But he hadn't yet worked up the courage to talk to his dad.

Still, the sooner they got a handle on this Lili thing, the better. And now that he counted back, Lili had been at his place for three weeks, and no one had mentioned her going home.

Maybe this trouble wasn't just a boy thing.

He shut his eyes. This would not be fun. But maybe it was the nudge his spineless self needed. "Yeah, I guess I can."

"Cool. See you soon."

The call ended, and Lili looked at him with an unreadable expression. "You're going to see Dad?"

"Just going to do a few rounds with him and Granddad in the boxing ring. I won't be long."

Natalie's gaze flew to him at the words "boxing ring."

Jem paused, focusing on Lili. "Do you want to come?"

She stuffed a packet of jelly beans into a bag. "No, thanks."

"Okay." He met Natalie's eyes, and she gave a tiny nod.

She'd remember what Dad's boxing ring meant.

Pure torture.

♡

The smell of rubber and sweat smacked into Jem's nostrils. Memories flew from the corners of his mind like disturbed bats. He trudged down his father's basement stairs and paused four from the bottom.

Thud-thud-thud-thud. Dad never broke his rhythm as he pounded his black boxing bag in time with "We Will Rock You" blaring from the stereo. And he wouldn't—not till the timer beeped and the three-minute round ended.

Jem gazed around the room while he waited to be acknowledged. The place had barely changed in seven years. A new boxing bag hung from the rafters, red and shiny compared to the worn black sack swinging next to it. The "ring," a makeshift square marked by old jump ropes tied together, still dominated the back half of the underground space. Dad's trophies lined the windowsill, next to a couple of Mike's.

Jem peered at the sill. There were no trophies for him—he'd never won any—but a familiar child-sized glove rested next to the golden lineup. Had Dad actually gotten sentimental over—

"Jeremy, stop gawking and get down here."

Jem stepped down the final stairs. "You couldn't leave the door unlocked for me, Dad? I had to climb the porch and get in through my old window."

"I'm a cop. I know better than to unlock anything."

"Then I don't feel bad about the foot-shaped dent in your gutter." He relished the way Dad's jaw ticked when he said "dent."

A black-and-white glove flew in his direction, and he caught it against his chest. "Quit yapping and suit up."

"Thanks, but I have enough trauma for one childhood." He dropped the glove to the floor and looked around for his brother. "Where's Mike? He's the reason I'm here."

"Coming." The steps rattled as Mike jogged down, wrapping black material around his wrist in a practiced move. "Sorry. Had to take a call."

Dad folded his arms and assessed Jem. Jem matched his posture and did it back. Dad's gray T-shirt steamed—he'd probably put in a good hour's training already. The old bulldog, built like a tree trunk, had the same muscular frame as always. A little thing like his sixtieth birthday was no reason to go soft. The only difference from seven years ago was the gray in his hair and a few wrinkles carved into his forehead.

That granite facial expression never changed. Unless Jem said something like . . .

"Nice to see you're keeping up with the exercise. They say a few leg raises each day wards off dementia. Some five-pound arm weights should help too." He lounged against a concrete pillar and crossed his ankles.

Dad jerked a hundred-pound barbell over his head and glared. "Why don't you step into the ring and we'll see who's got dementia?"

"Nice to see you still use humor as your defense mechanism." Mike clapped a hand on Jem's shoulder.

He winced. What a way to undermine it. "Nice to see you still love analyzing me."

"How's Natalie?" Mike stretched one arm, then the other. Quads next.

Jem stayed against the pole. "Overworked. Your wife's got her all wound up about this festival." He wrinkled his nose a little. Could he smell . . . cigarette smoke? Just a faint whiff when Mike walked past him. But Mike had quit years ago, before he was a pastor. Six-year-old Lili had learned about the dangers of smoking and begged him to stop, and he hadn't smoked since.

The smell faded. Must've been imagining things.

The smile drained from Mike's face. "That's Steph for you." He moved toward the boxing ring. "What brings you here? How's Lili?"

Jem picked the glove up from the ground, tossed it into the corner, and grabbed a couple of catching mitts from a steel trunk full of equipment. Maybe a light workout would help ease the tension tightening his muscles. The strain increased every time Dad looked at him. "That's what I wanted to talk to you about."

Dad dropped his barbell to the ground. "She's too much for you to handle?"

What was it about Dad's voice that made Jem feel like he was tied to the ring ropes, open to every blow that came his way?

He tightened his grip on the mitts. He wasn't fourteen anymore. He didn't have to prove himself. "She's fine, Dad. She's just a little quiet. I wanted to do some recon before I go poking around a woman's emotions."

Dad shrugged.

Jem ducked beneath the sagging rope and jammed the mitts on. He clapped them together, and the sound whipped through the air. "Jab, cross."

Mike punched his right hand, then left. Jem brought the mitts down to meet each fist, every blow sending a snap through the room.

"Jab, cross, hook, cross."

Mike pivoted his torso with the hook, and the impact knocked Jem back a step. Jem grinned. He'd thrown down the gloves as a seventeen-year-old after Dad criticized his technique one too many times. But he'd taken them up again when he moved to Chicago—and gotten pretty good at it.

His pulse quickened to the tempo of a Bruce Springsteen classic, and he shoved his right foot forward, strengthening his stance. "So, do you have any insights?" He raised his hands again, and Mike repeated the combination of punches.

"Into Lili? Ah—how is Grace doing? Those two were always joined at the hip."

"Grace moved to North Carolina last week, so that might be it. Lili's also hung out with Nick Kent a few times."

"Was that when I picked her up?" Dad slung his arms over the ropes. "Shift your feet, Jem. You're not stuck in the mud."

Jem bounced on his toes as sweat stung his paper cuts. But if he whined about paper cuts in the boxing ring, he'd never hear the end of it.

"Yes, that was then. Jab, cross, hook, cross, uppercut, slip." He rattled the combination off without a thought. It'd been cemented into his subconscious.

"She was crying," Dad said.

"What?" Jem dropped his mitts and Mike smacked him in the eye. Pain splintered across his eye socket. "Hey!"

"Whoops."

"Don't apologize." The coach's tone was back in Dad's voice. "Don't drop your guard, Jem. Why didn't you notice Lili that night?"

He ground his molars and raised the mitts again. Mike was Lili's father. Why was Jem getting the third degree? "I had Nat on the phone when she came in. A pipe burst and flooded her apartment."

Dad grunted. The short sound translated into so much. *Typical. Weak. Unfocused. Not trying.*

Jem threw down the mitts. A light workout just wasn't gonna cut it. "You know what? I'm in the mood to spar."

His jeans pulled tight as he climbed out of the ropes. He really wasn't dressed for this. And he hadn't entered a ring in the ten months since Olly had been born. But tell that to the vein he felt popping out of his forehead.

Jem rummaged through the trunk and pulled two faded red

gloves from the bottom of the pile. His old faithfuls. A crusty set of headgear completed the ensemble.

"Mouth guard?" Mike bounced on his toes and shadow punched.

"Don't have one. Don't need it."

The brothers tapped fists and circled. Jem feinted left, ducked Mike's cross, and delivered an uppercut to the ribs. Tempering the blow at the last moment, he hit him enough to hurt but not enough to wind him.

"Ooof!"

Jem bounced out of reach and grinned. "Gotcha."

Mike sucked in a breath. "Lucky punch."

"Got anything else you want to tell me before your pretty face is black and blue?"

The corner of Dad's mouth lifted. Jem's chest puffed out, just a little.

Smack.

A jab to the eye socket snapped Jem's head back, and he staggered against the ropes. The headgear protected him from any real damage, but it still didn't tickle.

"Gotcha."

Jem shook off the stars and resumed his stance. "It's on, big brother."

"I play the winner," Dad said, his tone full of challenge.

The warning voice in the back of Jem's mind shouted louder. If he took on Dad, nothing good could happen.

He shut the voice up with a jab to Mike's jaw.

His brother slipped the punch and grinned. "You can take a dive now, Jem. I know you don't want to face Dad."

Jem swung again, connected with Mike's ribs. "That's the only way you'd win."

The two ducked and weaved, but neither landed anything for a long minute.

Dad shifted his stance and covered a yawn, and Jem clocked Mike's chin with a fast left hook.

The timer buzzed, and Jem leaned against the cement pillar behind him. Pulling in deep breaths, he tried to not look like he was panting.

Mike rubbed his chin. "Someone's been practicing."

"Chicago. Before Olly."

Mike nodded, but his eyes focused somewhere around Jem's left knee. Finally, he looked up. "The truth is Steph and I are going through a rough patch."

Jem absorbed the information, tapping his glove against his thigh. So that's why Lili had been at his place three weeks and no one had mentioned her going home. He'd begun to suspect something was amiss between Mike and Steph, but actually hearing it saddened him more than he expected. "You think that's why Lili . . ."

"Probably. She's been avoiding me. Then she finally asked me out for ice cream, and I was stuck in a meeting. I don't think she trusts that I'm trying to fix this."

Jem dragged his glove over his forehead, and it came away shiny. He stole a glance at Dad, still stone-faced at the ropes. "How rough are we talking?" He sent up a fast prayer that Dad wouldn't turn into Judgey McPerfect Marriage.

Mike shrugged. "I'm trying to convince Steph to see a marriage counselor."

Jem winced. Saying the word *counselor* in front of Dad was like entering the ring with one hand taped to the top of your head.

"That's good."

Jem jolted, then turned to stare at his father.

Dad cleared his throat. "It's a good idea to get counseling. Before things get out of hand."

Wow. Was this one of those dreams where he was in a *Men in Black* movie? Had aliens taken over his father?

Mike shook his head. "She won't go. She's worried what the church will think if they see their pastors can't even hold a marriage together."

"That's bull." Dad looked ready to knock the lights out of any parishioner who dared disagree.

Muscles finally sated with oxygen, Jem stood up straight. Here was a sentence he'd never thought he'd say: "I agree with Dad."

Both other men snapped their attention to him. Obviously he wasn't the only one who never expected to hear those words.

He gestured in the direction of home. "Think of Lili. Family comes first."

Mike looked between them. "Even though I agree, that's a bit rich coming from you two." He turned to Dad. "Is Oliver going to grow up with his grandfather ten blocks away and never know him?"

Jem looked to Dad. This would be interesting.

Dad shifted on his feet. "Lili sends me photos."

Unbelievable. Of course he'd think that was enough. Jem barked a short laugh. "Believe it or not, Dad, kids need actual affection."

Dad's tone took on that I'm-right-and-you're-ungrateful quality he'd perfected. "I gave you affection."

"A hook to the ribs is not affection."

"I gave you time." Dad rose to his full height and glowered, even though Jem still outstripped him by a good three inches. "That's more than my father ever gave me. And if I was harsh, it's because I needed to straighten you out."

Jem rolled his eyes. "*If* you were harsh?"

The buzzer sounded, signaling the next round. Saved by the bell.

Mike bowed out of the ring and Dad stepped in.

Jem slapped his gloves together. He could do this. He wasn't a kid anymore. He was a man.

A man who'd picked a fight he probably couldn't win, just because Dad goaded him.

The CD in the stereo switched to Blur's "Song 2." Mike fist-pumped in sync.

Jem and Dad circled each other. Jem stayed light on his toes. *I can do this. He's got power, but I've got reach and speed.*

Dad threw a left jab, and Jem slipped the punch. Blocked two right hooks. Ducked a haymaker that could've knocked him flat.

If he got hurt without his mouth guard, Natalie would kill him.

Jem came up from the duck with a rip to Dad's diaphragm and two quick jabs to the head.

Dad fell back a step, then raised his gloves and spit on the floor.

Jem grinned. All that training would be worth it if he bested Dad in the ring.

A duck and two quick slips. Dad couldn't land a punch. Jem hit him with a quick one-two and drew his arm back for a right hook.

A sledgehammer slammed into his right ear. The force threw his head sideways—straight into the concrete pillar. His teeth crunched into his tongue, and he slid to the ground. His mouth flamed like he'd gulped boiling coffee and couldn't spit it out. Propped up in a semi-seated position by the pillar, he let out a deep groan.

"Jem?" Meaty hands touched his chin and the back of his head. The world shifted, and the grooves on Dad's face deepened to canyons. "Michael, get me some ice."

A clatter sounded from the stairs, presumably Mike off to do Dad's bidding.

Dad squatted before Jem and held up several fingers. "How many?"

"*Fwee,*" Jem spit a mouthful of blood and ripped the Velcro loose on his gloves.

"Show me your mouth. You didn't loosen a tooth, did you?"

Jem ran a finger across his teeth. The pain radiated from his tongue, not his gums. "Nuh."

"Bite it clean through?"

"I-uh-o."

"Stick it out."

Jem did, and blood dripped to the floor.

Dad snagged a clean towel from the corner and offered Jem the edge. "Put pressure on it. I don't think it went right through." A grin cracked across his features. "Looks like Chicago's not quite as tough as the old man."

Jem bit down on the towel. The ringing in his head eased, and the tunnel vision cleared. He'd had one or two harder knocks before, enough to know he wasn't seriously hurt. But few of those blows had been followed by concrete to the face.

Mike returned with a handful of ice wrapped in a tea towel. Jem leaned back against the pillar and shoved the ice between his head and shoulder.

Dad clapped him on the shoulder and stood. "I hope you can parent better than you can take a blow."

Jem glared at him from his spot on the ground. From his tone, it was hard to tell if Dad was joking or not.

"I'll give you a chance to prove it." Dad wandered a few steps away and stripped the faded red wraps from his hands as he spoke. "Dinner, Friday next week. Your place." He turned to Mike. "Get your keys. I'll drive Jem and his car home. You'll need to pick me up." He gave Jem a lopsided smile. "Natalie can deal with him."

Jem groaned and rested his head against the pillar. He'd rather pull the gloves on again.

But when Dad delivered him back to the apartment, Natalie met them at the door with a mumbled sentence about Oliver sleeping and her laptop charger being at home. She was gone so fast she didn't appear to see the bruise he felt forming on his jaw, nor raise her eyebrows at the presence of his father.

Even Dad took note, turning to watch her swinging ponytail disappear out the door as he pulled fresh ice from the freezer for Jem. "I was genuinely scared of facing her . . . but she didn't even notice." His tone sounded like that of a man saved from the noose.

Jem plunked down into a chair as the hackles on the back of his neck rose. Again. *Yeah, thanks for pointing that out.*

"She doesn't have to." He propped his feet on another chair. "She's not my girlfriend." Anymore.

Dad snorted. "And whose fault is that?"

Great. After that brief moment of sympathy on the floor of the gym, Dad was back into criticize mode.

"You could've had a family by now, not"—Dad gestured around the sparse apartment—"this."

A retort raced to the tip of Jem's tongue, hot and fast. He dropped his feet to the floor with a thud. So Olly wasn't family? And his leaving Natalie was straight-up selfish?

He ground his teeth. He needed to hold it in. He needed to forgive. He—

"Finfe I hated you fo much I had to leave, I'd fay the fault's at leaft firty perfent yourf." Jem stood and snatched the tea towel of ice from Dad's hand. If his sore tongue hadn't destroyed his pronunciation of *s*, that retort might've been more satisfying. "Fo fank you for da punch in the fafe, Dad, and good night." He wrenched the door open and held Dad's gaze.

Dad's eyes widened for a moment, surprised, before the granite mask slipped back into place. "Good night."

He walked out the door, posture stiff, and Jem swung it shut behind him, the pressure just short of a slam. He dragged his tired body to his bedroom door to check on Olly. Sound asleep. He made it to the couch and lay on it, eyes shut, the wrapped ice wet and cold against his jaw.

Dad's startled eyes replayed in his mind's eye. He'd actually looked . . . hurt.

And what Jem had said hadn't even been true.

Sure, he couldn't stand Dad controlling him. At twenty he couldn't comprehend letting Dad's God control him. But he'd made his own choices. Dad hadn't forced him to leave. Hadn't made him break up with Natalie.

Ironically, Jem's rebellion against Dad—and God—had driven him into some of the worst choices he'd ever made. That was just as bad as being controlled, if not worse.

He punched the cushion under his head, trying to mold it into a more comfortable shape. Tonight was another prime example of Dad's goading and Jem's resulting bad choices.

If he couldn't break this habit, what else would he mess up?

18

Today was the day.

Lili cringed at the footsteps echoing down the church hallway on Sunday morning. She dashed across the Kids' Church room, snatching up spilled candy and scattered markers as the footsteps drew nearer. If Nick was looking for her, she had no time to talk.

Sweat edged her hairline. She'd already handed out three hundred goodie bags for Natalie's Wildfire festival launch, run a Kids' Church class, and now had less than ten minutes to finish packing. After almost four weeks of instant messages and the occasional phone call, Dad had convinced her to go to lunch with him.

The door to the room creaked open, and a brown mop of hair poked through, followed by a pair of hazel eyes.

"Hey." Nick strolled in, a faded Nerd Machine T-shirt stretched across his broad muscles. "Why does this room smell like gummy bears and feet?"

She jammed a loose chunk of hair behind her ear and prayed none of little Bobby's boogers had attached themselves to her best cream shirt. "We played a game with the kids' shoes. And then we ate a lot of gummy bears." The sweet tang still danced along her tongue.

She grabbed two sweaters and one shoe—one shoe?—and tossed them into the lost property basket in the corner. She'd have to clean while she talked. She couldn't be late. Today wasn't just about lunch.

It was about convincing Dad it was time for her to come home.

Nick came a few steps closer. "You haven't been around much lately."

She scooped up a pile of craft supplies and scratched at the glitter tickling her finger. "Sorry, been busy." Busy proving to Dad that she could be a part of this family's healing process. Her grades had risen, she'd been an angel at Jem's house, and she had more responsibilities than ever at Kids' Church. If that didn't prove she could be a help to the family, what would?

Nick snagged a glue bottle that threatened to topple from the pile in her arms. "Busy? For an artist that's not very creative. What happened to our tutor swap?"

Lili glanced around. The corridor was empty. "I've just had some stuff going on at home."

"Oh. That sucks." The corners of Nick's mouth pulled up in a sympathetic smile. "It helps to talk to a friend."

She scooted toward the craft supplies cupboard. "You really don't want to hear all of it."

"Sure I do."

She turned around and almost bumped into him. His gaze bored into hers. The urge to spill her guts and drink in his compassion almost overwhelmed her, but she swallowed back the words. She couldn't risk ruining the one positive relationship he had in his family. "I'd cry."

"I'd grit my teeth and bear it."

Her hand went to her hip. "You're a weird guy, Nick Kent. Why do you want to get involved in a sixteen-year-old girl's problems?"

"Well, she fixes my shirts, for one." He nodded to her handbag. "I can see it poking out."

"Oh. Here." She plucked the shirt from her self-made denim-and-green-vinyl handbag. "Sorry it took so long, I accidentally sewed through to the front of your shirt the first time."

"That's okay." His fingers brushed hers as he took it. He paused. "I think you're worth getting to know."

Lili picked up a stack of memory-verse sheets and clutched them to her chest, hand tingling from his touch. She stared at the floor for a long moment. "It's a long story," she finally said. "But thanks for the offer. I'll . . . I'll let you know when I want to take you up on it."

"You better." He backed toward the door. "You've got my number." He exited, then poked his head back through the doorway. "You've also got some gummy bear in your teeth." He winked and left.

She ran her tongue over her teeth and scowled, then dumped the stack of papers in a recycle bin. One stuck to her chest. "Oh *nooooooo*." As she pulled at the sheet, pink chewing gum clung to her shirt, and the paper tore.

She prayed for a heavenly lightning bolt—or at least a vigorous zap from static—to avenge her shirt as she scraped the worst of the gum away with her fingernails. A sticky pink stain remained. She jammed her arms through the sleeves of her red cardigan just as her phone alarm went off.

Showtime.

She scooped up her handbag and jogged down the hall, around a corner, and down another corridor in the direction of the church offices. Her steps slowed as another figure walked toward her.

Recognition hit, and she jerked to a halt. "Miss Kent."

The woman stopped, then walked a few tentative steps closer. Her perpetual smile wilted. "Lili. Hi. How are you?"

Lili steamed at the fake politeness. "What are you doing here?" Sure, the woman was a member of the church, but to keep attending after Lili had caught her with Dad—that was just rubbing it in. And now, to be walking suspiciously close to Dad's office . . .

"Going to church." Miss Kent's tone tried for sunny but fell somewhere between limp and pathetic.

Lili folded her arms. "Go to a different church."

Devil-red lipstick shone like a beacon on the teacher's pale face. The same woman who encouraged her students to embrace their natural beauty. Lili curled her own lip in disgust.

"Lili? I've got dessert coupons." Dad appeared from his office door at the end of the hall.

Lili pushed past Miss Kent and stomped to her father. "Did you know she was here?"

She flung a hand toward where Miss Kent had been, but the teacher was fleeing back down the corridor.

Dad's smile faded as she approached. "No. I didn't even know she came this morning."

"Why was she down here then?"

"I have no idea. The ladies' bathroom is near here. Maybe that was it."

Lili scanned him. What were the signs of a liar? Pupil dilation or something? She squinted at his eyes. Nothing.

Dad gestured toward the door. "Did you want to come to lunch?"

She gave a cautious nod and headed for the back exit, which opened right next to where he parked his car. But with each step, the need to have everything out in the open pressed on her. She sucked in a big breath and released it. Was he still seeing Miss Kent? She couldn't fake her way through an hour-long lunch, not now.

As they slid into Dad's car, she spoke. "Am I allowed to come home yet?"

Dad's hand, poised to insert the key into the ignition, stilled. "That's what I wanted to talk to you about."

"What's to talk about? I've been good. How does keeping me away help anyone?" Her voice broke.

Dad turned to face her, eyes pleading. "Just another week and a half. Mom's away at a women's conference in Philly on the weekend, and I'm fully booked up. You'd just have to shift back to Jem's for four days anyway."

She pressed her lips together to stop them from trembling. "Then I can come home?"

Dad scratched his head. "I haven't told Mom yet."

She gaped. "About Miss Kent? You promised!"

"I know. I'm sorry. I'll do it before you get back." He fired up the engine and reversed. "I promise, kiddo."

She sulked back into her seat. He'd already broken one promise—not to mention possibly his wedding vows—so why should she believe him about this one?

A buzz sounded from Dad's pocket as he waited at the edge of the parking lot, indicating to turn right. He fished out his phone. "My battery's dying. Can you get my charger from the glove box?"

She opened the compartment and poked around. Just some registration papers and a brown paper bag. She tugged the bag open and peered in.

Cigarettes?

She whipped out the box. Icy tentacles wrapped around her lungs as she stared at the Philip Morris label. "Cigarettes, Dad? Really?"

His gaze darted to the pack. "What? I— That's not mine." He placed his hand over his heart. "I swear. I picked up a few people for church this morning. Someone must've left it in here."

The box crumpled in her fist as she squeezed it. Dad always prided himself on his honesty, but after recent events she wasn't so sure. "I remember you gave Mom your lighter when you quit. Did you buy a new one?" She held out a hand. "Empty your pockets."

Dad let the car roll forward a little. One last car approached, and then the coast would be clear to drive onto the road. "Lili, I really don't think—"

She cracked open her door and jumped out of the car onto the sidewalk.

Dad jolted, then lunged for her, but she darted away.

"*Show me.*" With every fiber of her being, she prayed those pockets were empty.

Dad pulled the door shut and glared at her though the window. He backed the car up to a safe place in the parking lot and jumped out. "Don't you dare do that again." His voice boomed loud enough for people in the parking lot to turn and look.

Her cheeks burned hotter than a forgotten iron. He made it sound like she was the one out of line. And this whole time, he'd been lying. About the cigarettes. About telling Mom.

About Miss Kent too?

"How could you?" Her plans for the day crumbled like stale cake. No way could she go home if this was still going on.

A new thought arose, and she held her breath to cut off the sobs that threatened.

If he was still doing stuff like this . . . did he even want her home?

Dad stepped closer and gentled his tone. "We're a family, Lili. We can work this out."

She shook her head. "Show me."

His expression darkened. "This is not what you're thinking. This whole thing is nothing. Stop turning it into an issue."

She lowered her own voice. "If you don't show me right now, I'm going straight to Mom."

He jerked back, shook his head, then reached into his pocket and pulled out a plastic blue lighter. He thrust it toward her. "Fine. Are you happy?"

The air left her lungs. A roar filled her ears, and every nerve ending turned cold. He had lied. He'd lied to her. "'This family tells the truth.'" She repeated the words he'd often spoken to her. Dad's face turned fuzzy as tears built up in her eyes.

"Lili, let me expl—"

She snatched the lighter from his fingers and, for the first time in her life, swore at him.

She fled through the parking lot, the cigarettes and lighter clutched in her fists.

She glanced back as she pushed through the back door of the church. Dad slumped against the car, dessert coupons on the ground.

She charged on and didn't stop till she reached the safety of the Kids' Church room, where she curled up in a pile of giant neon cushions as sobs tore free. Her whole body rattled. After a few minutes, she propped herself up on one elbow and pegged the lighter at the wall. Then the cigarettes.

Dad had quit when she was a little girl, had claimed that now even the smell of smoke made him sick. He'd always said how he was so glad prayer had helped him kick it. There'd been plenty of chances to smoke at school in the past, but she always steered clear. She couldn't disappoint her daddy.

She disentangled herself from the cushions and walked over to where the lighter and cigarettes had landed. What was the point? She'd been good her whole life, and it hadn't made any difference. Dad was choosing Miss Kent. Over Mom and her.

Maybe it was time to try bad.

She pulled one cigarette out of the packet, considered it.

Then strolled toward the church auditorium, lighting the smoke as she went.

She'd done it.

After the craziest working week of her life, Natalie had pulled off the Wildfire festival launch.

She sank into a chair in the church auditorium as the congregation hummed around her, still chatting after Mike's rousing sermon on integrity—and the Wildfire festival announcement. In six days' time, a team of motocross riders would wow crowds at Charlottesville High's football field, while those less interested in death-defying motorbike jumps could enjoy the gaming zone, graffiti art wall, free food, or the sports zone. Then Sam would close the event after the last big motorbike stunt with a short testimony to the crowd.

Six people, including two church elders, had congratulated her on the idea. She'd had a dozen people volunteer to help.

She breathed in deep, relishing the scent of twenty different old-lady perfumes. The scent—such as it was—of success. Nothing could ruin this happy day. Not even the weight of exhaustion pulling at her eyelids.

Someone coughed like their lungs had mutinied against their body. The sound plucked at her memory. She jerked her gaze up and scanned the auditorium. Lili?

She jumped up and searched the room. She looked past the Taylor triplets, past old Mrs. Prior and her KJV Bible with Chris Hemsworth photos taped inside the cover. There was Lili, on the other side of the sanctuary, coughing her lungs out.

Natalie dashed down the aisle, dodging parishioners in her path. Not easy in wedges and a just-long-enough-for-church skirt. Why was Lili coughing like that?

The smell hit.

Smoke?

Shock rooted Natalie's feet to the ground. She stared at Lili, bent over double, a glowing cylinder clutched between two fingers. Definitely smoke.

Natalie made it across the packed auditorium in five seconds flat.

"What are you doing?" She swiped the cigarette from Lili's hand. The smell coated Natalie's tongue in grit as she rubbed Lili's back and bent over to get a look at her face.

Hands on her knees, Lili tried to suck in air. Deep hacks sounded from her chest instead.

The eyes of two hundred churchgoers seared into Natalie. Steph was going to kill her.

Jem appeared by her side, face covered in purple splotches from Friday's boxing. He'd 'fessed up about the match on Saturday when she dropped in for the goodie bags and his puffy face scared her half to death. Now the discoloration emphasized the worried crease of his brow. "What's going on?"

"Code Beetroot. Take this." She shoved the cigarette at him.

He disappeared to do her bidding.

Natalie gripped Lili's arms. "Slow down. Deep breaths. Don't panic."

Lili nodded, eyes watery, and gulped in one breath, two.

A small crowd gathered around them. Not good. She grabbed Lili's hand and pushed a way through toward the doorway.

Lili still coughed, but at least it wasn't the rib-rattling sound from a minute before. Still, her arm trembled beneath Natalie's grip.

A familiar whistle sounded. She searched the room as she strode toward the door. Jem waved from twenty feet away, cigarette gone. He held Oliver but not the diaper bag. He tossed her his car keys.

She plucked them from the air one-handed and hustled outside.

At Jem's car, she grabbed a water bottle and shoved it at Lili. "Drink this. What were you thinking?"

Lili didn't respond, just chugged down the water.

Jem jogged over, juggling baby and diaper bag, as Lili emptied the rest of the bottle onto her hands. Natalie read the silent question on his face and nodded. Of course she was coming. She could get her bike later.

Lili finally got her breath back and slipped into the car without a word.

Natalie rubbed her temple as she eased into the passenger seat while Jem buckled Olly in. She had zero brain capacity to deal with drama today. What had possessed Lili to do such a thing?

Jem climbed into the driver's seat as Lili clicked her seat belt. He glanced at Natalie, eyebrows raised. The silent conversation continued.

What's going on with her?

She shrugged. *Don't know.*

Jem rolled his eyes.

She understood. She wasn't prepared for dealing with teenage girls either.

The car ride home was silent, apart from Olly's "Da-da-da-da-da" and an occasional splutter from Lili.

Natalie flicked a glance at Jem as he parked at home and shut off the car. Was she going to have to ask the obvious?

No, he was Lili's uncle. She kept her mouth shut.

Jem stayed silent as he got Olly out of the car. He had the baby out and diaper bag in hand when Lili's car door slammed.

"I caught Dad smoking, okay?"

Natalie, standing on the other side of the car, snapped her head around. Mike? Smoking? No way.

Jem's expression stayed neutral. "Okay."

"Well, not actually smoking. But I found his cigarettes. And lighter. He'd lied about having them." Lili opened her mouth, shut it. Gave her head a little shake. "It freaked me out. I've seen all those ads about lung disease. So I had one to show him. The same amount that he's worried about me, I'm worried about him."

Natalie leaned against the car, looking over the roof at Lili. Something about the way Lili hesitated . . . Was she telling the truth?

Jem nodded, face thoughtful. "It's good that you love your dad." Lili's face screwed up, like she was trying not to cry.

"But doing stuff that hurts yourself isn't the best idea. Even if you have a good point to prove," he said.

"I won't do it again." She dragged a hand across her eyes. "It nearly made me throw up."

"Good to know." Jem pulled her closer for a hug. "I love you, kiddo, you know that?"

"I know. Love you too."

He released her. "Let's go see if there's some leftover chocolate cake that can get rid of that taste for you, eh?" He winked at Natalie.

She followed on wooden legs. Whether Lili had a plausible explanation or not, she didn't want to be the one to face Steph.

Within half an hour they had both kids fed. They waited until they heard the customary gunshots from Lili's favorite TV show sound from behind her door.

Jem pulled out his phone and dialed Steph. Natalie bit her nails as he paced back and forth, phone in hand.

"Yes, Steph, I . . . That's right. She's okay. It just tickled her lungs a bit." Jem paused and listened. "We talked to her, and she said she found Mike smoking. She did it to show him how much it worried her." He held the phone out from his ear, and Steph's sharp tones carried across the room.

Natalie winced.

He glanced in her direction and offered a small smile. "Yes, Steph, I know it was a stupid thing to do, but that's what she said. Is there anything else you know of that would've made her do this?" He paced the room again.

Natalie looked around for something to do. Pick up toys. Dust. Anything. Her hands craved activity. She swiped a paper towel over the TV cabinet as Jem finished his call. He walked over.

"You realize Lili and I did the housework yesterday?"

"It's a distraction."

"Lili's okay, Nat."

She shrugged. She wasn't Lili's family, not even her nanny—her only responsibility was Olly. But the artistic teen had wormed her way into Natalie's heart, and the thought that they were missing something bigger here . . . It gave her chills. "Do you believe her reason?"

"Mike told me the other night he and Steph have been going through a rough patch. She could be upset over that."

Natalie's gaze snapped up. "A rough patch?" Mike and Steph? Impossible. They ran the church. She'd had dinner with them dozens of times. They were always happy. Affectionate. Perfect. "What are you going to do?"

"She made herself feel sick and embarrassed. I'd say that's punishment enough."

Would she have been harsher? She couldn't decide. "Are we bad at this . . . kid stuff?" She couldn't quite say "parenting."

Jem smiled when she said "we." "We're doing our best."

"Is that good enough?" She stared at nothing in particular. Mike and Steph were having troubles. Steph had never said a word. But there must've been signs. She'd been friends with Steph for years, working with her for weeks. How had she not noticed anything?

"Hey." He rested a tentative hand on her shoulder, then paused, like he expected her to shake it off.

She didn't. "I just . . . If something's been bothering her, I thought I would've noticed." She might not have been Lili's nanny, but she still spent hours each week with the teen. Her mind flashed back to Dad's cancer diagnosis. Different situation, but still, the signs had been there for months. In her grief over Jem, she hadn't noticed.

If she had, maybe they'd have caught it earlier. Maybe he'd have stood more of a chance.

She should have done more.

Tears welled before she could stop them. She fought to tamp them back down. This was stupid. A completely different circumstance. These emotions were nothing but irrational.

"Nat." Jem's hand slid from her shoulder to around her back. He embraced her, his hold gentle. It would be easy for her to pull away.

She didn't.

"She's fine. You're fine. She's a teenager. They don't make sense."

But this situation didn't just remind her of Dad's diagnosis.

She'd been completely blindsided when Jem left. What signs had there been then? She'd wracked her mind for years and identified several small indicators. But never enough of them to make sense of what he'd done.

Was this her destiny? To always try her best and never see the wreck coming?

Her emotions spiraled, locked-away memories of her darkest days spilling out. She hadn't been a good enough fiancée. She should have been a better daughter. Now her status as a friend looked shaky.

A hug was less embarrassing than crying in front of Jem, so she leaned into him, trying to pull herself together. She slid her hands around his waist and rested her forehead against his collarbone, his chin atop her head.

His arms stretched around her, the warmth of his palms soaking into her back. He felt solid. Warm. Safe.

Oh, I missed this.

The moment stretched out—whether it was seconds or minutes, she couldn't tell. Eyes closed, all she could sense was the strength in Jem's firm grip around her, then the gentleness of his feather-light kiss on her hair, the familiar scent of his skin beneath that sexy cinnamon cologne.

She could stay here forever.

"This is in no way your fault, Nat." The vibrations from Jem's voice rumbled through his chest into her. "Anyone with eyeballs can tell how much you care. You listen. You spent time with her on that sewing project. You're amazing."

"You're amazing."

Did he mean that? Because it had been seven years since she'd been able to believe it.

Before she could change her mind, she rose on tiptoe and planted a soft kiss on his cheek. "Thanks."

Jem didn't move, and a breath away from his face, neither did she. Locked in his tractor beam, her breaths came quick and shallow.

His blue eyes traveled from her lips to her eyes to her lips again, longing etched in his expression. His thumb made a lazy circle on her back and he leaned forward the slightest amount, forehead against hers, eyes closed as if in pain.

He wanted her. The realization broke over Natalie like the first drops of rain after a drought.

She kissed him.

Lips pressed against his, she slipped her fingers behind his neck and pulled his head down. Closer. Her other hand cupped his jaw for one Mississippi, two, and then Jem appeared to realize this wasn't just a dream.

His arms locked her against him, his kiss firm. He tasted of dark-chocolate peanut M&M's, mixed with the salt from her tears. He must've been pinching from her chocolate stash again.

She stretched on tiptoe to reach him better, threaded her arms round his neck. She was still hurt. She wasn't even sure if she forgave him. But that didn't matter right now. She pressed against him and poured seven years of loneliness into her kiss.

Drawing back half an inch, she drew in his scent, sugary with undertones of his cologne.

Jem dipped his head again and deepened the kiss, and every thought in her head melted into goo. Sweet, caramel goo. Nothing existed except his silky hair between her fingers, his arm tight around her waist, his fingertips tracing her jaw.

"A-hem." An adolescent voice sounded from behind.

Natalie leapt from Jem's arms and spun around. Her cheeks flamed with heat. What had she just done?

Lili stood in the entrance to the living room, arms folded and a Cheshire grin across her face.

Jem cleared his throat. "You're in trouble, young lady. You're not s'posed to be smiling." But he couldn't keep the sheepish tone out of his voice.

"Am I gonna have to keep an eye on you two?" Lili cocked her head. "Because I can't watch a baby *and* two adults. I'm only sixteen."

"Did you need something?" Jem's tone was pointed.

"Why, are you busy?" Lili smiled a devilish grin.

Jem threw Oscar the Grouch at her.

Lili ducked, laughing, and escaped to the kitchen.

Natalie's phone buzzed, and she grabbed at the diversion. That kiss had been a mistake. Jem had only been back in her life for four weeks. After seven years of heartache, that was not enough time for everything to be okay—or more than okay—between them.

Sam's caller ID flashed up, and she swiped and pressed the phone to her ear. "Sam? Hi . . . Yeah, the announcement went really well. We've already got people volunteering . . ." She reached for her notebook, discarded on the couch. "Is that the only change?" She flipped the notebook open.

But couldn't focus on it. Jem stood before her, flushed, eyes wide and blue and looking at her. Looking as uncertain as she felt.

The moment stretched, then Sam's voice broke back through. ". . . newspaper ads start Tuesday."

She scrambled to jot down her notes. In her peripheral vision, Jem walked away.

19

I am not going to kiss Jem. I am not going to kiss Jem.

Natalie repeated the mantra to herself as she took the steps up to Jem's apartment two at a time on Monday morning.

What had gotten into her yesterday? She and Jem weren't even dating. He'd decided he didn't want to marry her anymore, he'd left, and no amount of comforting hugs or even smoking-hot kisses could fix the hurt that'd caused.

She stood in the corridor and rapped on his door, rearranging her features into a neutral expression. The itchy tag of her most unflattering shirt—brown with a cartoon frog on the front—scratched against her skin. But the wardrobe was strategic. She had to get her head on straight.

The door opened. Jem stepped through it, caught her in his arms, and kissed her thoroughly.

Natalie slid her hands along his jaw and kissed him right back. Seven years had done nothing to dull the heat between them.

Whoops. She had to stop—in exactly five seconds. She leaned against him, fingers brushing the hair at the nape of his neck. Four . . . three . . . two . . .

Okay, maybe ten seconds.

A floorboard creaked to their left. Natalie jerked back. No one came. False alarm. Still, she pulled Jem's hands from her waist and stepped back. "I—That—I'm not doing this."

Jem quirked an eyebrow. "Kinda seems like you are."

Hands on her hips, she drew in a deep breath. "Momentary insanity. Nothing's changed. And this"—she pointed between them—"isn't happening again." She pointed to his bruised cheekbone and changed the topic. "How are you going to explain these bruises at work?"

After three days, the marks from his sparring bout with John still hadn't faded. When she'd suggested he try foundation yesterday, he'd squirted her with Olly's bathwater.

"I'll say I was in a bar fight. I need to increase my street cred."

Despite herself, Natalie smirked.

He leaned closer. "And nice try, but I'm still not distracted."

"Jem? Are you ready to go?" Lili's voice sounded from inside the apartment.

He groaned.

Natalie stepped farther away. "This isn't happening. And it's time to get to work."

Lili shuffled out the door, eyes half closed and bag on her back.

Natalie caught Jem's sleeve as he moved to follow his niece. "Don't forget, this weekend is the Wildfire festival, so I can't work on Friday. We have to set up for it. You told me to remind you at the start of the week." Even though she'd already told him a bunch of times.

He dropped a lid in a saucy wink. "I'll put it in my calendar." He blew a kiss, then followed Lili.

Natalie faced the open apartment door, rolled her eyes at her lack of willpower, then smiled at Olly in his high chair. Yes, it was time for work.

The rest of her day whizzed by as she did *not* watch the clock and count the seconds.

At 9:27 she finished changing the Wildfire advertisements for radio and print.

At 10:56 she lost three out of five crawling races against Olly.

At 11:39 she pressed Save on the festival schedule.

At 12:01 she pulled the clock off the wall and hid it in the fridge.

The rest of the afternoon was a flurry of activity as she prepared dinner, fed Olly, and helped Lili with math homework. Technically she didn't have to stay past 3:30 p.m., but the free Wi-Fi and food lived here. The least she could do was cook.

Steph called at five o'clock. "Nat, I've got a chance for you to score some points against Kimberly."

Natalie grimaced as she held the cell between her shoulder and ear and lifted a pot of water for spaghetti onto the stove. Not tonight. She'd been unable to sleep last night, emotionally disturbed due to recent events involving Jem and his lips. Plus, Steph had a bad habit of calling her last minute to work that night. Is this how it would be in the full-time position?

"Kimberly's come down with the flu, and she was meant to prep Sam's PowerPoints for his three school talks tomorrow. I didn't get to it today. Could you whip them up tonight?" Papers rustled. "He's giving another four during the week. Maybe while you're at it you could get them sorted too."

Natalie rubbed her forehead. She'd worked hours well above her internship commitment last week and had been up early this morning completing today's allotted jobs. She recalled the presentations she'd seen Sam give. "He doesn't always use a slideshow, does he?"

Steph hesitated. "He doesn't have to. We're just trying to put across a more professional appearance."

Natalie dug deep. "I've got commitments tonight, sorry." A commitment to eat her dinner and get some sleep. "I can do the rest of the week's presentations tomorrow, but I can't do tonight."

"O-kay." Steph drew the word out. "But Kimberly's really impressing the board. Don't give up too many of these opportunities." A meaningful pause. She probably expected Natalie to cave, like she always did.

Natalie pressed her nails into her palm. "See you tomorrow." She hung up and let out a breath. She'd done it. She'd said no.

Fifteen minutes later, she was shaking her hips to the sound of Lili's stereo as the pot of spaghetti boiled on the stove. She sang into a spatula, then pointed it toward Olly in his high chair. "Now clap your hands."

Lili clapped Olly's hands above his head as Natalie executed her best Beyoncé dance imitation.

The door flew open behind her.

"Uncle Jem!"

Natalie whirled around, midshimmy.

Jem stood framed by the doorway, shirt untucked. He grinned. "Don't stop because of me."

She hit the volume button on the stereo. "I didn't think you'd be home for another hour."

"I worked through lunch and took off early."

"That sounds awful." By Lili's expression, she couldn't comprehend skipping a lunchtime.

"I was motivated." Jem shot Natalie a meaningful smile, then plucked Oliver from his chair and kissed his cheek. "How's my favorite little man?"

Lili chattered to Jem about her day, and Natalie paused her spaghetti stirring to take in the picture. Jem, his collar unbuttoned and sleeves rolled to the elbow. Olly chanting "Da-da" and grabbing for Jem's cheek. Lili laughing at something Jem said.

Natalie pressed her lips together. Staying had been a tactical mistake. One she knew better than to make. Yet she wasn't walking out the door.

She was still staring at the trio when Lili's words penetrated her consciousness.

"I've got more homework to do." Lili disappeared into her room.

Jem caught Natalie's eye as he returned Olly to his high chair. A slow smile stretched across his lips as he strolled toward her.

She pointed the spatula at him. "Nu-uh. We talked about this."

He halted his advance. "Why're you here, then?"

"Free Wi-Fi."

"Are you working tonight?"

She hesitated. "No."

He smiled.

She tried again. "Free food."

"Try to sound convincing when you say it." He stepped forward and slipped his hands around her waist.

She didn't pull away. "We're not . . ." The words faded away as he trailed kisses from her cheek to the corner of her mouth. Her eyes slid shut. Traitors.

During her seven kiss-less years, how many times had she fantasized about feeling this way again? Wanted. Valued. Enough. She forced her eyelids to open. "I didn't think about you all day." A blatant lie if there ever was one.

A wicked gleam lit his eyes. "Guess I'll have to give you something to ponder." He lowered his head.

His kiss was slow and tender and left her wanting more. He rested his forehead against hers and smiled at her.

She was only human. She pulled his head back down and gave *him* something to think about.

Jem's hands were making a mess of her hair when two sounds registered in Natalie's brain.

The hiss of the spaghetti water overflowing its boundaries. And a sharp rap at the door.

"I'll get the pot."

"I'll get the door."

They spoke at the same time. Jem rescued the pot—he was a better cook than she was—while she opened the door.

A blonde woman with a figure Natalie could only dream of looked down at her from atop five-inch black pumps. She twisted a Louis Vuitton purse in her hands, damp marks scarring the expensive fabric.

"Can I help you?"

"Is this the home of Jeremy Walters?"

Jem's footsteps approached from behind. "Chloe?"

20

H i, Jeremy."

Natalie wracked her brain for any mention of that name. Chloe? No search results.

But she had blonde hair, apparent familiarity with Jem, and the way he said that name . . . A cold sweat broke over her.

Oliver's mother?

Be cool. You don't know for sure.

All she could croak out was an incredulous, "'Jeremy'?"

He pulled his dumbfounded stare from Chloe to her. "I didn't go by Jem in Chicago."

"Jem? What a cute nickname." Chloe's smile revealed two rows of blindingly white teeth. "May I come in?"

Natalie didn't budge.

"And you are . . . ?" The words emerged from glossy lips. The woman was a total Barbie doll.

Throat frozen, Natalie let Jem pull her inside and step into her place.

"What are you doing here, Chloe?" His voice carried a weird edge she'd never heard before on him. Cautious. Wounded. Suspicious. Uncertain.

Or maybe she was just projecting.

"You told me Olly needed a mother."

The words hit Natalie like a one-two punch.

Jem's jaw tightened. "That was the day he was born."

She acknowledged his words with a slight incline of her head. "I'm here now. Let's talk."

"Hallway. Now." He marched her into the outer hall and pulled the door shut behind him.

Hot and cold waves alternated through Natalie's body. This. Was. Not. Happening.

Should she eavesdrop? She stared at the peephole and debated whether she really wanted to hear.

"Who was that? Is Granddad here?" Lili emerged from her room.

"That's . . . that's Chloe. Oliver's—Jem's—" The words caught in Natalie's throat. "The woman who gave birth to Oliver." Oliver. The child that should've been hers. The child who'd squealed, screamed, and gurgled his way into her heart.

Lili's eyes grew wide. "Jem's ex?" She rushed to the door and pressed her ear against it.

Natalie was half a second behind her.

"I can't hear any screaming." Lili stretched on tiptoe to look through the peephole. "He should push her down the stairs."

Natalie stared at the closed door, unable to agree or disagree. What did this woman represent? Someone who genuinely cared for Oliver? On the one hand, she hadn't terminated her unplanned pregnancy. That had to mean something. But she had left Olly. That meant something too.

Was she a threat to Jem's custody? Possibly.

A threat to Jem's heart?

Unknown.

Natalie blinked. Not that she had—or wanted—any claim to Jem. Those kisses were just hormones, the result of a long dry spell, an emotionally charged week, and . . . well, mutual history and attraction.

But they were not the promise of any kind of future.

Lili pressed her ear to the door again, then gave up. She looked at Olly, gumming a rubber Marvin Martian toy and drooling up a storm. "Is she here to take Olly away?"

"No. She can't do that. Jem wouldn't let it happen." Natalie had no idea if her words were true. Surely Jem had full custody.

But then a mother often got sympathy in family court. And contact with his mother should be good for Olly. But what if Jem became an every-second-weekend dad?

Olly threw down his toy and cried. She scooped him from his chair and bounced him. He'd been unusually fussy this week. The two white stubs poking from his tender gums were probably to blame. Though usually teething put him off his food, and this week he'd been hungrier than ever.

"*Shhh*, bubby, *shhh*." She poked her finger in his mouth and let him chew it.

She peeked out the peephole again. Jem stood with his feet planted, arms crossed, profile toward her. Chloe waved her hands as she spoke. Neither looked happy.

"I think dinner's ready," Lili said from beside the stove. "It's a bit early, but I'm starving."

Noodles slopped into a bowl. Natalie kept her face pressed to the peephole.

"Do you want some?"

"No, thanks."

She couldn't even think about eating right now.

Natalie was trapped.

Her rapid steps echoed down the concrete corridor at Potted Plants 4 Hire, but the door at the end was locked. She was alone. Fear crushed in on her, a weight on her chest. Rubbing fog from a glass pane in the door, she peered through. Chloe stood with her back to the door, arms wrapped around a man. A man with broad shoulders, sleeves rolled to his elbows, and red highlights in his hair. Jem.

"Nat."

Her world shook. She threw a hand out. Instead of solid wall, her hand smacked something soft.

"*Ooof!*"

Her eyes popped open. The room was dark, but enough moonlight shone through the window to illuminate Jem kneeling next to where she curled up on his couch. His hand covered his right eye.

"Jem?" A warm weight against her torso registered. Olly.

The night's events rushed back. Jem had stayed in the hallway for hours. Lili went to bed early. Natalie had sat down on the couch for what she feared could be her last cuddle with Oliver.

She tightened her hold around the precious bundle, his head snuggled into her chest. She inhaled his scent—talcum powder and milk. She hadn't realized until tonight just how attached she'd become to Jem's baby boy.

"You nearly poked my eye out."

"What time is it?" She snapped the words, heart still slowing after the nightmare.

He pulled his hand from his face, eye still screwed shut. "Just after ten. You must've been tired."

She rubbed a hand over her face. Crying did that to a person. She lowered stiff legs toward the floor. "Where's Chloe?"

"Gone."

"For good?"

He stayed silent.

"Why is she here?"

"We just spent hours discussing that. I'm still not sure." His voice carried a dread that chilled her core.

Jem slid onto the couch beside Natalie but didn't reach for her. He just held his head in his hands.

She shifted Olly's weight against her. "Does she want to see him?"

"Yes."

"Does—Does she want to keep him?"

"I don't know."

"*Can* she?"

A pause. "I'm not sure about that either."

"You don't have full custody?"

"I started the process, but I was just trying to survive on my own as a parent. I could barely keep myself in clean clothes and fed for the first four months. Then the move happened and . . . I had an appointment with the lawyer next week to get things rolling again. But at the moment . . ." He let the sentence hang.

She didn't say anything.

"I know. I'm a horrible parent."

"I didn't say that."

"But you're mad."

She paused. He knew. She could tell. The volcanic wrath that had surged through her at the sight of Jem's former lover was nothing short of apocalyptic. An equal amount flowed in Jem's direction. And the thought that custody of this little ball of sweetness could go to the woman who'd abandoned him— She fought down anger at Jem for leaving the loophole open.

Instead, she searched for the right words. "I'm scared."

"So am I." A glint of light reflected on Jem's wet cheeks as he reached for Olly. It tore at her, anger notwithstanding.

She handed the baby over. "It . . . it's going to be okay."

Jem pressed his forehead against his sleeping son. His shoulder, pressed against hers, shook.

Anger could wait. She couldn't take the sight, the vibrations, of Jem crying.

She scrambled to her knees and threw her arms around him. Jem pressed his forehead against her shoulder. Tears, warm and wet, dripped onto her collarbone. One arm snaked around her waist. The other held Olly against them both.

"It's going to be okay." She laid her cheek atop Jem's head and rocked from side to side. Brushed her hand along his back, twisted his reddish-brown locks between her fingers. "We'll figure this out."

Meaningless words, all of them. Worse still because the "we" part was a lie, and they both knew it.

But there would be time for that tomorrow.

For the past several weeks, Jem had been there for her whenever she needed it.

She could be here for him tonight.

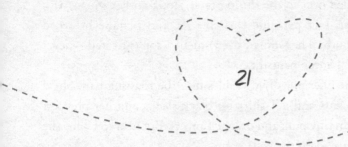

21

Someone was going to die tonight.

Natalie embedded a knife deep into the heart of a sweet potato as Chloe poked through Jem's kitchen cabinets. Even Lili, doing homework on the opposite side of the counter, rolled her eyes.

Chloe had only been in their lives for a day, but it felt like an eternity.

The woman opened a cabinet under the sink. "Where do you store your poisons?"

"Next to the milk." Natalie lopped off another slice of sweet potato.

Jem had said Chloe would drop by "in the late afternoon." When Chloe showed up two hours after he left, she'd been tempted to leave her in the hallway. Fear of a custody battle had been the only thing that prompted Natalie to open the door. And now, since she wasn't comfortable leaving Chloe alone with Olly and Lili, she was stuck here till Jem got home.

She'd tried to keep an open mind about the woman's qualities. If Jem had dated her, surely she wasn't the devil incarnate. But after six hours of the woman's snooping and condescending questions, she was tempted to relocate her nail file into Chloe's eyeball.

Chloe strolled over to the dining table, apparently content with Natalie's answer. Her perfume floated over and Natalie breathed through her mouth. The woman even smelled sophisticated—never mind the Ralph Lauren pantsuit.

Natalie tossed her pile of vegetables into the roasting pan. She'd swapped yoga pants and a T-shirt for black slacks and her prettiest blouse, covered in tiny pink and orange flowers. But next to Chloe she might as well have worn the yoga pants.

The day wouldn't have been so bad if Chloe had paid an ounce of attention to Olly. But she'd ignored him, instead fiddling on her phone or grilling Natalie on what kind of care the baby received.

Olly fussed in his high chair and gummed at his sippy cup, with only a few drops of water left.

Natalie refilled the cup. He guzzled it. She'd never seen the little guy so thirsty before. She glanced at Chloe, confirmed her back was turned, and ran her fingers over Olly's forehead. No fever. But he hadn't quite been himself the last few days. She made a mental note to tell Jem.

"Who put your festival program fliers together?"

Natalie looked up. Chloe had parked herself in front of Natalie's laptop, set up on the dining table, and scanned the draft flier she'd thrown together last week at 1:00 a.m.

Chloe shook her head at the screen. "Whoever they are, fire them. I studied graphic design in college, and this is atrocious."

"How many festival fliers have you seen before?" Natalie tempered her tone for Olly's sake, but her grip on the knife tightened.

Chloe didn't seem to notice any tension. "Tons. I run an event management business." She tapped at the keyboard with manicured nails.

Event management? Second to ministry, that would be Natalie's dream job.

And Chloe was successful in it. Figured.

After ten minutes of silence, Chloe pushed the computer away. "There. I've done the best I can."

Lili rolled her eyes.

Natalie sneaked a glance at the screen. Huh. Chloe's design didn't really look any better than hers had.

Though she was probably biased.

Her phone beeped again. Sam. Her lips twitched upward. He'd noticed her tension when she dropped into Wildfire that morning and sent her a hilarious GIF involving a puppy, a baby, and a puddle. They'd texted memes and GIFs back and forth all day long.

"Do you always spend this much time on your phone when you're nannying?" Chloe's imperious tone grated Natalie's tenuous grip on decorum.

"I have two jobs. This is my other boss. Jem's fine with it." The fact she had to explain herself at all increased her tension headache. She'd been clenching her jaw all day.

Natalie glanced at her watch. Jem should be home in a few minutes. And he was going to get an earful.

Chloe resumed her inspection of the apartment, opening the fridge. "Do you feed him organic food?"

"The moth he found on the floor was organic."

Lili snickered.

"What about baby education? Does Oliver know any sign language? Recognize numbers?"

"Jem reckons he can pass gas on demand."

A laugh escaped Lili before she covered with a cough.

Chloe sent her a look, then started on the freezer contents. Natalie slid her pan into the steaming oven as the door opened beside her.

"Hey, ba—uh, Natalie." Jem stumbled over his words as Chloe pulled her head out of the freezer. "Chloe. What are you doing?"

"Hi, Jeremy. How was work?"

The words hit Natalie like a slap in the face. They rolled off Chloe's tongue like she'd said them a thousand times before. Because she had.

Natalie clunked around with the oven as scenes flashed through her mind. Chloe greeting Jem when he arrived home. Eating dinner together. Kissing . . .

She blinked to clear the mental image but couldn't shake the inner turmoil so easily. It had burned her insides ever since she answered that knock on the door yesterday afternoon. Chloe's presence was an unforgettable reminder that Jem had chosen a whole different life over Natalie. And no matter how much she tried not to let it, it still stung.

She needed to move on with her own life. It was long past due.

Jem stared at Chloe a moment, then swung his gaze toward Natalie. "I need to talk to Natalie. In private." He grasped Natalie's wrist and tugged her into the hallway.

Her skin thrilled at his touch, the memory of his kiss sending tingles through her lips as he closed the door behind them.

But Chloe had those memories too—and far more.

Jem turned to her, face lined. "What is she doing here?"

She pulled her hand from his. "Driving me to the brink of homicide."

"Why did you let her in?"

"You said she was coming over." Natalie's pitch rose with her ire.

Jem shook his head. "This afternoon. Once I was home. Didn't I tell you that?"

Yeah, right, blame me. She folded her arms. "You forgot. Just like you forgot your phone. I sent you eighteen texts before I realized it was on the coffee table." She gritted her teeth. "Believe me, I almost threw her out ten times already. Why did you tell her she could come?"

Jem rubbed a hand over his face. "She wanted to make sure Olly was getting taken care of properly. She's in town for business till Friday."

Natalie wrinkled her nose. Surely he could see how unlikely that was.

"I said she could have a few supervised visits between now and then." He shrugged. "I thought maybe if I appeased her, she wouldn't press things further."

He had a point. Not that she had to like it. "Fine. I'll bar the door till you get here. Next time, *tell me* before you leave." She uncrossed her arms, irritation deflating a little. "Speaking of afternoons, I've got a ton of work to do this week, prepping for the festival. I can't stay late like today."

He leaned against the wall and nodded. "I'll tell Lil not to answer the door to Chloe unless I'm here. And I'll make sure Chloe knows she's not welcome before five thirty."

She rubbed her temple. "What are you going to do about Friday?"

His brow creased. "Friday?"

She pinned him to the wall with her stare. "Don't tell me you forgot your Dad too."

His face blanked. "That's this week?" His eyes widened. "Nat, I'm begging you."

"I'm not getting you out of it." Fixing other people's problems was starting to get old.

He ran a hand through his hair, giving it that bed-head look. That Chloe had seen. Natalie folded her arms again.

He groaned. "This week. Of all the weeks."

She shook her head. "You'll have to deal with it yourself."

Jem clasped his hands together like he was imploring her. "You've always been so good at keeping Dad civil—at least more civil. I'll get down on my knees if I have to."

"I'm working at Wildfire all day."

"But you'll be off by dinner, right?"

"Chloe's a stranger. That'll keep him civil."

Jem looked at her like she'd suggested he bungee jump naked from the Empire State Building. "Dad and Chloe in the same room? I'm not a lunatic."

She pressed her lips together. She should say no. She needed to say no.

"Please."

"No Chloe?"

"No Chloe."

She shut her eyes. "Fine. But as a friend only. And I'm not cooking."

He rested his hands on her shoulders. "Thank you."

She gave a pointed look at them.

He removed them, palms up in defeat, expression a tad . . . sadder.

Natalie marched inside, grabbed her stuff, and flounced back out the door and down the stairs, leaving Jem alone in the hallway. She would not let that puppy-dog expression get to her. No siree.

Her phone vibrated as she reached the ground floor.

Incoming call. Sam.

"Heeeeey, Natalie." A slight undertone of nervousness scored his words.

She attempted a lighthearted tone as she exited the building and made for her bicycle. "I'm still looking for a GIF to top that kangaroo freaking out at a mirror."

"Good luck. It's unbeatable." They chuckled, and the silence stretched to awkwardness. Natalie unchained her bike. "Were you after something?"

Sam cleared his throat. "Look, I wouldn't normally do this, but, well, Steph tells me you're open to the possibility. Would you like to have dinner with me this week?"

Natalie's breath caught. She'd gotten a slight ego boost from Steph's teasing, and the memes today had been fun, but she hadn't actually expected him to ask.

She glanced up to the second-story window that glowed with a homey light.

Time to move on.

"Sounds great. I'm free Thursday."

♡

"I want to go home and sleep for a year. Instead I have to have dinner with a scary police captain."

Natalie stood three feet in the air on a ladder on Friday afternoon, hands full of canvas. Limp hair stuck to her forehead, the ends tickling her ear. She swiped her head on her shoulder to shift it.

As if her weighted eyelids and the thought of dinner with John Walters wasn't bad enough, her watch had now ticked five minutes past when she was supposed to leave.

Sam, stripped down to his undershirt on the opposite side of the ladder, hefted the canvas into place on the metal frame they'd just built. Charlottesville High had allowed them the use of their football field for the festival tomorrow, and they'd been working for hours to prepare for it. They still had another tent to go. Three barbecues to unload. Dozens of last-minute jobs.

Worst of all, her cherry cordial M&M's had run out.

Sam tied the canvas down, and she couldn't help but notice how well defined his biceps were. How chirpy he'd been all day despite the draining workload. How fun their date last night had been at a restaurant that specialized in chocolate fondue.

Why, oh, why had she agreed to leave this attractive man and go spend the evening with her ex and his cranky father?

Natalie stole another glance at her watch. Jem would soon be wondering where she was—if he noticed she wasn't there. He'd been so distracted with Chloe this week he'd barely said two words to her. Though she had made sure to mention her date with Sam on Wednesday. Jem had done a decent job of masking his reaction, but she'd still been able to tell it bothered him.

Not that she cared.

She opened her mouth to beg early leave from Sam. She hated to go while Kimberly was still working—the woman was unstacking chairs on the north side of the field—but it couldn't be helped. Natalie could return to finish these jobs early tomorrow morning. The festival didn't start till lunchtime.

But Sam spoke first.

"I have a request that might seem a bit odd."

"Okay." Her tone made the word more of a question.

"I want you to come speak at a Christian leader's network breakfast . . . in Washington."

She gaped at him. The ladder wobbled. "Are you serious?"

He grinned. "You're surprised? You've done an incredible job with this." He indicated the rest of the field.

Her fatigue evaporated like morning mist before a sunrise. "Really?"

"I'd love for you to tell the leaders in Washington about the festival idea."

She was late. She should say that she needed to leave. But . . . "You're sure they wouldn't rather hear about it from you?"

He shook his head. "It'd be good to have a fresh perspective in a guest speaker. I think you'll be a natural. And your work really has been amazing. You've kicked things up a notch around here. Everyone's noticed."

She beamed even as her arms turned to limp spinach trying to hold up the canvas. She *had* kicked things up a notch this week—and it was killing her. She'd almost fallen asleep over her cheese sandwich at lunchtime.

But now—totally worth it.

"Steph was a bit concerned when that soccer ball mishap happened, but I told her she had nothing to worry about." Sam shot her a smile that had probably weakened the knees of many a church choir girl. "I knew you'd pull through."

Heat filled her cheeks. "Thanks."

He gave the knot a final tug, and Natalie released the canvas. It held.

She scooted down the ladder. "When is it?"

"Not for another eight weeks. I just wanted to flag it with you early. Will you be able to get the time off from Jem?"

"I'll work something out with him." Maybe Mom could babysit Olly?

"How is Jem?" Sam descended his ladder and coiled a leftover rope.

"Grumpy and worried." She grimaced. Chloe wasn't common knowledge at the moment. "This dinner thing with his dad has him freaked out," she covered. "Plus the baby's been a bit sick and his niece is going through . . . a phase, I guess. He worries."

"That doesn't sound like the makings of a fun evening."

"It's not."

"Well . . ." Sam picked up the ladders and walked with her toward their pile of supplies under the main tent. "If you need a cheer-up afterward, I could be persuaded to drop by Bloop. Frozen yogurt fixes everything."

"You've got a serious sugar addiction." She laughed the words—it wasn't like she could judge. In fact, they'd bonded last night over their mutual love of all things sweet.

Sam grinned back. "Fifteen cavities and counting. The yogurt is my attempt to get healthy."

"You're a guy after my own heart."

He checked his watch. "You should probably go if you want to make it to Jem's on time. Text me if you want that yogurt."

She gestured to the piles of gear that surrounded them. "Are you sure? I could stay a few more minutes or come early tomorrow."

He gave her a poke toward her newly repaired car. "Go. And say hi to Captain Walters for me. He's offered to help run security at the festival."

She shuddered for any teen planning to misbehave and grabbed her duffel bag. "Thanks, Sam."

He waved her off, and she headed for the women's bathroom. A fresh pair of jeans, soft coral sweater, and a few swipes of mascara transformed her from a mess of sweat to a semirespectable human being.

Her hand trembled as she shoved her makeup back into her duffel. It'd been a crazy week, between extra visits to Mom and Dad—Dad'd had some bad days lately—and the festival prep work. Though not even her ridiculous workload the past few days had stopped her from checking her phone for a text from Jem. She'd received three. One to confirm Chloe would visit Olly every evening, one asking why the clock was in the fridge, and a third that said R we OK?

She'd started typing a response no less than seven times. And seven times she'd backspaced it and shoved her phone into her pocket.

Every molecule in her body screamed for home and bed before she could even contemplate sorting through her emotions. But she'd promised Jem she'd be there. She kept her promises.

She eyed herself in the mirror, noting the bags beneath her eyes and the dull flop of her hair. "One more night. I just need to survive one more night."

Then Chloe would be gone and she could focus on Sam and Wildfire and staying entirely professional with Jem.

22

Tonight had to be perfect.

Steam rose around Jem in the shower as he mentally ticked off the tasks to be done before his dad arrived. The roast was ready, vegetables in the oven, thanks to Chloe.

He'd been forced to work late, and while Lili could handle Olly, she barely knew a bread knife from a butter knife. So he'd asked Chloe a favor—a small favor, considering the gray hair she was giving him.

So far, nothing disastrous had happened. Nat wasn't due to arrive for another half hour. And when he'd left them five minutes ago, both kids had been alive and in clean clothes.

He shut off the faucet after a record-breaking short shower and flicked water from his hair dog-style. What was he missing?

This was ridiculous. He was having dinner with his father, not the president. He exited the shower and reached for his towel.

Peas! He'd forgotten a green vegetable, and Dad's favorite was peas. Jem was writing the word on the steamed mirror when a voice sounded through the wall.

"Chloe. I didn't expect to see you tonight."

Jem pulled the towel from his wet head. Was that Natalie? He glanced at his watch, sitting on the bathroom cabinet. Oh boy. He'd misjudged the time. He couldn't have a catfight fifteen minutes before Dad was due to arrive. Even without Chloe here now, he was already in hot water with Natalie. Hearing her talk about going on a date with Sam had been about as much fun as twelve rounds in the ring with Dad. And now this.

Chloe had to go, ASAP.

He jumped into his jeans. Natalie's footsteps—more delicate than Chloe's high-heeled elephant feet—tapped from the direction of the kitchen. She should cross in front of the doorway in three, two, one.

He pulled the door open, shirt still on the edge of the bathtub. "Hey, Nat."

She jolted, arms full of a stack of his novels she'd borrowed. "Hi." Her frown smoothed out into a more neutral expression.

He did a mental fist pump and scooped his shirt from the bathtub. She didn't look too mad. "Sorry I'm late—"

"Jeremy, can you taste test this for me?" Chloe breezed past Natalie and entered the bathroom, ladle in hand. "I'm not sure if this gravy tastes right."

He yanked his arms through his shirt sleeves. Natalie shook her head and turned away.

"Excuse me." He brushed past Chloe and followed Natalie to his room, buttoning his blue plaid shirt as he went. She dumped the books on his bed and kept her profile to him, wisps of dark hair curling around her face. Her pinky-orange sweater accentuated her slim curves, and the scent of flowers and vanilla hung in the air. But tension rolled from her in waves.

He took a tentative step closer. "Chloe's here, and I know I promised she wouldn't be. But she's leaving right now, and I needed her help."

"What does it matter to me?" She tried to walk past him.

He blocked her path with a hand to the wall. "Work kept me late, and she offered to help get dinner going. If she wasn't here, everything would've been late." And Natalie, of all people, knew he needed tonight to go well.

But instead of an understanding smile, all he got was an eye roll.

"There's always something." She ducked under his arm and escaped.

He whirled to face her retreating back. "What's that supposed to mean?"

"Figure it out, Mr. Journalist."

"Are you kidding me?" Frustration laced his tone. What did she want from him? He couldn't make Chloe disappear, as convenient as that would be. And this whole cold-shoulder thing smacked a little too much of John Walters for his taste. She couldn't change him—or his past—no matter how much she wanted to. "Stop being ticked off and just *talk* to me." He took two steps after her.

She spun and nearly bumped into his chest. "You want to talk?" Her voice rose, then bit off. She glanced in Chloe's direction and shifted her tone to a furious whisper. "I had better places to be than here. And you know that her being here is—" She bit off whatever she was going to say. Inhaled and exhaled. "You promised." She speared him with a look, half frustration, half disappointment. "Guess I of all people should've known better than to trust your promises."

The words landed like a heavyweight's punch to the gut. Jem lost whatever it was he'd been going to say.

He should've known. Despite all the history, the attraction, even kissing—he'd never be able to make up for what he'd done. Not for her, and not likely for Dad either.

Though he'd lost Dad's good opinion long before he ever left Charlottesville.

A knock sounded at the door. He tamped down the urge to punch something. "We're not finished here." He stalked over to the door, wrenched it open. "Hi, Dad."

Movement at the dining table caught his eye.

Oh no.

Chloe was still here.

♡

"Who haven't you introduced me to, Jem?"

Dad strode into Jem's kitchen, his pressed cream shirt and suit pants somehow more terrifying than his gun and taser.

Jem sweated as Dad plucked a fussy Oliver from his high chair and nodded in Chloe's direction. "That's, um—"

"Chloe Kingston." Chloe stepped forward with a glowing smile.

Jem relaxed. At least she hadn't said—

"Oliver's mother. I thought it'd be nice to get to know Olly's family at dinner."

Jem clenched his jaw. Of all the manipulative, low-down . . .

Dad's polite expression dropped. "Oliver's—" The baby launched a day's worth of food onto Dad's shirt. Chloe jumped backward.

"Olly!" Jem pulled the baby from Dad's hands. Oliver screamed.

Jem rushed him to the kitchen sink in case there was more, but Olly seemed to have emptied the entire contents of his stomach onto Dad. Perfect. What a great start to their first dinner in years. "Sorry. The doctor gave him antibiotics on Tuesday, but they're not doing much."

Dad held his shirt away from his body. "No wonder he's sick. He smells like all he's had today is sweet juice."

"He had a tiny bit of watered-down juice at lunch, that's all."

Dad glanced at the mess dripping from his front, brows raised.

Jem's hackles rose.

Natalie rushed forward, towel in hand. "Come to the bathroom, John. I'll see if Jem has any shirts that might fit you."

She tossed another towel to Jem, and he caught it one-handed.

Spreading it on the counter, he stripped off Oliver's miniature button-down shirt and jeans, doing his best not to smear the mess everywhere. Not much success. He picked Olly up, wearing only his diaper, and held the bundle of towel and clothes in front of him in case he spewed again.

By the time he reached the bathroom, Dad was shrugging on Jem's biggest flannel shirt.

Nat took the baby from Jem's arms. "I'll bathe him. You take care of dinner." Water already rushed into the tub.

He let Dad pass him out the door, then spoke to Natalie. "We'll wait for you." Mad or not, he wouldn't be rude.

She laid Olly on the bath mat and stripped off his diaper. "Don't be silly. I'll heat up a plate." The corners of her mouth pulled down as she looked at the diaper in her hand. Her lips pursed.

Jem fought the urge to snap at her. "What?"

"When did you last change him? This feels like he's worn it all day."

He closed his eyes and prayed for strength. She was trying to pick a fight. He'd changed it less than an hour ago. Still, he had to be the bigger person. "I can change him. You go get some food."

She set the diaper aside. "No way am I letting you hide in here while I sit out there with Chloe and your father."

Hide in here? Jem bit back his response and left the room without a word.

As he reached the kitchen, Chloe pulled a pan of vegetables from the oven. The piercing wail of a smoke alarm cut the air. Oliver's cries turned to shrieks.

Jem reached up to the ceiling and yanked the alarm free. A flick of the finger and the battery disconnected. He wrinkled his nose against the smell of burnt parsnip.

Chloe grimaced. "Sorry, Jeremy. I thought now Natalie was back she was in charge of the cooking."

A low mutter sounded from the bathroom.

Jem pulled a hand down his face, stretching his cheeks. What else could go wrong? "Let me see what we can salvage."

In ten minutes he had Chloe, Lili, and Dad seated at the table, dinners before them.

Dad poked at a scorched carrot and cleared his throat. "So, Chloe, what brings you to town?"

Jem tensed at his guarded tone.

"My business brought me to Charlottesville for a few days, and I wanted to check on Oliver." Chloe's tone didn't give away whether she was pleased or dismayed with what she'd found.

Jem stabbed a potato. He just had to survive until she flew back to Chicago tomorrow morning. Hopefully with an agreement to sign over full custody.

"And what business are you in?" Dad forked a piece of potato into his mouth with a grimace.

"Event management, with a little marketing thrown in. We ran some promotional events for Victoria's Secret last month." She sent a too sweet smile toward Jem. "That's how Jeremy and I met."

Jem choked on a mouthful of roast. And prayed to never hear the words "Victoria's Secret" in front of his father again.

Chloe continued, oblivious. "He was reporting on a promotion the company held for a children's charity, and we reconnected. I'd known him from college. He was the bartender at our favorite hangout."

Dad glowered. "Bartender?"

Jem swallowed. "Only for a few months. Had to pay tuition somehow."

"That wouldn't have been a problem had you stayed here and gone to UVA."

"I know." Jem kept his tone pleasant. Alcohol had always been a sensitive issue, ever since Dad first found a beer can beneath eighteen-year-old Mike's bed. The verbal explosion had made such an impression on then six-year-old Jem that teenage Jem had made sure to never get caught.

Until he'd decided he didn't care anymore.

Dad hacked at his meat like it was Jack Daniel himself.

Natalie returned to the table, a freshly scrubbed Olly on her lap. The only seat left was next to Chloe. She took it with a stony glance at Jem.

Chloe eyed Oliver's mouth and edged away.

Jem clenched his fork and left the table. Could no one in this room act with a little maturity?

He fetched Natalie's plate and slid it before her. Everyone ate in silence for several moments, tension thicker than Chloe's floury gravy.

Dad weighed his heavy stare on Jem, then snapped at his granddaughter. "Lili, don't just push food around your plate."

She jolted.

"Don't take it out on Lili when you're mad at me, Dad." Jem couldn't keep the edge out of his voice this time. He looked over at his niece. Maybe she had Olly's bug? "You feeling okay, Lil?"

"Fine." Her tone was flat, but her eyes sparked.

The beginnings of a migraine prodded his brain.

Nat reached for her cup and found it empty. She indicated her hands, full of baby and dinner. "Could you grab me a drink, Jem?"

"I'll get it." Dad hefted himself from his seat before Jem could respond. He rummaged through the fridge. Jem turned when a *glug-glug-glug* sounded at the sink.

Dad held a wine bottle upside down over the drain.

Jem slammed his cutlery onto the table. Lili jumped.

Of course Dad would take the overbearing and judgmental route. "Dad, what do you think you're doing?"

"Don't cause a scene. I'll pay you the ten dollars this is worth. I just don't want alcohol in the home of my grandchildren."

Jem thrust his chair back and stood. Dad just couldn't let him have one night without criticism. Or some attempt to control him. "I knew you'd find something."

Dad didn't respond, just let the liquid chug away.

"You know it's *cooking* wine."

"Doesn't mean people can't drink it."

Jem took a step forward. "You are so unbeliev—"

"Stop it!"

A chair crashed against the wall. Every head swiveled to Lili.

She threw her napkin on the table. "If you're just going to keep hating each other, then leave. There's no point pretending we're a happy family."

She flew from the table, past Dad, and into her room. The slam of her door echoed through the apartment.

Jem glared at his father. "Happy?"

"Jem, beetroot." Natalie's voice carried warning.

"What?"

She narrowed her eyes at him. "We have company."

He knew that tone. She wasn't worried about Chloe. She wanted to cool him down.

Chloe's high-pitched giggle cut through their silent interaction. "Don't worry about me, Nat. I've heard all about John."

The look Natalie sent Jem almost boiled the flesh from his bones.

Dad set the now empty bottle next to the trash can. "I'll take my leave now." He paused by the door. "If your mother was here, what would she say?" He left.

The silence stretched.

A chair squeaked on the floor.

Chloe stood and took her purse from the kitchen counter. "I'll talk to you before I go to the airport tomorrow." She exited quietly.

Jem's stress levels hit new heights. What did her thoughtful expression mean? Had his family's dysfunction just given her ammunition for a custody fight?

Natalie handed Oliver to Jem and headed to the bathroom.

Jem looked at his son. The child had hit a growth spurt and slimmed down in the last few weeks. The thinner face made him look older.

"Is it just me, or is everyone overreacting today?" he said to the baby. Movement caught his eye. Natalie.

♥

"Is that what you think I'm doing? Overreacting?" Natalie stepped farther into the dining room, a growl entering her voice. Heat rushed up her neck and poured into her face.

The man had smashed her heart to smithereens, tempted her again, then thrown her into a spin with his ex-girlfriend. She'd done tonight as a favor, and he'd broken his one promise. And *she* was overreacting?

"I didn't mean it about you." His unconvincing tone betrayed him.

Like having ex-lovers around was something that should be easy to deal with. Like she didn't have better options.

She folded her arms. "How would you like it if I marched Sam in here and told you I slept with him?"

Jem's face went white.

The time bomb that'd been ticking in Natalie's brain all week exploded into a hot rush of fury. "Of course I didn't. But how did that feel? You know what? Just forget it." She grabbed her handbag and keys. This was too hard. "I can't do this anymore. Consider this my resignation."

He swallowed, plopped Olly down in his playpen. "Just like that? You're leaving?"

"As if you can talk about leaving." She stomped toward the door. "Look, I thought maybe I could forgive you, but—"

"No, you didn't."

"What?" She spun to face him.

He stepped closer and lowered his voice. "You thought you could forget. Not forgive. There's a difference." He strode away from her toward his bedroom.

Natalie set her jaw. Typical Jem. Walking away from her. She stormed out and slammed the door.

Beyond the closed portal, Oliver cried again.

23

Natalie's sobs had just hit the ugly-cry stage when her phone rang. Still parked at Jem's apartment block after that disastrous dinner, she fumbled around the passenger seat, eventually reaching under an inflatable frog—a festival prop—to pull the vibrating cell out.

"Hey, Nat, do you remember where we left that paper bag full of bolts?" Sam's cheery voice sounded from the speakers. "Once I find it, I thought I'd go grab a tub of Strawberry Sensation if you're still up for it."

She opened her mouth to reply, but a sob came out instead.

"Nat?" Sam's tone changed to concern. "Are you alright?"

"I'm okay," she gasped, but couldn't manage much more.

"I'll come get you. Are you still at Jem's?" He'd given her a lift from there once before when her car was on the fritz, so he knew where it was.

"Yeah."

"I'll be there in five."

She dropped the phone atop a pile of candy wrappers in her console and rested her forehead against the steering wheel. Slapped the dashboard three times.

How could she have let this happen? Jem reentered her life and here she was again, crying in her car. Maybe this time she'd learn her lesson.

Vehicles zoomed past, and she sat up. Sam would be here any minute. She dug through her glove box for a tissue and found only her emergency stash of personal products. Well, this was a different type of emergency, but an emergency nonetheless. She wiped the mascara from her cheeks and blew her nose, then hid the mess back in her glove box.

Headlights spilled over the dark asphalt ahead, and a rusty Chevy pulled in beside her. She walked around to where Sam wound down his window and surreptitiously swiped her sleeve past her nose.

Sam had donned his red flannel shirt again. It matched the faded paint on his truck. He leaned out the window and scanned her. "This looks serious. Do we have a Dreamy Dark Chocolate situation on our hands?"

She leaned on the hood of her car. "I'm sorry, I shouldn't have called you. You've still got so much to do." And she was crying over her ex. In front of the guy she'd gone out with this week.

"I called you, remember? And it'll keep. Get in. It's cold out." He reached across and popped the passenger door handle.

She slid into the warm vehicle and glanced around. "So this is how you roll."

Dress-up costumes covered the back seat, a layer of sports equipment sprinkled on top. A crate of snack foods leaned against the left rear window, and a black duffel bag with drumsticks poking out was jammed into the foot well.

Something crunched beneath her foot, and she tried not to look.

"You never know when you'll need a feather boa and a hockey stick." He backed the Chevy onto the road. "Your dad okay?"

"Yeah."

"Jem? Oliver?"

"They're fine . . . physically, anyway." Well, except for Olly's flu.

She picked a piece of lint from her sweater. "It's not a very interesting story."

Sam tutted and shook his head. "Everything about you seems to be interesting. And you and Jem have a . . . well, a unique situation." A tactful way to put it, without a hint of malice for her ex. Her esteem for him rose another notch.

She gave a short, humorless chuckle. "You could say that." She paused, trying to think of a way to be honest without saying, "I'm crying about my ex and the woman he moved on with." She smoothed a hand over her jeans and tried. "Obviously my relationship with Jem is long in the past." Because kissing didn't count as a relationship. "But working for him reminds me of a pretty rough year after our engagement ended." She twisted her fingers together. Should she say more?

"And . . ."

"And?"

He slid her a look. "You've worked for him for weeks. There must've been a trigger that made tonight harder."

She bit her lip. "Oliver's mother is back in town. And that makes bad memories . . . amplify."

"Ouch." He glanced at her.

She sighed. "I'm sorry. You don't want to hear about this."

"Hey." He nudged her with his elbow. "What kind of friend would I be if I didn't?"

She came uncorked. "I mean, we were long over when Chloe became pregnant, but that doesn't mean . . . It's still not an easy thing if your ex-fiancé has a baby with someone else, right? Especially someone so perfect. I don't know. Maybe I did overreact." She sniffed and tucked her cold hands beneath her thighs. "I said I'd tried to forgive him, and Jem got mad. He said all I'd tried to do was forget. I don't even get what the difference is."

Sam flashed his turn signal in the opposite direction of Bloop.

"Where are you going?"

"If we're going to get deep, yogurt won't cut it. I need real sugar. I need a Macca's soft serve." He pulled into a McDonald's drive-thru line behind a dusty van and faced her. "So you want to understand forgiveness? Nice to see you picked an easy one to test me on."

She smiled. No wonder kids found him easy to talk to. "More or less."

"Any part specifically you're struggling with?"

"I've tried it. Every day I tell myself that I forgive him, that I'm past this. It doesn't work."

"What would make it feel better? Besides rewriting the past."

"I'd want him to feel the same thing I felt!" The words burst out with more venom than she'd like. *Rein it in.* She took a calming breath. "But I know it wouldn't help. I'm not normally this bitter."

Sam passed a few coins through his window to the drive-thru operator and accepted two cones. He passed her one and took a generous lick of his own.

When he'd parked the car in the lot, he gave her his full attention. "You're right, it wouldn't help. It would be fair, but it wouldn't bring back what you've lost. It would just make two sad people and wasted years."

She took a lick from the top of her soft-serve swirl. "But how do you just let something like this go?"

"First of all, I think we should establish that no one's equating forgiveness with necessarily trusting Jem." Sam waited till she met his eyes before continuing. "When a person hurts you, you don't have to give them the chance to do that again. Jem's right. It's different from forgetting."

She licked a drip that threatened to spill from her cone. Sam had finished his in about three bites. "But how do I get past the I-hate-Jeremy-Walters stage?"

"Have you tried saying it out loud?"

She blinked. "What?"

He twisted her cone to show her another imminent drip. "Say it out loud. 'I forgive Jeremy Walters.'"

"I—" The words stuck in her throat. She breathed out a shaky laugh. "This is ridiculous." She'd thought the words a hundred times. Why was it so hard to say them?

"Harder than it sounds, right? Pray about it. Forgiveness doesn't come naturally." He turned the ignition. "No one ever said it was easy. Only possible—with some divine help."

He dropped her back at her car and said goodbye with a friendly wave.

Natalie jumped behind the wheel and cranked the engine. A headache from crying pounded on the back of her eyeballs, and she had a week's worth of sleep to catch up on before the barbecue tomorrow. She could deal with the Jem problem after a solid eight hours in oblivion.

She zoomed along the dark streets toward home and cranked the radio. The Fray's soothing lyrics calmed her nerves.

Red-and-blue lights flashed in her rearview mirror.

She bit back a curse and slowed until she found a spot to pull over. Footsteps crunched in the gravel behind her as she rolled down her window. "Sorry, Officer—" Her words halted as she looked up at the man by her window. "John? What are you doing?"

"I volunteered for a shift and sent an officer back home to his family." He gave a grimace that was maybe intended to be a smile. "Nothing like a good deed to cheer you up."

"He just wanted to impress you, you know." The words escaped before she could stop them.

"With what? His former lover, burned food, or the child sick on sugar?"

"Would it kill you to tell him he's done a good job? Or at least tried to?" Mad as she was, even she could see that.

John set his jaw. "When he does a good job, I'll tell him."

"Are you just trying to punish him for leaving you?" Realization slapped her as the final word left her mouth. *Hypocrite.* She swiveled her gaze to the road ahead. "Forget it. Just write me the ticket."

John handed her the fine and crunched his way back to his car.

Tears streamed down Natalie's face as she completed the short drive home, then wet the pillow beneath her cheek as she fell asleep.

The fabric was still damp when her ringtone jerked her awake. The alarm clock beside her bed glowed 1:53 a.m.

She snatched up the phone. "Hello?"

"Natalie." The shudder in Lili's voice catapulted her out of bed and halfway into her jeans before the teenager finished her sentence. "We're on our way to the hospital. Olly's really sick."

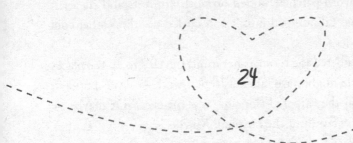

24

*D*ad was missing.

Lili's footsteps echoed against the tiles in her empty house. It was almost 2:00 a.m. Jem had dropped her here on his way to the hospital, assuming—as she had—that Dad was home. She twisted the hem of her purple polka-dot pajamas between her fingers, worrying her lip as she surveyed the living room.

She'd checked the whole house. Her parents' bedspread lay undisturbed, Dad's keys weren't on the hook by the door, and his favorite shoes were missing.

"Dad?"

No reply.

Something creaked, and Lili started. Phone in hand, she double-checked the locks as she called her father's cell. The call rang out and dropped to voice mail. "Dad, Oliver's sick so Jem dropped me home. Where are you? I'm getting worried." She tried the church phone next as she felt her way down the dark hall. Same result.

She reached Dad's office, felt through the doorway, and hit the light switch. Yellow light flooded the room, illuminating his massive cherrywood desk and leather chair. The desk matched his bookcase, both new pieces Mom purchased during last year's redecoration. But the chair, with worn patches rubbed on both armrests and the seat, matched nothing. Lili jumped into it and curled up, the leather cool against her bare legs.

Her eyes wandered the room as her mind traveled to all the places Dad could be. He might have fallen asleep at work—he was prone to stretching out on the carpeted floor to "rest his eyes." Or maybe he was with a church family at the hospital. Maybe . . .

A familiar plaster finger caught her eye, resting in the ajar bottom drawer of Dad's desk. She nudged the drawer open.

A hundred webbed cracks ran through the painted plaster cast that sat atop a pile of old Bible-study workbooks. She picked it up and held it inches from her face. It was an enlarged impression of her father's handprint at double size, painted shades of red. Inside his palm was Mom's handprint, dotted with a pattern of light-blue shades, at one and a half times its real dimensions. Mom's hand contained Lili's real-sized handprint in a swirl of purple.

She'd seen this artwork not just crack, but shatter, the day she'd busted Dad with Miss Kent.

Something red caught her eye in the drawer beneath. She peered down. The lid of a super-glue tube.

"Dad, you fixed it?" She ran her fingers over the artwork.

She placed the art back in the drawer and eased it shut, then returned to Dad's chair and rested her forehead on his desk.

She could have been wrong, that day in the church when she smoked. Maybe Miss Kent really had been in the bathroom. Maybe Dad had told the truth about his cigarettes.

The super glue, and hours he must have spent using it, didn't lie. She'd thought Dad's fling with Miss Kent meant he didn't care about their family—Lili included—but this . . . Maybe she had been wrong.

Her intestines twisted like a well-wrung cloth. Where was Dad? What if he'd crashed his car or something? She had to tell him she was sorry.

An idea sparked, and she grabbed for Dad's keyboard. Her fingers flew across the keys until the login screen for Dad's Find My Phone service came up on the screen. She typed *Lilianna* into the password box and hit Enter.

The computer searched for his location, and Lili chewed her fingernails and prayed.

An unfamiliar address popped up. The hair on the back of her neck raised. She copied the address, dumped it in the Google search bar, and brought up the Street View image of a house. A rosebush peeked over its fence and white wicker furniture rested on the porch.

Miss Kent's house.

Lili punched the desk and screamed.

Then she dialed Mom's number.

♡

Natalie gunned her Bug to its limits on the way to the hospital. Who cared if John prowled the streets? He could kiss her taillights.

She screeched to a halt in the hospital parking lot and scanned for Jem's Camry. There. She sprinted across the asphalt.

Jem held Olly, bundled in a blanket, in his right arm as he locked the car with his left.

Natalie screeched to a halt beside them. "Is he alright?" She reached for Olly, and Jem shifted him so they held him together.

The little boy opened his eyes, and a small smile lit his face. He lifted a hand in her direction, but it fell back against the blanket.

Jem tucked his fingers back into the warm flannel. "He got really lethargic after you left, and I googled his symptoms. I need to make sure it's not something serious."

"Where's Lili?" Natalie brushed her finger over Oliver's smooth cheek. No fever.

"I dropped her at her parents' on the way over. Steph's away at the conference in Philadelphia, but Mike should be home. He didn't answer his phone, but most people don't at 2:00 a.m. I made sure Lili got into the house before I left."

Natalie's skin pinched into goose bumps as a sharp breeze blew from the north. She'd run out the door in yesterday's jeans, flip-flops, and the first T-shirt she grabbed from a pile of unfolded laundry.

Jem ran his hand over her upper arm. "You don't have to be here if you don't want. I'm sorry. I shouldn't have had Lili call you."

Natalie tightened her grip on the baby. "Don't be stupid. Of course I should be here."

He gave her a brief squeeze. "Let's get inside."

The antiseptic hospital smell speared Natalie's senses as they crossed the threshold. Panic clawed at her throat. Every time she smelled that scent, something painful happened. Dad's diagnosis, his relapse, and that close call they'd had two years ago.

She glanced around the room as Jem spoke with the nurse. Cold, sterile, unsympathetic. Just like the woman Jem was talking to.

The nurse handed him a form and pointed to a chair. "Fill this out and wait over there."

"Are you serious?" Natalie leaned forward. "He's only a baby. He's sick."

The woman didn't even glance up. "Tell that to the guy whose friend can't aim a nail gun." She nodded toward a patient.

They swung their gazes to a disheveled man hobbling through the heavy doors that separated the emergency department from examination rooms. He held an ice pack to his groin.

Jem paled. "We'll wait."

He led Natalie to two plastic chairs and passed Oliver to her. Olly didn't stir, just lay limp in his blanket.

"I thought the doctor said antibiotics would fix it, and that if he's still eating and drinking, it would be okay," she said.

"I know. I told Lili I'm being paranoid." Jem kept his focus on the paperwork.

"What aren't you saying?"

He signed the final box and stood. "Google is scary."

She cuddled the baby against her chest. What if he had some sort of childhood cancer? Possibilities swarmed her mind like fire ants. She curled around the bundle in her lap and tried to pray, but no words came to mind.

You know what you have to do.

Eyes closed and face buried against Olly, she paid no attention to Jem until he brushed her side as he sat down. She unraveled herself and shifted so Olly lay half on her lap and half on Jem's.

They watched his son, cradled between them.

"Jem, I have to tell you something."

He shifted, Chicago Bears hoodie warm against her bare arm. "I'm sorry about tonight."

"No, that's not—I mean, yes, I'm sorry too. But that's not what I wanted to say." She pulled back till she could look him in the eye. "I talked to Sam after you left—"

His left eye twitched.

"—and I ran into your dad. Between the two of them I got reminded of some things. I did some serious thinking. And . . . I . . ." She took a deep breath and shot up a prayer for help. "This is something I need to say out loud: I forgive you."

He stared at her. "What?"

"I understand what you meant about the difference between forgetting and forgiving, and I forgive you."

A glassy sheen came over Jem's eyes before he blinked it away. "Thank you," he whispered.

She smiled at him for a moment. Saying it didn't mean it wasn't hard anymore. It didn't mean she entertained the thought of a future with Jem. No, she couldn't get sucked into his vortex again.

But it was a weight off her soul.

He shifted Olly onto her lap, gripped the hem of his hoodie, and pulled it over his head. "Here." He swapped it for the baby.

She pulled the fleece on, inhaling Jem's scent as she did so. Still warm from his body, it enveloped her frame.

Jem, wearing his blue shirt from dinner, shifted so she could lean against him and still reach Olly.

She placed her index finger in the baby's palm and closed her eyes.

When she opened them again, it was to squint up at the cranky nurse.

"They're ready for you now."

The nurse led them to an examination room and pointed to two even more uncomfortable plastic chairs. Natalie jigged her foot against the ground as the woman grilled Jem on Olly's symptoms.

Jem rattled through Olly's unusual thirstiness, vomiting, and lack of energy. "The doctor gave us antibiotics, but they didn't do anything." He paused. "Tonight my father noticed that his breath smells sweet. And when I checked on him at 1:00 a.m., he'd saturated the bed . . . and that smelled sweet too."

The lines on the nurse's face deepened. She hefted her body from the chair, ducked beyond the curtain, and returned with a small black machine in one hand, a pen-like object in the other. "Hold out his hand."

Natalie frowned as Jem did so. "Why?"

The woman held the pen up to Olly's hand and it clicked. Olly jolted, screamed.

"What are you doing?" Natalie reached for Olly, but Jem grabbed her hand.

The nurse held a thin strip of paper up to the red spot below his thumb, then inserted the paper in the handheld machine. The machine beeped, and the nurse's eyes widened. "Excuse me. I need to get the doctor." She swept past the curtain.

Natalie grabbed Olly from Jem's arms and bounced him against her shoulder. "What was that all about? Why is the sweet smell important? You didn't tell me that before."

Jem rubbed a hand over Olly's back as he settled back down. "When I googled all his symptoms, the computer lit up with a hundred thousand results, pretty much all saying the same thing."

"What?"

"I think he has—"

The curtain swept aside, and a man with a gray mustache and brown toupee strode in. "Mr. and Mrs. Walters," he said.

Natalie didn't correct him.

"I need to run some more tests for confirmation, but you should know . . . we think your son could have diabetes."

25

ili? What time is it?" Mom's groggy voice brought a wave of tears to Lili's vision. Dad's computer screen blurred. "M—Mom, it's about Dad," she sobbed.

A crash sounded at the other end of the connection. "What's wrong? Is he alright? Just let me switch on the lamp. I knocked it over." A rustle sounded, then a click. "What's going on?"

"I-I should have t-t-told you earlier, but he said he was going to talk to you. I wasn't certain, and I thought—or I hoped—he was telling me the truth, b-but—"

"Lili, tell me what's happening." Mom's voice was firm but not harsh.

She gulped back a sob. "Dad's having an affair."

The clock on Dad's wall ticked—one, two, three, four.

"I know."

"You *know*?" Lili sucked in a breath, then another. A tingle buzzed through her fingers, and her head floated two inches above where it should be. Was she hallucinating right now? How could Mom have *known*? "F-for how long?" The photos on the wall twisted and danced. "Mom, I feel dizzy."

"You're hyperventilating, Lili. Slow your breathing down."

She stared at Dad's bookshelf as she counted to three, breathing out, then in. A silver-framed photo of their family at Disney World sat at eye level. Mom, green from one too many Space Mountain rides, Dad with half a churro shoved in his mouth and looking cross-eyed at the camera, and eleven-year-old Lili laughing at him. Happy.

Now never again.

She twisted the cord of her pajama pants round her finger till it turned purple. "What are you going to do?" Her voice wobbled.

"I need you to do something for me, Lili, and you might not understand at first, but I want you to promise me."

Poor Mom, knowing something this awful and pretending nothing was wrong. Anything she could do to help . . . "Okay. Promise."

"Don't tell anyone."

Was she *serious*? "What? Why? People should know what two-faced liars they are." She stabbed a pencil against a notebook, and the lead snapped off.

There was a pause. "You know who she is?"

Lili's insides clenched at the waver in Mom's voice. "Yeah."

"Don't tell me. I don't want to know."

A question burned to escape. "Are you going to get a divorce?" She held her breath.

"Not if I can help it."

She breathed easier even as disgust curled her lip. "How can you stay with him after what he's done? Do you still love him?"

"It's complicated."

"No, it's not."

"I can't be a divorced woman!" The words flew out of Mom like a squeezed watermelon seed. "I'll lose my job, my ministry."

The church fallout was going to be . . . Yikes. But Mom hadn't done anything wrong. "Dad will, you won't."

"Who goes to a divorced woman for relationship advice, Lili? The church wants good role models to be its leaders, not people who couldn't keep their family together. No one would look at me the same." Mom's voice cracked. "And I've only ever worked in the church. I don't know how to do anything else. I don't even have friends outside our congregation."

Tears slipped from beneath Lili's eyelids as she looked at the Disney World photo again. It had all been a lie. Dad didn't want them anymore.

"I'll do it on one condition," she said.

"What?"

"Don't look in Dad's office when you get home."

"Deal."

♡

Lili seized an armful of papers from the bottom drawer of Dad's filing cabinet and tossed them into the air. A papery blizzard raged around her. She'd just emptied the entire cabinet in less than two minutes.

Pain registered. A paper cut sliced down her index finger, thin and red. Her throat ached the way it always did before she cried. Sermon notes and church budgets fluttered down around her.

She curled up on the paper-covered floor and sobbed till the tax return beneath her face turned soggy.

How could Dad have done this? Did he care that little for her and Mom?

She pounded the floor and screamed again. She'd tried to be the perfect daughter. Her grades were flawless, and even her math had improved. With the exception of the smoking incident, her behavior had been exemplary. She had no bad friends. No boyfriend. Didn't party. Wore a skirt to church every week and had taught Sunday school for two years.

Apparently that wasn't enough to make Dad love her.

Fire surged through Lili's veins. She bounced up from the floor and attacked Dad's desk drawers. When a notebook, calculator, and stash of jellybeans fell from drawer number three, a small black cylinder rolled from the top of the pile. She dropped the drawer and grabbed it. Red lipstick. Definitely not Mom's.

Lili pulled Dad's leather-bound Life Application Bible from the towering pile of books on the edge of his desk. A small nudge sent the rest of the pile crashing to the floor. She plopped the Bible in the center of the desk. Uncapping the toffee apple-red lipstick, she scrawled across the page.

Liar.

The lipstick worked like a giant crayon, its red stain smudging the holy pages.

Her gaze landed on the cream office wall before her.

Cheater.

Dad's massive bookcase covered the third wall, and his filing cabinet and a cupboard blocked most of the fourth. But the back of his door was an untouched canvas.

I hate you.

She squished the remaining lipstick against the wall, then dropped the pulverized red mash. A sweep of the hand sent Dad's bookshelf photographs tumbling to the ground, and she yanked every book from its place. The corner of an Old Testament commentary landed on her big toe. She yelped and jumped backward. Biting back a curse word, she clenched her fist against the roll of pain.

A thought whispered from the back of her brain. Why not curse? It wasn't like God loved her either.

Lili shouted every curse word she knew and looked around for anything left to destroy. A pair of scissors suggested themselves from Dad's desktop. She picked them up and turned to Dad's chair.

Dad's favorite leather chair.

She pressed the blade against the leather. A hot tear splashed onto her hand. She gripped the scissors tighter.

She could do it . . .

She should do it . . .

Throwing the scissors aside, she collapsed to her knees, face pressed against the seat. Her tears soaked the yellow foam that poked out from cracks in the worn cushion.

This chair belonged to the father who'd smuggled her chocolate-chip ice cream when Mom sent her to bed without supper. The man who'd danced with her at the elementary school ball. The one who bought her new paints last November, for no other reason than to see her smile.

She couldn't destroy it yet.

Lili dragged the back of her hand across her face and rose on unsteady feet.

She screenshot the Find My Phone map, printed it, and laid it on the keyboard.

Uncapping a red pen with her teeth, she scribbled on the bottom of the page.

> Dad, Oliver was really sick so Jem dropped me home. I got worried when you weren't here.
>
> I'm not worried anymore.
>
> P.S. Mom knows.

She dropped the pen on the desk and left the room, shutting the door behind her.

26

A warning alarm buzzed close to Jem's ear. He jerked his head up from where it rested on the hospital wall. What piece of medical equipment was that?

He squirmed upright in the large window seat of Olly's hospital room, Natalie's head limp on his shoulder. Careful not to wake her, Jem viewed the machines in the room. Predawn sunlight filtered through the window, devoid of warmth. Despite the tubes coming out of Olly, so small and still in the hospital crib, he couldn't figure out which contraption made the racket. They'd been shifted to a private room sometime around 3:00 a.m., so the alarm couldn't be coming from anyone else's machine.

The sound rang out again, and he looked at the pocket on his hoodie—the one Natalie was wearing. It vibrated.

"Nat, wake up." He jostled her and brushed the navy hood back from her head.

She sat bolt upright. "What's wrong?"

"Answer your phone."

She fumbled for it. "It's Mom." She looked at Olly, clearly torn.

"Go. I'll watch him."

She pressed the answer button. "Mom?" She slipped out of the room.

Jem stood and stretched, working out the kinks from a night spent in chairs that made a torturer's rack look comfortable. Resting his hands on the rail of Olly's crib, he gazed at his son.

Olly wore a baby-sized hospital gown—Natalie had held on to his blue "I'm Dad's favorite" onesie ever since the nurses changed him out of it. His white-blond hair blended in with the pillow, cheeks barely a few shades lighter.

Jem stroked the soft skin of one of them, noted the lack of chubbiness. Olly had lost much of his baby fat in recent weeks. Jem had attributed the change to a growth spurt—he'd seen friends' babies suddenly grow up instead of out. But the doctor said the change—as well as Olly's ravenous hunger and thirst—had not been due to growth but the fact that his body could no longer draw energy from his food. It was Olly's internal reserves, stored in fat, that had kept him going so far.

His own stomach growled, and he winced. His son had been starving, and he hadn't noticed. How could he have missed the signs?

He expelled a breath and shook his head. Even the family doctor had gotten it wrong, prescribing antibiotics.

Footsteps sounded in the hall, approached the door.

"What did your mom sa—" The words froze in Jem's throat.

Chloe stood before him, hair tousled and no trace of makeup on her face. She wore gray sweats and had mismatched ballet flats on her feet.

Jem stared. He'd never seen her in such a state, not even when they were dating.

"I got your message that he was here. What's wrong?" She made no move toward Olly, but a tremor rang in her voice.

"They say he has diabetes." His voice came out wooden, just fact, no emotion. He couldn't make it sink in.

She swore.

Still comprehending that she'd shown up—looking like this, no less—he took her elbow and led her to his chair, taking Natalie's seat himself.

Chloe's eyes remained glued to the little boy on the bed. "Is he going to die?"

Jem flinched. "It has risks, especially if his blood sugar drops too far, but if we manage it carefully he should be okay. But he'll have to take insulin for the rest of his life."

Her hand went to her stomach. "Is it genetic?"

"I think so. Dad's brother has the same thing." That little fact had clicked in his brain somewhere around 4:30 a.m. as he stared at his son in the dark.

She looked at Olly, still motionless on the bed, and her face crumpled. "Richard t-told me this w-w-was a bad idea." She kept talking, but it came out in a mumble he couldn't decipher.

"As in your ex, Richard?" She'd mentioned him—quite a bit, now that he thought about it—back in Chicago.

"Now my fiancé." She pulled a ring from her right hand and slipped it onto her left. The diamond sparkled, even in dull fluorescent light. "We got back together not long after . . ." Her eyes darted away from Olly. "We got engaged two months ago." She shrugged. "He doesn't want to do the blended-family thing, but I had to come check on Oliver."

Jem's neck heated. The guy was pressuring her to stay away because he didn't want to do "the blended-family thing"? What kind of man did that?

Memories crashed through him—comments she'd made sitting outside the doctor's office, an offhand remark from her mother. Chloe had been two years younger than him—twenty-four, newly graduated and ambitious—when she fell pregnant. He'd known she was under pressure from outside forces not to be a mother. But he hadn't realized to what extent. A fresh wave of gratitude flooded him that she'd given him his son.

He grasped her hand. "The question isn't what Richard wants. It's what's best for Olly, and for you. You . . . can be a part of his life."

The words didn't want to come out. Sharing custody would mean less time with his son. Probably another move.

But like he said, it wasn't about him.

Her eyes filled again, and she dashed a hand across her face. "I'll— I'll remember." She drew a deep breath and calmed herself. "Where's Natalie?"

He blinked at the change of topic. "On the phone with her mother. She's been here all night."

"She's a good woman."

"She is." His gaze went to the door Natalie had disappeared through, and he silently thanked God that he'd asked Lili to call her last night.

"She's a good mother."

Jem looked back to Chloe. Where was she going with this? "She's . . . not my girlfriend." He couldn't quite bring himself to say "seeing someone else."

"I hope I haven't messed that up for you."

"I've messed up plenty on my own." His tone was rueful.

"You're a good father."

Yeah, a father who didn't notice his son had a chronic disease. He ran a hand over his face. "It doesn't feel like it."

"I mean it." She stopped and looked at Oliver. "And I'm sorry about this week. I know I was demanding. And awful to Natalie." A wry smile poked through. "I'll admit, some of it was on purpose. I wanted to see how she did under pressure. How you both did."

A flicker of movement caught his eye, and his gaze darted to the door. A Natalie-shaped shadow shifted, then stilled. He scratched his lip to cover a smile. "I wondered."

"I think Natalie nearly skinned me once or twice, but that's good. She'll fight for what she wants. And tell her she's got a knack for graphic design. I was just being catty. This festival she's organizing sounds terrific." A chuckle burst out. "And tell her I'm impressed that Olly can pass wind on demand."

Jem's mouth opened, but no sound came out. What had gone on during that day she'd spent with Nat?

"Thank you," he managed.

Chloe ran a hand through her hair, straightening the mess. Her tone changed to businesslike. "If you don't want to, you never have to hear from me again. Richard doesn't want me getting involved. But . . . if it's okay, I wouldn't mind an email with a photo every now and then."

Both relief and grief swelled inside. Yes, things were less complicated if she stayed away. But Olly would miss out on knowing someone who—ideal circumstances or not—was important to him.

But it was her decision.

"That's okay." He touched her arm. "I'll be honest with him and tell him who you are. If he wants to meet you—again, that is—it'll be up to him."

She nodded, scrubbed her sleeve over her face. "I have a plane to catch. I'll send you the official paperwork from Chicago." She paused. "If it wasn't for Natalie, I'd stay, but I think the two of you have him well covered."

"I'll let you know how he does."

She looked toward the door, then back to the crib, her face pinched. "I didn't want to get attached . . . but could you give him a kiss good-bye for me?" She rushed from the room before Jem could respond.

He stared at the empty doorway. Shook his head. That was the second time in two years Chloe had left him and Oliver in a hospital, alone.

Natalie's head poked around the doorframe. He smiled.

Not alone.

"How long were you standing there?"

"Long enough. I hid around the corner when she left." As she drew closer, the tear tracks on her face reflected rising sunlight.

He fought the urge to reach for her. "Hey, it's okay. I know this is major, but he'll be okay."

She shook her head. "It's not that." She lifted her watery gaze to his. "Mom said Dad's had a bad turn."

♡

Natalie picked lint from Jem's hoodie as she paced the hospital hallway, waiting for Dad to be transferred to his room. She checked her watch. Nine fifteen a.m. Two hours and forty-five minutes until the festival was due to start.

She sniffed. Her nose had turned into a tap. Where was a tissue when you needed one?

Sam's phone went to voice mail again.

"Natalie."

She whipped around to the sound of Steph's voice from behind.

Steph's heels clacked on the floor as she approached, arms outstretched. "I got your message. How's your dad?"

Natalie accepted her hug and used the moment to clear her throat. Never mind last night's fiasco, her stress over Olly, gritty eyes from no sleep, and now a terror that gripped her every time a doctor walked past with a grim face.

Now was not the time to be emotional.

"I'm waiting to hear. But I needed to talk to you about the festival. I'm not going to be able to leave."

The words were hard to say. Surely this would only increase Kimberly's lead in their race for that permanent position. But there was no question about where she'd spend today.

With Dad.

Steph nodded, face grim. "I thought you'd say that. I teed up Kimberly, just in case. She can run things with Sam."

Natalie rubbed her irritated eyes and nodded. It couldn't be helped.

"But I thought you should know—" Steph hesitated, then placed a gentle palm on Natalie's arm. "I've been chatting with some of the board members. They're beginning to lean in Kimberly's direction."

Natalie swayed against the wall behind her. How much bad news could a body absorb in twenty-four hours?

Steph shrugged. "Sam's in your corner, obviously. But he only has so much influence. I just thought you should know."

Natalie closed her eyes and counted to ten. The world was too loud, her feet in these flip-flops were too cold, and she was one stubbed toe away from lying down in the middle of this floor and having a good cry.

Deep breaths.

As she tried to regain her zen, a thought hit her. "Aren't you supposed to be at a conference?"

Something flickered across Steph's expression. Come to think of it, she didn't look too hot either. Her face showed more lines than usual, and she radiated tension. She wrapped her cashmere jacket more tightly around her. "I came home early. Just got in, actually. Lili's in the car."

"Okay. Good." At least they knew Lili was fine for now.

"Nattie." Mom rounded the corner of the corridor, today's sweat suit a lime green that clashed with her red Sketchers.

Natalie straightened. Steph squeezed her shoulder. "Just let me know when you can come back. You can still give Kimberly a run for her money."

Maybe. But her underdog status was now obvious to all.

She nodded her thanks and walked toward Mom, who looked calm. But Mom had been a nurse. She always looked calm, no matter how bad the news was.

Natalie dug her nails into her palm as she approached. "How's Dad?"

"Asking for you."

She breathed a sigh of relief. He was responsive, then.

"And?"

"And he's more worried about you missing your festival than he is about the fact I couldn't rouse him this morning."

Natalie smiled, despite herself. "That sounds like Dad."

"Were you able to organize something?"

"Kimberly's going to take my place." Hopefully not in more ways than one.

Mom nodded. "I'll tell him. He doesn't want to hurt your chances for this job. He's so excited about it."

Natalie's smile turned fragile. "Tell him it'll be fine. I've got it under control."

Had she claimed to leap tall buildings in a single bound, it could not have been more untrue. But one thing was certain: as soon as Dad recovered, she'd work harder than Kimberly ever could to make sure she got this job.

27

Jem needed a plan, and the only one he could think of depended on the sleep-deprived woman sitting at his kitchen counter. And his ability to convince her.

Meanwhile, the pink-and-purple-clad *Mommy and Me* workout instructor on Jem's laptop screen made this exercise look way too easy. She held her bow-adorned baby in front of her and executed ten squats in a pristine living room. "A-one, a-two . . ."

Jem kicked a stuffed toy out of the way on the living room floor, held a fussing Oliver out in front of him, and tried to follow suit as Natalie heckled from her stool at the counter.

"You're doomed. He's teething."

From the corner of his eye, he could see her flip open a tiny mirror from her handbag and apply lipstick.

"Focus on the main topic here," he puffed out between squats.

He'd had an epiphany at some point during the long hours in the hospital this week, reflecting on that mess of a dinner with Dad. He'd never been able to please his father. But that didn't mean Dad couldn't be a part of Olly's life.

Enter Natalie.

She'd been a lifesaver this week, coming with him to the hospital's training sessions in between visiting with her dad. Her father had given them a scare last week when he lapsed into unconsciousness, but now he was back at home.

Jem wobbled on squat number eight. "Just one playdate. Take them both to the park or something. Let them spend some time together."

She fluffed her hair, the scent of fresh perfume drifting over to Jem in the living room. "Do you pay me extra if I nanny both your son and your father?"

"I pay on a per-diaper basis."

Squats done, he held Olly closer and bounced him. This kid did not enjoy being used as a dumbbell.

Natalie scowled at a spot on her shirt. He tilted his head as he watched her. "What are you getting ready for? I thought the reason I had to be home early this afternoon was Lili's after-school tutoring and your appointment." What kind of appointment required this much fussing?

A knock sounded at the door.

Natalie flushed a little. "Actually, the appointment is . . . well, a date with Sam. He's flying out to Georgia tonight to speak at some schools, so we're just catching a quick bite before he heads to the plane."

Oh.

Great. Because it wasn't like he thought of her kisses every five seconds. Why wouldn't he love to see her new boyfriend pick her up for a date?

She moved toward the door. "I was going to go down. I didn't think he was coming up."

She opened the door, and the young preacher was there, all smiles and exotic accent. He nodded in Jem's direction. "How are ya, mate?"

Jem regretted every friendly chat they'd had about boxing. "Just peachy, thanks." He held Olly out again and raised him above his head, if only for something else to look at.

Natalie and Sam departed, and Jem huffed to himself. Watching Natalie date Sam was about as delightful as second-degree sunburn on a long-haul flight. Who had he been kidding with this Natalie solution for Dad? She'd be gone as soon as she landed that job at Wildfire—which seemed likely, now that she was dating the founder.

He kicked at Oliver's plush Daffy Duck. It wasn't a fair thought. She'd get the job on merit. She was a fantastic organizer. But he had to be mad at something, and being angry with himself was getting boring.

No, it was time to face facts. He'd never fix things with either Natalie or Dad.

He looked at his grizzling son. "Come on, Olly. Enough with this *Mommy and Me* rubbish. Let's run like men." He pulled on his worn sneakers, left a note for Lili, who'd returned to his apartment when Oliver came home from the hospital, and wrestled Oliver's stroller downstairs. At least the bouncing kept the baby entertained.

At the ground floor, his phone buzzed. An email from work.

Congratulations! You have been awarded the Team Player of the Year award.

He blinked and read it again. The newspaper's annual award ceremony—and he was getting an award?

He took off down the street at an easy jog and rolled the news around his mind like a Gobstopper candy.

He'd done it. After that confidence-rattling layoff and a rough start, he'd proven his worth as a reporter. The career had been his dream since he first visited the newspaper office as an eight-year-old with Gramps. His mother's father had been a journalist back in the days when newspapers were printed using linotype machines, and young Jem had been captivated by his stories—by the man, really.

Jem passed the one-mile mark and slowed to a walk. Parenthood had left him horribly out of shape. And the thought was one that required energy to ponder.

Gramps had been the best. There hadn't been anything particularly amazing about his grandfather to an outsider, but Jem well remembered his childish wonder at how someone could be so old and know so much. Getting to "help" Gramps in the garden, fixing Gran's chair, or walking the dog had been the pinnacle of his young existence.

Olly needed that.

Jem picked up his pace again.

Two miles later, as Jem wrestled the stroller back up the stairs, he'd come to a decision. For now, he was giving up on running. But he'd give Dad one more shot.

He cleaned himself and Oliver off in the shower and was still in his room fastening the last snap on Olly's jumpsuit when a key scratched at the door. Must be Lili.

But when the door opened, he didn't hear the usual ten steps across the dining nook and kitchen and then the bang of Lili's door.

He peered out into the living area, Olly now content in his arms. "Natalie?"

"Forgot my laptop." She called the words out, then pressed her phone back to her ear. "Yeah, Mom, I'm here. What did you say?"

Jem scanned her for hints as to how the date had gone. Sam must be on his plane by now. She didn't look either upset or ecstatically happy. Jem pressed his lips together. These were the times in life when a Sherlock Holmes would come in super handy.

Natalie froze, phone still glued to her ear.

Jem crossed the room. What was wrong?

A hand flew to her mouth as she listened to whatever her mother was saying. "O-okay. I'll be right over." She lowered the phone, tears in her eyes.

"Nat?" Jem dropped Olly in his high chair. "What's wrong?"

"It's Dad." Tears spiked her eyelashes. "The test results came in. The cancer's back, and he doesn't have long."

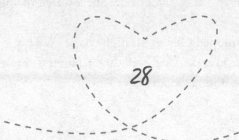

28

I've got you now."

Lili slammed Miss Kent's laptop lid down at the sound of a voice near the art room door.

It had been a week since they rushed Oliver to the hospital, since she learned the truth about Dad and Miss Kent. In that week, she'd successfully cold-shouldered her father and snooped around for evidence he was still seeing her trampy teacher. But had she been busted?

Nick sauntered through the doorway, wearing a Captain America T-shirt and thumbs hooked in the straps of his backpack.

She released a breath, then eyed him. "Firstly, who wears both straps of their backpack? I can't teach you art *and* how to be cool."

"Cool wishes it could be Nick." He approached where she sat behind Miss Kent's desk. "Speaking of art, are you going to pay up? I gave you a math lesson last week." He looked around the room. "And why are you sitting here in the dark?"

"I'm doing one last favor for Miss Kent." She grabbed her backpack and Nick's arm and hustled him out of the room. Alone, she could go undetected, but Nick's noise would blow her cover. She'd tested Miss Kent's door every day for a week, and today was the only time it had been left open. She'd had to be quick and quiet. And now, all for nothing. She hadn't found anything incriminating.

"I'm dropping art next semester." Though truth be told, she'd been skipping it already.

"What?" Nick stopped and grabbed the sleeve of her navy-blue shirt. "Are you crazy?"

"I'm just not feeling it anymore." A now familiar ache came over her throat. After the past week, between Dad and Oliver, she'd thought she was cried out. Obviously not. She pulled her arm from Nick's grasp. "It's no big deal." She picked up the pace and tried to keep her tone normal. "People's likes and dislikes can change."

"Yeah, but this is brain-transplant territory. What's going on?"

My family is ruined, and it's your precious aunt's fault. She took a deep breath. "I can still help you with your art projects if you want. I just don't want to do it myself anymore. You can drive me home, and we'll work on your assignment there." She exited through the outer doors of the school and looked around. "Did you bring the truck today?"

"Uh, not exactly. Mom . . . misplaced the keys. I hot-wired it a couple times, but people looked at me funny." A single bicycle remained on the rack outside. Pink and glittery, with streamers. "Riley loaned me her bike."

Lili mustered up an enthusiasm she didn't feel and jogged over to the sparkling monstrosity. Any change in topic was welcome, even if it came in the form of a Barbie bicycle. "Let's ride double. It'll be fun." Her voice came out flat, even to her.

Nick came closer and cocked his head. "What's going on?"

Distract and evade. "I'll bet you a free movie choice that I can ride this thing faster than you."

"No way am I risking another movie bet with you. If I ever have to see another Selena Gomez chick flick, I'll remove my eyes with a pencil." He unlocked the bike and removed the handlebars from her hands. "Is it stuff at home?"

She froze. How had he—

"It must be a bit depressing there at the moment, with Oliver and Natalie's dad."

Thank goodness that was all he was referring to. "Oh. Yeah, it is." That wasn't a lie. Jem's house had been quiet and sad all week. Natalie and Jem had barely been there. The hospital was giving them a crash course in how to care for a diabetic baby, and Natalie had spent a lot of time camped by her father's bedside.

"Why don't you go back to your parents?"

"I'm doing the cooking and cleaning for Jem while they're busy at the hospital." Lili and Mom had worked out that lie, after Lili slammed Jem's door in Dad's face. He'd come to Jem's and begged her to come home, even though Mom told him not to. Lili had refused to go, and Mom was quick to invent a cover story for extending her stay at Jem's.

Enough of this line of questioning. She jerked the bike from Nick's hands, took a few running steps, and jumped onto the seat. "Catch me if you can."

"Hey!" Nick scrambled after her, laughter in his voice—with a hint of concern.

She pumped her legs till the wind's cold rush raised goose bumps on her arms and drew water from her eyes.

Nick's voice faded, and she slowed to let him catch up. At least now she could blame the wind for her wet cheeks.

The regular *thump* of Nick's jog approached from behind. She twisted in the seat to look at him.

"Lili, watch out!"

The last thing she saw was a flash of black-and-white.

Lili opened her eyes. The grill of a police car loomed above.

Had she seriously been knocked down by a *police* car?

A door slammed and a pair of navy-blue legs appeared.

"Oh, sweet pumpkin pie, don't tell me she's dead," a high-pitched voice said.

She peered up at a barrel-chested policeman. She closed her eyes again. She must have a concussion.

A hand touched her shoulder. "Can you move your toes, darlin'? Did you break your neck?"

Wriggling each digit, then limb, Lili took stock. The side of her face ached like it had been hit by—well, a car—and her left ankle throbbed, but other than that her body responded as normal. "I think I'm okay."

"I'll call you an ambulance. It'll be here in a jiffy." The officer reached for the radio attached to his shoulder.

"No." She grabbed his pant leg. If she went to the hospital, her parents would come. The three of them would be in the same room.

No one wanted that.

"I feel fine. It's just a bruise. I didn't even get knocked out. See?" She sat up and moved her arms and legs to prove it.

Nick sprinted up and threw himself onto the grass beside Lili. "Are you okay? I could see him coming, but I couldn't do anything."

The officer shook his head, his spectacular mustache quivering with the movement. "I must have been too busy singing Kelly Clarkson to notice I'd put it into Drive instead of Reverse. Mmm, but that girl can sing."

Nick stared at him. "Are you serious? Do you know who her grandfather is?"

The man's face lit up. "Is she related to Kelly Clarkson?"

"Not unless Kelly Clarkson is also the granddaughter of Captain Walters."

The mustache drooped as the man's face went slack. "Oh my. Oh no. Oh, I'm so sorry."

Lili pushed herself up from the ground. She'd be fine, as long as she avoided a scenario with all her family in the one hospital room.

Nick grabbed her forearm as she rose and steadied her.

"It's fine. I'm not even hurt. I won't tell Granddad. Though I don't know how you'll explain that scratch."

Pink sparkles shone from a scrape across the grill, but the bike seemed to have escaped major damage.

"Oh, I'll just wash off the sparkles and say it was Mom's scooter again. But you—" The man faced Lili again. "You have to let me take you home."

"No. Uncle Jem will ask questions. Then he'll start thinking about hospitals."

"Lili," Nick said, "I think—"

"Go." Lili nodded at the policeman. "The only way I'll tell my grandfather is if you keep standing here arguing with me."

The man snapped his mouth shut. Opened it again, then nodded. "Yes, ma'am." He pointed to Nick. "You take care of her now, you hear?"

The car scraped against the curb as the man reversed, then rumbled down the street.

"What was that all about?" Nick touched Lili's arm.

She shook her head.

He shrugged. "I'll take you to the church. That's closer than Jem's. Your parents can take you home—or to the doctor."

"No, I'm going back to Jem's." She took a step and winced at the spikes of pain jabbing her ankle. But apart from the whole Dad issue, she seriously hated hospitals. Nothing was broken, just mega bruised.

She'd survive.

Nick lurched forward, but she pushed his hand away.

"Did you break it?"

"I'm not tough. If it was broken, I'd be squealing. It's just sore."

He watched her hobble another step. "It's, like, three times as far to Jem's. The bus has already gone."

She took another step. "That's fine."

"You'll barely make it to the end of the block, and you know it." He crossed his arms, feet planted next to the fallen bike. "Why are you being stubborn?"

She looked at his bike. "We can ride double." That should get her out of this pickle.

"No."

Her gaze snapped to his. What was his deal? "No?"

"You haven't been yourself for ages, but something's even more different this week. What you're doing isn't healthy."

She jammed a hand onto her hip. He had no right to judge. "And what am I doing?"

"Bottling it up. Whatever's bothering you, you haven't even told Grace."

"Who says I haven't told Grace?" Not that it was any of his business anyway. And if he kept poking around, the truth would explode from her like Old Faithful.

He spread his hands. "*Grace* did. She messaged me last night to say she's worried about you."

Yikes. She wasn't doing a good enough job of faking it in their phone conversations. And she hadn't realized that Nick and Grace still kept in touch.

Lili sucked in a breath. Nick's tone, a mixture of caring and concern, was nearly her undoing. Time for one last-ditch effort. "So what if I am? It's my life, not yours."

"We're just worried about you. We care."

Her eyes filled. "Nobody cares." Not Dad—if he did, he wouldn't have done this. Not really Mom, who was basically leaving Lili to deal with this on her own. Not even Uncle Jem, who hadn't noticed that something was seriously wrong.

Not that she could really blame him—he'd been a tad distracted this week.

Nick watched her face. "What do you mean?"

She took in his expression, his intensity. Nick had noticed. And he'd taken the time to try and talk to her, even though she was being awful to him.

He cared.

"My dad's having an affair." The words burst out. She gulped in a breath of pure relief. *Finally*, somebody knew.

Nick's eyes widened. "*What?*"

"I suspected just before I went to Jem's. I found out for sure the night Olly was diagnosed."

Nick shook his head. "I can't believe it." He rocked back on his heels, pushed his fingers through his hair. "I always think of him as the guy who helped Aunt Trish and Stephen, you know?"

Lili kept her eyes down.

"Do you know who she is?"

She plucked at the hem of her shirt. No matter how much she hated her traitorous teacher, she couldn't destroy the one good relationship Nick had with someone in his family. "No."

Nick shook his head. "I can't believe it. That sucks. That really, really sucks. I'm so sorry, Lili." He reached for her, and she wilted into his hug. He squeezed her. "I wish I could say something that would make it better."

"Nothing makes it better."

"I know."

"But things about your life suck too, so at least I know you understand." She took a shuddering breath and pulled back. "You can't tell anybody. Mom made me promise not to tell."

Nick frowned. "That's not fair to you."

True. "She doesn't want a divorce."

"So your uncle doesn't know?"

"No one. You seriously can't breathe a word, especially to your aunt."

He cocked his head. "Why her especially?"

"Just . . . because she's the one you're most likely to talk to," she covered. *Yikes. That was close.*

"I can keep a secret." His face darkened. "Sometimes too many."

Lili cocked her head. Golden boy Nick had a dark side? "What do you mean?"

Nick fiddled with the bike's bell. "It's just . . . when Stephen got busted for dealing, I'd known what he was doing for ages. Like, two years at least. And I never said anything, not to Mom, not to Aunt Trish."

She curled a hand on his forearm. It made her melt a little, that he confided in her. "You didn't want to rat him out. That's fair enough."

"But it would have been better for him in the long run. He would've gotten help earlier, the addiction wouldn't have been so severe. But he made me feel helpful."

That didn't sound good. "Did you—"

"I had nothing to do with the drugs, but I'd cover for him with Mom. Say he was out with friends, tell her all the people dropping by were Jehovah's Witnesses or something." He shrugged. "She never paid much attention, so it was easy. Stephen would grin and say he couldn't survive without his 'fixer.' I had this need to fix everything for him." He gave a rueful smile. "Or so my therapist said." He kicked at a piece of grass. "The truth is I didn't do what was really best for him because I was afraid he'd hate me. Now that he's getting better, I'm afraid he hates me because I didn't speak out."

She rested her head against his shoulder. Even though their pain was different, it helped to have someone to share it with. "You'll just have to not make that mistake next time."

"I guess not."

They stayed in that loose embrace for a moment longer before Lili stepped back. "Will you take me back to Jem's now? I'm still avoiding my parents."

"Sure. Hop on the handlebars. I'll pedal." Nick unclipped Riley's Disney Princess helmet and dropped it onto Lili's head. "This would have come in handy fifteen minutes ago."

She clipped on the helmet, and Nick pushed on the pedals. He kept the pace slow and careful, so it was after four when they hobbled up the final stair of Jem's apartment block.

"Do you want to come in for a drink?" Lili asked.

By the end of the ride, Nick's face had taken on a pink hue that almost rivaled the bicycle. "That would be good," he said.

Lili unlocked Jem's door and entered the apartment. She froze in the doorway.

Natalie clung to Jem, standing next to the fridge, sobs shaking her whole body.

Jem looked over her head to Lili, tears in his eyes. *"Nat's dad's dying,"* he mouthed.

Lili shot a glance to Nick.

He grasped her fingers. "I'll stay."

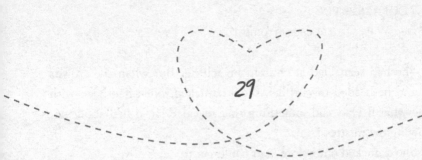

29

Dad had stopped calling.

Lili lay on the kitchen floor and stared at Jem's cracked ceiling, alone in the apartment, a week and a half after telling Nick the truth—or at least part of it. She'd made it upstairs after the bus dropped her off, but had no energy to go further. Nightmares had plagued her all night.

The dreams followed a similar pattern. She woke, got out of bed, and walked from her room to find all the furniture gone. She'd search every room, but the place was deserted. She'd been left alone. Sometimes the house was Mom and Dad's, sometimes Jem's, once even school. But the panic each time was the same.

Still stretched on the floor, Lili pulled her phone from her pocket and scrolled through her messages.

5 OCT AT 10:10AM
Dad: Mom agreed to go to counseling. Really wanna chat about this with u. Call me?

6 OCT AT 2:37PM
Dad: This silence isn't helping anyone Lilianna.

7 OCT AT 5:26 PM
Dad: Will I see u at church tomorrow?

She had seen Dad at church, preaching. But when the crowds left and he headed toward her, she'd panicked. Nick had been with her—what if Dad said something that revealed she'd lied about not knowing the mistress?

She'd ducked out before Dad could get to her.

9 OCT AT 9:13AM
Dad: Sorry to miss you at church. House feels empty without you.

10 OCT AT 12:10PM
Dad: WILL YOU TALK TO ME??

Her phone hadn't vibrated in two days.

She hovered her thumb over Dad's contact icon. Her stomach spun like a waterspout—the sensation had kept her from eating all day.

She'd checked her phone every five minutes during class, waiting for it to vibrate. She didn't actually want to see him in person—had convinced Mom to keep him away. But his desperate attempts to get her attention had been comforting, in their own way.

She dropped the phone onto her stomach and slapped the linoleum floor with an open palm. She wanted to talk to Dad. She wished she could. But other than scream expletives at him, what else was there to say?

Hot tears pressed against her eyes. *No.* She'd cried enough lately to fill Olly's bathtub.

She sat up and looked around the quiet home. She needed sugar, but Nat had changed where she hid her M&M's stash again. She needed sleep, but the nightmares waited behind her eyelids.

She needed to forget.

Lili scooted on her backside toward the pantry, her black leggings picking up crumbs that Jem hadn't had time to sweep this week. She pulled the door open.

Jem had never replaced that bottle of cooking wine Granddad tipped out, but a dusty bottle with a ribbon on it rested on the bottom pantry shelf at Lili's eye level. A goodbye present from Jem's old workmates—though he'd once said he never had the heart to tell them he didn't like white wine.

She pulled it from the shelf and considered it. Its lid was a screw top, not the cork that popped like in the movies.

She unscrewed the lid and took a sniff. Her nose wrinkled, and she blew the air back out. Her father never drank, and she'd always imagined alcohol tasted like cream soda—sweet and bubbly. This smelled more like the cough medicine she'd spat out as a kid.

Still, everyone had to be hyped up about something. Maybe this would make her feel better. She put the bottle to her lips and tipped it up. She chugged down four mouthfuls before the taste made her pull the bottle away and shiver.

"*Blaucgh*." The stuff tasted like it smelled. But a warm fizzing sensation unfurled in her stomach as the liquid made its way down.

She tipped the bottle back up and forced in another few mouthfuls.

By the time a knock sounded at her door, most of the bottle was gone.

Lili spun around on her backside as the knock sounded again. Jem and Nat had both been out, then planned to meet at their weekly basketball game. They weren't due home for ages. Nat had Olly with her. She looked at her phone. Two missed messages. She slapped her hand to her forehead. Nick!

She scrambled to her feet, then gripped the bench as the room spun. Sitting on the floor, she'd had a pleasant buzz going on in her head. Now the world tipped off-kilter.

After a moment her balance returned, and she followed the straight line that ran in the pattern of the lino floor to the door. Sobriety test passed. No problem.

She pulled the door open. "Hey, Nick."

He stood two feet back from the door, hands pushed into his jeans pockets, gaze fastened to the next apartment down from Jem's. "I'm eighty-seven percent sure I just saw an elderly woman check me out."

Lili doubled over in giggles.

"Do you have weird neighbors . . . or am I that hot?"

She broke into another round of laughter.

He walked around her to enter the apartment. "I'm glad you find it funny. This is going to come up in my next counseling session."

Lili shut the door and leaned on it, gasping for breath.

He peeked into the cookie jar Natalie had bought last week. "Are you on a sugar high or something? 'Cos I want in on some of that action. What about those birthday-cake M&M's of Natalie's you told me about?"

She regained her breath and stood up straight. "I think she's on to me. She moved the stash again. I managed to get Jem blamed for most of the ones that went missing."

"Got your art brain ready?"

"No. Why?"

He gave her a weird look. "That's why I'm here. You're teaching me some of this art junk."

"Oh, I totally forgot." *Whoops.* They'd arranged for this on Saturday.

Nick spotted the bottle on the floor. "What's this?" He picked it up.

Uh-oh. "Just some stuff Jem cooks with," she covered.

He stepped in close to her and inhaled. All teasing drained out of his face. "Lili, what have you been doing?"

She looked down. "I just had a taste." He had no way of knowing how empty the bottle was before she got to it.

"Your breath says otherwise."

She jerked her head up. "How can you tell?"

"Think about the house I grew up in, Lili. I can tell." He frowned. "Is that why you're so giggly? It shouldn't hit you that hard. Have you eaten or slept?"

"I've been having nightmares." Her eyes puddled with tears. "It's just been so hard. I thought skipping art class would make things easier, and I thought about going home, I really did, but the thought of Dad bossing me around or trying to ground me—it's just so stupid."

"Hold up. Go back. What does art have to do with it?"

"And I've managed to avoid seeing him so far," she rambled on as if Nick hadn't spoken, "but I still see *her* all the time, and she smiles at me like nothing's wrong and—"

"Lili, are you saying your Dad's sleeping with an art student?"

"No," she scowled.

Nick's face changed.

Realization hit, and Lili slapped her hands over her mouth.

He put a hand on the counter, as if to steady himself. "Are you saying"—he paused, like he couldn't make the words come out of his mouth— "that . . . Aunt Trish?"

She shook her head. "No, no, ah—"

"I thought you said you didn't know who she was."

"I, um—"

"All this time, you've been thinking my aunt Trish was sleeping with your dad?"

She gave a small nod.

"Not Aunt Trish. She's the good one. She's a Christian."

She narrowed her eyes. "Christians can make mistakes too."

He shook his head. "Not Aunt Trish."

"What are you saying? That I made it up?" Her voice neared ultrasonic.

"There's no way she would do this."

"I caught them making out in the art room."

His eyes nearly popped out of his head. "That . . . that doesn't mean anything."

"I traced his phone back to her house."

"They could have been working stuff out for Stephen."

"At two in the morning?"

"*No!*" He slammed the countertop with his fist.

She jumped.

"You told me you didn't know who it was. You either lied then or you're lying now."

"I didn't want to hurt you! I know how important she is to you. But it's true." Her tone turned to pleading. How could he think she'd make this up? All this time, all the secrets, and now, when it was finally out, Nick wouldn't even believe her?

He stared at her. "Don't say that."

Her emotions spiraled as her voice rose. "Don't say what? That she's been banging my dad and then saying hi to me at school? That she's been lying to everyone? That's she's a hypocrite?"

"*Shut up.*" Nick took a step forward.

Lili backed into the door. She felt behind her for the handle, wrenched it open. "Get out."

He shook his head and stomped past her, out into the hallway. He turned around, as if to say something, but she slammed the door in his face.

Then she walked over to the bottle and chugged the rest down.

Lili curled around the porcelain toilet bowl as her stomach spasmed.

Maybe it hadn't been the best idea to drink almost a whole bottle of wine on an empty stomach and no sleep.

A knock sounded at the door.

She retched again.

"Lili?" Granddad's voice sounded concerned.

Oh no. Granddad had to pick today, of all days, for a surprise visit. The wine bottle was on the table, and she hadn't locked the door after Nick.

Another contraction of her abdomen kept her on the floor.

"Lilianna?"

The apartment door whined as it opened. A moment's silence, punctuated only by her gags.

"Lil." Quick footsteps approached the bathroom, paused at the door. "Oh my—"

She couldn't turn to see him, but thick fingers gently grasped her hair from behind, shifting it out of the way.

She lost what was hopefully the last of her stomach contents, then sank back on the tiles, eyes stinging with tears.

After a moment, Granddad grasped her arm and supported her weight as she stumbled to the sink. She twisted the faucet on full blast and shoved her face under the stream. Cool, cleansing heaven. She kept her face under the rush of water for long moments after she'd already rinsed her mouth and washed her face.

Finally she raised her head, water dripping from her chin and wet wisps of hair. She risked a glance at Granddad.

"Your elderly neighbor just asked me if I was one of those police strippers." Granddad's face held no mirth, his mouth set in a straight line. "And then I find my granddaughter drunk. I can smell it on you, Lili. Is this upside-down day?"

Despite the situation, her lips twitched in a smile. "You don't get old ladies hitting on you regularly?"

Steam practically sizzled from his scalp. "This is not funny, Lilianna."

Her gaze fell to the floor. "Yes, Granddad."

"Where's your uncle?"

"At basketball with Natalie."

"What are you doing?"

"Nothing. I wasn't drunk. I've been sick all day."

"So you decided to treat it with a bottle of wine? I saw the bottle. I can smell your breath."

She shrugged. She couldn't tell him the real trigger for her behavior. If his reaction to a little alcohol was anything to go by, news of Dad's affair would destroy this family—permanently.

Granddad perched on the edge of the bathtub. "What's going on?"

"Nothing. I—I just had a fight with Nick." Her lip trembled. "I think he hates me."

"That's it? You had a fight with a boy?" His tone indicated that was *not* a good enough reason.

"It—It was a big one."

He gave a huff as he stood. "I'm taking you home."

She pulled her gaze from the ground. "I am home."

"No, to your parents'. Your uncle clearly doesn't have his head on straight."

Her eyes widened. "What about my things?"

"Grab what you can fit in your duffel, and you can get the rest later." He strode from the bathroom, and after a moment there came a clink of glass against metal. Probably the bottle landing in the trash.

Lili ran her fingers through her hair, heat expanding through her chest and face. Another adult trying to boss her around. And his life in no more order than hers—one son a cheating hypocrite and the other estranged.

She sat on the bathroom floor, drew her knees to her chest, and locked her arms around them.

After a minute, Granddad stomped back in. His face slackened. "What are you doing?"

"I'm not going."

His eyes narrowed. "I'll put you over my shoulder and carry you."

Boldness, perhaps from the residual alcohol, pumped through her veins. "I'll scream. Mrs. McCarthy next door has a taser and wandering hands."

Granddad drew in a slow breath, his intense gaze burning holes into Lili. Rage built behind his eyes, tinged with something else. She recognized it from her own reflection. Fear.

She pushed herself up off the ground. "What are you going to do? Shout at me, like you do to Uncle Jem? Throw me out of your family unless I behave like I'm perfect? Tell me you don't love me anymore?" She folded her arms. "Whatever. I don't care."

Had she performed a spontaneous jazz number, Granddad couldn't have looked more stunned.

After a moment he wiped the frozen-fish look off his face and replaced it with a scowl. "You're talking crazy." He strode to the door, then turned back, face set. "I'm walking down to the car. If you're not there in five minutes, I'm coming back to handcuff you and sit you in lockup for underage drinking." He glared at her. "Don't think I won't. Just ask your father."

She watched him go, stood still for a full thirty seconds. Then she dashed to her room and stuffed her laptop and clothes into a backpack.

Few things could be worse than going home.

But one of them was sitting in lockup.

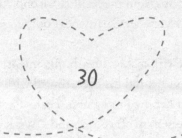

30

Red-and-blue lights whirled in Jem's rearview mirror. The flashes caught his gaze as he drove one-handed through Charlottesville's darkening streets, reenacting his winning three-pointer to Natalie with the other.

"Are you serious?" He checked the mirror again. "I'm not even speeding. If this is Dad again, this has got to be some sort of abuse of power." He let the car roll to a stop on the side of the road.

He even had good news to share with Dad, but he'd rather not do it in the glow of police lights.

Natalie looked over her shoulder, her chocolate-colored ponytail bouncing with movement. "It's your dad. And he looks crankier than a librarian with a wedgie." She stuffed a McDonald's bag, three soda cans, and a diaper under her seat.

Jem swiped dust off the dash and hit the windshield with a squirt of water.

Their teamwork was instant. Synchronized. Unspoken. There'd been a weird energy between him and Nat for the last few weeks. They'd relied on one another during the drama of Olly's injections, finger-prick tests, and the haze of grief around Phil's diagnosis. They'd both spent a lot of time this week at the Groves home with Phil.

But she was still dating Sam.

A rhythmic crunch of gravel indicated Dad's approach. A moment later his starched shirt blocked the view from Jem's window. He tapped the glass.

Jem wound down the window while rolling his eyes. A rush of cold air swept in, cooling the sweat on his body. "You know they've invented these wonderful things called cell phones, Dad."

"You should try answering yours once in a while. License and registration, please."

Great, he was snippy already. As he reached for his papers, Jem eyed the awards-night invitation perched in the cupholder where he stashed his phone and spare pacifiers. Maybe not the best time to extend his olive branch of inviting Dad to the ceremony. But they hadn't seen one another for weeks—how could he possibly be angry about something?

He handed his license and registration over. "My name is Lucius Alfredo, and this is my friend Kathy Cupcake. What's going on?"

"I could say the same to you." Dad took the wallet and stepped back. "I'll check your details. Wait here."

"What the— He's not— *Augh*!" He thumped the steering wheel. "I swear, he does this just to drive me insane."

Natalie pulled his phone from the console. "You missed six calls."

"What?" He grabbed the phone. All the calls had arrived during the game.

Natalie twisted the heat control. A blast of hot air hit Jem's face even as chills rippled through his body. What was so urgent that Dad would call him six times?

His father reappeared at the window and held Jem's wallet up but out of reach. "I have Lili in the back of my car."

"What? Why? What's wrong?" Jem twisted to try and see her, but Dad's car was parked at an angle that blocked his view.

"I was returning her to Mike and Steph's."

"You were . . . Excuse me?" A firecracker lit in his brain. "What gives you the right—"

"I have every right," Dad snapped. "The only reason I've brought her back to you is because they're both out."

Jem gaped at him. "Who made you the policeman of parenting?"

"Your apartment is no place for an unstable teenage girl. You've got Oliver's sickness, the drama with his mother. Natalie's got her own crisis—"

Jem's knuckles whitened on the steering wheel. Dad, controlling everything. Again. "The decision for Lili to live at my house is between Mike, Steph, and me."

"Mike hasn't seen Lili in two weeks. How is he supposed to have confidence that—"

"Steph takes her out to lunch all the time. They know exactly how she is."

"I found her drunk."

Jem opened his mouth, but no sound came out.

Beside him, Natalie leaned forward. "You what?"

"She was throwing up. Your bottle of wine was empty. And I could smell it."

Jem narrowed his eyes. "You're telling me you found Lili drunk. I haven't even bought more cooking wine— Oh." There was that gift bottle he'd received from his old workmates. But he still shook his head.

Dad reared back. "Are you calling me a liar?"

"I'd like to hear Lili's version."

Dad's lip curled in a sneer. "This is why I took her to Mike and Steph's. I knew you wouldn't be concerned about this." He shook his head, as if he wondered why he'd ever expected better.

The words struck like a hook to the ribs. *Failure.*

Jem pushed the inner voice aside and glanced at Natalie. "Could you please get Lili?"

She slipped out of the car and jogged toward the police vehicle.

He counted to five, jaw clenched. "I never said I wasn't concerned—"

Dad cut him off with a slash of his hand. "When are you going to stop goofing around and realize this stuff is serious?"

Jem's last thread of restraint snapped. "When are you going to stop inventing reasons to criticize me so you feel better about your own crappy parenting?"

Dad drew himself even more upright. "How dare you—"

"No, how dare you, Dad?" He spat out the long-held-back words. He was a man now. Dad had no right to lecture him anymore. "You had your chance and you screwed it up. Stop messing up mine."

Lili and Natalie slid through the passenger-side doors at the same time.

He raised his eyebrows at his father. "You going to give me my wallet back?"

"Not until you—"

"You know what? Keep it."

Jem hit the gas and squealed away. His father, a lone figure in the side mirror, grew smaller and then disappeared altogether.

Shaking his head, Jem tried to shake off Dad's judgmental words. And the niggle of guilt at his own response. He flicked a glance at Lili in the rearview mirror. "What happened, Lil?"

There was a long pause. "I felt sick all day, and a friend at school told me that a little bit of wine settles your stomach. They're into those organic remedies and stuff. I was at home, and Tylenol wasn't working, and I saw a bottle in your pantry. So I had half a cup. Granddad caught me and went berserk." She shrugged. "You know how he is."

Jem made eye contact in the mirror again, but Lili broke it. Fresh worry poured in. Was she telling the truth? "So if I go home and check the bottle, will there only be half a cup missing?"

"Uh . . . Granddad poured the rest down the sink and threw out the bottle."

"Of course he did," Jem muttered.

Natalie glanced at him.

Jem pulled into his apartment block's parking lot and shut off the car. He shifted in his seat to face Lili, who stroked a sleeping Oliver's hand. Had she been acting different lately? Between Olly's diabetes and Phil's terminal diagnosis, he couldn't remember. His stomach churned, twisting and flopping in that spot below his diaphragm. Maybe Dad was r— *No.* That thought wasn't worth finishing.

He wasn't like Dad. He could actually communicate.

"Lili." He waited till she looked at him. "You know you can tell me if something's going on."

She squirmed in her seat. "I know."

"Is there anything? Anything at all?"

"No." She stopped her squirms and held his stare.

He sighed and dropped his gaze. "Okay. Make sure you tell us if anything ever comes up. And no more organic remedies." He shook his head. "I have no idea if it settles your stomach or not, but you won't taste alcohol again until your twenty-first birthday. Am I clear?"

"Fine." Lili unclipped her seat belt and shot from the car into the building.

Jem leaned his head back against the seat.

Natalie twisted to face him. She still wore her blue-and-gold basketball uniform, and the intense game had put some pink back in her cheeks. But concern darkened her green eyes. "Do you believe her?"

He scrubbed a hand over his face. "What else can I do? It's her word against Dad's. And he's proven more than once he has his own guilt-driven agenda. Have you noticed anything odd about Lili's behavior?"

She shrugged. "I've barely noticed the sun going up and down for the past few weeks."

He grimaced. The timing was horrendous. Between Natalie's grief over her father's life expectancy, concern for Olly, and her new workload, he was already worried about her. She was slipping away, and he seemed powerless to stop it.

He pushed his fingers through his hair. "We'll just have to keep a close eye on her."

She nodded, then snagged the envelope that he'd shoved into his cupholder, the word "Congratulations" stamped on the front. "What's this?"

He tried to smile, but his facial muscles felt heavy. "Can you believe I was going to drop by Dad's place tomorrow and tell him about this? I got nominated for a journalism award. That's the invitation to the gala dinner."

"Are you serious? That's amazing."

Jem pictured his father's probable reaction. "He'd find something to criticize."

Natalie shoved his shoulder. "Forget trying to please him. You don't have to prove that you're good enough to anyone."

Jem widened his eyes in mock pain. But her words soothed the roiling tension inside. She had a point. Maybe if he could just remember that, he could stop doing stupid things around Dad.

He rubbed his forehead. He'd only resolved to try again with Dad last week. Hadn't taken long for that to fall apart.

Natalie pulled the elegant invitation from its envelope. Jem allowed himself the luxury of watching. Natalie had kept her word about forgiving him these past weeks, and it no longer seemed to take just three seconds for her to hate him again.

They were definitely up to at least seven.

That was it. Jem set his jaw. If Natalie could do it, so could he. Next time he had a run-in with his father, no matter what went down, he would not react. He would not be goaded. He would not explode. He would forgive.

He shot up a prayer for divine help. This would require nothing short of an act of God.

Natalie, reading the invite, widened her eyes. "This ceremony looks like it's going to be gorgeous."

The sparkle in her expression fully erased Jem's mental image of Dad standing alone on the roadside. "Well . . . you could come. As a friend." His pulse quickened at the thought, though she was certain to say no.

She hesitated. "I thought you'd need me to watch the kids."

Jem's mind scrambled for solutions. "Lili can babysit. Maybe Steph can help too, keep an eye on Olly's sugars. We won't stay late." His voice was at its most coaxing. Was it a dog move to invite another man's girlfriend to his award ceremony? Maybe. But if Sam wanted her, he could fight for her.

When Jem had first come back to town, he'd dreamed of winning Natalie back in the same way he dreamed of a tropical holiday home or a full night's sleep. Not gonna happen. Then she'd kissed him, and for one magnificent day he'd hoped—until reality crashed back in. Things had happened so quickly, Jem hadn't had the chance to tell Natalie how he felt.

Now she'd been dating that Australian preacher for weeks, but she wasn't exactly turning cartwheels with happiness. So maybe there was still a chance.

Natalie deserved to know how he felt about her. Then she could choose. He just needed the chance to tell her.

"I'll have Wildfire work."

"Take one night off. Between Wildfire and your dad, you're beyond stressed. This will be good for you."

Natalie pressed her lips together, face awash with indecision. "Maybe."

"It's next Saturday. You've got time to decide." Jem unbuckled Olly and pulled him from the car seat, lips moving in a silent plea to God.

He'd given her ten days to decide.

Ten days for him to pray.

♡

Natalie really should have been moving faster.

She folded her arms over her worn duffle coat in a vain effort to keep the wind out as she walked to Bodo's on Saturday morning. Her faux-leather knee-high boots tapping on the pavement restricted her speed to a degree, but as much as she'd like to blame them, the cold headwind, or the college student who nearly ran her over on his skateboard, she couldn't. It was her own fault.

She didn't know what to do.

Bodo's came into view, and her speed decreased even more. The bagel eatery had become her and Sam's favorite hangout. But before she arrived, she needed to make a decision. What would she do about Jem's invitation?

Was it fair to go with him to his awards ceremony while she was dating Sam? Should she tell Sam? Should she say no? Should this be such a debate if she was meant to be over Jem? And did that even matter because committing more to Sam was probably what would cleanse Jem from her brain?

Her mind had run a marathon already, and it was only noon.

She crossed the Bodo's courtyard with a grimace. It was clear what she should do. She should ask Sam out next Saturday night. They could go ice skating, something that the Australian had never done, and it would probably prove hilarious. With Sam, the night would be light, fun and easy.

So why couldn't she get more excited about it?

She paused outside the door.

Because she wanted to see Jem dressed up. She wanted to sit next to him and smirk at the host's bad toupee, wanted to share Jem's dessert and cheer when he won.

Because she was insane.

He'd blindsided her by leaving once. What made her think it wouldn't happen again?

She pulled the door open with determination. She'd ask Sam to go ice skating. It was the only rational decision.

She looked around the restaurant. No Sam. *Huh.* She checked her watch. Twelve-oh-seven p.m. And she'd thought she was late.

The door opened behind her.

"Kim, I'm meeting Natalie. I've gotta— We can talk about it later, but I'm not keen on the idea."

She turned and encountered Sam's apologetic smile. He mouthed, *Sorry.* Kimberly's voice still emanated from the phone, and Sam rolled his eyes. "I'm hanging up now. See ya later." He ended the call and tugged a seat out for Natalie. "Sorry about that. She wants to pitch new ideas for Wildfire."

Natalie took her seat as a vise gripped her chest. She'd put in more hours than ever on Wildfire work since Dad came home from the hospital. Was Kimberly getting an edge with this?

Or really, more of an edge?

Sam seated himself across from her. "She has . . . Well, she has a lot of ideas." His tone did not indicate that it was a compliment.

"Too many?" Natalie hazarded a guess.

Sam's smile turned rueful. "You could say that."

An interesting tidbit of information. Natalie tucked it away for further pondering later. She picked up a menu and pretended to consider it while she tried to form her next sentence. "So, next Saturday night—"

"Actually, I wanted to talk to you about, well, future Saturday nights."

Natalie put the menu down and paid sharper attention. "Yes?" His tone, his expression . . . What was wrong?

A pained expression crossed his countenance. "I'm not certain if we should be spending them together."

She blinked. He was breaking up with her? Her brain scrambled for a response, and the best it came up with was, "Umm . . . okay?"

"It's not that I don't enjoy hanging out." Sam leaned forward. "I do. It's just I get the sense . . ." He trailed off and appeared to search for the right words.

"What?"

"It seems like there's some unresolved stuff between you and Jem. I'd rather not get in the middle of that."

Oh no. Jem was not wrecking this for her. She matched Sam's pose, elbows on the table, leaning forward. "It only seems that way because we have history. But that's in the past." Where it would stay.

Sam looked skeptical.

"You don't believe me?"

He shrugged. "I believe you. I'm just pretty sure it's not in the past for Jem." At her look, he smiled. "I saw his reaction when I picked you up the other day. A bloke knows."

Natalie opened her mouth, closed it. Jem . . . Jem wasn't over her. The thought filled her with an expanding sensation of joy, a hot-air balloon lifting off in her heart.

Sam's comment shouldn't have this effect on her. She'd suspected how Jem felt. The evidence was there. His kiss, before Chloe. His invitation now. The strangled expression he got each time she mentioned Sam. She'd known. She'd fought it.

But Sam saying it aloud sounded ten different kinds of wonderful. She was a terrible person. She'd just told Sam this was in the past.

The man before her held up his hands. "But that's just Jem. I believe you. And honestly, Nat, on paper I think we're great together. But in practice, I think we're missing a little . . . zing."

She couldn't argue. Had felt it herself, though she'd told herself that it could come with time. "I get that," she admitted.

"But you're a terrific friend. I think we can still work together great at Wildfire."

She smiled and said all the things you're meant to say in a breakup and meant most of them. After Sam left, she stared at the napkin holder for so long that someone tapped her on the shoulder and asked if she was okay.

Natalie jolted, turned.

Kimberly.

The younger woman slid into the seat Sam had vacated, concern in her expression. "You can tell me to go away, that's fine. I just wanted to check."

Natalie sighed. She wanted to hate Kimberly. The woman stood ready to steal her dream away in a matter of weeks. But though Kimberly could be focused to the point of abruptness, there was no denying she had a kind heart.

Natalie tore the edge of the corner of a napkin and debated how much to tell her. "Sam and I just decided to stop seeing each other."

Kimberly's expression was entirely empathetic. "I'm sorry. That sucks." A worried expression crossed her face. "I wasn't stalking you guys either, by the way. Sam said he was meeting you, but I didn't know it was here. He just said the other day that he loved the bagels here, so I decided to try it out." Her words got more rushed and awkward the longer she went.

Natalie shrugged. "It's fine. The breakup was . . . relatively mutual."

Kimberly leaned forward. "I'm sure he'll be fine at work, if you're worried about that."

Natalie debated her next words, then threw caution to the wind. Once the Wildfire decision was made, she and Kimberly would have little reason to meet again. Sometimes a near stranger could be the best sounding board. "It's more the reason we decided to call it. Sam thinks that my ex, Jem, is interested, and I can admit to being . . . tempted. Sam could see that." She worked at tearing the napkin into a strip like Mom did with those Australian Minties candies she loved. "But Jem already broke off our engagement once. Don't you think it's crazy to trust him again?"

Kimberly tapped a fingernail against the table. "You won't be surprised to know that relationships aren't my strong point. But I do believe that some people change. And some don't. The trick is working out which is which."

She smiled and left, and Natalie stayed until her napkin was one long piece, like a perfectly peeled apple skin.

"The trick is working out which is which."

Could Jem have really changed enough for her to entrust her heart to him again?

There was only one way to find out.

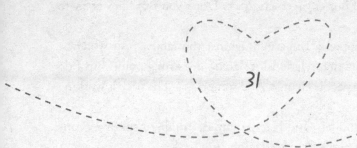

31

If Natalie wasn't careful, this special night would end before it began.

She rose from the edge of her mattress in red strappy heels and took a cautious step. She hadn't worn heels in a month, hadn't worn a six-inch stiletto in . . . ever. She moved forward at a slow pace and made it to the mirror propped on top of her dresser.

Still upright. Good.

Twenty minutes left to do hair and makeup before Jem got here for the gala. Bad.

She sashayed to the bathroom as fast as her shoes would allow, fighting the bubbles that fizzed in her stomach. Jem's quiet delight when she'd accepted his invitation last weekend—and happened to mention her breakup with Sam—had spun her insides into cartwheels ever since. She jammed a hairpin into place, her dark tresses curling in a messy bun. The bathroom light flickered, and she held her breath. Eyeliner was challenging enough in the light—the bulb couldn't fail her now.

Eyes done, she leaned into the mirror, made an O with her lips, and applied a generous layer of Certainly Red. Eye shadow and blush came next.

A familiar deep voice floated through the open window. Jem talking to someone . . . on the phone, maybe?

A few swipes of mascara and a spritz of Beyoncé's latest fragrance, and she was ready. She smoothed a wrinkle in the pleated chiffon skirt of her cream dress as she walked to the front door. Hopefully Jem wouldn't notice the crease. She'd already ironed it three times.

She pulled the door open.

Jem stood on her front porch, phone to his ear, navy shirt undone at the neck, and a charcoal-gray tie tossed over the shoulder of his matching suit jacket. He flashed Natalie a grin and a wink and pulled the phone slightly away from his mouth. "Beetroot," he whispered, eyes apologetic.

She stepped closer and tugged the tie from his shoulder. The scent of his cologne filled her senses. It wasn't his usual fragrance—this one was smoky, sweet, and rich. Yummy.

With a slight tremble to her fingers, she fastened Jem's collar, hoping he couldn't see the pulse hammering in her throat. She looped the tie around his neck, his breath tickling wisps of hair against her cheek, and tied the knot. She kept her eyes fastened on her task but felt his gaze on her.

"When did this happen?" he said into the phone. "No, I guess you can't. We'll head over there now. Okay. Bye."

He lowered the phone, and a slow grin spread across his lips, mere inches from Natalie and level with her forehead.

She met his eyes. "Hi."

"Hi." His gaze wandered over the full length of her and back up again. "How have you been?"

"In the two hours since I last saw you? Just dandy." She'd gotten conditioner in her eye, cut her ankle shaving, and burned her finger on the curling iron, but Jem's appreciative smile made it totally worth it.

His hand slid down her bare arm, grasped her fingers, and lifted her hand above her head. "Twirl."

She obliged, her skirt fanning out.

The spin tested the limits of her balance, and Jem caught her against his chest. "Gorgeous." His gaze caressed her face, then dropped to her lips.

Her eyes widened, and her chest rose with a deep breath. She pulled back. "We should probably get going."

He shortened his strides to match hers as they walked across the stepping-stone path toward the car. "If it's okay, I need to check on Dad before we go. That call was Mike. He sounded pretty worried about him."

"Why can't Mike go?"

"He's sitting with a church family at the hospital. Their kid is sick."

She wobbled on a stepping stone and grasped Jem's elbow. "How was Olly? Was Steph okay? Does she have your mobile number?"

"His sugar was 8.5 at the last test, and he seemed totally normal. Steph can handle it. You just have to concentrate on having a good time."

Natalie returned his smile. A good time. They'd been few and far between in the past few weeks, between worrying over Dad and Steph's near constant phone calls about Wildfire. The ministry had been insanely busy in the past few weeks—the festival had been a runaway success under Kimberly's watchful eye and created a lot of speaking opportunities for them to follow up on. But if her phone rang tonight, she'd throw it out the window.

They got into the car and zoomed toward John's house. Natalie frowned as they approached the colonial-style home. There wasn't a single light on. It didn't even look like anyone was home. "What exactly did Mike say was wrong?"

"He didn't." Jem slowed to a stop in John's red brick drive. "He just said he sounded upset on the phone when Mike called him."

Jem stepped out of the car, and Natalie followed suit. A crash sounded from inside the house, and they double-timed it up the path.

"Dad?" The front door opened without a key. Jem motioned for Natalie to stay on the porch. "Dad, are you there?"

Natalie stood on tiptoe to peer inside. She stared at the sight in front of her.

Had a hurricane gone through the house?

Usually a meticulous housekeeper, John had pizza boxes and fast-food bags scattered all over the floor in the hallway entrance. Natalie squinted, but it was too dark to see what else lay beyond the street-light's glow.

"Daaaaaaad!" Jem hit the lights and crunched his way into the house, kicking rubbish aside as he went. Still no response.

Natalie picked her way along behind him, trying not to trip over a KFC bucket in her ridiculous heels. When she caught up to Jem, he'd flicked the lights on in the living room and was staring at a big lump in the recliner.

John, as she'd never seen him. Bloodshot eyes, greasy hair, and a haggard expression like he hadn't slept for days. He still wore his wrinkled captain's uniform, and his lap was covered in photos. Old photos.

In fact, the entire room was. Boxes covered the couch, overflowing with old frames, albums, and loose prints. Polaroids and yellowed newspaper articles laid scattered across the floor.

John blinked at them through bleary eyes, then sat up in the recliner. "What are you doing?"

There was that captain's bark they all knew.

Jem bent and plucked a newspaper article from the ground. "Mike called me. He said you were upset. He didn't say the house had been taken over by squatters on a bender. What's going on?"

John directed a fierce frown in their direction, then waved them away and closed his eyes. "I'm unwell. Just leave. Lock the door behind you."

Natalie looked from the other man to Jem. This didn't add up.

John could be on his deathbed, and his garbage would still be perfectly sorted between compost, recyclables, and general waste. Not scattered across the floor.

But Jem wasn't looking at his father. His attention was focused on the newspaper clipping in his hand.

"'DUI kills mother.'" Jem read the faded clipping aloud, still squatting where he'd picked it up.

John bolted upright. "Put that down."

Jem jerked back, though he was already out of his father's reach, and rose to his feet. "'A *single*-vehicle crash has claimed the life of local mother Barbara Walters, thirty-nine.'"

He paused.

Natalie leaned on his arm to look over his shoulder and read the article. That wasn't right. Single vehicle? Hadn't a drunk driver hit her car?

John slumped back into the chair.

"'Walters' station wagon allegedly hit a tree on Preston Avenue about 7:40 p.m. Thursday,'" Jem continued. "'Police allege Walters had a—'" His voice failed. He cleared his throat. "'A blood alcohol reading of point two five at the time of the crash.'"

That wasn't a story she'd heard around the family dinner table before. Her eyes zeroed in on the number. Point two five. Point-three should be enough to knock a grown man unconscious.

He kept reading, voice wooden. "'An ambulance was called to the scene, but she was declared dead on arrival.

"'Walters was the wife of local police Lieutenant John Walters. She leaves behind two sons, Michael, seventeen, and Jeremy, five.

"'A funeral service for Walters will be held at the Charlottesville Christian Church on Friday.'"

Jem's hand dropped to his side. "Dad? You wanna explain why that's not the story you told me?"

John didn't answer.

Jem worked his jaw. Uh-oh. Natalie unbuckled her fancy shoes and stepped out of them. No point staying dressed up tonight. Instead of an awards ceremony and a chance to probe into New Jem, she'd witness the next chapter of the lifelong conflict between him and his father.

Old Jem.

His muscles bunched beneath her hand, still on his arm. Emotions flitted across his face, like he was struggling to contain himself. She braced for whatever came next.

But then his expression cleared. He lifted his head. His voice came out measured, under control. "I forgive you, Dad."

"What?"

"What?"

Both Natalie and John fastened their attention on Jem's face.

Jem shrugged. "I don't know why you lied about this. I understand nothing about your approach to parenting . . . and other human beings. But you should know that I forgive you for the past. That's all." He carefully placed the article inside one of the photo boxes. "I'll go now if you want."

Natalie gaped. That was the last thing she'd expected Jem to say. Berate his father for dishonesty? Sure. Demand answers? A given. But forgiveness? It wasn't a move in their family's playbook.

Jem moved toward the door. Natalie moved to follow him.

"She found it hard to cope." John's voice cracked on the last word. They both paused.

"There was a bad patch after Mike was born, then again after you. Except it was worse the second time."

Jem swiveled. "What really happened?"

The question was quiet, nonjudgmental.

"She started drinking. Too much." He cleared his throat. "But she covered it well. I didn't realize the extent until . . . Well, I was meant to be home that evening but got held up at the station. She needed groceries, and she decided to leave you with Mike for an hour and drive herself to get them." He shrugged. "They didn't know exactly how it happened. But she hit a tree."

Motion caught Natalie's eye.

Trembling. His hands were trembling. "Today would've been our fortieth anniversary."

That explained the photos. Natalie bent and gathered the nearest ones, tapping them into neat piles and placing them inside the patterned box she found upturned behind the couch.

Jem remained where he was. "Why didn't you tell me?"

A photo slipped from John's fingers, bounced on the carpet. "You were just like her. Even down to your blasted freckles. She was so carefree, always the life of the party. If I'd kept her more grounded, not encouraged her antics, maybe she wouldn't have . . . Maybe things would have been different." He shrugged. "So I tried to, with you."

Natalie set the box of restacked photos on the couch.

Jem walked out of the room.

She picked up her shoes. Was he leaving? Should she follow?

"Don't forget to lock the door!" Dad called the words out after him.

Jem banged around the kitchen and returned with a garbage bag. He scooped up three Big Mac boxes. "I'm not leaving, Dad. I'm cleaning this place up. How long has it been since you were at work?"

"I took a couple days off."

Natalie looked around the room with fresh eyes. John never took vacations. This wasn't just a bad night. What did you do when the most capable person in the world had a breakdown?

Jem nudged her. "I'm sorry. I don't think I should leave him like this."

She just smiled. It was okay. Tonight's plans had changed.

♡

Natalie drew a pattern in John's living room carpet with her bare toe. Dimmed light bathed the room as Michael Bublé crooned on the stereo. Were it not for the sixtysomething police captain snoring upstairs, the place would be downright romantic.

Jem, tie long gone and shirtsleeves rolled up, tossed the last candy wrapper into the trash. He glanced at Natalie. "Sorry tonight didn't go as planned."

"Award ceremonies are boring anyway." She tried for a light tone.

"Yeah, I'd much rather scrub floors." Jem looked at his wet socked feet with disgust.

Natalie rolled her eyes. "It would've been easier if you knew how to mop properly." He'd sloshed way too much water out of the bucket, and it still lay in pools on the tiled floor. Amateur.

But it'd been a good strategy for helping his father. She'd agreed that leaving John alone in this state wasn't a great idea, and neither was staying in that living room where John remained alternately silent and belligerent. So Jem had stayed quiet and gotten to work.

Together they'd cleaned up the trash, mopped the floors, put in a load of wash, and fitted fresh sheets onto John's mattress. Jem had finally talked his father into going to bed and getting some real rest. It looked as though he'd been sleeping in that recliner the past couple of days.

And all the time, the thought that had taken root in Natalie's brain when Jem said "I forgive you" had blossomed into a full-blown notion.

Jem had changed.

Her fiancé all those years ago would never have said those words to John. Much less meant them. But everything Jem had done tonight indicated his determination to build a bridge between himself and the prickly lump of stubbornness he called a father.

If Jem could change toward his father, was there a chance that their relationship would be different this time too?

One thought nagged at her. What had sparked this change? What had even brought Jem back to his faith? He spoke so little of his metamorphosis in Chicago. She needed to fill in some puzzle pieces.

So, as she followed Jem down the basement stairs to fetch the finished load of laundry, she voiced the question.

"Fill in some pieces?" He echoed her words as he crossed to the washer. "You want to talk about what we both did in the last seven years?"

"We know what I did," she answered quickly. No need to delve into her string of meaningless jobs and mind-numbing years.

A mistake she wasn't going to repeat.

"You mean you want to go over why I left?"

She paused. She'd avoided this conversation since Jem's return. Why would she want to hear a list of reasons explaining why he'd stopped loving her?

But maybe this needed to happen. She braced herself. "Okay."

32

Jem was silent for so long as he hauled the clothes out of the washer and carried them upstairs, Natalie wasn't sure if he was going to tell her at all.

Back at ground level, he fetched a drying rack and positioned it by the north windows where they'd catch the morning light. He had the third sock hung on the rack before he spoke. "The Miss America pageant."

"Excuse me?"

"That's what Dad and I were fighting about that tipped me over the edge. He was into me over why I hadn't been to church that Sunday." The corner of his mouth tipped up. "I was doing college assignments, but just to see his eyes pop, I told him it was because I wanted to watch the Miss America pageant."

Natalie gave a low whistle. She could well imagine the reaction that'd get.

Jem shrugged. "It was the latest in a series of fights. We'd been building to it for a while. I know we were trying to save for the—well, to save money—but staying with him instead of moving out was pretty much a terrible idea."

She remembered. Money or not, she'd warned Jem of that at the time.

"I think Dad suspected what I was hiding: there was not one single part of me that wanted anything to do with God. I had twenty years of resentment toward Dad for always bossing me around and never giving me the benefit of the doubt. I thought God was the same." He finally met her eyes. "And I knew your greatest dream was to build on your father's legacy with his ministry."

Natalie swallowed. He'd expressed parts of this—in far less coherent fashion—standing on Mom and Dad's back porch on that terrible Thursday night when he told her he was leaving for Chicago. She could still smell the scent of burned vegetables that'd emanated from the house. She'd found out later Mom was too busy eavesdropping to remember she had dinner on the stove.

Jem touched her hand, fingertips barely grazing her skin. "It wasn't your fault. At all."

Natalie managed the barest of smiles. "Obviously. Keep going."

He pulled a pair of John's pants from the hamper. "I agonized over it, but I couldn't escape it. Our lives were headed two totally different directions. You wanted to spend your life working for God. And I wanted to spend mine running away from Him." He shrugged, eyes on the wet clothes. "It's no excuse. But at the time, I didn't think it was a choice. I couldn't imagine spending my life serving—or pretending to serve—a God just like my father. And I couldn't marry you, knowing that. So I left." He shook his head. "It sounds even worse when I say it out loud."

Natalie cleared her throat. All this time, and she'd thought he'd been disappointed in her. That somehow she hadn't measured up. The thought was so hard to dislodge, she had trouble fully believing his explanation. "And then?"

"Fast-forward five years, and the life that I thought would make me happy just wasn't working out. I had my degree, my job, a girlfriend.

No dad or God to make me feel guilty. And I was miserable. Then one day I got a postcard from Charlottesville. I thought it was from you."

She snapped her gaze up. "I didn't—"

"It was my cousin. She puts the tails on her *f*'s like you do." He hung the last shirt, placed the hamper on the kitchen counter, and pointed to the door. "Want to finish this conversation on the porch?"

She shook her head. "Finish the story."

He leaned back against the counter, hands in his pockets. "I was ready to drive back here overnight. It was a wake-up call. I was miserable. I'd thought giving God control would ruin my life, but I'd ruined it just fine on my own. So I broke up with Chloe and went back to church. Then Chloe came back a few weeks later with her news." He offered half a smile. "At first I thought God was punishing me. I stopped church again for a while. But the pastor reached out, and we talked about it. He helped me realize that me projecting Dad onto God was totally wrong. The road back started for real from there."

Natalie gripped the back of a dining room chair. It was true. She'd ignored the signs when they were younger, but the distance between Jem and God had been real. Things were different now, she could tell. But still . . . "What changed now? You and your dad have fought the entire time since you got back. Something's different."

He smiled. "You."

"Me?"

"You forgave me. Every day, each time you got mad again. I want Olly to have a grandfather. And if you can forgive me, maybe I can forgive him." He picked up his keys. "Come on. I'll take you home."

She followed him out the door, and they drove back to her apartment in silence. Natalie pulled the bobby pins loose from her hair and rested her head against the seat, processing the conversation they'd just had.

She'd asked God for an indication about whether Jem had changed.

She'd gotten it.

He walked her to the door and waited as she fished out her keys. "Did I tell you that you look amazing tonight?"

Sweat dampened her dress, her hair was an unruly tangle, and her shoes were . . . *Whoops*. Still somewhere at John's house. "I'm a mess."

"You're a hot mess." He offered his hands. "We might not get the filet mignon I was hoping for, but would you still care to dance?"

She held still and studied his face, a combination of boyish freckles and the faint worry lines of a new parent. Tired as he was, a sparkle still danced in his ocean-blue eyes.

Jem's actions tonight soothed the doubts she'd had about the change God had wrought in his heart. A man who loved like this—in the face of rejection, disappointment, and hurt—was a man she might be able to trust again.

He wiggled his fingers at her.

Natalie stepped into his arms and pulled his head down.

She slipped a hand along the slight stubble on his jaw, her face a breath away, then brought her lips to his. She kept her kiss sweet and light, and after a moment Jem's hands rested on her upper arms. Her fingers brushed Jem's hair as she reveled in being in his arms again. He'd made mistakes, yes. Did the thought of being hurt by him again still terrify her? Completely.

But she was tired of being apart from him when every inch of her wanted otherwise.

Pulling back a fraction, she opened her eyes and smiled at him.

The sparkle in Jem's eyes had fanned into a blaze. "Uh-uh. Come back here." He caught her lips once more, one hand on her waist and the other cupping her jaw. He deepened the kiss, and a flare alighted deep inside Natalie. She stood on tiptoe and wound both arms around his neck, tasting the lemonade he'd pinched from his father's fridge.

Jem held her tight, kissed her as if he'd been waiting to do this for years. He kissed her cheeks, her temple, her forehead, then brushed her lips again.

Natalie dragged her eyes open as Jem finally rested his forehead on hers. One hand gripped his collar, the other slid along his neck.

Jem drew in a ragged breath, opened his eyes. "Is this another I'll-kiss-Jem-but-then-tell-him-it's-not-happening-again thing?" His arms tightened around her. He brushed her lips again, spoke with his mouth barely touching hers. "'Cos I'd really like to convince you otherwise."

She smiled and pulled his head back down.

33

*C*ould today get any worse?

Lili's foot slipped on wet asphalt as she pushed against the trunk of Natalie's car. To passersby, it looked like Smurfette and Gru from *Despicable Me* were pushing a green VW Bug—steered by Big Bird—off the side of the road, still fifteen blocks from Jem's place. Or at least, attempting to push. The car didn't budge—just like the cold wall of silence between her and Nick for the past week.

Lili's hand slid on the slick bumper, and her eight-inch fake nose hit the trunk and squished her real nose.

Beside her, Natalie turned, blue trickles running down her face as rain eroded her body paint. "Are you okay?"

"I think I just broke Gru's nose."

Natalie rubbed her temples like she had a headache. "I can fix that. As long as the bird stays out of the rain, we'll be fine. Let's push."

Lili returned her attention to the steaming vehicle before her, torn between praying for help and pleading with God to keep anyone she knew from seeing her.

Natalie had enlisted her mother's and Lili's help in an elementary school skit earlier that afternoon for Wildfire. Natalie had been freaking out at the thought of stepping out in front of the kids—apparently her public-speaking fear extended to seven-year-olds—and she'd begged Lili to help.

It had sounded great at the time—Lili had a free period at the end of the day and needed a distraction from moping about Nick.

But now with her change of clothes at home and cold water soaking through the shoulder padding that formed Gru's figure, she wondered why she'd said yes.

Natalie threw her weight behind the broken-down car, and Lili pushed beside her. The vehicle gained some momentum, and as they pushed, Natalie's mom steered the car onto the shoulder of the road.

Lili executed her best Gru victory dance, complete with a shuffle and stanky leg, and a truck slowed beside her and beeped its horn. She froze as Nick's dual-cab pickup rolled to a stop.

You have got to be kidding me.

The two of them had barely spoken in a week, and this was how he found her?

His window wound down, and he peered through the rain at her. "Please tell me I can be Buzz Lightyear."

She folded her arms and tried to look as dignified as she could in a bald cap and prosthetic nose. "What are you doing?"

"Offering the Nickelodeon channel a lift home."

"We're not Nickelodeon characters."

"Nick!" Natalie's blue face appeared in Nick's other window.

He jolted, then grinned and lowered the glass that separated them.

"Can you give us a lift home?" she asked.

"Jump in," Nick said with a sly glance toward Lili.

Natalie and her mom jumped into the back seat, and Mrs. Groves tried to pull the door closed.

"Your tail feathers are sticking out," Lili said.

Mrs. Groves gathered her plumage as Lili pushed the door shut behind her. She dragged herself around to Nick's passenger seat.

Nick exchanged pleasantries with the older women as they started off toward home, before a country music station filled the silence. Natalie and her mom started discussing Natalie's internship, and Nick glanced at Lili. "How are you?"

"Fine." She kept her tone neutral.

"Grace is kinda worried."

"Why?"

"She said you failed your math test, and you've been acting weird. Why haven't you told her about . . . the stuff?"

"Who says I haven't?"

"She did. She had no idea why you'd failed or what was going on."

Lili huffed. "She's a gigantic blabbermouth." A blabbermouth who'd grown increasingly snippy that Lili was keeping a secret. They'd barely even messaged this week.

"Look, I wanted to say I'm sorry about—"

"Not here," she hissed with a look toward the melting Smurf and oversized bird in the back.

"Fine. We'll talk in code." Nick glanced toward the back seat, but Natalie and Mrs. Groves were engrossed in their discussion. "I'm sorry I didn't believe you about *blank*. It's not that I really thought you would lie, but it was just a lot to take in—she's like my mom, you know? More than my real mom is. But, well, I asked her."

Sitting in the truck, the massive shoulder and body padding she wore puffed up around Lili. She shrank into it like a turtle and clenched her hands together. "I don't care."

"She admitted it."

She snapped her head toward Nick. "She what?"

"But she said it's over. He ended it. The day your Mom got back from her conference. She said they were only actually together for about a week. The week Chloe was here."

Her eyes slid shut. *No.* If that witch was telling the truth, that meant Dad hadn't lied at the beginning, when he said the kiss was a one-time thing. Maybe he'd been fighting the way he felt.

It meant Lili's behavior on the Sunday she smoked could've been what finally pushed him into Miss Kent's arms.

It meant the whole shemozzle might be partly her fault.

And since Dad had still only made feeble attempts to contact her, he probably resented her for it.

"She said she's sorry," Nick said. "She's been lonely for a long time."

Lili's jaw dropped. He was making excuses for her?

"You can take your apology and shove it *blank blank blank blank blank*. That *blank* is lying to you." She folded her arms. "And I don't want anything to do with anyone who has anything to do with *her*." Tears pressed against her lids. She wiped her cold nose against Gru's scarf. Hopefully everyone would think it was just rain.

Nick stayed silent for a minute, eyes fixed on the road. "I'm sorry to hear that," he eventually said, eyes blinking at a rapid pace.

They pulled up outside Jem's apartment and Natalie and her mom exited the car.

Nick touched Lili's forearm as she reached for the door handle. "If this is it, I wanted to tell you that I'm sorry I hurt you."

She pulled her arm away and kept her focus on her lap. "You didn't."

A pause. "That's a relief, then. And I wanted to thank you. Your art tutoring really helped improve my grade. I have a college scholarship interview in two weeks. It's a new thing Wildfire's doing."

"Yay for you." Her tone said the opposite. She got out of the car. "Goodbye, Nick."

She slammed the door shut and walked into Jem's building without looking back.

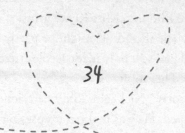

34

J em gritted his teeth and focused on super-gluing the cracked television remote back together and not his father's mouth shut.

Dad, seated at the kitchen with Olly in his high chair, alternated between playing "high-speed police chase" with Olly's car toys and criticizing every element of Jem's parenting.

"He keeps grabbing for my phone, Jem. Do you let him play with yours? Experts say children under two shouldn't have any screen time."

Jem tuned him out and squeezed glue onto the remote, trying not to drip it on the couch. He probably should have laid down a newspaper or something to do this.

Last Saturday night seemed to have been a turning point for Dad, who appeared both embarrassed at the state they'd found him in and quietly appreciative of the forgiveness Jem offered.

"Quietly" because he never actually said so. But he had come around to visit Olly a couple times this week, so Jem read between the lines.

But that didn't mean he'd had a brain transplant. He still seemed convinced that Jem couldn't parent without his sage advice. And with him around now more than ever, that meant more "advice" than any human should have to bear.

"Shouldn't he be saying more than 'da-da' by now?"

Jem squeezed the tube too hard. A big dollop of super glue landed on the couch.

He needed to get out of the house.

He checked his watch. When were Natalie and Lili getting home from that school skit? He'd been so excited about taking off his time-in-lieu and spending time with Nat that he'd forgotten she had her own job to do. Plus, he'd wanted a chance to talk to her. It was only week one of their relationship 2.0, and it already seemed something was bothering her. Was it him? Work stress? Worry over her father's cancer?

If only he could get away from Dad for five minutes to find out.

A key scraped in the front door. Jem bolted up. If that was Nat, then item number one on the agenda was dragging her into the hall-way for a kiss and then a complaining session about his dad.

But Lili entered, stripping off the remains of some kind of costume.

Jem placed the remote and the glue on the table, careful not to spill any more. "Hey, Lil. How was your day?"

She stomped into her room and slammed the door without a response.

Dad looked at him with raised eyebrows. *You going to stand for that?*

Jem held back a groan. Parenting his own baby was hard enough. Adding his brother's teenager to the mix pushed the intensity to eleven.

Natalie came through the door—and she was blue. Literally.

Jem stopped. "What's going on?"

"I think she and Nick are fighting."

That'd been question number two on his list, but he nodded like that's what he'd meant.

Natalie rubbed her neck, smearing the blue. "My car's not work-ing. Again. Can you come take a look?" Her voice was strained. That stupid car. It caused her far more trouble than it was worth.

But she'd just given him an out. He looked at Dad. "Would it be okay if you watched the kids for an hour?" He'd given Dad the rundown on Olly's diabetes earlier this week, and as a cop Dad knew his way around first aid pretty well.

Dad harrumphed. "I suppose. It'll give me a chance to look around this apartment for signs of mice. There's something about the smell in here . . ." He sniffed the air.

Jem clenched his teeth. It was like Dad didn't even think he tried. Like he didn't wake at three in the morning and worry about whether to pick Olly up straight away when he cried or to let the baby know he wasn't at his beck and call. Should he have tried harder to feed him a variety of vegetables during that month that Olly wanted nothing but his bottle, rice pudding, and applesauce? Should he not let him play with his phone when they were in public and the choices were (1) give him the phone or (2) let him scream the house down?

Whatever. Jem grabbed his keys and followed Natalie out the door. One hour, child-free, to spend with his girlfriend and find out if he was a part of the problem or solution regarding whatever bothered her.

And an hour to forget his failings as a parent.

♡

Natalie focused her nervous energy into jiggling her leg as the wind did its best to blow them off the road en route to her stranded car.

After a trial period, the Wildfire board had green-lighted Kimberly's youth drop-in center idea. Were she a more unselfish person, she'd feel happy for her colleague and the kids who'd benefit. But the approval was one more indicator of what the board's decision in one month's time would be.

She rubbed a hand over her face, fingers running over the uneven texture of an impending breakout. Great. Stress-induced pimples. Just what every girl still wanted to be dealing with at twenty-six.

Jem placed a hand on her knee, stopping the jiggles. "Nat. I just said your name three times. What's up?" He laced his fingers with hers, but it did nothing to take the edge off the tension coiled through her.

What was up? Only a lack of a college degree, the world's most boring résumé, and a father's legacy going down the drain. She fiddled with the wet hem of her costume and told him about Wildfire's decision.

"Why is this internship so important?"

"What?" She snatched her hand back. How could he even ask that? Did he know her at all?

With a glance at her reaction, Jem shrugged. "I mean, I know it's a great opportunity. But why does it have to be this one in particular? Why youth ministry? You're fighting so hard for this career and, well, sometimes I wonder if you really enjoy it."

She stared at him. Didn't enjoy it? She loved it. Couldn't he tell?

Her phone rang. She narrowed her eyes at Jem. "Saved by the bell."

Jem pulled over by her Bug and grabbed her keys from where they sat in the cupholder.

Natalie stayed in the car and pressed the phone to her ear. "Hey, Dad. Sorry I'm late." She'd meant to spend an hour with him this afternoon, as he was often too tired in the evenings.

His voice crackled over the storm interference. "That's okay, bubs. You've gotta hustle for this job. You're so close!"

She winced. "Actually, it's not the job. My car broke down."

"I'll come help."

She tried not to laugh. He could barely get out of bed, and he wanted to come help fix her car. Dads.

"It's okay. Jem's here. He's looking at it now."

"Make sure Jem doesn't mix up the jumper lead cables."

She smiled. It wasn't a battery problem, but okay. If only she could tape these conversations, full of Dad-ish concern and love. She treasured each one. While she still could. "Okay."

"And tell Sam that I live-streamed his talk at that school down in South Carolina. You guys are doing fantastic work. I'm so proud of you."

Her eyes slid shut as hot emotion rushed into them. "Thanks." She croaked out the word. Dad was the only person more excited about this internship than she was.

She was so close. And it was about to slip through her fingers.

They said their goodbyes, and after a moment to collect herself, she stepped out into the rain and joined Jem where he stood, staring at the engine of her car.

"Any luck?" She had to raise her voice to be heard over the rain.

"King Tut has more life in him than this car does." Lightning lit the sky as he lowered the hood. "I think it's time to call it quits, babe."

Thunder crashed around them. "No!" The word came out too harsh. She bit her lip. She had to hold it together. But everything was spiraling out of control.

He raised a quizzical brow. "I'm talking about the car."

She crossed her arms. "But you mean it about the job too, right? I can't believe you'd even suggest it."

His brow creased. He ran a hand through his wet hair, spiking it up. "You hate public speaking. You've said it yourself."

"I do it anyway."

The exasperation in his tone increased. "I can still see it's torture every time. I'm just not sure why it has to be *this* job if things aren't working out. You could do party planning. Event management. There's options."

He just didn't get it. And without living her life for the past seven years, he probably never would.

Natalie pointed her finger at him. "You went to college for four years and walked straight into your dream career. I vacuumed floors at UVA and answered phones for a store that rented out plants. This is my chance at something meaningful."

His expression softened. "Your dad's work is not the greatest thing about him, Nat. And it's not your responsibility to *be* him."

She placed her hands on her hips. "You think I don't know that? This is what I want. I'd have thought you would've supported me."

Jem's expression darkened. "I didn't know that asking the question meant not supporting you."

She refocused on the car. "I'm going to have to call a tow truck. Let's go." When he turned away, she swiped at her eyes, though by this point any tears were indistinguishable from the rain.

Dad's devotion to ministry wasn't *the* greatest thing about him. But it was the trait people remembered. The trait they said she shared with him.

And soon it would be all she had left.

Tense silence reigned in the car on the sodden ride home. Jem beat her upstairs to the door and opened it.

He sucked in a breath. "What happened?" The words were directed inside the apartment.

She hustled up the last few steps and slid past where he stood in the doorway, into the apartment.

John bounced a crying Olly, his expression thunderous. "You left that super-glue tube on the table. He can stand and reach things now, Jem. He got ahold of the tube and he's glued his eye shut."

Natalie clapped a hand over her mouth and peered at Olly's face. Yep, his closed left eye had a translucent layer of glue on it.

John held up a sodden washcloth. "Apparently warm soapy water can remove it. But the kid's lost half his eyelashes and has screamed blue murder the entire time. I hope you're usually more careful than this."

Jem palmed his forehead and muttered so low she barely caught the words. "Why do I even try?"

35

Lili was cornered.

She stood on the front steps of school on Friday afternoon and gaped at her father, standing two steps away on the sidewalk. What was he doing here? Around them, students streamed past on their way to buses and cars. He'd picked his ambush location well. She couldn't exactly shout at him here.

"Hi, Lili." Dad's smile had "fake" written all over it.

Lili folded her arms against her black tunic and leveled a glare. "What are you doing here?"

"I came to give you a lift home." His tone was lighter than whipped meringue.

She clenched her jaw and glanced around. If only Grace was still here with her beat-up Honda. Not that they were talking at the moment, anyway. Grace had gotten sick of Lili's evasive answers and blown up at her five days ago. Not one message since.

And since she hadn't spoken to Nick since last Friday's fight, her list of friends was shrinking.

Lili shuffled to the edge of the stairs to let other students past. But she kept her distance from her father. "I don't want to talk to you."

"This is important. And if you want to yell at me, at least come to the park where your friends won't hear you." He strolled toward the street, a leafy park on the other side.

After a moment she scurried down the stairs. "What's so important that Mom can't tell me tomorrow? She's taking me out to lunch. I thought she told you I needed space." It had been six weeks since she'd trashed Dad's office, but each time she saw him the rage bubbled up again.

There was a break in traffic, and Dad headed across the road.

She huffed and followed.

In the park he sat on a sunny bench and indicated the seat next to him.

She stayed standing.

"Mom is helping Sam prepare for his next Wildfire tour," Dad said, elbows resting on the pinstriped knees of his suit pants. "But we wanted to discuss this with you before we went to Jem tomorrow, so she asked me to come see you this afternoon."

"What are you discussing with Jem?" Lili's insides seized like plaster of Paris.

Dad held her gaze. "It's time for you to come home."

She stepped back. "I don't want to."

He flinched like she'd struck him. "I know you're mad."

"Mad? You think I'm just mad?" A buzz started in her ears. He acted like this was an emotion she'd just get over.

"But whatever you feel, this isn't about us. It's about Jem. He's had you for more than two months now. He needs his home back."

A tidal wave of despair washed over Lili and leaked from her tear ducts. Her one happy-*ish* refuge was about to disappear.

Dad's voice turned pleading. "Come on, Lili. What are people going to start thinking about our family if you stay there much longer?" He stood and rested a hand on Lili's shoulder.

She jerked away.

"We wanted to warn you before we talk to him. Pack your things tonight, and we'll collect you tomorrow." He opened his mouth like he wanted to say something, then sighed. "Do you want a lift back to Jem's, or would you rather take the bus?"

Lili shook her head and stormed off. He hadn't even said he missed her.

She stomped for five steps. Dad would stop her at any moment.

Nothing happened.

She twisted to look back. He walked in the opposite direction, shoulders slumped and hands in his pockets.

Her hands trembled as the beast inside strained to break loose from its chains. Were Dad within reach, she'd pound at him with all she had.

Instead she stumbled forward a few more steps and dropped down, sitting on the curb. Hidden from the school by a blue Fiat, she bawled. The gut-wrenching sobs built until they almost cut off her breath.

She couldn't go back to that house, couldn't live with her parents, couldn't help them pretend to the world that everything was okay.

They were liars.

And it seemed Mom and Dad cared more about their pretend life than they did about what it was doing to her.

Lili leaned her forehead against the cold metal of the car and fought for control.

Breathe. Just breathe.

A glint of metal caught her eye. She lifted her head, slid her hand into the wheel rim of the Fiat, and pulled out a hide-a-key.

She turned it over in her hand. She'd seen a similar one before, tucked under the flowerpot at Miss Kent's—

Wait. She tipped her head back and scanned the car again.

Miss Kent's car.

She scrubbed a hand over her face, jumped to her feet, and checked the street. The after-school rush had cleared, and no one was paying her any attention.

No one but her and that baby-blue Fiat, calling her name.

She slid the key into the lock and turned it. The mechanism clicked beneath her hand.

Her lips pulled into a smile.

♡

It wouldn't be long before someone caught her snooping.

Lili rummaged around the car's console with one hand and with the other poked another piece of chicken from her uneaten sandwich through the air vent of Miss Kent's car. She didn't dare risk taking the vehicle for a joyride, not with a police captain for a grandfather. But this was better. Another chance to snoop, plus the decaying meat should provide a nice counterbalance to the car's usual too sweet air freshener.

The console revealed nothing but Nickelback albums and lip balm. Disappointing. She went for the glove box next. Might be a good place to stash the remains of her chicken sandwich.

As she tugged it open, a lemon-yellow box tumbled out. With its wide satin ribbon, it looked like a present. A quick tug loosened the ribbon, and Lili flicked the lid of the box away. She frowned at the contents.

Who gift-wrapped a thermometer?

She plucked the thin piece of plastic from the box and turned it over. There was no screen for the numbers, just a strip of white with two blue lines on it.

Her fingers shook as her vision tunneled onto those two thin lines.

Miss Kent was pregnant.

Lili dropped the pregnancy test like it burned her and flung the box into the back seat. She rubbed her hands on her plum jeggings.

A baby. Her teacher was going to have a baby. With *Dad*.

Possibilities tumbled through Lili's mind. Had Dad known? Had this happened on purpose?

The world spun as she hyperventilated. Pins and needles ran through her hands and feet.

"Lili? What are you doing?"

She jolted at the voice next to the car and jerked her gaze to the driver-side window.

Nick tapped on the glass, a frown denting his forehead. His button-down shirt and tie looked out of place with his unruly brown hair.

She grabbed her backpack and the pregnancy test and thrust the door open. He jumped back to avoid it.

"Did you know about this?"

"What?" Nick focused on what she held beneath his nose. Color drained from his face. "Oh, God." The words didn't sound like profanity, more of a plea.

"She's pregnant. She's *pregnant*."

"Trish, what have you done?" He ran his hands through his hair.

Lili's ire toward him eased. At least he looked upset.

"I can't believe she didn't tell me." Nick mumbled the words to the plastic stick in her hand.

It fell to her side. "You've been talking to her?"

"I had dinner at her house last night."

Lili's stomach twisted. So he'd chosen sides too.

Nick pulled his gaze from the pregnancy test to her face. "What's with that look?"

She shook her head, felt her face contort in an effort to keep tears away. "Nothing. You made your choice." She threw the test at him. "I hope you're all very happy together."

Grabbing her backpack, she took off down the sidewalk.

"Lili, wait!"

She kept on, fury giving her speed.

Behind her, footsteps slapped on the path, then a car door slammed.

The familiar sound of Nick's pickup roared to life, and moments later his vehicle slowed to a jogging pace beside her. "Where are you going?"

"Anywhere but here."

"I don't have long. I'm on my way to my Wildfire scholarship interview. But I can give you a ride home."

"I don't have a home anymore." As she said the words, their truth sank deep into her soul.

Traffic backed up behind Nick as his pickup crawled beside her. "Lili, please. I have to go. Let me take you to Jem's."

"No." She slowed to a walk, tight bands around her chest. If only Grace was in town. Then she could at least crash at her place for a couple of days.

Cars zoomed past Nick, beeping. He ignored them. "Then where are you going?"

An idea formed in Lili's brain. She walked on, shaking her head.

"Lili."

"I told you, anywhere but here. Now leave me alone." She picked up her pace but veered right, into the park, away from the road.

She stayed there till Nick's pickup rumbled away, scanned the road to make sure he'd really gone, then backtracked and headed southwest. Just because Grace was out of town didn't mean she was out of reach. Maybe it was time she told her friend what was really going on.

Lili pulled out her phone and checked her banking app. Just enough money, if her calculations were correct.

Legs pumping, she reached the bus station in ten minutes. She stood outside its glass doors and stared at the square brick building.

Her plan wasn't a great one—her parents would be furious, and God wouldn't be real impressed either.

But the alternative was returning home. And that was unthinkable.

She pushed through the doors and approached the counter.

"How much is a ticket to Raleigh, North Carolina?"

36

Natalie banged on Mom and Dad's front door on Friday afternoon with more force than necessary. She was forty-five minutes late. Forty-five minutes she wouldn't get back with her father.

Oliver, sitting on her hip, yanked a handful of her hair and cried.

Natalie looked down at the armload of party supplies she held for Dad's party next week. The three grocery sacks and a box of plastic utensils and paper plates would've been a lot easier to carry if she had the use of both arms.

But Lili hadn't shown up for babysitting duties this afternoon. She was probably just off with Nick again, and Jem had forgotten to tell her to come straight home. And Jem hadn't responded to Natalie's six phone calls, hence the lateness.

Oliver yanked again. Natalie dropped the party supplies with a huff and disentangled his fingers. "*No*, Oliver, we do not pull hair."

He released her hair and went for her earring.

The sound of locks flipping rattled through the door. It pulled back to reveal Mom, today in tangerine sweats.

Natalie dumped the baby into her arms. "Take him."

Mom bounced the fussy eleven-month-old as Natalie gathered her

288

things up again. "Dad's excited to see you. He wants an update on the internship. When do they make the decision?"

In just under a month. But nothing in Natalie felt jubilant at the impending deadline. She scooped up the last of her things and followed Mom inside. "Don't get too excited."

Mom frowned but didn't press further. With her spare hand, she held a plate out to Natalie. "Anzac bikkie?" The Australian cookies—or biscuits, as Mom called them—were a staple in this house.

Natalie shook her head. "No, thanks." The news she'd received an hour ago had banished her appetite. Or what little appetite she'd had lately, anyway. She'd heard that the stress-causing-ulcers thing was a myth, but she could swear one was forming right now.

Mom carried Olly down the hallway to the bedroom and sat him on the empty side of the bed, beside a dozing Dad. As she paused *Goldfinger*, playing on his little TV screen, she leaned in Natalie's direction and murmured, "Don't let him jostle Dad."

Natalie nodded and pulled up a chair, close enough to keep one hand on the baby.

Dad opened his eyes and shifted with a wince.

Natalie grimaced. In the past week his pain levels had started outstripping what the medication could handle.

His gaze focused on her. "Nattie. Talk to me. Did the board approve your proposal?"

She did her best to sound upbeat. "They decided the funds were better spent on Kimberly's youth drop-in center. It's yielded more results than the festival did."

"Oh." He looked crestfallen. "What does that mean for your chances of getting the job?"

The upbeat tone was harder to maintain this time. "It's not a great sign, but it's not over yet." Her one advantage was that Sam seemed to genuinely enjoy working with her while Kimberly got under his skin.

Dad gripped the handle over his bed, let it go, and shoved his coverlet aside. At least shoved it as far as he could without moving his torso. "That doesn't sound right. Let me talk to them."

Olly tried to crawl toward Dad. She kept a firm grip on the back of his little baby shirt and held him in place. "They've already—"

"Don't they know how much you've given up?" He tried to shift around in the bed. "I shouldn't have let you drop out of college. What will you do if you don't get this?"

Oliver strained against her grip, reaching for Dad. She stood to adjust her hold on him. Dad normally liked Olly to sit next to him and let the little guy chew on his finger, but today he seemed too agitated to even notice. "It's going to be fine. Don't wo—"

Oliver slipped in her grasp. His momentum threw him forward, colliding with Dad's torso.

Dad cried out, back arching with pain.

Natalie yanked Oliver away. "Mom!"

A clatter sounded. Mom's uneven gait echoed at a run. She burst through the door. "Phil? What happened?"

Natalie cradled a flailing Oliver to her chest and tried to explain through tears, snot, and overwrought emotions.

Mom began rifling through pill bottles after the first choked sentence as Dad clutched at the pillow beside him and moaned. This from a man with a pain threshold worthy of Chuck Norris.

Natalie ran for the door through blinding tears and didn't stop till she had reached her chained-up bicycle outside. She sat Olly down and tried to enter the combination with shaking fingers, but the lock wouldn't release.

Olly's indignant shrieks turned into whines, and he crawled away.

"Oliver!" She grabbed him and plopped him between her feet. "Stay still."

She tried the lock again. No luck.

Oliver pulled himself upright against her leg and took two wobbly steps toward the mailbox.

Her self-control snapped. "*Oliver!*" The shout probably could've been heard by Jem at work, or wherever on earth he was. She jerked the waistband of Olly's pants till he plopped back down on his bottom. He wailed.

She froze.

Olly had walked.

Olly had walked without holding anything for the first time.

And she'd shouted at him for it.

She sank down to the ground, kept one hand on Olly, and buried her face in the other and sobbed. What was she going to do? She couldn't keep this up. Everything expected of her for this internship, nannying Olly, taking care of her parents, keeping an eye on Lili, dating Jem—it was too much.

One more month and you could have the job, and it'll all be worth it.

She envisioned Sam's phone call in a month's time, telling her that despite Kimberly's visionary plans for the ministry, her unmatchable work ethic, and her sharp mind, Natalie was the woman for the job. She waited for the rush of excitement at the thought. The thought of being part of a team, speaking into young hearts, of networking with others with a similar passion.

None came.

She pressed her spare hand over her eyes and blocked out the world. *God, is this how it plays out? You dangle my dream in front of me and then yank it away?*

Her phone rang. She dragged it out of her pocket. Steph. Uh-oh. "Hey, Steph, I know I'm—"

"I've got a minivan and eight middle schoolers here, but no Natalie."

She dragged her sleeve over her nose. "I had an issue with Dad, but I'm on my way."

"I know your dad's sick, Natalie, but are you committed to this? Do you really want it? Because I think you can take Kimberly, I really do, but only if you're one hundred percent in." Steph sighed and ended the call.

Natalie sniffed back her tears. If anyone on the planet was one hundred percent in, it was her. She wouldn't lose this job because of a lack of commitment.

She tried the lock again. Bingo.

With Oliver in the bike's baby seat, she pumped her legs in the direction of Wildfire and made it in record time. Not that Steph looked impressed.

Within thirty minutes, she had the kids raking leaves and weeding Mrs. Hillman's jungle of a backyard. Today was the launch of Kimberly's latest initiative, Love Thy Neighbor. The citywide community-service project had started with the eightysomething grandmother of one of the drop-in center kids.

Kimberly's team of kids was attacking the front yard and had already tamed an impressive amount of it.

Natalie gritted her teeth and got to work cleaning out an ancient garden shed, first in the waning afternoon light and then under Wildfire-supplied floodlights. A teen girl more suited to babysitting than manual labor entertained Olly on the enclosed front porch. After two hours, Natalie stood back and surveyed her progress. Respectable. She walked over to the door of the porch. Time for the teens to head home. The door opened from the inside, and the girl—Lauren? Laura?—handed a sleeping Oliver over to Natalie. "He started getting sleepy in the last half hour." She scampered off to the waiting minivan.

Natalie brushed a hand against Olly's forehead, and he opened his eyes in a series of long blinks. Hmmm. Unusual for him at this time of the evening. She checked her watch. Almost six. "Olly?"

She searched back through her mind for signs of unusual behavior. He'd had a good appetite at lunch, and at his afternoon sna—

Oh no. She'd forgotten to give him his snack.

Ever since Olly's diagnosis, their lives had revolved around precisely planned meals, insulin injections, and sugar tests. If she'd mistaken a hypoglycemic episode for sleepiness, Olly's low blood sugar could knock him unconscious or . . . worse.

She scrambled for the blood test kit in Olly's bag.

♡

Jem leaned back in his chair at the local school board meeting and tried not to visibly wince. When a distracted teen driver had run over his foot in the Walmart parking lot this morning, he'd thought that'd be the low point of the day.

But as today's fiery meeting entered its third hour, he was tempted to reevaluate.

Under normal circumstances the debate over raising the school levy would've fired up his journalistic juices. But Olly had kept him up half the night, and to top it off, the achiness all through him indicated he was getting the flu.

Fingers cramping, Jem stopped scribbling in his notebook for a moment and flicked his phone over. Seven missed calls. The last from Dad. He fumbled to play the voice messages as he sneaked out of the room, heart racing. Was something wrong with the kids?

He berated himself as he limped up the corridor. What if Olly had caught his flu? What kind of parent didn't check his phone when it was on silent?

There were six messages from Natalie, her irritation levels rising with each one. Lili hadn't shown up to take Olly. He frowned. He'd definitely told Lili this morning. Had she forgotten? Or had something happened? He shoved his notebook into his back pocket and limped faster.

Dad's message: "Have you found my granddaughter yet? Natalie called me. Ring me back *ASAP*." Aggravation leeched through his words.

Jem rubbed his forehead. Dad seemed to think he was incompetent enough without this happening.

He phoned Mike as he reached his car. Maybe once they found Lili and things calmed down, he should have lunch with his older brother. Mike could always make him feel better about his inability to measure up. "Hey, Mike. Is Lili with you?"

"I'm at the church. She's not at your place?" Mike's voice had the sharp tone of an alarmed parent.

Jem slid into the driver's seat. "I'm still working. Natalie said Lili never showed up to take Oliver. Nat had to take him to Wildfire with her." The car's Bluetooth took over the call. He set the phone down and backed out of the parking lot. "I'll go home and check. She might have shown up. Do you know that Nick kid's phone number?"

"Nick who?"

"Her . . . friend." Their relationship status was something he hadn't been able to figure out yet. "They spend a lot of time together." What was that kid's surname? His brain struggled to fire. Nick was the brother of the one who— "You know his aunt."

"Excuse me?" The words seemed to come out with more force than was warranted.

"Trish Kent. You did all that work for her nephews. Anyway, you obviously don't have the number." Jem barely registered a stop sign. He mashed the brake pedal down with his sore foot. *Ouch.* "Have you seen Lil lately?"

"At school this afternoon. You know, she's developed a real sass since living with you."

Jem pulled a face. Where had that come from? "In case you hadn't noticed, she's sixteen. If you're concerned, maybe you should do something about it since you're her actual parent." He shook his head. He loved having Lili, but it seemed to also mean taking the blame for any hiccup in her behavior. Why was he the one being held responsible?

"Sorry that my failing marriage is inconveniencing you." Mike's words dripped with bitterness.

Any fragment of good humor in Jem's mood vanished.

"What's your deal, man? She's your kid." The words slipped out of his mouth, and he winced. It sounded like he didn't want her.

"Nice to know how you really feel. I guess Steph shouldn't have blown off a marriage-counseling appointment to babysit Olly while you and Natalie went on a date. He's your kid." Mike's tone made it sound like Jem spent all his time out on dates.

"That's not what I—"

"Guess I shouldn't help you pay to employ your girlfriend anymore."

"Mike, I—"

"I shouldn't have trusted you with her."

The words cut through to Jem's soul. In this dysfunctional family, Mike had always been his ally. Now it seemed he'd let his brother down too, though he wasn't sure how.

The phone beeped. Incoming call. Natalie. He pulled the car over.

"Mike, calm down. This is Natalie, she probably knows where Lil is." He changed calls before Mike could respond.

"Nat, tell me some good news."

A pause. "Jem, you should come."

She was crying.

37

Natalie flinched as Jem's car jumped the curb in front of Mrs. Hillman's house. He jumped out of the car and limp-ran over the yard.

Natalie shivered from her spot on a tree stump in the deserted yard. Kimberly had ferried both her and Natalie's charges back to Wildfire for their parents to pick them up.

Jem reached them, face pale under the full moon and streetlight. "How is he?"

Natalie handed the baby over. "He seems alright. I checked his sugars again. They're better." He'd been teetering on the edge of consciousness by the time she got some juice into him, about to slide into a hypoglycemic episode.

Jem held the baby up to the streetlight, inspected him, then cradled him against his chest. "Should we take him to the hospital?"

Oliver chattered to himself and waved his toy car around, now perked up with sugar in his system.

She sat back against the tree stump. "I called the doctor. Only if you want to."

Jem sighed and sagged against a nearby tree.

She rubbed cold hands against her jeans. "I'm so sorry. I forgot to give him his snack."

Jem was quiet for a long time and didn't look up from the baby. Finally, he met her eyes. "I don't think this arrangement is working out, Nat."

Chills spread through her. "What do you mean?"

"The ministry. Nannying. If you're going to nanny Olly, now with his health issues, he needs your full attention. It doesn't work having you cart him around to all your Wildfire work." His tone ended on a frustrated note.

Natalie fought for calm. She was three and a half weeks away from Wildfire's decision. How could she find another job to work around the internship for only three and a half weeks? And if she didn't get her paycheck, she didn't pay rent. With the loans she'd already taken out for Mom and Dad, borrowing wasn't an option. "Jem, think about what you're asking."

His expression turned to steel. "I'm asking to not get phone calls like this." He headed for the car.

She scrambled after him. She'd expected fear, some anger, but not this reaction. "It was one mistake."

He buckled Olly in, straightened, and spoke to her over the roof. "It's a pattern. You seem to be the only one who can't see it."

"What's that supposed to mean?" Her voice squeaked.

He got into the car and she followed suit. "You're obsessed with getting something you don't even really want. And now it's affecting Olly."

Natalie's mouth fell open. "And who are you to tell me what I want?"

He rolled his eyes. "I'm someone with my eyes open!"

Unbelievable. "Are you just jealous of all the time I spend with Sam?"

Jem flashed her an incredulous look. "I can't believe you would even say that."

She pinched her forefinger and thumb. "I am this close, Jem. I let go of what was important once before. I was so distracted with you and the wedding, and then my chance to work with Dad was over before I knew it."

A call came over the car's Bluetooth. Natalie glanced at the phone's screen. Mike. Jem hit the Reject button. "So Olly staying conscious isn't what's important?"

Natalie clenched her jaw. "Stop twisting my words. I feel like I've been in the wilderness for seven years, and this job has given me a purpose again. It's not a just a job. It's who I am."

Jem shook his head. "I can't argue with that."

Her ire calmed a fraction. "Thank you."

Jem barked a laugh. "I mean I can't argue with such a ludicrous statement. You are not a job."

"Easy for you to say!" Natalie rifled through the console for a tissue. "You have your career, education. You have options. You weren't here. You don't know what it was like." She couldn't go back to that. The unending sensation of being forgotten. Left behind. Not only by Jem but by God too.

No tissues. She gave a disgusted huff and slammed the console shut. "What kind of parent doesn't have tissues in his car?"

Jem stopped at an intersection and glared at her. "I'm not forcing you out of Wildfire. Change your hours, reduce them, find a different job. There's options."

She gaped at him. He made it sound so easy. He had no idea.

He set his jaw. "I might not be a good enough parent to have unending supplies of tissues, but this is my line in the sand." He rolled through the intersection and pulled into his apartment complex's parking lot.

She crossed her arms. "I can't believe you're not supporting me on this."

"I'm doing what's best for my kid. If you're too caught up trying to impress your dad and Steph to see that, then we have a serious problem."

"Well, if you can't support my dreams, then *we* have a serious problem." The words flew out without forethought.

Jem turned the car off and faced her, a frown carved into his forehead. "Wait—What are you saying?"

She stared back, unable to wrap her brain around the words they'd just said. Was that how he really felt? How *she* really felt? "What are *you* saying?" She gulped. Strike first. "I'm saying this is a deal-breaker." She'd been distracted from her calling by Jem once before, and look what that had gotten her.

Never again.

Besides, he'd cave. He'd see how unreasonable he was being and give in. He had to.

Jem stared at her. "An ultimatum, Nat? Really? I didn't tell you to quit Wildfire. I just asked you to change your hours. And you threaten to break up with me." His voice was quietly furious.

She matched his level of indignation. "You might as well have, and you know it. It's not possible. Kimberly's already got a major advantage over me."

Jem threw his hands up. "Maybe that's because she's the better one for the job."

Natalie flinched. The comment hung between them for a long moment.

He didn't believe she could do this. He didn't believe in her dream.

He didn't believe in her.

She got out of the car and slammed the door.

Oliver cried.

She stomped toward where she'd chained her—*Oh*. Her bicycle. They'd left it at Wildfire.

Whatever. She'd walk.

Behind her a car door opened. "That's it, Nat? You're going to run away?"

She snapped over her shoulder at him. "Guess it's my turn."

"If you think this tantrum's going to change my mind, you're wrong."

She spun and planted her hands on her hips. "If you think I'm quitting Wildfire, you're insane."

"Fine!"

"Fine!"

So, this was how it ended. In a fireball.

Natalie kept walking, if only to keep Jem from seeing her cry.

Behind her, Jem's phone rang again.

Jem: "*What?*"

Mike's voice came over the car's stereo system, reached her through Jem's open door. "Have you found Lili yet?"

Lili. Natalie stopped and looked up to Jem's apartment window. Dark.

She changed directions. She'd make sure Lili was okay.

Then she'd officially break up with Jem.

Jem punched in Nick's number and paced the living room while Natalie phoned the school administrator's home number from the kitchen. Tense lines formed around her pursed lips. He pulled his eyes from her and forced his mind to focus on the ringing phone. One problem at a time.

The phone sounded its fourth ring.

Come on, pick up.

He'd already tried Steph, Dad, and the school. Lili had better be with Nick, or Natalie would get a front-row seat to his full parental panic mode.

"Hello?" Indistinct chatter sounded in the background.

Jem pressed the phone closer to his ear, even though it was already on full volume. "Nick, it's Lili's uncle Jem. Is Lili with you?"

"No, sorry. I'm with Aunt Trish at Wildfire. For my scholarship interview. Well, I'm waiting to go in. They got delayed."

Jem pressed a hand to his forehead. Worry clawed his insides. "Okay. You don't know where she is?"

"I saw her at school earlier, but I haven't seen her since."

The kid's voice sounded uncertain. Weird. Was there something he wasn't saying?

He waited a moment, in case Nick volunteered anything.

Silence.

Jem sighed. "Alright. Let me know if you hear from her."

He pulled the phone from his ear.

A faint sound came from the speaker. He jammed the phone back against his head. "Sorry?"

"I just had to walk a few steps from my aunt. Do you know . . . I mean, has Lili told you . . . Did she talk about what's going on?" he asked.

Knew it.

"Do you know?" Jem's voice was urgent.

"There's stuff going on with her parents. She's pretty torn up about it." Nick kept his words hushed.

Jem's mind spun with scenarios. "I know they've been fighting, but this sounds more serious."

"It is."

So something had been happening for a while. But there must've been some kind of trigger—"Did something happen today?"

"Yeah." Nick's tone indicated that was all he would say on the matter.

Jem went for another tactic. "Do you know where I can find her?"

"No. She just said she wasn't going home. Actually, she said she didn't live at your house anymore."

What? Where had that come from?

Across the room, Natalie caught his expression and lifted an eyebrow. But he had no answers. Yet.

He plugged his spare ear and turned away from her. "That doesn't make any sense." But it didn't sound like he'd get more from the kid. Did Mike know something? "Either way, I'd better keep looking. Good luck, Nick."

"Wait." Nick jumped in before Jem could hang up. "I'll put off this interview and come to your apartment. There's a bit of a story. I think you need to hear it."

"What is it, Nick?" Jem channeled Dad's captain voice for that one.

Nick's voice dropped quieter again. "Her mom wouldn't let her say anything, but . . . her father's been having an affair. With my aunt. And today we found out my aunt's pregnant."

Jem almost dropped the phone. Mike. Responsible, older-brother, church-pastor Mike.

Had gotten a woman other than his wife pregnant.

That explained his bad mood.

"Thanks for telling me." Jem choked the words out.

A female voice sounded in the background. "You're Nick, Lili's friend."

Steph.

Uh-oh.

Nick's voice, wary. "Yes, ma'am."

Steph's voice grew a little fainter, like she'd turned away from the phone. "And you're Lili's teacher. You're . . ." Her voice trailed off.

The phone beeped. Call ended.

Bad. Very bad.

Jem grabbed his keys and dialed Dad's number.

"Where's my granddaughter?" The voice barked from the phone so loud that Jem had to pull it away. He scooped up Olly in one arm, made eye contact with Natalie, and jerked his head toward the door. Braced himself for the reaction he was about to get.

"You need to get Mike and meet us at Wildfire. I think Lili's run away."

38

Natalie wrung her hands and sneaked looks at Jem's stony profile as they zipped toward Wildfire in the evening traffic. The words he'd spoken still wouldn't compute.

Mike, a cheater.

Steph, a liar.

Lili, alone through it all.

How could she have missed the signs?

Natalie replayed every conversation she'd had with Lili in the past three weeks. The girl had seemed off, sure, but that was easy to put down to her fight with Nick.

But the whole time her family had been falling apart, with Lili forbidden from saying a word about it.

Natalie scrubbed a hand across her face. "That day your dad said she was drunk . . ."

"I know." Jem's voice was tight.

He'd barely looked at her since he passed on Nick's message. Resentment rolled from him in waves. Not that he seemed to blame her for the Lili situation, though she'd clearly misread it.

No, with the Lili situation, he was just worried. But he *was* mad about Olly—and her reaction.

She folded her arms and slouched in the seat.

Jem swung into the parking lot, his wheels over the painted line. He yanked the keys from the ignition without bothering to correct.

She touched his arm as he twisted in the seat to unbuckle Olly. "She's going to be okay."

He brushed her hand aside. "Let's go."

She sat still as he exited the car, a hollow ache blooming in her chest.

Jem poked his head back inside. "Are you coming?" He shut the door before she could respond.

Scrambling out, she peered over to the five people staring one another down in the parking lot. What was Lili's teacher doing there, and why was Nick standing between her and Steph?

Realization hit. She was Lili's teacher. She was Nick's aunt. She'd probably come with him to Wildfire for the scholarship interview.

And she was the mistress.

"Oh no." She dashed to catch up with Jem, who'd reached his father's side.

As she arrived, Mike was telling Jem the story of his encounter with Lili that afternoon. "We planned to talk to you tomorrow," he finished.

Jem turned to Nick. "And you saw her afterward?"

"She was in front of the school."

"And she'd just found out about the pregnancy?"

Steph's face twitched at the word.

Natalie winced.

Nick nodded. "Yes, sir."

"Did she say anything about where she was going?"

"She just said she wasn't going home. That was it."

Natalie glared at Mike. What had he done?

"We're going to search in pairs," Jem said. "Whoever finds her, call us." He pointed to his father. "You take Steph. Natalie, Mike. Nick, you're with me." He gave each pair a zone of Charlottesville to tackle. "Go to malls, cinemas, and fast-food places first. And any place to do with art."

"I've got the force looking too," John said, nodding to a police car cruising past.

"Good. Let's go." Jem stepped away from Natalie's side.

She shivered. No reassuring touch to the arm. He just went.

She walked on wooden legs toward Mike. Red scratches stretched across his cheek. She could only imagine what Steph's reaction had been. "You're despicable."

"I know." He looked at his wife, then Trish.

Natalie followed his gaze. Trish stood alone among the pairs, her arms wrapped around her middle.

Nick hugged his aunt. Natalie was close enough to hear his low words.

"Go home, Trish."

She mumbled something in response.

"It's going to be okay. I'm going to be a great cousin for this baby." She nodded against his shoulder, sniffed, and left.

Natalie's stomach turned. Nick, Lili, even the baby, had nothing to do with this mess. But they would suffer for it, nonetheless.

When Trish's Fiat pulled away from the curb, Mike unlocked his car.

Natalie climbed in, and they headed toward the downtown mall. Silence reigned during the drive and the first part of the search. They checked the Paramount Theater, Splendora's, the children's museum, and the Freedom of Speech Wall. Nada.

As they hiked back to the car, Mike's phone buzzed in his hand. He hit the answer button and set it to speakerphone. "Jem?"

"Nick had a brainwave." Jem shot the words out rapid fire.

Natalie perked up. They'd found her?

"We tracked her through her phone, same as she did to you," Jem said.

Mike winced, and Natalie deflated. Jem didn't sound excited that he'd found Lili's location, so it mustn't be good.

"Where is she?" she asked.

"I just sent a screenshot of the map to Mike's phone. That's where she was ten minutes ago. We lost her signal—she must have switched her phone off."

Mike pulled up the image.

"Where is she going?" Natalie studied the pinpoint on the map, at least a hundred miles from Charlottesville.

"She's on the interstate to Raleigh," Mike said. "Grace lives there."

"Things haven't gone well with Grace's dad, and her grandmother in Washington has cancer." Nick's voice came over the phone. "Grace and her mom have gone to take care of her for a couple months. Grace mentioned it to me the other day. But I don't think Lili knows that."

♡

They were losing time.

Natalie folded her arms against the icy chill of the November night wind as she leaned against Jem's car, the heater inside still humming to warm Olly. They'd regrouped at the parking lot of Jem's apartment.

Across from her, Jem and Nick leaned over Jem's phone. Both had loosened ties and frustrated expressions. They'd been trying to pick up Lili's signal again.

"This isn't working," Jem lowered the phone. "Mike and Steph, are you sure Raleigh is where Lili would be heading?"

"It's the only thing that makes sense." Steph shivered as she spoke.

Mike offered his coat to her.

The look she gave him could have frozen an Eskimo.

Mike shrugged his jacket back on. "She doesn't know anyone else in that direction."

"I can contact the bus station and find out if she bought a ticket," John said. He wore only shirtsleeves but seemed unaffected by the plummeting temperature.

Jem nodded. "But for now, we're running out of time. If she is on the bus, the schedule says she should arrive a bit after 9:00 p.m. And she doesn't know that Grace has moved. If Lili isn't able to contact Grace for some reason, she could be stranded."

"You'll never beat her to the bus station." Natalie studied the map on her phone.

"The bus could've been delayed. They often are."

"We can take a squad car," John said. "Faster."

"I'll follow in the Bimmer," Steph said. Her gaze cut to Mike. "You can ride with your father."

"I'll go shotgun with Steph," Jem said.

"Whoa." Natalie took a step forward. "Is everyone going? Won't that be overwhelming? She might just stay on the bus."

"We can't take Oliver. One of us will have to stay home." Jem's face shuttered as he spoke. His expression wiped every time he was forced to speak to her.

"You're her uncle. You should go," she murmured. Then, louder, "But I don't think all of you can show up and expect things to go well." She stared down Mike. "Especially you."

Steph stood straighter. "I'm her mother—I need to be there."

"She's angry with both of you." Jem spoke at the same time.

"Just put her in the police car and don't give her a choice." John started toward his car.

Natalie put two fingers in her mouth and whistled.

Everybody stopped.

"Lili hasn't been able to be honest with any of us lately. Except Nick. I think we should ask what he thinks."

The boy's eyes widened.

Steph pursed her lips but nodded.

Nick scratched his head. "I understand Mrs. Walters wanting to be there. You, too, Mr. Walters. And if you stay home, she might think you don't care."

Steph flashed a triumphant look toward John.

"But I also don't think she'll come quietly if you show up at the bus station. She's still pretty raw." His eyes landed on Jem. "You've got the best shot."

Natalie nodded. "Mike and Steph, you guys could go, but get a couple of motel rooms and stay there while Jem talks to Lili. That way she has the option of seeing you and knows you care. But if she can't handle it, Jem can just drive her straight home or stay in a different room."

"Best idea we've had yet." John pulled out his keys. "Mike, get your backside in here."

Jem snagged Nick's elbow. "If you have to leave, that's fine, but I'd like to have you with me if you're willing."

Nick pocketed his keys and nodded.

Jem approached Natalie. "I'll text you to find out his sugars." Jem inclined his head toward where Olly dozed in the back seat.

She looked down. She'd deserved that. "Okay."

Jem didn't move.

She scrounged the courage to lift her face again. "We will find her, you know. She'll be okay."

"Physically, maybe. But we can't fix her broken heart." He shook his head. "I'll let you know when we're on our way back. If you don't want to be here, then . . . See if your mom can babysit Olly instead."

Her eyes filled. Why did he give up on their relationship so easily?

Then again, if he didn't support her dream of working at Wildfire, did she want that relationship?

He walked away and slid into the passenger seat of Steph's car. The vehicles pulled away. Natalie stayed, propped up by the car, until they disappeared into the dark night.

She hit her speed dial. "Mom? I need you to come over."

39

The bus arrived at Raleigh right on time.

Lili shifted her head from the window as they rolled into the North Carolina capital, ran her fingers over the curtain imprint on her cheek. Her nap for the past hour had been bliss—except for the BO wafting from two shaggy-haired guys sitting in front of her—but now reality crashed back in.

Miss Kent was pregnant.

She'd run away.

Grace had no idea she was coming.

She powered on her phone. Its battery low, she'd switched it off hours ago. Hopefully she'd have enough juice left to call a taxi.

She screwed up her eyes against the screen's glare as forty-three missed calls flashed up. She swiped past all of them, found a cab company's number, and punched it in.

By the time the bus pulled into the station, her cab waited by the curb.

She shot from the bus to the taxi, frigid night air raising goose bumps on her arms.

"Where to?" The cab driver's frizzy black hair and red goatee reminded her of an artist's impression of Lucifer. Lili pressed back into her seat and gave Grace's address.

As the cab pulled away, her phone vibrated in her hand. The screen went black. Battery dead.

Lili hugged her backpack as they zoomed down the road. Her heart rate accelerated. She should have warned Grace she was coming. Then, at least, if this guy turned out to be a serial killer, someone would notice her absence. What had she been thinking? She was sixteen, alone in a strange city at night. According to the *Law & Order* reruns she'd seen, that basically guaranteed her kidnapping.

She watched for street signs and landmarks, searching her memory of Google Maps to try and gauge if they were going the right way. The cab made an unexpected turn left, and her hand shot to the door handle. Was this guy driving her to some abandoned cabin in the woods?

They turned again, right this time, and passed a sign to Grace's cul-de-sac. She released her breath and eased her hand from the door handle.

The lights in Grace's house were out as Lili exited the vehicle and paid the cabbie with her last twenty-dollar bill—save for a glow in the kitchen window. The taxi pulled away, and she stood in the driveway for a moment, gathering her courage.

She should have warned Grace, had almost done it six times during her first few hours on the bus.

But while Grace's mom was generally a chilled-out person, she couldn't run the risk that she'd meet her at the bus station and buy her a ticket home.

If she just arrived on their doorstep, they couldn't turn her away.

Something brushed her leg. Lili leapt across the drive, slapped a hand over her mouth to contain her squeal.

A cat meowed, then sauntered off, its black body barely visible.

The shot of adrenaline energized her. She strode up the driveway, toward the front door. Muffled voices floated from the kitchen window.

Unfamiliar voices.

". . . supposed to pay for a boat when . . . Sarah's tuition?" a woman's voice rasped, with the trademark throatiness of a chain smoker.

Lili backed a step away from the house. Who was Sarah?

A man's voice responded, ". . . extra shifts, and Ray told me—"

"Ray?" The woman barked a laugh. "Max, you'd believe anything that man says."

Lili bolted away from the door, down the drive to the mailbox. She must have the wrong number. Her stomach clenched as she read the address, then turned to view the house again.

It was the address Grace had given her months ago.

But it seemed it wasn't Grace's house anymore.

"Who's there?" The front door of the house cracked open, and yellow light spilled onto the porch.

Lili sprinted down the cul-de-sac as fast as her legs could take her.

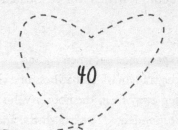

40

Natalie hit the DVD pause button at her mother's distinctive *knock-knock, knock-knock-knock* on Jem's apartment door.

Shane West and Mandy Moore's faces froze on the TV screen. She sniffed and shifted a heavy blanket and *A Walk to Remember* DVD case off her lap so she could get up.

She'd known moving her DVD collection to Jem's house was a good idea—she just hadn't expected to use her I-need-to-cry playlist so soon.

Knock-knock, knock-knock-knock.

"I'm coming." Natalie kept her voice hushed. Oliver slept feet away in his crib in Jem's room.

Mom had been dealing with Dad's pain meds again when Natalie called, and then it'd taken quite a few phone calls to find someone to come and stay with Dad.

Natalie did a quick calculation of the time since the others had left for Raleigh. They should have arrived by now. Jem still hadn't messaged.

She pulled the door open.

Mom stood on the other side, holding up a jumbo packet of plain M&M's. "It sounded serious."

Tears bubbled. She wilted into Mom's arms, inhaling the scent of her vanilla body wash between sobs.

Mom nudged her inside and pushed the door shut with her foot. "Tell me what happened."

Natalie perched on a stool by the counter and spilled the story. Thirteen crumpled tissues sat by the M&M's bowl by the time she finished.

Mom listened without interrupting, just stroked the back of Natalie's hand. When the words stopped, she chewed an M&M and let Natalie sop the moisture from her face.

"So . . . that escalated quickly," Mom said in a dry tone.

Despite her tears, a chuckle escaped Natalie. "I guess."

"Do you really think Jem doesn't support you? I mean, was there anything before today?"

"He asked me once if I really did enjoy the job. He didn't think I would, in the long run."

"And do you?"

Natalie opened her mouth for an enthusiastic *yes*. But something gave her pause.

Her panic about the presentation.

The stress of that elementary school skit.

Sam's announcement that the permanent job would involve even more travel and public speaking.

"I don't adore every single part of it," she conceded. "But that's life. No job is perfect. I love the organization side of it: preparing for that festival, promoting the ministry, doing all the back-office jobs."

"And you have a gift for that." Mom nodded and spoke around the handful of M&M's she'd just popped in her mouth. "But you can use that gift in areas other than Wildfire. There's a new wedding-planning business in town. You'd be great at that."

"No!" The word popped out with more force than she'd intended.

Mom blinked. "That hit a nerve." She pushed the M&M's bowl

aside. "Is it possible—and I'm not saying that you did, I'm genuinely asking—that you overreacted to Jem's request because you can't bear to think about anything jeopardizing Wildfire?"

"Maybe a slim possibility." Natalie hiccupped.

"And why is that?"

"I always planned to take over Dad's ministry, and then that wasn't possible anymore. Wildfire is my second chance. I'd make Dad proud, Steph proud. And I'd be making a difference in the world. It's what I always expected of myself."

"Ah." Mom appeared to ponder Natalie's words for a moment as she slowly chewed, lips stained from choosing all the blue M&M's. "And what if Kimberly beats you to that job? Who are you then?"

Natalie shook her head. "I can't even think about that."

"And do you think that's a warning sign?"

"Huh?"

"Jem has no desire to break up with you, Natalie. He's just trying to do what's best for his son. *You* escalated that fight. You overreacted at the first sign of a threat to your job because you see it as a part of your identity."

Natalie squirmed, searching her brain for a way to refute what Mom said.

"The truth is you are far more than a job, a ministry, or even a calling. You are a person created and saved by God, no matter what your job is or what you do in life."

"But if I—"

"Hear me out." Mom paused her with an upraised hand. "If God has told you to work at Wildfire, then let nothing stop you from doing that. Quit working for Jem and trust God to find you what you need. But if you're working for Wildfire because you feel like you're letting yourself and everyone else down if you don't . . . maybe you should have a look at what you're allowing to shape your identity."

"But Dad—"

"Your Dad knew you had *already* made something of yourself. Before Wildfire. You know what makes God happy? A life that seeks after Him, that loves Him.

"You sacrificed your own plans for us, and that kind of sacrificial love doesn't go unnoticed." Mom tightened her grip on Natalie's hand. "God wants obedience. And He has called some people to ministry, but He's also called others to work in business or raise kids or do a hundred other things. It's not the job that matters, it's the obedience.

"I don't think He'll be disappointed, whichever path you choose. But don't choose an option you don't really want just because you think there's an expectation you should."

Natalie shook her head. "Dad always thought—"

"You want to know what Dad thinks? I found this the other day." Mom dropped Natalie's hand and rummaged through her handbag. She pulled out a creased piece of notepad paper covered in Dad's distinctive scrawl.

"He wrote this two years ago, when we almost lost him. But then he pulled through, so he put it away until the right time. I forgot until I was poking through some papers yesterday."

Natalie unfolded the sheet, fingers shaky.

G'day baby,

Tears blotched the page at the first words. Dad's gravelly voice filled her brain as she read. She shifted the page so her tears wouldn't stain it.

I am so proud of who you are.

When you were born I was overwhelmed with the fact that I was responsible for raising this little baby into a godly and wonderful woman. I wrote these verses down that day:

"For I am convinced that neither death nor life, neither angels nor demons, neither the present nor the future, nor any powers, neither height nor depth, nor anything else in all creation, will be able to separate us from the love of God that is in Christ Jesus our Lord." Romans 8:38–39

God has been very faithful and has guided us both along the way.

I'm so proud to be your dad, and to see you grow into the capable, compassionate, loving, wise, beautiful, and passionate woman that you are has been my greatest joy in life. I know sometimes you feel restless, but you've already made me so proud. I know you've made the Lord proud too.

I know you wish we could remain together, but I know for sure God has a purpose and plan in all things.

I look forward to seeing everything God has in store for you, whether in this world or the next.

> I love you more than you'll
> ever know,
> Dad

She dropped the page and bawled. Her throat ached and her diaphragm hiccupped with the force of her sobs.

He was proud of her. As she was. No work required. And so was God.

Soft arms slipped around her shoulders. Mom's forehead pressed against her ear. Moisture dripped onto her neck.

They stayed like that a long time, until Natalie's phone beeped in her pocket. She tugged it out. A message from Jem flashed onto the screen. "Oh no."

"What?" Mom peered at the phone.

"Lili wasn't at the bus station or Grace's old address." She reread the message as she spoke, hot and cold waves running through her body. "She's missing."

41

*G*od hated her.

It was the only explanation that made sense.

Lili folded her arms against her chest as tight as she could, her tunic and jeggings no match for this weather. She kept her steps fast but light so her Docs didn't make too much noise. It had to be coming up on midnight, and the only people out were ones she didn't want to meet.

Yellow light spilled from behind. A car turned onto the street. Lili dove behind a large bush in the yard of a two-story home. If someone saw her, they might wonder at a young girl alone at night and stop. If they did, she would run.

But she didn't have the energy to run anymore.

She curled into a ball, a blade of grass tickling her nostril. Silent tears watered the sweet-scented bush as she waited for the car to pass.

What did I do to make You so mad at me, God?

So maybe she shouldn't have run away. That didn't explain why her parents stopped caring, why Miss Kent got pregnant. What had she done to start this whole chain of events?

The car whooshed past, and she pushed herself into a sitting position. Cold from the ground seeped into her bones. Like the despair in her soul.

She was lost. No one to come find her. And disoriented in the middle of suburbia, she had no way to call for help.

Would she be left out in the cold forever?

"God, if You care, please let Jem show up right now." She squeezed her eyes tight and clasped her hands in a way she hadn't prayed since she begged for a Rapunzel Barbie. She peeked one eye open. Nothing.

Something brushed her back.

Lili shot to her feet. As she twisted to race back out to the street, a glimpse of dark fur trotted past.

She paused. Was that . . . the same cat?

When the cat headed down the street, she shrugged and followed it. No better plans had presented themselves.

The cat traveled on silent paws, hooked a left, and kept going another two blocks. Lili power-walked to keep up with it, a layer of sweat breaking over her goose-bumped skin.

Three blocks past I-can't-believe-I-can-barely-keep-up-with-a-cat, the animal padded into the front yard of a large brick structure. A wooden sign stood out front. Lili peered at it. A church.

The main sanctuary stood before her, majestic even in the dark. A low wrought-iron fence ran around the church.

She eyed the building. She'd have to break in. But it looked safer than a bush. And an old church could mean old locks.

She scanned the street for onlookers. Nothing but the streetlights standing guard. She crept closer, clambered over the fence, and raced to the back of the building.

A board creaked under her foot as she mounted the bowed back porch. A window stood at waist height. She cupped her hands against the ice-cold glass and peered in. An office, strewn with papers, and a pile of books stacked on the desk like a Jenga tower. The next window revealed a room with four filing cabinets and boxes of devotionals.

Lili checked every window on ground level, then returned to the back entrance. A wooden door stood in front of her, its frame warped. Her tentative fingers reached for the handle, turned it. Locked. She pulled her student ID from her backpack. She'd overheard Uncle Jem mention his breaking-and-entering skills to Natalie once.

She slid the card between the door and the jamb, but nothing gave. Wriggling it higher up, she tried again. No luck.

At least no one seemed to have seen or heard her. Courage building, she rattled the door. It shifted in its misshapen frame. Up. The trick was to move it up.

Setting her shoulder against the rough wood, she yanked the door up by its handle and threw her weight against it.

It popped open and banged against the internal wall. Momentum threw her inside. Off balance, she dropped to her knees. Held her breath. Listened.

All clear.

Movements slow, she rose and reached for the door. The cat ducked inside before she closed it.

Not brave enough to turn on any lights, Lili pulled her shoes off and slipped through the building on silent feet, guided only by the street-light glow. The corridor on her right led to the filing-cabinet room.

She'd wake early tomorrow, but just in case, this looked like the most boring room in the place. No one was likely to come here in a hurry. And it was close to the back door for a fast escape.

The box of devotional books sat inside the room, beneath a built-in desk jutting from the wall. She crawled under it, between the heavy book box and the wall, and lay on her side with her face to the door. The cat slid in beside her, curling up against her chest.

Burying her fingers in its fur, Lili closed her eyes and prayed for morning.

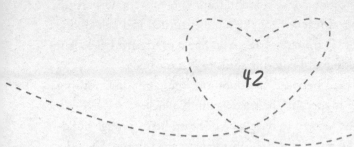

42

God, we need a miracle here.

Jem scrubbed a hand across his face and slapped his cheeks. Now was not the best time to fall asleep, as he rolled along Raleigh's Capital Boulevard past Home Depot. A streak of light blue ran along the horizon, stars dimming in the east. The night surrendered to morning.

And still no Lili.

The scent of Canadian bacon and salt tempted him. "Hand me another McMuffin?" he asked Nick, who munched on his own in the passenger seat.

Nick rummaged in the bag for another, passed it along, and returned his gaze to the window.

The kid had kept watch all night.

At 2:00 a.m. they'd regrouped with Mike, Steph, and Dad. With the motel rooms already booked, they'd agreed to take shifts. Mike would search in one car, Jem in the other. The rest could sleep until seven, when they would change shifts.

Nick had climbed into the BMW's passenger seat before Jem could refuse. Now he was glad. A poke from Nick had kept him from hitting a street sign at least once. Nick had helped Jem search every street near Grace's old address, every park, every fast-food place. He checked for Lili's signal regularly, but she'd never popped back up.

Now they were less than an hour from the shift change, and no good news. Lili had spent an entire night out here somewhere, cold, alone, and believing herself unloved.

Jem shoved the rest of his McMuffin back into the bag. He had another park to search.

They pulled up at Spring Forest Road Park and left their heated car for the predawn chill. They had to find her here. He was running out of ideas.

They swept through all the trees, then met at the yellow playground equipment. It was the last place left in the park where she could be hiding.

"Lili?" Nick poked his head into an enclosed slide, then scampered up a curved metal ladder to check a tunnel. He shook his head.

Jem pressed a fist to his forehead. No. He'd failed her.

Nick trudged with him back to the car, steps dragging.

They climbed into the vehicle and turned toward the city center. They could check the food places close to Grace's old address again. But the shift change was coming soon.

Nick leaned his head against the seat. A yawn escaped.

Jem glanced at him. He strove for an upbeat tone. "At least when we do find her, you'll look very dashing."

Nick looked down at his button-down shirt. He'd ditched the tie hours before. "I had a scholarship interview when you called."

"That's right, I'd forgotten. How did it go?"

"You called before I went in."

Jem slowed. "Wait . . . You mean you blew off a scholarship interview to help search for Lili?"

Now that he thought about it, he had a vague memory of Nick saying "scholarship." But it had been hard to hear over his own brain screaming, *Where is my niece?*

"I was going to tell them I needed to reschedule." He shrugged. "We'll see if they let me."

They stopped at an intersection. "You're a good friend."

Nick ducked his head. "Anyone else would do the same."

"No, they wouldn't. I hope she sees that."

"At the moment I'm not sure." Nick's tone rattled Jem. What had he let happen to his niece?

Nick pulled his phone from the console, where it charged. A sharp intake of breath drew Jem's attention.

"I've got her signal. She's four blocks away."

43

"Lili?"

Lili pulled her gaze from the game on her phone. She'd lost her mind. She could have sworn she heard Jem calling her name.

"*Lili?*"

She jumped to her feet, dropping her phone. It still dangled from the charger she'd found a few minutes ago.

A creak sounded from the direction of the front door. Lili charged through the sanctuary, pawed at the locks, and wrenched open the door.

Uncle Jem stood on the steps, face lined, the rising sun shining on his hair like a halo.

Lili threw herself into his arms.

"Thank you, God." Jem's murmur barely penetrated her consciousness. He squeezed her tight, let her cry into his shirt.

He'd come for her. Someone loved her enough to come for her.

She hung onto Jem with all her strength. They stood like that for a minute before Jem sat her down on the top step.

"Just let me message your parents and Granddad. They're out looking too. And Natalie will be worried sick."

"They are?" She dragged a sleeve past her nose.

Jem tapped a message into his phone. "We split into shifts so we could search all night."

"How did you find me?"

"It was Nick's idea. He used the Find My Phone thingy. He said you did the same thing to your dad."

She grabbed Jem's arm. "Nick? He's not here, is he?"

He slid his large hand over hers. "He searched with me all night. He's in the car. He thought I should talk to you first."

She scanned the road. No car.

"We parked on the other side," Jem said, pointing around the corner.

"I can't believe it. Mom and Dad too?"

"Mom and Dad too."

Tears welled again. "I thought no one wanted me."

Jem's face twisted, like he was about to cry too. He opened his arms, and she leaned against his chest, face tucked into his shoulder. "I know. Nick told us everything. Your parents finally came clean. I'm so sorry, Lil."

She couldn't hold back the sobs any longer. Jem rocked her as she cried.

"I had no idea your dad told you to come home. I've loved having you, and if you want to stay at my house and your parents are okay with that, then I'd be a lucky guy." He squeezed her tight. "You are *very* wanted."

"Dad replaced me," she choked out. "Miss Kent is—"

"I know. He did the wrong thing. For what it's worth, his mistakes have nothing to do with you. He made some selfish decisions." Jem pulled back and gripped her shoulders. "But no matter what he's done, you are still loved. Don't forget that."

"I don't know what I did. Dad doesn't care. Mom doesn't care. God doesn't care."

"That's not true, Lili."

"It feels true."

"I know." Jem sighed, then glanced toward the corner. "Nick gave up his scholarship interview to come find you."

"He what?"

He gestured toward the car and Nick. "Nick made a big sacrifice. Now, do you think he doesn't care about you?"

"Of course not." Where was he going with this?

"What if things started to go wrong? Would you assume he didn't like you then?"

"To give up that interview . . . That's huge. I don't think I could ever doubt that he's my friend."

"Don't you think the same applies to the Person who died instead of you?"

She blinked. It was nothing she'd done. God loved her no matter what.

She pushed away from Jem. "I need to talk to Nick."

"Okay."

She strode across the dewy lawn and around the corner, but faltered when her parents' BMW came into view.

Nick sat with his head back against the headrest, still in the same shirt he'd worn for his interview yesterday. His head jerked in her direction as she approached. He climbed from the car, caution written across his face.

"I'm sorry," she blurted, stopping three feet away from him.

He tilted his head. "For what?"

"For making you miss your interview. For yelling. For not trusting you."

He extended his hand. "It's okay."

She flew past his hand, wrapped her arms around his middle. Cried for the billionth time in the last twenty-four hours.

Nick's arms locked around her. Secure. Somehow, weirdly, it

didn't just feel like Nick was hugging her. It was almost like God was too.

"It's okay," Nick repeated. "Everything's going to be okay."

For the first time, she believed him.

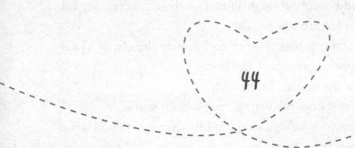

44

Natalie wasn't here.

Dad steered the police cruiser into Jem's parking lot. Riding shotgun, Jem leaned forward and scanned the lot. No Bug. No bicycle. But her mother's Volvo was parked in the next-to-last space.

The rat that had gnawed at his intestines all the way home from Raleigh clawed past his diaphragm and sank its teeth into his heart.

He hadn't been enough for her.

"I'm sorry, son." Dad spoke in a quiet tone.

Jem bowed his head and clenched his fists together. For the past twenty hours, all he'd been able to pray was, *Please, please, please, please, please.*

Now it became *No, no, no, no, no.*

No one to hide his carrots and replace them with Snickers. No partner on the court. No backup with the kids. No best friend.

The car stopped, and Nick and Lili piled out of the back seat.

They'd breakfasted at a small cafe in Raleigh with Lili's parents. The table had run out of napkins by the end of it, between everyone's tears. Although there had been apologies all round, Lili had been firm in her decision to stay at Jem's, at least for now. He'd been relieved. Mike and Steph, though joined in their concern for Lili, oozed resentment toward one another.

And if the coming nights were going to be lonely, it always helped to have another person in the house.

He exited the car on stiff limbs.

Beside Nick's pickup, the young couple embraced.

"I'll see you tomorrow," Nick said to Lili, then fired up his truck and rumbled down the road.

"Guess I'll head too," Dad said, one foot still in the car.

Jem turned. "Would you like to come up for a drink? Of juice?" he added, at his father's scowl.

Dad's expression softened. His skin carried a grayish hue from fatigue, eyes bloodshot. "Sure." He paused at the door. "Why don't you head up, Lil? I want to talk to your uncle."

She took the keys from Jem and disappeared inside.

Jem rubbed his temples. Exhaustion weighed down every cell of his being. Couldn't whatever his dad had to say wait? He needed to get everyone fed and watered, then hit the sack.

"What happened with Natalie?" The question was cautious, not demanding.

Jem paused. They didn't have a talk-about-relationship-problems kind of dynamic. But what the heck. He didn't have the energy to object. He sketched their argument out in the briefest of terms.

Dad nodded, face thoughtful. "Do you remember the day you gave up on me?"

Jem blinked. "What?"

"I rode you all the time. But you still always tried to please me, at least to a degree. But there was a day when that stopped."

Jem shifted on his feet. Yeah, he knew. "The ski trip."

Dad nodded. "The ski trip."

One of his top-five least-favorite memories. He'd been sixteen. Dad hadn't loved the idea of the school ski trip, but after a decent amount of nagging he'd set his terms. Better grades. Impeccable behavior. And Jem had to pay for it himself.

Against all odds, he'd met the criteria. But when the time came for Dad to sign the permission slip, he put it off, lost it, found a dozen excuses.

Jem crossed his arms. "You goaded me into that fight."

For the first time, Dad admitted, "I did."

"You thought I'd never be able to do as you asked."

Dad gave a slow nod.

"And because you still didn't trust me, you wouldn't let me go. So you goaded me into getting into a fight about it, then grounded me as punishment."

"That's the long and short of it, yes."

"And you bring this up why?"

Dad stroked the stubble on his cheek, the sound scratchy. "I broke something in you that day. You gave up. You decided that no matter what you did, you were doomed. And it didn't just affect your relationship with me." He gave a meaningful look.

"That's ridicu—" Jem's voice trailed off. Did it make a terrible kind of sense? He'd ended his engagement with the love of his life. Then broken up with her a second time after only two weeks of dating. Even the ease with which he'd broken up with Chloe probably wasn't natural.

Dad folded his arms. "You believe you're destined to fail. But it's not true. You're a good son. A good dad. You could be a good husband too."

Jem stared at his father. He could not have been more surprised had his father stripped naked and performed the chicken dance. Was that what Dad really thought? He couldn't even make himself believe it. "I've got two kids in my house, and yesterday one ran away and the other nearly went unconscious."

Dad shrugged. "Stuff happens. But you try. That counts."

He clapped a hand on Jem's shoulder, apparently at the end of his emotional-honesty tolerance for the day. "Let's go get this drink."

They trudged up the stairs together. When Jem reached the door, his hand faltered.

He didn't want to be in this apartment if Natalie wasn't going to be with him.

But I've got Olly. And Lili. And I know You still love me, Lord.

The strains of "I Believe I Can Fly" greeted him as he opened the door. On the television, Michael Jordan walked down the gangplank of a spaceship. *Space Jam.* One of Natalie's childhood favorites—and he'd caught her playing it "for Olly" more than once.

"Karen?"

"Jem?"

He stopped breathing.

Natalie looked up from her spot in the living room, eyes wet and Lili still wrapped in her hug.

A hand squeezed Jem's shoulder. He turned.

Dad grinned and backed toward the stairs, giving a two-fingered salute as he went.

Jem looked back at the girls. Hope fluttered its wings, but he anchored it to the ground. She might have only stayed from concern for Lili.

Natalie and Lili separated long enough to perch on stools at the kitchen counter, and Lili spilled the story of her midnight breaking-and-entering, then Jem's rescue. Natalie listened with wide eyes.

Jem stayed frozen in the dining nook.

Then Lili yawned wide enough to swallow a cat and said, "I want to go to bed."

Natalie gave her another hug, and his niece disappeared into her room. Her door clicked shut.

Jem turned to Natalie, standing by the end of the counter. Her hair shone in its customary ponytail, and she turned jeans and a faded hoodie into a delicious ensemble. He took a step closer, then another.

She didn't meet his eyes.

Hope sparked, then fizzled.

"Jem—"

"Nat—" They spoke at the same time.

"I need to apologize," he jumped in. "I'm sorry what I said. I was freaked out over Olly."

A small smile softened Natalie's expression. He held his breath. Was that a good sign?

"You're forgiven. I've done some soul searching myself." She twisted the cords of her hood between her fingers. "You were right. This job isn't about God, it's about me. And if I really want to go for it, then I have options. But I think I need to pray about the path ahead."

And did that include him?

Natalie took a deep breath, and he braced himself.

"In light of that, I want to talk about us."

No. No, no, no, no, no, no, no.

But he forced a strangled "Okay" past his lips.

She smiled. "I love you."

He rested his hands on her waist, unable to speak. She loved him. All the mistakes, all of the drama, all of the heartache. All his screwups. And she still loved him.

Dad's words returned to him. *You try. It counts.*

This time he'd not only try, but he'd believe they could make it. This family, for all of its dysfunction, would be a group of people who stuck by each other.

Thirty-six hours of stress and no sleep had left his brain full of cotton balls. He opened his mouth, but no sound came out.

She tipped her head to one side. "Speechless? Finally?"

He drew a finger along her jaw and tipped her chin up. "Not quite."

He dipped his head, and her eyes fluttered shut. He kissed her, long, sweet, and slow, and the "Hallelujah Chorus" roared.

Epilogue

"Oliver just ate his flower."

Natalie turned at the sound of Lili's exasperated voice behind her, one hand holding her cream chiffon skirt above the grass.

"I'll fix it." Mom scooped a finger into the toddler's mouth, removing three mushed petals and a leaf.

The four of them stood outside a barn door on a rural property owned by a church family. The May sun warmed Natalie's bare shoulders as she adjusted the sweetheart neckline of her gown for the millionth time. Bunting, tacked to the outside of the barn, fluttered in the gentle breeze. The heels of her nude pumps sank into the rich soil as the smell of fresh grass and springtime filled her lungs.

Today was her wedding day.

She brushed a chewed piece of stem from Olly's miniature gray suit. The little boy waved a hand at her. "Momma, uppa."

She grinned. Would that ever stop feeling weird? She gathered her son into her arms and pressed a kiss to his soft cheek. By this time next week, she'd probably forget that he'd ever called her anything else.

"Are you ready?" Mom held out her bouquet, a Lili creation of brilliant pink roses, hydrangeas, and spray roses mixed with an array of wild greenery that gave it an enchanting, untamed feel.

Natalie placed Olly in Lili's arms, careful not to brush his lipstick-stained cheek against the girl's mint-green dress. She rubbed his cheek with her thumb to remove the strawberry-frosting-colored mark, then took her flowers from Mom. "I'm ready." A grin broke across her lips as she spoke.

Mom passed Lili a single long-stemmed rose.

Lili fired off a text to Nick, tucked her phone under Oliver's vest, and a moment later the sounds of Ed Sheeran's "Thinking of You" filled the air.

"Good luck, Nat." Lili leaned in for a hug, Olly between them. She pecked Natalie's cheek, straightened her dress, and disappeared through the door.

Mom adjusted Natalie's veil, which swished down her back from its diamanté clasp in her curly updo. Mom had abandoned her neon sweat suits in favor of a classy satin number, mint green to match Lili's dress. Her right hand cradled an eight-by-ten photo of Dad. "I'm so proud of you, honey. We both are."

Her face blurred in Natalie's vision. Thank goodness for water-proof mascara. "Love you, Mom."

Mom kissed her cheek, and Natalie caught the scent of her White Diamonds perfume. "Time to go get your man." She offered her left elbow.

The music hit its cue. Natalie drew a deep breath and stepped through the door.

Candles lined the "aisle" down the center of the barn, and the massive double doors at the other end had been thrown open to display the rolling green hills of a Charlottesville spring.

Nick, John, and Mike stood together on the right side of the candlelit circle at the end of the barn. Steph, Lili, and Olly waited on the left. Natalie beamed at the group.

Despite tension between Steph and Mike—especially with the impending arrival of Trish and Mike's son—the pair had put aside their differences for Nat and Jem's special day. And Natalie was grateful, because somehow she and Jem were closer to both of them than ever.

Life hadn't been smooth for the pair—they'd both resigned from the church, and Mike moved into his old bedroom at John's the day after they brought Lili home. Steph seemed to go into hibernation for a time, but she'd recently rejoined Asylum to lead the Love Thy Neighbor initiative. Lili had stayed with Jem over the past months, but after the wedding she planned to move back in with her mom.

And Lili and Nick . . . Well, the two made a team like Natalie hadn't seen since her and Jem.

The six of them formed a V formation at the end of the barn with Sam, dapper in his black suit, standing in the center with his Bible in hand.

But they all faded away as Jem beamed at her, devastatingly handsome in his gray vest and open-collared white shirt.

She kept her gaze locked on his as she glided across the swept concrete floor, glad that the group of witnesses was small as tears puddled in the corners of her eyes. With limited funds, she and Jem had agreed an intimate ceremony was best.

After the vows, a decadent morning tea waited on lace-covered tables—complete with white chocolate M&M's—and then she and Jem would spend their five-day honeymoon in the Shenandoah Valley. Mom couldn't wait to bond with her new grandson as she cared for him during their absence.

Although she'd done plenty of bonding already as Olly's new nanny. Mom had actually been the one to suggest the arrangement. After Dad passed in his sleep six months ago—a week after laughing his way through his Crocodile Dundee party—Olly had been the perfect distraction.

And the only person enjoying their new job more than Mom was Natalie. She'd taken the part-time wedding planner job she'd been offered just two weeks after she resigned from Wildfire. Turned out official ministry wasn't the only place God could use her. One of her coworkers had already begun attending church with her, and she had a client who seemed to love asking questions about God as much as she loved changing her mind about table settings.

The Wildfire job had gone to Kimberly—much to Sam's chagrin. He'd revealed to Natalie when she resigned that she'd been his first choice. Kimberly was brilliant but drove him nuts. But Wildfire seemed to be surging forward, so their partnership was obviously working somehow.

Natalie swept her eyes past the people she loved as she stepped up to Jem and took his hand.

There were no easy answers for any of them. Olly still had diabetes—always would. Dad wasn't here. Lili's half sibling would grow up with a splintered family, as would Lili.

But as Jem's twinkling gaze swept down the length of her and back up again, one overwhelming truth filled her mind.

God was faithful.

She intertwined her fingers with Jem's. Her cheeks heated under his appreciative observation.

Sam began the ceremony. "Dearly beloved, we are gathered here today . . ."

The words faded away as Jem squeezed her fingers.

She sent him a sultry wink and thanked God that, at the end of it all, love would win.

A Note from the Author

G'day!

Thanks for letting me share Natalie, Jem, and Lili's story with you. This book is special to me—I wrote Natalie's and Lili's journeys of betrayal and healing as I experienced those emotions (though in far less dramatic circumstances) in my own life. Anything useful in these pages comes from the wisdom of parents and friends who helped me work through the questions that I think many people ask in their twenties—What do you do when someone you looked up to betrays what they said they believed? What if they had been an example of faith—how does that affect your relationship with God? With the church?

In the years after this experience, a friend told me about similar struggles. She prefaced the conversation with "you're going to think I'm not even a Christian." But I think these questions are both natural and common—it's what you do with them that matters. And God is much bigger than the mistakes of His followers.

I hope you enjoyed this story, and can I just say that Nick is still my favorite character I've written to date? The boy loves Batman and Nirvana and knows how to hotwire a car. I just don't know how I'm going to top that.

A NOTE FROM THE AUTHOR

Hopefully you'll join me back in Charlottesville AND in rural Australia (woot woot!) with my next book, *A Girl's Guide to the Outback*.

Catch ya later!
Jess

Acknowledgments

G od. You give me the passion for stories, the ideas, and the energy to create them. Plus, there was the whole saving my soul and loving me for eternity thing. Thank You.

Mum, you are the person who picks up the phone when I'm at my most discouraged and listens every time. Thanks for always being there.

Dad, you taught me to work hard, not give up, and that only cleaning your office once a year was a good idea. I follow your example in all three.

Thanks to both Mum and Dad together for, knowing that I'm a "words person," writing the beautiful letter you gave me when I moved out of home. It formed the basis for the letter Natalie got from her dad. I still reread it. It makes me cry every time. Thanks for being great parents.

Bek, Jake, Jack, and Abby. I am so lucky to have you as my siblings. Hanging out with you guys is my favorite thing to do.

To Mumma, my grandmother. When I was a broke boarding school supervisor you helped me buy a new computer because you believed in my writing. I must've done at least three drafts of this book on that computer. Thank you.

My agent Chip MacGregor, you took a chance on a young Aussie

ACKNOWLEDGMENTS

and invested years into improving my work before we saw any pay-off. Thank you.

My mentor Rachel Hauck, your wisdom and time are deeply appreciated. Thank you.

My brainstorming partner and *StoryNerds* podcast cohost Hannah Davis: without your input my editing process would've been astronomically more difficult, and my upcoming book ideas not half as good. You're a kindred spirit.

Grace Olsen, you dropped what you were doing to read my whole book and give me feedback in that last week of editing. It helped calm my first-time writer nerves so much. Thank you!

My editor Jocelyn Bailey, I had no idea until I received your notes just how much a fantastic editor can improve a book. You were spot-on, and you delivered them with such kindness to my fragile writer's heart. It's been a delight working with you.

Melissa Tagg, I vividly remember our first meeting because you encouraged me so much! Thank you for supporting this newbie writer.

All my critique partners over the years, especially Nico Bell and Iola Goulton. I owe you dozens of critiques. Thanks for all the encouragement.

To the friends and family who have taken time to pray for my writing. It blows me away that other people could care enough about my scribblings to take the time to pray for them. Thanks.

Discussion Questions

1. When Lili found out about her father's affair, she felt betrayed both as a daughter, and as someone who looked up to her father's example of faith. Have you ever felt let down or betrayed by someone you looked up to? How did that affect you? How did it affect your relationship with God?

2. Natalie felt like her life wasn't living up to her own expectations, her father's, or God's. Have disappointed expectations ever affected how you think God feels about you? Did your perception match how the Bible says God feels about you?

3. Natalie believed that both Sam and Steph were more fulfilled and pleasing to God than she was because of the work they did. How do you think Sam was really doing? How was Steph?

4. Have you ever felt envious of someone else's life, only to realize that they had struggles just like you?

5. Jem felt he could never meet his father's expectations and that reflected on his perception of God. Have your parents' imperfections ever affected the way you view God?

6. Jem didn't realize for a long time that his father's attitude was

an overcorrection from what he felt were past mistakes. Have your efforts to avoid your own or others' past mistakes ever pushed you too far the other way?

7. How did Jem's relationship with his father affect his relationships with others in his life?

8. How did Jem begin to establish healthier relationships?

9. Natalie's identity was wrapped up in her career and service to God. How did that impact her emotional health and choices?

10. What did Natalie let go of, and what did she embrace, to become happier?

11. How did Nick's sacrifice for Lili help her move past her father's mistakes?

Don't miss Jessica's next novel coming January 2020!

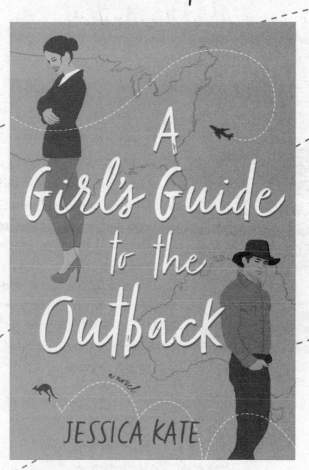

AVAILABLE IN PRINT, E-BOOK, AND AUDIO

THOMAS NELSON
Since 1798

About the Author

© April Hildred - aprilphotography.studio

Australian Jessica Kate is a sassy inspirational romance author and screenwriting groupie, whose favorite place to be—apart from Mum and Dad's back deck—is a theme park. She cohosts the *StoryNerds* podcast, travels North America and Australia, and samples her favorite pasta wherever she goes. But the best (so far) is still the place around the corner from her corporate day job as a training developer.

Visit her online at jessicakatewriting.com
Instagram: jessicakatewriting
Facebook: jessicakatewriting
Twitter: @JessicaKate05